SONG OF VINES

A JACK AND THE BEANSTALK RETELLING

THE SINGER TALES
BOOK 6

DEBORAH GRACE WHITE

LUMINANT PUBLICATIONS

SONG OF VINES: A JACK AND THE BEANSTALK RETELLING

By Deborah Grace White

Song of Vines:
A Jack and the Beanstalk Retelling
The Singer Tales Book Six

ISBN: 978-1-922636-72-0

Luminant Publications
PO Box 305
Greenacres, South Australia 5086

http://www.deborahgracewhite.com

Cover Design by Karri Klawiter
Map illustration by Rebecca E. Paavo

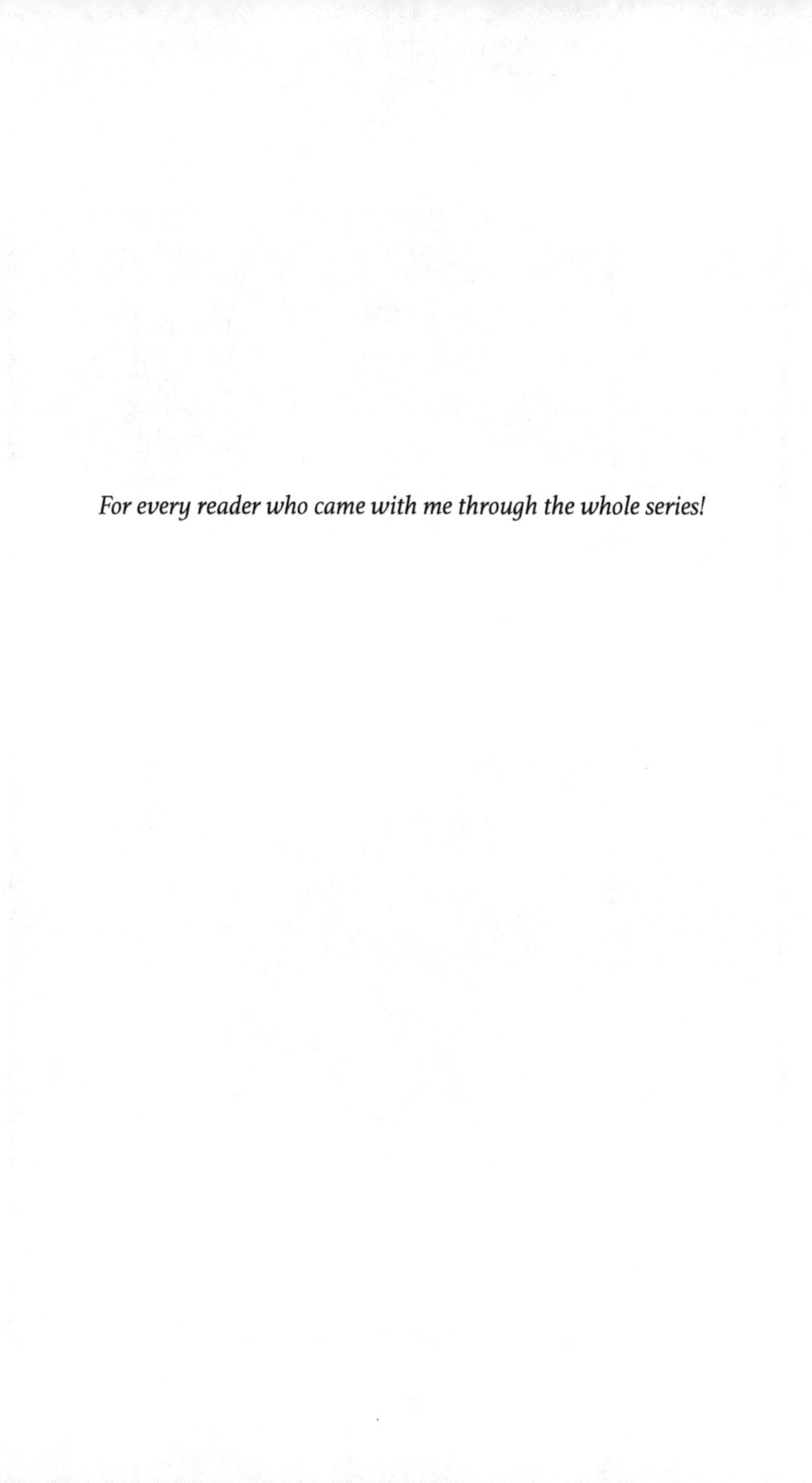

For every reader who came with me through the whole series!

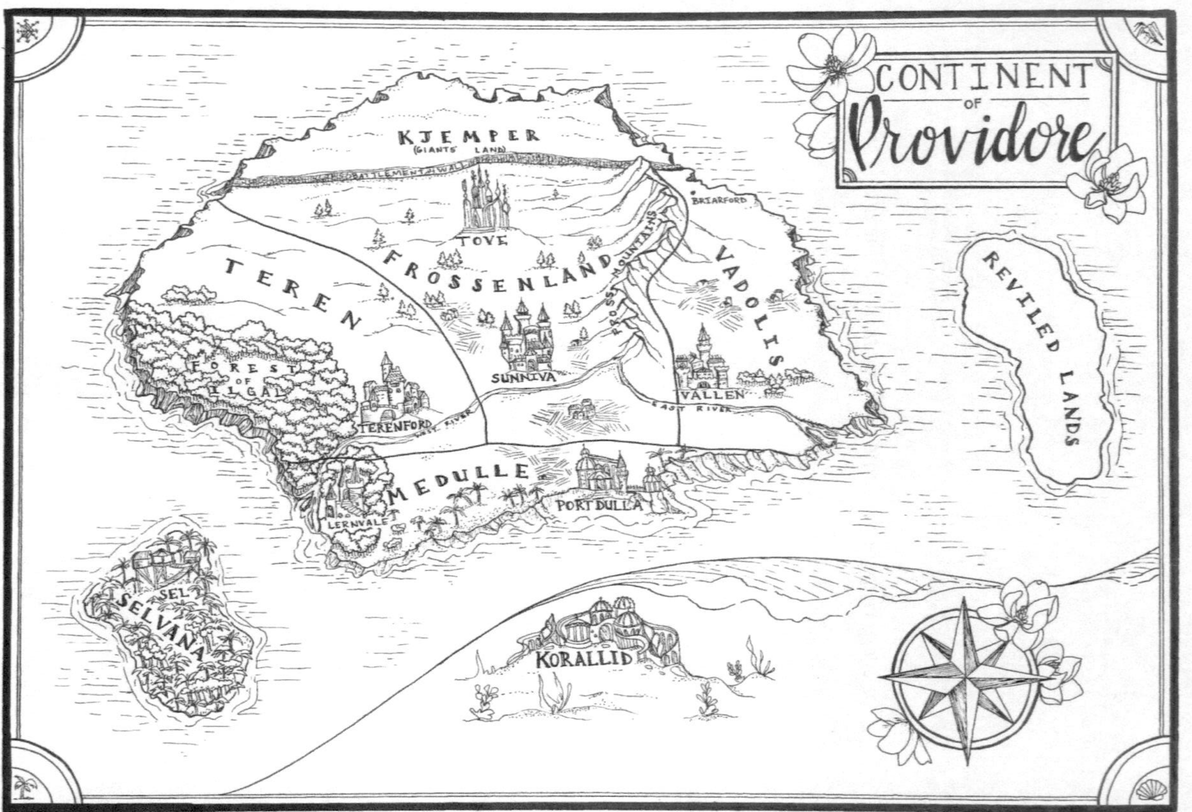

CONTINENT OF Providore
KJEMPER
(GIANTS' LAND)
BATTLEMENT WALL
TOVE
BRIARFORD
FROSSENLAND
FROSS MOUNTAINS
VADOLIS
TEREN
FOREST OF ILGAL
SUNNIVA
VALLEN
EAST RIVER
TERENFORD
EAST RIVER
MEDULLE
LERNVALE
PORT DULLA
REVILED LANDS
SEL
SELVANA
KORALLID

CHAPTER ONE

Jacinta

Jacinta stepped through the door into the tiny cabin she shared with her mother, relishing the rush of warmer air that met her. It was bitterly cold outside.

"And it's technically still summer," she muttered to herself, stamping her feet on the mat.

"What's that?" Her mother's voice sounded irritable, which meant her joints must be paining her.

"Nothing," Jacinta told her, forcing her voice to be cheerful. "This is the last of the wood, so I'll have to take the ax out later."

"You have to do no such thing," contradicted her mother. "Jacinta, summer isn't even over yet! We don't need a fire at all hours of the day and night."

"We do, Mamma," said Jacinta patiently, depositing the wood in the little crate near the fireplace. "You're ill. You just have to accept it."

"Well, I refuse to accept it," said her mother staunchly. "I don't have any patience for colds."

"Well, you may not have patience, but you do have a cold," Jacinta informed her. "And the sooner you accept that you need to rest, the sooner you'll recover from it and be back to your full strength."

Her mother sighed, leaning back and setting her rocking chair into motion.

"You need my help, Jacinta. We can't afford for me to sit around here, wasting wood on unnecessary fires."

"I'm managing, Mamma," Jacinta insisted. "Let's be honest, the place doesn't require a great deal of tending anymore."

The older woman didn't respond. Like Jacinta, she was probably thinking of happier, easier times. When Jacinta's father had been alive, they'd had a small farm, even a few sheep of their own. Now there was nothing left but the cow. They'd even had to eat the chickens to make it through the previous winter. The poor birds were too cold to lay, and work was too scarce. Jacinta was painfully aware that they'd made their way through their reserve of coins, as well. Each morning she woke worrying about what they would eat that day. It had never been that way when she was a child.

"Any milk?" her mother asked quietly.

Jacinta shook her head. "Nothing again."

"She's getting too old," the other woman sighed.

"Perhaps her joints plague her, like yours," said Jacinta, nudging her mother's chair so that it rocked back.

"My joints are just fine," her mother insisted.

"They're not." Jacinta frowned at her. "Winter is months off, and you're already sore. Do you think I can't tell? At this rate, you won't be able to spin the wool in the colder months."

"Well, then you'll have to take over," said her mother matter-of-factly.

"Yes." Jacinta's tone was emotionless. "I will."

Her mother studied her face. "I know it's not exciting work, Jacinta. In fact, I know better than anyone that it's mind-numbingly dull. But we have to eat, and there's no sense shying away from reality. We're fortunate to still have two neighbors who are managing to keep sheep alive, *and* who are willing to hire us to spin their wool. I'm sure they have plenty of other options. We don't."

"I know, Mamma," said Jacinta quickly. "Of course I'm ready to do more of the spinning if necessary. I wasn't trying to shy away from anything."

"Hm." Her mother didn't look convinced. "If you say so, Jacinta. It looked to me like you had that far-off look you get when you're dreaming silly dreams."

"You were mistaken," said Jacinta shortly. "My thoughts were and are very much on our present situation."

Her mother nodded, apparently accepting this response. "Such a shame you didn't inherit your father's gift," she said.

"Yes," Jacinta agreed, stoking the fire. It didn't really need attention, but she was putting off the chores awaiting her on the other side of the single room that served as kitchen, bedroom, and living area. "I miss the sound of singing in the house."

"So do I, but that's not what I meant," her mother responded. "I meant that if you'd inherited the gift of songcraft, it would have made things easier these last four years. And it would also give you greater opportunities. It would take you to Vallen, like you've always dreamed."

"I don't want to go to Vallen," said Jacinta quickly, her voice a little too sharp at this mention of the capital city of their kingdom of Vadolis. "My home is here in Briarford, and I don't want to abandon it. The capital has no interest for me."

"Hah!" Her mother's voice was grim and unimpressed. "The strength of your response proves my point, Jacinta. I knew I was right—you were dreaming. You're thinking of that prince, and I tell you, those sorts of dreams are the worst way to lose yourself!"

"I'm not dreaming about anything," said Jacinta, her own

voice becoming irritable. "My friendship with Mariella and her brother is a relic of the past. It has nothing to do with my life now."

"Then why did you give the blasted cow a royal name?"

"I wasn't naming the cow after the royals," Jacinta protested. "I named her after me. Just a little joke, Mamma."

"That's even worse," her mother said. She shook her head. "And irreverent, frankly. On which topic, you'd do well to remember to refer to them as Princess Mariella and Prince Matthias, or as Their Highnesses. You could get yourself into trouble if people heard you calling the royal family by their given names so casually."

"There's a much easier solution, Mamma," said Jacinta wearily. "I don't have to remember to use the correct titles because I simply don't refer to them."

Her mother looked ready to press the point, but Jacinta forestalled her. She simply couldn't bear to have this conversation. Standing abruptly, she plastered a smile onto her face.

"I've just remembered that the weekly market is on today. I meant to go first thing, but I got distracted foraging. I'll go now—there'll still be some produce."

Her mother eyed her shrewdly. "I won't claim to be averse to the idea of fresh produce with dinner, but how are you going to pay for it?"

Jacinta hesitated for a moment, then strode over to her bed in the corner. She knelt beside it, pulling out a fur muffler. It was made of soft mink fur, and in spite of her best efforts, the feel of it in her hands brought a lump to her throat.

"You're going to trade that?" her mother demanded. "What happened to sentiment?"

"We can't eat sentiment," Jacinta said practically. "And I've held on to this for far too long. It's time for it to be useful to us."

Her mother's brow creased. "Colder weather will be on us soon, Jacinta. You'll miss it."

Jacinta shook her head, refusing to acknowledge any truth in the latter part of her mother's words. "I'll manage in the winter. This is a luxury item we don't need."

"Too much of a luxury to trade for a few vegetables," her mother said. "Surely there won't be anything in the Briarford market that would allow you to get the true value of a mink muffler of fine enough quality for royalty."

Jacinta laughed, the sound unnatural. "I doubt it is, Mamma. It's not as though it ever belonged to Mariella. Matthias gave it to me for my birthday when we were children."

"I remember," her mother said.

"My point is, it was intended for me," Jacinta explained. "It was fit for a child whose parents worked at the manor. Not for royalty."

Her mother's dark eyes searched hers for an uncomfortably long moment. "Don't do this in anger, Jacinta. Things done in anger can't be taken back once tempers have cooled."

"I'm not angry, Mamma," Jacinta said seriously. "I used to miss my friends, but those days are a distant memory now. They didn't wrong me, because they owe me nothing. Emotion has nothing to do with it." She drew in a breath. "The truth is, I found nothing edible when I was foraging. Nothing at all. The ground is too hard, the air too cold. And as winter approaches, it'll get even worse. I swear the land is more barren every year. The chickens are gone, our reserves are almost out, and even the cow isn't giving us milk. We have nothing but some dried meat, and we've been given no spinning work for at least a fortnight. I can't afford to hold on to trinkets which might help put food in our bellies."

Her mother said nothing for a long minute. Jacinta thought

she could see a heaviness in the older woman's eyes, but eventually her mother gave her head a little shake.

"You're right, Jacinta. We must think practically. See you're not cheated at the market."

"When have I ever been cheated at the market?" Jacinta asked, affronted. "I pride myself on being a very shrewd bargainer, I'll have you know."

Her mother gave a wry chuckle. "I'm not denying it, but even shrewd bargainers can slip up."

"Not this one," Jacinta assured her.

Pulling on her jacket, she made for the door. She had her hand on the knob when a low but building rumble caused the two women to freeze, their eyes finding each other.

"Brace yourself," Jacinta's mother said grimly.

Jacinta did as she was told, pulling open the door and using the doorframe to support her lean form. A familiar sense of dread washed over her. The rumbling before the tremors was the worst part because everyone could feel it coming, and there was nothing anyone could do to alleviate its severity. And this one sounded big.

Sure enough, Jacinta had barely gotten into position when the ground began to shake. This tremor was more violent than usual, and Jacinta could hear their wooden hut rattling alarmingly. The legs of their simple table thudded across the floor inside, something smashing as it bounced off the surface.

Then, suddenly, it was over. Everything went still again, the earth no longer rumbling under Jacinta's feet.

"Are you all right?" she asked her mother.

"Of course I am." The older woman relaxed her grip on the arms of her rocking chair. "Have I ever been thrown into a panic by a tremor before? Off to the market, if you want to catch anything fresh."

Jacinta nodded, slipping out the door without another word. Her mother was right that the tremors had become commonplace, but Jacinta wasn't so sure it was true that they shouldn't be letting it worry them. They'd been getting steadily worse. She'd thought so for years, even before they became destructive. But in the last year they'd worsened considerably. It was now common to have shaking violent enough to break things and even damage buildings.

As she stepped around the outside of the house, Jacinta's eyes flicked up as they always did. Not that there was anything much to see. They lived on the outskirts of Briarford, the actual town located to the south of their home. But the door of their hut faced northward. Which meant that Jacinta's view was dominated by an enormous wall of hewn stone, stretching up much higher than any human castle, so high she had to crane her neck back to catch a glimpse of the top. The stones were cut to an impossibly large size, weathered and worn but still immovable.

Battlement Wall.

It had been built generations ago by the Frossians, inhabitants of the kingdom of Frossenland which stood to the west of Vadolis, on the other side of the Fross Mountains. The purpose of the wall was simple. To keep the giants out.

And this monument to human innovation was all that separated the humans of Providore from the vicious, brutish giants who occupied the continent's frozen northern wastes, a land they called Kjemper.

Almost the entirety of the wall constituted Frossenland's northern border. But a tiny section continued on the Vadolisian side of the Fross Mountains. And that tiny section was found in Jacinta's backyard.

There was a reason the hut had been incredibly cheap to rent. No one in Briarford liked to live on the northern edge of the town, with Battlement Wall looming ominously above at all hours of the day and night.

People had felt that way even when the giants were believed to be as incapable as humans of crossing the wall. The fear and superstition that surrounded the wall had become even more marked in the year since the supposedly dead Prince Herleif of Frossenland had appeared to claim his throne, with tales of how the giant queen had breached the wall and murdered his father. Rumor was that the murderous queen's son now ruled the giants, but they had no reason to think him any less dangerous than his mother. Needless to say, Jacinta and her mother didn't receive many callers.

But the wall itself didn't trouble Jacinta. From all reports, everything had been quiet for a year, since King Herleif and his bride returned from the land of the giants. She figured that even if the giants decided to breach the wall again, they would surely target their attack on Frossenland, perhaps to seek vengeance on the Frossian king for whatever exactly went on in Kjemper a year ago. She couldn't imagine them having much interest in a dull corner of Vadolis.

It wasn't as though the Vadolisian royals set foot anywhere near Briarford anymore.

No, Jacinta's biggest irritation with the wall was that it blocked out so much of the sky, and its shadow made it difficult to grow anything in their tiny yard.

She turned her back on Battlement Wall, pausing to bestow a friendly pat on the still milkless cow.

"You need to dig deep for me, Princess, and soon. Things are getting desperate, and we can't keep a cow who produces no milk."

The inappropriately named cow gave no reply, chewing her mouthful of bristly grass in an imperturbable way.

With a sigh, Jacinta turned away, her quick stride taking her south toward the town. She would have liked to have brought her ax, to hunt for promising wood for the fire along the way. But arriving at the market with an ax in her hand was the type of behavior the good people of Briarford frowned upon. Part of shrewd negotiating was not alienating the people you did business with.

Jacinta slowed her pace as she neared a wide creek that ran along the edge of town and into a nearby copse of trees. There were handy stepping stones which made crossing it easy, especially at this time of year. It was memories that made her steps falter. Her eyes strayed to the copse, remembering how many happy hours she'd spent playing there as a child. She'd lived at the fancy manor house then, albeit in the servants' quarters. Trekking to the northern part of town to gawk at the wall and play giant battles among the trees had been a regular adventure. She'd never imagined she'd be living in a tumbledown hut out this way.

Caught off guard by a rush of nostalgia, as sharp and bracing as the gust of wind that was sweeping past her, Jacinta knelt at the water's edge. She dipped her hand into it, feeling the icy chill of water that had flowed down from the still-snowy peaks of the Fross Mountains. Impossible not to get lost in memories.

"Ooh! That's so cold!"

The sandy-haired boy scrunched up his nose, his smattering of freckles scrunching up, too.

Ten-year-old Jacinta laughed gleefully, splashing water at him with her boot. "Don't be a baby, Matthias. It's summer!"

"The fact that you northerners call this summer is a travesty," Matthias said with dignity as he stepped out of the stream into which his foot had slipped. "And you can't call me a baby! I'm twelve years old."

"And a prince," Mariella added helpfully, hopping lightly over the familiar stepping stones without repeating her brother's disaster.

"Yes, and that," Matthias said, latching on to his sister's addition as if it had only just occurred to him. "You can't call a prince a baby, Jacinta, you little rat."

"And yet, it seems I just did," said Jacinta, grinning impudently.

Matthias shook his head ruefully at her, and Jacinta found herself looking him over. He certainly didn't look like a baby. Privately, she thought he looked so much older and more sophisticated than last year. Perhaps his bulky fur coat contributed to that. She'd waited all year to see her familiar, favorite playmates again. And now that they were here, they were a perplexing mix of familiar and entirely new. At least, Matthias was. Mariella remained the same cheerful friend she'd always been.

"Besides," Jacinta added, trying to match the somber tone Matthias often used to such comedic effect, "you're not a prince at all. You're a common servant boy, remember?" For a moment she held her breath, wondering if this older version of Matthias would resent the game they'd played every summer since she could remember.

But she needn't have worried. The prince's face creased in a smile as he blew a tuft of his sandy hair out of his eyes. "Of course, Your Highness, how could I forget?" He swept a courtly bow that Jacinta was secretly very impressed by. "Princess Jacinta, how may I serve you? Shall I lie down across this stream and allow you to use my body as a bridge so as not to get your gown wet?"

Mariella giggled, but Jacinta's eyes went wide. "Do your servants really do that for you?" she demanded.

That sent both siblings into gales of laughter.

"Of course not!" Mariella told her. "We do get spoiled quite a lot, but it's not that bad."

"Some of them probably would if Father asked them," Matthias said fairly. "I know loyalty is good and all, but their devotion sometimes makes me wonder if they have any personality at all."

Mariella sent him a coy look. "Forget water, some of the girls in court would probably lay themselves as a bridge over hot coals if they thought it would catch your attention."

"Ugh, don't remind me." Matthias gave a shudder. "This is supposed to be a holiday, Mariella. The whole point of coming to Mother's estate up in this frozen wasteland is so that the court can't follow us."

"Hey!" Jacinta folded her arms, genuinely offended this time. "This happens to be my kingdom, servant. I won't have you calling it a frozen wasteland."

"Sorry," said Matthias, his quick gaze taking in her expression. "I'm very fond of the frozen wasteland, if it helps," he offered.

Jacinta's frown deepened. She wasn't sure it did help.

"He's right, Jacinta," said Mariella, not unkindly. "It gets colder and more barren here every year." She slipped her arm through her friend's, squeezing. "But he's also right that we're fond of it. We love coming here. We both look forward to our month with you all year, don't we, Matthias?"

"We do," he confirmed, his smile so open and genuine that Jacinta felt herself thawing.

"Well, I suppose I won't have you beheaded, then," she conceded.

"Father doesn't do beheadings, actually," Matthias informed her. He pulled an apple from his pocket, polishing it on his coat before taking a bite. "He thinks it's barbaric."

"Well, here in my northern kingdom, we're not afraid of being a little barbaric," sniffed Jacinta.

Matthias grinned. "What would be really great is if you could come to Vallen with us when we go home. Wouldn't it be such fun if Jacinta visited us at our castle, Mariella?"

"It would be the best!" the princess gushed. "Do you think your parents would let you, Jacinta?"

Jacinta felt her face heating with pleasure at the invitation, and immediately tried to hide the emotion. "I don't know if I want to come," she said jokingly. "It sounds like the people in Vallen are crazy. Why else would girls lie across hot coals for fun?"

Mariella let out a trill of laughter. "Oh, not for fun. To try to snag Matthias."

"Snag him?" Jacinta asked, bewildered.

Matthias wasn't laughing along with his sister, his expression pained instead. "Can't you drop it, Mariella?"

"Matthias doesn't like me teasing him about it," grinned the ten-year-old princess. "He's embarrassed."

"So would you be," muttered Matthias, kicking a rock. The twelve-year-old did look uncharacteristically awkward.

"Embarrassed about what?" Jacinta demanded. "What do you mean they want to snag him? Snag him for what?"

"For romance," said Mariella, as if it was the most obvious thing in the world. "They like him. They're all trying to flirt with him."

"Romance?" Jacinta said blankly. "That's the silliest thing I ever heard."

"I'm glad I'm not the only one here with an ounce of sense," Matthias said approvingly. "It's absurdly silly, Jacinta, you can't even imagine what fools they're making of themselves."

"It's not that silly," said Mariella defensively. "Even Mamma says you'll change your tune one day."

"Never," vowed Matthias.

His sister rolled his eyes at him. "So you're never going to get married and produce an heir to carry on the kingdom?"

Matthias scowled. "I'll consider it. In twenty years."

That earned a giggle from Jacinta.

"Well, half the girls I know are already considering it," Mariella informed him. "They probably want to be a princess one day. I heard two arguing the other week about which one of them was going to get you to kiss them."

"Urgh." Matthias grimaced. "Tell me their names so I can make *sure neither of them ever, ever, ever," he shuddered dramatically, "tricks me into kissing them."*

Mariella grinned. "Letty and Simone."

"I'll burn it into my memory," said Matthias staunchly.

"Are we going to talk about romance all day?" Jacinta asked disapprovingly. "I thought we were playing giant wars."

"Your Highness, you're right," said Matthias, his tone once again solemn. "Please allow us to apologize most humbly, Princess Jacinta. Lead us fearlessly into battle and save our fair kingdom from the pillaging brutes."

"Well," said Jacinta, unsheathing an imaginary sword. "I think I will."

The eighteen-year-old Jacinta stood with a sigh, wondering as she crossed nimbly over the creek why she'd allowed herself the indulgence of childhood memories. Perhaps it was the muffler in her hand. She glanced down at it, remembering the cheerful smile on Matthias's face when he'd presented it to her as a birthday present, only days after that memory by the stream. She'd never dreamed at the time that it was to be their last summer in Briarford.

If Mariella's protestations in later correspondence were to be believed, they'd known nothing of their parents' intentions, either. But then, who could say whether the prince and princess had ever been really honest with their secret summer friend? Not that it mattered now. It had been years since the last letter from Mariella, and Jacinta had spoken the truth when she told her mother that the once-treasured friendship bore no connection to her current life.

And a good thing, too, a prideful voice in Jacinta whispered. She wouldn't want them to see her as she was now, too thin from months of eating less than her appetite demanded, gown patched and worn, hands weathered. She had enough pride to think it far better for their paths to remain diverged.

She found the market still decently abustle, and quickly set about assessing the wares. She would like fresh produce, as she'd told her mother. But she would be wise to also acquire some food that would keep longer.

Jacinta moved along the line of stalls, nodding greetings to the vendors, all of whom were known to her. Sometimes they had visitors to the market from other towns, but it didn't look to be the case this week.

"What are you trading today, Jacinta?" A thin-faced man hailed her. "Selling that cow at last, are you?"

"Not yet," said Jacinta. "I'm still hoping she'll rally."

"Hm. Ever the optimist, aren't you?"

A chuckle went around those in earshot, and Jacinta tried not to let it sting. She knew the man meant nothing malicious by his words, and the onlookers were right. She wasn't known for her optimism.

"I have something better than optimism," she informed him. "And that's determination."

"Well said," a woman chimed in. "And I'll give you that, child. You must be the toughest and most determined girl in the village."

"True, true," agreed the thin-faced man. "I wouldn't bet against you, Jacinta. But I can't go giving you produce for free, you know. Times are as tough for my family as for yours."

Privately Jacinta doubted it, but she was too proud to reveal just how desperate their situation was becoming.

"I wouldn't expect you to," she assured him. "I'm willing to trade this." She held up the muffler, then added, "for the right price."

"Ooh, is that mink?" someone asked. She stepped forward and examined it. "Where did you get something like this?"

"I've had it for years," Jacinta said casually.

"It was probably a gift from the royals, was it?"

Jacinta held in a wince. She'd hoped no one would piece that together.

"The royals?" The high-pitched new voice made Jacinta look around in confusion. She couldn't see the speaker. "Is this girl a friend of Vadolis's royal family?"

"No, of course not," said Jacinta quickly, still looking around. "Not at all."

The speaker stepped forward from behind a nearby stall, and the reason for both her unusually high voice and her hidden presence was revealed.

She wasn't a human at all. She was an elf.

With the alabaster skin and emerald eyes of her kind, she stood at about half Jacinta's height, the tapered tips of her ears slightly pink in the cold air. Long, pale hair was pulled back into a braid, and she was dressed for travel. Apparently at least one traveling vendor had come to the market in Briarford this week.

"Greetings," Jacinta said, inclining her head politely to the elf. She didn't know a lot about the diminutive creatures, but she knew enough to tread carefully around them. They were shrewd and calculating, and had access to magic in ways even human singers didn't.

"Greetings," the elf responded, her eyes curious as she studied Jacinta.

On closer inspection, Jacinta could see the silver in her pale hair. The elf wasn't young, then. And considering they aged much more slowly than humans, she was probably much older than Jacinta guessed.

"So you don't claim friendship with the royals?" the elf asked.

"Of course not," said Jacinta, trying to sound as though the idea was absurd.

"She used to be friends with them," chimed in the woman who'd spoken earlier.

"Really?" A few surprised murmurs sounded around the group, and Jacinta's hand curled into a fist around the fabric of her gown. This wasn't at all the direction she'd wanted the conversation to go.

"Friends is an exaggeration," she said, trying to speak dismissively. "Back before my father died, my parents both worked at the manor house, remember? Before it was closed up. The royal family used to spend a month there each summer, and so the prince and princess and I crossed paths occasionally. That's all."

"Ah yes, of course," said the first vendor brightly. "I often wonder what's become of them. Princess Mariella was always such a bright little thing." He raised an eyebrow at Jacinta. "Didn't she come for your father's funeral? I remember thinking she looked all grown up."

Jacinta swallowed, then nodded. How did the day suddenly turn into a barrage of painful memories? He wasn't wrong, though. The princess had indeed come to the funeral four years earlier. They'd both been fourteen at the time, and Mariella had certainly seemed much more grown up in her finery than Jacinta had felt in her simpler mourning gown.

"Very gracious of her, I'm sure," said the man approvingly. "That must have been a real honor for your family, especially given..." He trailed off, seeming to realize he was straying into uncomfortable territory. Jacinta had long since shown the town's inhabitants that she wouldn't tolerate slights against her family.

"Indeed," Jacinta agreed tightly. "We were very honored."

"Did Crown Prince Matthias come to the funeral, too?" asked a woman known for being a busybody.

Jacinta paused for a moment to collect herself. "No."

"Well, I daresay he had more important things to attend to

in the capital," said the vendor tolerantly. "He's a young man now." He glanced toward the closed-up manor house, which Jacinta knew to be locked up, the halls silent and the furniture shrouded in holland covers. "I do miss the business those royal visits used to bring to our town, though."

"Yes, it's a shame," agreed someone else. "I remember a time when..."

Jacinta let her mind wander, uninterested in reminiscences about how much more prosperous Briarford used to be. It wasn't as though any of it was news to her.

"Jacinta, is it?"

The elf's high voice drew her attention again, and she nodded.

"My name is Valwynn."

"I'm glad to make your acquaintance," said Jacinta, inclining her head again.

She was as surprised by the elf giving her a name as she had been to see the creature in the first place. Elves were rare in the practically magic-less northern region. Their business was mining magic from the ground, after all. Most Vadolisian elves had moved further south, to the rest of the kingdom, where the ground was fertile and the magic correspondingly plentiful.

Everyone knew that the more fertile the land, the more power poured from the ground. That was why the lush jungles and forests in the southwest of the continent were in danger of being overrun by wild magic, while the northern reaches of Providore were as barren of magic as they were in other ways.

"I would like to trade for that," Valwynn said, pointing to the muffler in Jacinta's hand.

"You would?" Jacinta blinked at the elf in surprise.

She was about to say, *What do you want for it?* but remembered in time that she needed to tread very carefully. Bargains with elves were bound by an inherent magic, and that wording might make it sound like she'd agreed to a trade.

"What do you propose to give me if we were to trade?" she asked instead.

Valwynn smiled at her wary tone, as if reading Jacinta's thoughts. But she didn't seem offended by the hesitance.

"These beans." She drew one slender, long-fingered hand from her pocket, holding it open to show Jacinta five green and apparently unremarkable beans.

"Beans?" Jacinta repeated blankly.

"That's right," said Valwynn. "They're magic beans, of course."

"Of course," Jacinta repeated. She was at a total loss for what to say. "I don't think I will, thank you," she settled on, in her politest tone. "They would be eaten up far too quickly."

The elf showed a flash of impatience. "They're not for eating, silly child. They're for planting."

Jacinta frowned. "Do they grow into something I can eat?"

"No," Valwynn said, still seeming irritated. "Of course not. Is food all you think of?"

Jacinta bit down the retort on her lips, her stomach complaining at all this empty talk of food.

"What are they for?" she asked. "What does the magic do?"

"I don't think I'll tell you that," said the elf comfortably.

Jacinta curbed her impatience with an effort. "Then I'll decline to trade my muffler for them."

The elf narrowed her eyes, not as if annoyed, but in contemplation. "What about the cow you mentioned? Would you trade her for my beans?"

"You want my cow?" Jacinta demanded, more perplexed with every turn of the conversation. Without thinking it through, she blurted out, "She's not even giving us milk at present."

"I don't care about that," said Valwynn airily. "I have a fancy to keep the cow as a pet."

Jacinta gave her head a little shake, wondering if she was dreaming. This was by far the strangest encounter she'd ever had at the market.

"My answer remains no," she said in a respectful tone.

"Hm." The elf looked disappointed but, alarmingly, not defeated. "I'll have to give this some thought."

Leaving the elf to those thoughts, Jacinta turned away to barter with the safer and more predictable humans. She had no idea what this Valwynn was thinking, but she could only shudder at the thought of what her mother would say if she went to market with either her valuable muffler or their sole cow and came home with nothing but a handful of beans.

CHAPTER TWO

Matthias

Matthias strode up the corridor, trying to ignore the sunshine pouring through the windows as he scanned the parchment in his hand. It was a perfect day for riding, or perhaps some training in the castle's open-air training yard. But he had too many responsibilities that were unwilling to wait.

Oh, to be a common man rather than a prince and heir to a kingdom.

Or just to be a child again. He'd thought himself unfairly hampered as a child. How little he'd grasped what his future was to be.

Finishing the parchment, Matthias raised his eyes, scolding himself for these thoughts. He didn't really regret his position. He just found it hard to resist the lure of sunshine on days such as the present one, especially with the knowledge that summer was drawing to an end.

Another summer gone by without a visit to Briarford.

The stray thought surprised him. It had been eight years since he'd spent a summer in the northern town, enjoying the break from normal responsibilities at the manor belonging to his mother's family. He'd never gone as an adult, only as a child. Why did the absence of the once annual trip still make him feel every year as though the summer was incomplete?

It was another foolish thought, one he shouldn't allow to distract him from the day's tasks. He rounded a corner, swiftly changing course to avoid walking into a pair of gorgeously dressed and adorned young noblewomen, who greeted him with modest smiles that didn't fool him for a moment.

Lady Letitia and Lady Simone.

He had changed a great deal since those golden summers of his childhood. But some others he could name hadn't changed at all. Reluctantly, Matthias forced himself to stop, bowing to the two young women and greeting them courteously.

His mother's exhortations prompting him, he even bestowed the briefest of kisses on the back of the hand Lady Letty offered him. The gleam of triumph that flashed through her eyes wasn't precisely attractive, but he couldn't deny that she was very pretty in her stylish gown and fashionably curled hair.

"If you'll excuse me, ladies, I'm expected elsewhere," he said, in his usual cheerful way.

With a definite feeling of relief, he strode away toward his father's study. The guards flanking the doors nodded to him, and he didn't slow his pace at all as he walked in confidently.

"Good morning, Father," he said brightly.

"Matthias." King Fidelius nodded without looking up. "Sit."

Matthias obeyed, leaning back comfortably in the chair.

"Did you read the letter from King Ryker?" his father asked.

"Just now," said Matthias.

"What did you think of his request?" King Fidelius looked up at last, pinning his son with a calculating look.

Matthias held in a sigh. He wished his father would converse more naturally with him, instead of constantly setting obvious tests.

"I have mixed reactions," he said. "I do feel for him, and all of Teren. It's a dire situation, with the magic of the Forest of Ilgal having grown so wild. Obviously it would be a huge blow for Teren if the forest became uninhabitable. And I'm delighted for them that they believe they've found a solution. In ordinary circumstances, I would be glad to send any of our singers who were willing to assist with the process. And I would say it would be worthwhile for the crown to fund their travels, as an investment in our relationship with Teren."

"But?" the king prompted.

Matthias settled more comfortably in his chair. "But it's not ordinary circumstances. If the Frossians are to be believed, the giants could breach the wall and mount an attack at any time. I don't think we can spare singers at present. Any willing to assist the crown are already occupied in very valuable work."

"I agree," said King Fidelius approvingly.

Matthias hesitated, wondering how good a mood his correct answer had put his father in. Was it a good time to try again?

"Speaking of the threat from the giants, Father," he said casually, "I still feel we could be doing more to prepare."

"We're shoring up our defenses in both magical and military ways," said the king. "We have agents in Frossenland, including in the northern region, ready to provide the most current information on any developments. Things are well in hand."

Matthias shifted in his seat. "But northern Frossenland is not the only place where Battlement Wall keeps the giants out. If you would allow me to lead a small force, I could examine the stretch of wall that falls in our own kingdom, ensure that there are no weaknesses that could be exploited by—"

"You're not going to Briarford," said the king shortly. "No matter how many times you ask, or how well you think you disguise the question. Leave it be, Matthias. Your place is here."

Matthias fell silent, frustration washing over him. His father wasn't an unreasonable man, generally speaking. Matthias had never been able to understand why his parents were so reluctant for him to go back to the northern town where their family had spent many happy months in his childhood. His duties as crown prince had increased in recent years, but it wasn't as though his time was so full he couldn't afford the occasional trip away from the capital. It was true that the distance to Briarford was considerable, but that hadn't been a barrier once. No one had ever properly explained to him why their annual visits had ceased.

"I intend to write a reply to King Ryker along those lines shortly," Matthias's father went on. "You're welcome to read it before it's sent if you're interested."

Matthias gave a non-committal grunt. He knew his father was eager to expand his training in all matters of state, but checking over correspondence wasn't exactly how Matthias would choose to spend his time.

"The other matter I wanted to discuss with you is this exchange program at the Academy of Song. I understand that you've agreed to take on the first Frossian apprentice?"

"That's right." Matthias nodded. "He's due to arrive today, fresh from the Academy of Song in Sunniva."

The king nodded. "Apparently he comes with high praise from his instructors at the Frossian academy. I've been informed that our academy will send an apprentice to Frossenland when an appropriate candidate is selected."

"It will be interesting to learn if our academies take a different approach to the study of songcraft," Matthias mused.

"I'm sure it will be of great interest to those at the academy, but that's not your focus," King Fidelius reminded his son. "The technical side of things wouldn't mean a great deal to you or I anyway. Your role is to help this young singer—what's his name again?"

"Hagen," Matthias supplied.

The king nodded. "To help Hagen settle into life in the castle, and give him a positive experience of Vadolis. A castle apprenticeship is prestigious, so we can assume this apprentice has the favor of both his king and his academy. The relationship with him could be a key one in promoting goodwill between our kingdoms."

"I know, Father," said Matthias. "I'll do my best to make us look good."

The hint of amusement in his voice didn't awaken any responding humor in his father.

"I trust you will not need to work hard to achieve that aim," the king said coolly. He leaned back in his chair. "Frossenland has become strong again under King Herleif's leadership. If we are to have trouble with the giants for the first time in centuries, it will be in our interests to have a strong alliance with Frossenland." He rapped a knuckle absently against the polished mahogany of his desk. "It's a shame that King Herleif was already married when he reappeared. If we'd known he was alive all that time...a marriage alliance between him and Mariella would have been perfect."

"I'd say that opportunity has well and truly passed us by, Father, given that King Herleif and Queen Adrienne have just christened their first child. Besides," Matthias pointed out, "I'm not sure how Mariella would have felt about that. Herleif is quite a bit older than her, and I don't remember him as the romantic type. Mariella wants to be swept off her feet."

"Mariella will be no such thing," said his father curtly. "This is why we need to find her an appropriate match. It's past time for her to stop daydreaming like a child."

Matthias frowned. "Surely there's no great hurry, Father. She's only eighteen. And why shouldn't she marry for love? She's not the heir."

"She is a member of the Vadolisian royal family," said the

king austerely. "She will marry as her parents see fit." He bent a stern eye upon his son. "As will you."

Matthias raised his hands in a gesture of surrender. "I'm not arguing, Father. Why do you always speak of my hypothetical marriage as if I need to be scolded into making a sensible choice? When have I shown a tendency to be attracted to ineligible girls?"

"You can't deny that your habits haven't always been circumspect when it comes to who you associate with," his father said. "When you were a child, you spurned friendship with every courtier's son, and instead tried to befriend the servants' children!"

"They were so much more fun to play with," Matthias said reminiscently. "And often much kinder friends than the noblemen's children. They didn't have hidden agendas."

"Of course they did," said his father dismissively. "You were just too naive to see it. You're proving my point."

Matthias sighed, running his fingers along a stack of parchments on the desktop. "I don't think I am, though. I've been very dutiful and obedient in this area for many years now."

With one glaring exception, but he had no intention of making his father aware of that incident. He'd gotten away with it at the time, and given it had been four years, he'd ceased to be afraid that his parents would learn of it. He wasn't even sure if Mariella knew about it.

"Well, never mind that," the king said. His voice turned dry. "I believe the Frossian apprentice is a commoner, so you should find him an acceptable friend."

Matthias chuckled. "As long as you don't try to arrange a marriage alliance between me and their thirteen-year-old princess, I'll promise to be friends with any Frossian you like."

His father gave a wry smile. "You can consider yourself safe."

He made a gesture of dismissal with the words, and Matthias

wasted no time in leaving the study. He was pleased to have been assigned to show the Frossian apprentice around. It was a much more interesting task than his usual duties.

It wasn't long before a servant came to find him with the news that the singer had arrived. Matthias strode toward the castle's wide entranceway, not wishing to keep the newcomer waiting. He paused at the end of the corridor, however, taking the opportunity to survey his charge while the steward spoke with him.

The young man had hair so pale it almost looked white, and a rather square jaw. He was stocky and strong—if Matthias hadn't been told he was nineteen, he would have guessed older.

Hagen also looked ill-at-ease. It wasn't anything blatant. He was calm, and his replies to the steward seemed to be respectful and confident. But there was an air about him that Matthias recognized from watching many people come through the castle. If Matthias was reading him correctly, he felt out of place and not of sufficient importance to be there.

The prince found himself warming to the apprentice. It would have been unsurprising if the young singer had been egotistical, since he was presumably among the best at his craft in order to have been selected for this honor. If he was humble enough to feel out of place in a castle, he was likely of sufficient moral character to actually belong there.

"Hagen?" Matthias gave his friendliest smile as he walked across the entranceway. "Welcome to Vallen."

The singer started slightly, but recovered himself quickly in a bow.

"Allow me to introduce His Highness, Crown Prince Matthias," said the steward helpfully.

Hagen bowed again, and Matthias waved it off. "No need for bowing and scraping." He smiled. "We'll likely spend a fair bit of time together. I've been tasked with settling you in here at the castle."

"I'm honored, Your Highness," said Hagen, his low voice carrying the melodic quality so common in singers.

"Are you tired from your journey?" Matthias asked. "Do you want to settle into your rooms straight away, or shall I take you on a tour of the castle first?"

"I'm all right," said Hagen, clearly wishing to be accommodating. "I crossed East River last night. It was an easy ride to Vallen this morning."

"Excellent," said Matthias brightly. He nodded to the steward. "I'm sure someone will see that your things make it to your rooms." He looked around the entryway. "Where are your things?"

"Here." Hagen swung a rucksack from his shoulder and held it in front of him, looking uncomfortable.

Matthias blinked at it, good manners asserting themselves just in time to prevent him from blurting out, *That's all?* His father hadn't exaggerated when he'd called Hagen a commoner. It was heartening. Prestigious apprenticeships were often given to any singers within the nobility, regardless of talent. It reflected well on King Herleif and his Academy of Song that the magical exchange to the castle in Vallen had been offered to a commoner without wealth.

It also reflected well on Hagen's abilities.

"Walk with me, Hagen," said Matthias, when the steward had relieved Hagen of his lone bag. He led the other man across the entryway and up a corridor. "Where in Frossenland do you come from?"

Hagen cleared his throat. "Originally from the north, Your Highness. My family lived in Toveham for generations. But when I was twelve, we moved to the capital." He paused. "Sunniva, I mean. Of course, Tove used to be the capital a long time ago, which might be why my family settled there initially. I don't know our history that far back."

"Living in the north must have been frustrating for you, with your gift," Matthias commented. "Magic being so scarce in the region, I mean."

"Yes," Hagen commented. "I made more progress on my songcraft when we moved further south."

"Is that why you moved?" Matthias asked curiously.

Hagen hesitated for a fraction too long. "One of the reasons."

Matthias decided not to push. "Out that window, you'll see the royal training yard," he commented, waving a hand. "I'll take you past there later. There's another training yard at the Academy of Song, which your mentors will probably take you to. Magic of any kind isn't allowed in the castle's training yard. It's purely for unembellished physical combat."

Hagen nodded his understanding, and Matthias moved on with the tour, showing him the formal dining hall for special celebrations and his father's public receiving room. Hagen responded respectfully to anything directed at him, but he didn't offer much. Matthias refused to be daunted, taking it as his personal mission to draw the other man out.

"I have some experience with the frozen north myself," Matthias commented as they went out a side door and into a small, private garden. "Our capital was never anywhere but Vallen, but my family used to spend a month each summer in Briarford. It's a small town right in the shadow of Battlement Wall."

Hagen raised an eyebrow. "The people must be tough. Even Toveham wasn't in sight of the wall. Not many in Frossenland would be willing to live that far north."

"Yes." Matthias's eyes glazed over as a steady trickle of memories made their way through his mind. One particular resident of Briarford had been the toughest friend he'd ever had. But thinking of her would just bring him pain. "They're indomitable. My mother's family has an estate up there. It's not where they live—they moved their main residence to an estate further south a long time ago, as the northern region grew colder and more, well..."

"Barren," Hagen supplied, his voice emotionless.

"Yes, that," said Matthias. "So the house was empty most of the time, but still maintained. Like I said, we used to stay there every year." He frowned. "Until we just stopped. It was when I was twelve as well, incidentally."

"The age we all abandon the frozen north," said Hagen. He spoke lightly, but there was an edge to his words.

"Yes, so it seems." Matthias studied his face, familiar and uncomfortable thoughts in his mind. "Do you think it felt like an abandonment? To those you left behind?" He paused. "To the residents of Briarford?"

"I don't know," said Hagen, seeming surprised at the prince's searching question. "I've often wondered. My parents worked in the castle in Tove, and I can't deny it was a blow to them when the royal family stopped spending time there. I wouldn't be surprised if others felt the same about us leaving. My father was set against it. But we were far from the first ones."

"Did your father come around?" Matthias asked curiously.

Hagen was silent for a moment before he answered. "No. I don't think he would have ever moved. He died when I was a boy. We moved after that."

Matthias winced at his clumsiness. "I'm sorry," he said. "I shouldn't have pried."

"Not at all," Hagen assured him. "It's no secret."

Matthias nodded, his thoughts returning to his own northern region as he thought over the other man's words. "There's no castle in Briarford, but I believe the manor house was closed up after we stopped using it."

Hagen nodded wisely. "Which likely meant a number of locals were out of work."

"But they would have found other work, surely," said Matthias quickly. "If they worked in a nobleman's manor frequented by the royal family, wouldn't that carry a high recommendation?"

Hagen shrugged. "Only if there's other work to be had, which likely there wasn't." He gave Matthias a curious look. "If you'll forgive me speaking plainly, Your Highness, maybe you don't know the state of the frozen north as well as you think you do."

Matthias ran a hand over his chin, lost in thought. How many times in those early years after they stopped going to Briarford had he imagined confronting her, and demanding an explanation? Now he wondered uneasily if her side of the story might cast a different light on things.

He gave his head a little shake. But no. She'd had every chance to tell him if she or her family were in trouble. Why was he even thinking about this? It had been so many years. It was all water well under the bridge, flowing far beyond his reach or interest.

"Well, I should probably show you to your rooms," he said, returning his attention to Hagen. "I'm sure one of our resident singers will be wishing to give you a proper induction. We can finish the tour later."

The Frossian followed him back into the castle, keeping stride in silence.

"You're to be accommodated in the same wing as the castle singers who take responsibility for—"

"Matthias!" A bright voice cut him off. "There you are!"

His sister's petite form skipped into view, her auburn hair cascading down from where it had been carefully pulled back, and her face as cheerful as ever.

"Mariella." Matthias smiled at her. "I'm glad we've run into you. I've just been showing Hagen around."

"Hagen?" Mariella asked, turning eyes bright with interest onto the newcomer. Her expression was open and friendly, stripping away any rudeness in the way she and Matthias were speaking of their guest rather than to him.

"The singer from Frossenland who's come to take up an apprenticeship in our castle as part of an exchange between the academies," Matthias prompted her. He turned to his new charge. "Hagen, this is my sister, Princess Mariella."

She swept into a dazzlingly graceful curtsy, her eyes never leaving Hagen's.

"I'm delighted to make your acquaintance," she told the Frossian. "I hope you'll enjoy your stay here, and that the exchange will strengthen the ties between our kingdoms."

She straightened, her smile brighter than ever.

"Now that those formalities are done, and I've said what I should, we can forget about matters of state. You don't look like a nobleman, so I'm sure you didn't come here hoping to get mired in politics." Her eyes sparkled. "Not if you have any sense in you." She cocked her head to one side. "Will you sing for me?"

"Mariella," laughed Matthias. "Give the poor man a minute to settle in. He's barely arrived from Frossenland."

"I didn't mean anything arduous," said Mariella innocently. "Just a little song. Our resident singers are much too serious. They'll never sing without proper royal cause." She narrowed her eyes in disapproval, the effect far from intimidating.

Matthias glanced at Hagen, who'd remained silent throughout the princess's greeting. He looked a little dazed by the flood of words. "Ignore my sister, Hagen. There's no need for you to stretch yourself."

"It wouldn't be a stretch at all," said Hagen, recovering

himself and offering the princess a belated—and rather clumsy —bow. "The magic in your kingdom is plentiful and responsive."

He cleared his throat, then let out a low, wordless melody. After a few notes that seemed to hang, throbbing, in the air, he added words, a simple invocation to beauty. Matthias listened, spellbound, to the enchanting sound. So few people were born with the ability to sing, and there was no way for anyone else to learn it. A person was either a singer or not a singer. No matter how he tried, Matthias knew he'd never be able to make his voice create melody like Hagen was doing. And he always enjoyed hearing singers at work.

For a moment he'd forgotten even to wonder what magic Hagen was working through the song, until his gaze followed the apprentice's to the floor beneath their feet. Through a tiny crack in the polished stone of the corridor, a green tendril was poking. Before their eyes, it grew, a bud developing on the end before unfurling into a common daisy.

The song died off as Hagen bent down and picked up the bloom, holding it out to Mariella. "For Her Highness," he said. "I had to work with the options dormant underneath us, or I would have called forth a blossom more appropriate to a royal castle."

"No, it's beautiful as it is," beamed Mariella. She turned the flower over in her hand, enchanted. "Thank you." With deft fingers, she slipped the daisy into her hair.

Matthias glanced at Hagen, noting with relief that the singer seemed pleased with how his efforts had been received rather than irritated at being put on show like a performing animal.

"Well, it was lovely to meet you, Hagen," Mariella said. She raised her eyebrows in farewell to her brother. "See you at the meal, Matthias."

She turned on the words, nearly colliding at the closest corner with one of the castle's two resident singers.

"Your Highness." The silver-haired man sounded tense as he bowed to Mariella.

"Ah, excellent timing," Matthias told him brightly, as his sister moved out of sight. "I was just going to have a message sent to you. Your new apprentice has arrived. Allow me to introduce Hagen."

The man approached, considering Hagen with an expression that even Matthias found forbidding.

"That explains it," he said curtly. "I thought I heard singing. You're Hagen, are you? We were told to expect you today." His eyes flicked between the pair. "What songcraft were you exercising, young man?"

"Nothing of import," said Hagen quickly, his voice gruff now. "I apologize if I sang out of turn."

"I'll be the judge of its importance," said the singer sternly. "What was the song?"

Hagen cleared his throat. "A simple growth song, calling a dormant plant from the ground beneath us and making it bloom."

"Hm." The experienced singer looked unimpressed. "I suppose we'll have to examine the foundations for root damage."

"No, there's truly no damage," said Hagen quickly. "There was no substantial root system. I called out a simple daisy."

The singer eyed him. "It seems things are done differently in Sunniva, Hagen, but in Vallen, apprentices do not sing without authority from their masters. Particularly in the castle."

"Yes, sir," said Hagen, his frame stiff with discomfort.

"It really wasn't his fault," Matthias interjected. "My sister pressed him to sing for us, and politeness dictated that he oblige. I realize I don't understand the craft, but it seemed to me like he chose the least impactful option he could find."

"Hm." If the resident singer's expression softened, it was only minutely. "Thank you for your interest in my apprentice, Your Highness," he said, with a bow. "I'll be glad to take charge of him from here."

"Yes, of course." Matthias sent Hagen what he hoped was an encouraging smile. The apprentice didn't see it, his focus on the corridor where Mariella had disappeared.

"Do you mind giving me one more minute with Hagen?" Matthias asked, concerned at the guarded look on Hagen's face. He didn't want the young singer to form the wrong idea about Mariella.

Hagen's supervisor stepped backward, allowing Matthias to draw Hagen further down the corridor.

"I'm sorry my sister's request got you in trouble," Matthias said quietly. "She seems foolish, and dare I say it, a bit flighty, but she's not." He felt an unpleasant heaviness settle on his heart. They all had their defenses. Mariella's were effective in their own way. He shook off the thought, trying to speak more cheerfully. "The truth is she has a very good heart. Better than mine, in fact."

The melancholy threatened to descend again as, for the second time that day, he found his thoughts drifting to a certain funeral in Briarford four years earlier. Mariella hadn't faced the same obstacles he had, it was true, but she'd undoubtedly handled the situation better.

"Neither you nor the princess has anything to apologize for, Your Highness," said Hagen, in his low, steady voice. He hesitated a moment before adding, "And I didn't think her foolish or flighty."

Matthias rewarded this diplomatic answer with a vague smile. "I'm glad to hear it. I'll see you again soon, Hagen."

He strode off down the corridor, his thoughts far away. He'd been looking forward to meeting Hagen, and getting a closer view of how an apprentice in songcraft was trained. What he hadn't counted on was the singer's heritage—both as a northerner and the child of a family formerly employed at a royal, northern retreat —and the wounds that heritage would poke at.

Wounds he'd thought long healed but which, judging by the emotions swirling through him, were still much more raw than he cared to admit.

CHAPTER THREE

Jacinta

Jacinta stared up at the imposing stone fence. It was still solid and impenetrable, in spite of the overgrown creepers and other signs that it was no longer being maintained.

Well, impenetrable for those who didn't know it as well as she did. She turned away from the unyielding iron gates, running a hand along the stones of the wall as she made her way around the edge of the property.

This isn't so bad, she told herself. *I can handle this.*

She knew she was deceiving herself. Of course the trickle of emotion she felt at seeing the walls of the estate was manageable. She didn't have much sentiment attached to the outside. That view bore no relation to her childhood—she'd spent all of that inside the walls, looking out. The manor was where the real pain awaited her.

But she didn't care. She'd mostly been sensible in staying away these last several years, and she was ready to be foolish. Ready to put herself through the pain of remembering.

What did it matter now, anyway? If she and her mother were

going to starve, what did she have to lose from the emotional risk of reliving happier times?

Perhaps she was being dramatic. She and her mother would manage—they always found a way. But she had to acknowledge to herself that she couldn't remember their situation ever being so desperate before. The food she'd bartered her precious mink muffler for was gone, and much too quickly. Princess had produced no more milk, and worst of all, both of their neighbors had informed them that they were sending their wool to be spun in the next town over.

Someone there had a magically enhanced spinning wheel, apparently, and the job was much more efficient.

It wasn't in Jacinta's nature to give in to despair, but she truly couldn't see a way out. Her mother was mostly recovered from her illness now, and she'd visited every home and shop in town, offering their services as cleaners, or assistants, or anything at all. No one needed help. Or at least, no one could afford to pay for it. Times were hard for everyone, and with winter coming, the whole town knew they'd get harder.

All they had was a cow who didn't produce milk. Her mother thought they'd need to eat her, but Jacinta wasn't sure she could bring herself to eat Princess. She'd have to take her to the markets the next day instead. She could fetch a good price for the cow, and if they were wise, they could make it stretch. The buyer may well have the same grim plans for the cow, but at least Jacinta wouldn't see it. A pang of hunger lanced through her stomach, the familiar complaint easy to ignore. She'd reached the place now, and she stepped back from the wall to study the tangled vines growing around its base. It had been undisturbed for a long time.

Stooping, Jacinta ripped at the brambles. They didn't come away easily, and her hands had many scratches by the time she'd cleared the area enough to reveal the grate beneath. She gave it an experimental wobble, and a smile crossed her face. Still loose.

Jacinta was taller than she had been in childhood, but otherwise not much larger. Small benefits of barely scraping by, she supposed. The rusty grate came free in her hand, and she used a stick to clear the cobwebs from her passage. Her gown would get filthy, no doubt, but it didn't matter.

Lying flat on her stomach, she crawled forward, pulling herself hand over hand through the small, ground-level opening. She emerged into the manor's garden, scrambling to her feet and brushing leaves from her skirt.

She raised her eyes slowly, drinking in the familiar landscape. The gardens were sadly neglected, the once-neat rows overgrown, and the trees in desperate need of pruning. It wasn't beyond reclaim. Her father would make short work of tending his once-loved landscaping back into shape with his song if he was here. But she didn't want to dwell on what he'd think if he saw this sad sight. She also didn't want to reflect on how the total lack of maintenance spoke clearly of the owners' disinterest in ever returning to their holding in the frozen north. She was here to remember happier times.

Jacinta made her way toward the house. The ivy had grown a little wild over the walls in the years since the place had been locked up, but the manor's facade was still imposing. Not that Jacinta had found it that way as a child. It had been familiar. It had been home. She'd always taken pride in the majestic appearance of the country residence.

She followed the outside of the manor around to the back, to the servants' entrance. This had been her true domain. She looked hopefully through the kitchen garden, gratified to find a few plants still producing edible fruit. She pocketed some peas in their pods, and even managed to dig up an onion that must have self-planted. She could make them into a passable stew for the evening's meal.

As she deposited them in her pocket, her fingers brushed against cool metal. She drew the key out as she approached the kitchen door. Her mother didn't know the fate of the supposedly lost spare key. Jacinta would have been in terrible trouble if either of her parents had realized she'd intentionally kept it. But she had no regrets. This wasn't the first time she'd snuck in since the house was deserted. Although her head knew she had no right to be there, her heart couldn't quite accept that she wasn't entitled to visit the place that had been her home for so much of her life. It wasn't as though the owners were using it, or had any interest in its maintenance.

Jacinta hovered in the doorway of her old room, the small but comfortable space now looking bare and dead. It wasn't anyone's home anymore. None of her personal effects remained —she'd taken them all when she and her parents had moved out. It had been so sudden, and she still didn't understand it. When the royal family departed after that final summer visit, her parents had packed up and sought a place to rent in town. In spite of Jacinta's tears and pleading, they'd been adamant. And they'd never explained their reason.

Of course, the rumor mill had given plenty of reasons. Jacinta remembered her outrage when she'd first heard the whispers that her parents had actually left because they'd been fired by the king and queen for misconduct. She'd hotly defended the claim in the marketplace. But when she took her indignation home to her parents, their reaction had been unsettling. Neither of them had scoffed or contradicted, as she'd expected. She still remembered how their faces had closed off, and how unyielding they'd been in redirecting the conversation.

She wished they'd just been honest with her. She still felt that it would be easier to accept that they really had been dismissed for misconduct than to wonder what had actually happened, certain of nothing but that her parents weren't giving her the full picture.

She'd been tempted to ask Mariella in a letter if it was true, but she couldn't bring herself to do it. What if the princess didn't know, and the news caused her to stop writing? She'd wanted to keep the one friend she still had, even if she was far away and out of reach. The people of Briarford had turned a cold shoulder on her family when the rumor spread. It was years ago now, of course, and most had long forgotten the gossip. But there was no denying that the loss of reputation had cost her family dearly in finding more work at the time.

And, of course, all the old stories had resurfaced on her father's death, most likely spurred by the unexpected presence of the princess at his funeral. But at that time, Jacinta had been too swallowed in her grief to really care.

Besides, her father's death was the circumstance that made her realize how little any of it mattered. Once they lost him, they wouldn't have been able to stay anyway. The house was fully closed up by then, and she and her mother would never have been able to keep it in even the most basically inhabitable state without his songcraft to aid them.

Thoughts of that grief-ridden time inevitably brought to mind the last visit Jacinta had made to the abandoned manor house. It had been four years ago, the day of her father's funeral. Still reeling from his sudden death and unsure she could face the ceremony, she'd fled to the sanctuary of her former home. She'd been only fourteen, but clad in her expensive black gown —the last new garment they'd been able to afford—she'd felt much older. She'd felt as though her childhood was over forever. Looking back, she'd been right.

Wandering the halls in her grief, she'd felt as much a ghost as her father. Just as the eighteen-year-old Jacinta was doing, her younger self had walked through the formal parlor with its furniture swathed in covers and into the part of the manor where the royal family had once spent their visits.

Dust swirled under her feet as she passed now, marking her passage into the very corridor where Matthias's and Mariella's rooms had been located. The siblings had always been close. She knew from hearing her mother mention it to her father that they'd specifically requested rooms with an adjoining receiving room between them.

Feeling as though she was walking through her memory of the day of her father's funeral, Jacinta came to a stop in that room, remembering the many happy hours she'd spent with the pair of siblings there. Playing checkers on rainy days, challenging each other to dares, reading aloud...Matthias had always kept her and Mariella in stitches with his dramatic portrayal of even the driest text. Technically, Jacinta wasn't supposed to be in that part of the manor, but it was rare for a single day to pass during the royals' visit without either Mariella or Matthias sneaking her in.

When the weather was fine, of course, they didn't sit around. All three of them couldn't wait to get out in the sunshine, exploring the woods, conquering imaginary giants, and running barefoot through the gardens.

As she surveyed the still, muffled scene of her childhood memories, Jacinta relived her visit there four years before, the day of the funeral. Much as she resented her own weakness, part of her wished she could once again be startled by the sight of a tall, young man stepping out of the bedroom she'd thought empty.

. . .

"Oh, I'm...I'm sorry," Jacinta stammered, eyes widening as she took in his finery. Had the manor been sold at last to another noble family? "I know I'm not supposed to be here."

"Jacinta?"

The familiarity of the voice had stunned her into stillness, her eyes traveling more slowly over the young man's features.

"Matthias?" Her own voice came out a whisper, hardly able to believe the evidence of her eyes. For a moment, all she saw was the playmate and confidante of her childhood, and without thinking it through, she threw herself toward him.

He received her into his arms willingly, and Jacinta let herself relax, the burden of the last four years of struggle and the more crushing weight of her recent grief seeming suddenly lighter.

"I've missed you." The words were whispered into her hair, their simple kindness bringing tears to Jacinta's eyes. An insidious voice in her mind retorted, then why didn't you write to me? but she silenced it.

The memory of the years that had now stretched between them and their childish friendship had intruded on her moment of peace, however, and she drew back. She dabbed self-consciously at her eyes as she cast another look over him. How had she seen her childhood friend? The Matthias of her memory was long gone, replaced by a handsome and confident young man. Not just a young man. A young prince. Out of the reach of her friendship in every possible way.

"You're so...grown up." The words tumbled out without her permission.

Matthias let out a laugh that made her heart ache with all the memories it carried. "So are you." He fell quiet as he once again considered her. "It's strange, isn't it? I'd know you anywhere, and yet... you're so different."

Jacinta cleared her throat, overwhelmed by the emotions passing through her. "Are you supposed to be here?" she asked.

The prince's expression became more guarded, and he shook his head.

"How did you even get in?" Jacinta demanded. She cast another look over him, her cheeks inexplicably warming as she took in how broad his shoulders had become. "You don't look like you'd fit through the grate anymore."

Matthias grinned. "I remember that old grate. I definitely wouldn't fit now." His eyes passed over her form, and Jacinta felt her cheeks heat further. To her relief, he didn't comment on the ways in which she'd grown. "It's not just you I've missed," he said, looking fondly around him. "I've missed this place. We were so happy here, weren't we?"

"Yes." The word came so softly, Jacinta could barely hear her own voice.

"I have to admit, it's a bit of a shock to see it in its current state," Matthias commented. "It's become so dilapidated."

"Yes," Jacinta repeated, something inside her hardening. "It's a good reflection of what's happened to Briarford. And my life."

"Jacinta." Matthias's face softened at once. "I'm so sorry about your father. I was devastated when I heard. I can't imagine how much you're hurting."

That snide voice sounded in Jacinta's head again, questioning how sad he could really be about her father's death. She knew it wasn't fair. It might not even be true that his parents had fired hers, and even if it was true, that didn't make it Matthias's fault. But her emotions were such a tangled mess, she didn't trust herself with words.

"It's his funeral today," she said hollowly.

"I know." Matthias nodded. "That's why I'm here."

She raised her eyes to him in amazement. "You came to attend his funeral?" Her heart swelled at this public declaration of honor. Surely the wagging tongues would stop bringing up rumors of her family being disgraced in the eyes of the king and queen if the crown prince attended her father's funeral.

But this optimism waned as Matthias squirmed before her eyes. "I can't actually come to the funeral. I'm sorry, Jacinta. I...I would like to, but I..."

"But you what?" she asked, her eyes narrowing. "You're too ashamed?" The rumors must have been true—her father was a disgraced man in the sight of the royals as well as the people of Briarford.

"Of course not," Matthias denied quickly. After a moment's hesitation, he stepped forward. Lifting a hand that—in spite of his confident demeanor—shook slightly, he touched her dark braid, causing her heart to jump erratically. "Jacinta, I'm not ashamed. I just have pressures on me that you don't...that are hard to explain. Things that weren't part of my life here, but that control so much of it in the capital."

"But you're not in the capital," said Jacinta, a note of pleading in her voice. "You're here, with me. Like old times."

"I wish it was like old times," said Matthias regretfully.

"It can be," Jacinta insisted. She glanced out the window. "I have to go, Matthias. The funeral will be starting any minute. Will you come with me?"

Matthias hesitated, then shook his head. "I'm sorry."

Jacinta stepped back, disappointment settling like lead in her stomach. But it was unreasonable, she told herself. She'd never dreamed Matthias would appear as if by magic to comfort her on her day of grief. She had no right to be disappointed that he was only willing to do it privately.

"I understand," she said dully. "You have many demands on your time. I must go, though."

"Jacinta."

Matthias's face was so deeply unhappy, it tugged at her heart. She turned, waiting for him to say more, perhaps to tell her that he'd changed his mind, and would come to the funeral and hang any damage to his reputation.

"I really am sorry for your loss."

The inadequate words hung between them for a moment before Jacinta nodded.

"Thank you."

She hurried away on the words, more shaken by the encounter than she cared to admit. It was too much. She was already dealing with the loss of her father. She couldn't wrestle with her emotions regarding this new, older, more complicated Matthias as well.

Jacinta came back to the present, a shiver passing over her as she stared at the place where she'd last seen Matthias. It was so long ago. Why did the emotions still feel so fresh? She was being foolish.

She'd been so confused by Matthias's behavior, unable to comprehend why he would travel such a distance for the funeral only to not attend. It wasn't until she arrived at the ceremony and received a second shock in the form of Mariella that she understood. Matthias must have escorted his sister on the trip from the capital. Far from mollifying Jacinta, it made the whole situation harder to swallow. If Mariella wasn't ashamed to be seen with the mourners, why should he be?

But then, Mariella had been willing to write to her when Matthias hadn't.

Jacinta's conflicted feelings had only intensified when Mariella told her, after a long and comforting embrace that somehow felt very different from Matthias's, that the prince had wanted to come but had been unable to.

The awkwardness in the princess's voice had made Jacinta grit her teeth. Clearly Mariella had no idea that Jacinta was aware of how close Matthias had come to attending. And she didn't intend to inform her. No need for the princess to know her lies weren't believable.

If they had been lies. Both of them had made it sound like the decision might not be in Matthias's hands. Jacinta didn't know much about how the royal family operated in their normal life. Perhaps they had much stricter rules regarding the crown prince than his younger sister. Perhaps he had to be more cautious with whom he was seen, and how his reputation might be affected.

Thinking about it with the hindsight of four years, Jacinta reached the same conclusion she had at the time. What difference did it make? She didn't blame Matthias either way. He'd owed her no obligation to attend her father's funeral, any more than she'd been entitled to expect letters from him. But blame or no blame, it was still added to the long list of things that stood between them. Of painful circumstances that soured the once-happy memories of their childhood times together.

Jacinta turned her back on the familiar rooms, making her way out into the weak sunlight. She didn't want to spend her time with ghosts. She had much more pressing concerns to focus on if she wanted to ensure she and her mother stayed among the living. She needed to let go of sentiment. It was time to barter Princess.

In that spirit, she took the cow to the market with her the following day. Her heart was heavy, and not because of her mother's dire comments that they were in desperate straits to be giving up their last animal.

It hadn't been meant as a criticism—her mother agreed with her assessment that the time had come to barter Princess. That wasn't why Jacinta felt sad. The truth was, foolish as it may seem, she was very fond of the cow. Princess had been with them for years, and had been the recipient of many heartfelt confidences from a younger Jacinta. It was deeply depressing to think of her being butchered, but given she'd stopped producing milk, Jacinta could see no other likely outcome of her sale.

She tried to turn off her emotions when she reached the market, knowing they wouldn't aid in shrewd bargaining. A number of neighbors had been aware that the mother and daughter were close to bartering their cow, and Jacinta saw a few pairs of eyes light up as she and Princess approached. To her irritation, the neighbors in question seemed determined to cheat her. Either that, or her estimation of her cow's value was vastly different from theirs.

Jacinta refused to budge in the negotiations, painfully aware that her own and her mother's survival depended on her trading Princess not just for food, but for an ongoing source of food. A chicken or two who were actually laying would be ideal, but there were other options she'd accept.

None of which anyone seemed prepared to offer.

Jacinta had just stepped away from one stall to collect her thoughts when a child spoke up from behind her.

"Having trouble?"

"Yes," said Jacinta, without turning around. "You could say that."

"Do you want to sell your cow for a lot *more* than it's worth, instead of less than it's worth?"

"Yes, that would be great, thanks," said Jacinta with a hint of sarcasm. Bargains like that weren't possible in the shrewd marketplace of Briarford.

"Done." The voice turned instantly from whimsical to businesslike, and Jacinta spun around, uneasy.

To her alarm, she saw that the high-pitched voice had come not from a child, but from an elf. The very elf who'd approached her in the markets the week before.

"Valwynn?" she asked warily.

"That's right." The elf beamed at her. "I'm so pleased we've been able to make an arrangement after all. I'll have the cow now."

Cold horror dropped into Jacinta's stomach. "No, no, no," she said quickly. "I wasn't making a bargain with you. I was just...talking."

"Talking is precisely how bargains are made, child," said the elf, in a tone of humorous indulgence. "And I'd like to fulfill our bargain immediately, thanks."

Jacinta shook her head quickly. "There wasn't a bargain. You didn't even say what you'd give in exchange."

"Yes I did," contradicted the elf. "I said I'd give you a lot more than it's worth. And that's precisely what I'm going to do."

"What is this merchandise that's apparently worth much more than my cow?" Jacinta asked, although she had a horrible feeling that she already knew.

Sure enough, the elf opened one hand, holding it palm up to reveal five small beans.

Jacinta let out a groan. "I can't trade my cow for beans!"

"On the contrary," said Valwynn happily. "You've just done so."

"What am I supposed to do with those?" Jacinta demanded.

"Excellent question," nodded Valwynn. "I was going to give more specific instructions, but I've found out where you live, and I'm pleased to say it simplifies things considerably. Just plant them anywhere near your home, and all should be fine."

"All will not be fine!" Jacinta cried, gripping Princess's halter more tightly. "Please, Valwynn, I'm begging you to release me from the bargain. I didn't mean to enter into it!"

"Intention has nothing to do with it when it comes to elf bargains," said Valwynn comfortably. "The point isn't what you meant to say, but what you actually said. You're bound to the bargain now, same as I am." She rattled her fist. "Here."

Jacinta stared down at the five vivid, green beans in the elf's palm. "Please." Her voice was hollow. "I can't go home with just those. I have to make a proper trade. My mother and I will starve otherwise."

"Nonsense," said Valwynn unconcernedly. "Haven't I just told you that all will be fine?"

"Fine for whom?" Jacinta asked, her anger growing.

Maddeningly, the elf laughed. "You are a shrewd one," she said. "I'm glad I chose you. Hopefully, all will be fine for many, if you do your part with half an ounce of sense."

"My part?" Jacinta was almost wailing in frustration now. "My part in what? What is it I'm supposed to do?"

"I've already told you," said the elf. "Plant the beans."

"How will that help feed me and my mother?" Jacinta demanded.

The little elf shrugged. "Oh, well, that's not my affair, is it? That part's up to you. I'm sure you'll manage beautifully, though." She held out a hand imperiously for Princess's halter. "You don't want to break the bargain," she prompted, when Jacinta still didn't hand it over. "Trust me when I tell you, it's not worth unleashing the magic attached to bargains."

Fingers numb, Jacinta held the halter out. Her eyes were miserable as they rested on Princess's docile countenance. How had she made such a catastrophic mess of this trade?

"Excellent! And here are your beans."

The elf's cheerfulness was grating against Jacinta's misery. Silently, she held out a hand to receive the meager offering.

"It's a good trade for the cow, at least," said Valwynn pleasantly. "If she's producing no milk, another buyer would probably butcher her for meat, but, like I said, I think I'll keep her as a pet."

And with a tug on Princess's halter, she turned and skipped —positively *skipped*—out of the market, leaving Jacinta ready to tear her hair out.

Mutters were beginning to grow around her, soon turning into chuckles at the sight of the elf leaving with the cow and Jacinta clutching a handful of beans.

"Got done by an elf, did you, lass?" asked an older woman with a titter. "Ah well, happens to the best of us."

The ones who'd attempted unsuccessfully to barter with Jacinta for Princess looked more inclined to be angry than amused, and she decided it was time to make herself scarce. Cheeks burning in humiliation, she hurried out of the market toward home.

She was dreading telling her mother what had happened, and debated making up some story. But no good would come of lying.

"Jacinta?" Her mother's voice greeted her while she was still in the yard. "Is that you?"

"Yes, Mamma," said Jacinta, coming into the hut.

"What did you get for the cow?" her mother demanded.

Jacinta swallowed around the lump in her throat. "I...I made a terrible mess of it, Mamma. I was trying to negotiate, but I got tricked by an elf."

"An elf?" her mother demanded, startled. "What's an elf doing at the market in Briarford?"

"I have no idea," said Jacinta helplessly. "But she was there last week, too, so I should have been more on my guard. I'm so sorry, Mamma."

"Sorry for what?" her mother asked with a dash of impatience. "What exactly is it that this elf tricked you into doing?"

Jacinta drew a deep breath. "She trapped me with words into trading Princess for...for these."

She held out the beans, and for a long moment of painful silence, both women just stared at them.

"Beans?" her mother asked blankly. "Am I seeing right?"

Jacinta sighed. "Yes. Apparently they're magic beans."

"What do they do?" asked the older woman skeptically.

"The elf declined to tell me." Jacinta's voice was hard. "She just said to plant them near our home somewhere."

Her mother let out a long breath, surprising Jacinta with her calm. "Well, I suppose you'd best do what you were told."

"But, Mamma..." Jacinta stared at her. "Don't you realize what a disaster this is? Without Princess, we have nothing! How will we survive the winter?"

"My hopes of surviving the winter weren't high," said her mother prosaically. "You're a shrewd bargainer, Jacinta." She glanced at the beans. "Well, usually. But even you can't get a season's worth of food from one cow in a market where no one has anything much to spare. Even if anyone had a laying chicken to sell, there's no guarantee that chicken would keep laying through the winter."

Jacinta bit her lip. None of these thoughts were new to her, but hearing her mother say them so unconcernedly was difficult.

"Besides," the older woman went on, "we don't have nothing." There was a hint of humor as she nodded at Jacinta's still outstretched hand. "We have those beans. Now go on."

Still a bit stunned by her mother's calm response, Jacinta went out into the yard. She wasn't inclined to take things as philosophically as her mother. Inside, she was still seething with anger at the elf's perfidy, and despair at their hopeless situation.

Still, she may as well plant the beans. The elf had bargained on the basis that they were worth more than a cow. Given the elf was bound by the bargain, that must be true in her eyes, although that gave no guarantee that Valwynn's assessment of value would bear any relation to what Jacinta and her mother actually needed to survive. But if they grew into anything, it would be better than nothing. And if they really were magic, maybe they'd exceed Jacinta's expectations.

Not that she had any high hopes as she cast her eye around the yard, looking for a likely spot to plant them. The wall loomed over her as always, its shadow bringing an extra chill to the already cold air. Jacinta's gaze fell on the outhouse, which stood between their hut and the distant wall.

"This is what I think of your beans," she muttered to the absent elf as she strode across the yard. Kneeling down behind the outhouse, so that the hut was obscured from her view, she planted the beans in the hard, frozen earth. At least the soil here would be better fertilized than elsewhere, she thought, wrinkling her nose at the thought.

A tremor shook the ground as she covered the beans with the upturned soil. It wasn't by any stretch the strongest she'd felt, but it was still enough to make the outhouse rattle. Jacinta ignored it. The tremors were the very least of her concerns.

Her work done, she stepped back. "You really will be magic if you can grow in this hard soil," she informed the now-buried beans. "I can't say I'm holding my breath."

Disgruntled and hungry, she turned her back on the scene and strode toward the house. They were almost out of wood, but tonight they'd have a fire. It wasn't as though they could eat the wood. If they were going to starve, they may as well be warm.

CHAPTER FOUR

Matthias

Matthias grunted in effort as he parried the attack. Sweat beaded on his forehead, and his muscles strained. He'd been in the training yard since the sun rose, and it was starting to tell. His moves weren't as tight as they had been when he started, and his arms were weary. Slipping in under his guard, his opponent landed a hit.

The prince stepped back, acknowledging it with a gesture. The member of the royal guard with whom he was sparring drew back as well, wiping an arm across his forehead.

"If you hadn't been born a prince, you'd make a formidable royal guard, Your Highness."

Matthias laughed. "You're too generous," he said. "That's the third bout I've lost in a row."

The guard smiled. "If I'd been fighting with barely a break for four hours, I'd likely be unable to raise my sword at all."

Eyeing the muscular and well-trained guard, Matthias doubted that was true. But he appreciated the man's attempt to spare his feelings.

"Been watching me disgrace myself, have you?" he asked

lightly. A page boy trotted up with a towel, and Matthias accepted it gratefully, his chest heaving with his breaths.

"Not at all, Your Highness," the guard contradicted. "I've been watching you give an excellent account of yourself." He hesitated, giving Matthias the distinct impression he meant to say more, before dipping his head in a bow.

"What is it?" Matthias asked. "You can speak freely."

The guard hesitated again, then seemed to decide he was genuine. "I hope I'm not out of line to say it, Your Highness, but you look to me like a man who's trying to use training to get something off his mind."

Matthias grimaced.

Accurately taking it as acknowledgment, the guard continued. "Many a man does the same when his mind is troubled. But in my experience, all it does is prolong facing whatever is weighing you down." He gave a disarming smile. "And makes your sword work sloppy, because your mind is elsewhere."

"You're bold," Matthias laughed, "calling your prince's sword work sloppy."

"I'm sorry, Your Highness, I didn't mean—" the guard started in alarm, but Matthias waved him off with another laugh.

"I spoke entirely in jest. You said nothing you shouldn't have, and my sword work *was* sloppy in that last bout." He shook the man's hand to acknowledge a good fight. "Thanks for the advice. I'll try to face my giants head on."

The guard grinned in good-natured acknowledgment, moving off to seek a match with another guard.

Matthias stood for a moment, debating whether to find a new opponent himself or take the guard's advice. The man wasn't wrong. Matthias had been unsettled ever since his conversation with Hagen the day before, and try as he might, he couldn't seem to exorcise his doubts or discomforts. All he could think of was Briarford...and what he'd left behind there.

"Good morning, Matthias." The bright voice made him turn, one eyebrow going up as he watched his sister traipse across the training yard. "You missed breakfast."

"I wasn't hungry," he informed her. "Aren't you banned from the training yard, Mariella? I thought Mother said it was unseemly."

"I won't tell if you don't," the princess said lightly. She cast an eye over his uncovered, sweat-soaked chest, her cheerful features contorting into a grimace. "I see what she means, though. Who wants to be greeted with that first thing in the morning?"

Matthias threw the sweat-covered towel at her by way of reply, causing her to squeal in dismay and dodge to avoid it. It landed in the dirt just as another page boy materialized at the prince's elbow with a fresh one.

"Thank you," Matthias told him, with as much dignity as could be mustered by a royal prince who'd just ditched a towel at his sister's head.

"Firstly," he told his sister, "it's not the first thing in the morning. It must be ten o'clock by now. I've been up since dawn."

She just shrugged, glancing with interest around the yard full of training guards. "You have my sympathies."

Matthias shook his head, his lips curving in spite of himself at his sister's banter.

"Secondly," he went on, "what are you doing here, Mariella?"

"I'm looking for Hagen," she told him brightly. "The new singer apprentice from Frossenland. I thought he might be with you."

"No, I haven't seen him today," said Matthias absently. "That reminds me, though, I should seek him out. I'm supposed to be taking him under my wing, and he might need a bit of extra encouragement after yesterday." A frown broke over his face as he thought about his sister's words. "Hold on. Why are *you* looking for him?"

"Well, he's very handsome," Mariella informed him artlessly. "Didn't you see him? Those muscles, Matthias!" She delicately poked one of her brother's arms, so that the contact between the tip of her finger and his sweaty skin was as minimal as possible. "Puts your lean frame to shame, don't you think?"

"Thank you, sister dear," said Matthias dryly.

He studied Mariella, wondering what mischief she was up to. She wasn't given to flirting, generally speaking. In spite of her carefree air, she was much too wise to bring down their parents' ire, as would undoubtedly happen if the princess was observed flirting.

"And yes, I saw him," Matthias added sternly. "I saw him get in trouble for the magic you pressured him to perform. Don't get him in more hot water, Mariella."

"I won't," she said earnestly. "I heard about that, and I felt bad. That's one of the reasons I'm looking for him. I want to apologize."

"And the other reason is that he's handsome?" Matthias asked sarcastically.

She beamed up at him without the slightest hint of apology. "Precisely. Now go and wash. You smell."

"Thank you," said Matthias in his most courteous voice.

His sister just grinned shamelessly at him.

"I'll tag along and wait in your receiving room," she decided. "I'm trying to dodge my tutor. Apparently my knowledge of our trade history with Frossenland is lacking." Her eyes danced as she smiled up at Matthias. "I spent all our lessons asking questions about the giants instead of studying trade treaties. It's honestly amazing how little we know about Kjemper and their ways. It seems unwise for us to be so ignorant, given the threat they now pose."

"Yes, it probably is unwise," said Matthias absently, dunking his fresh towel into a barrel of cold water and bathing his face. "I suppose the downside of Battlement Wall is that it keeps out information as well as the actual giants."

"But there must be ways through it, especially if we use magic," said Mariella enthusiastically. "Imagine if we sent spies into Kjemper, Matthias! It would be just like our childhood games come to life."

"It would be much too dangerous," said Matthias discouragingly. "A death sentence for whoever was sent in there."

Mariella glared at him. "Where's your spirit of adventure? You're no fun."

Matthias sighed. "You're right. I used to be more fun, didn't I? Growing up is tedious work." He gave her a sympathetic look. "I hate to tell you this, Mariella, but your future promises many more studies on trade treaties than adventures with giants."

"Ugh." Mariella's youthful face was so full of world-weary resignation that Matthias had to laugh.

"So I suppose you're seeking Hagen out to ask him to fill you in on our trade history with Frossenland?"

Mariella's eyes danced at this suggestion. "An excellent excuse, should I need one. Thank you, Matthias." She lowered her voice conspiratorially. "One good turn deserves another. You should put on your shirt sooner rather than later. I saw a number of noble girls hovering a corridor over, waiting for you to emerge from your training."

"Heavens preserve me," said Matthias in alarm. "Thanks, Mariella." He hastened over to where he'd left his tunic, Mariella trailing in his wake.

"Don't you like being admired?" she asked curiously, as he slipped the garment over his head.

"There's nothing sincere about their admiration," Matthias said, his voice curt. Mariella was far too ready to talk about romance, in his opinion. It wasn't a topic he enjoyed discussing with her.

"But don't you like the idea of falling in love and getting married?" the princess pressed.

Matthias took his time answering, pulling on his jacket and lacing it. "With the right girl, I suppose. But I'm unlikely to find her, and even if I found her, I probably wouldn't be allowed to marry her, so I can't see how it benefits me."

Mariella regarded him with interest. "You sound like you're speaking of a specific person. Is there something I don't know, Matthias? What experience do you have of romance?"

A fleeting memory passed through Matthias's mind, years old, but as fresh as the day it had occurred. A slim form held in his arms, a face pressed into his chest. His hand tentative on a braid of dark hair.

"I'm not speaking of anyone specific," he said gruffly.

Honestly, it was embarrassing that when asked about his experience of romance, his mind flew to a fleeting encounter when he was sixteen. With a girl who, if he'd read her demeanor correctly, hadn't parted from him with a very good opinion of his character. A conclusion that was supported by her failure to ever respond to the letter he'd sent trying to more comprehensively explain his decision not to attend the funeral.

"I didn't think I was particular," he told Mariella, determined not to dwell on these thoughts. "I didn't even think I was looking for anything specific. But I must be, on both counts, because I can't seem to find what I'm looking for in anyone."

"Hm." Mariella looked more thoughtful than ever, and Matthias felt uneasy under the shrewdness of her gaze.

Now fully clothed, he made his way across the training yard. Mariella, heroine that she was, stuck close to him as they passed a group of hopeful young noblewomen, whose eyes lingered on Matthias's tousled hair and the glimpse of loosely laced tunic visible under his jacket. Pretending to be deep in conversation with his sister, he was able to get away with a smile and a nod in their direction. Even that was enough to make them burst into giggles as they passed.

"They do rather make idiots of themselves, don't they?" Mariella observed, once they were out of earshot.

"They really do," said Matthias. He frowned in memory. "Do you remember the last summer we spent in Briarford? When you were teasing me about the girls of the court chasing me, and I was complaining that it was a nuisance?"

"Yes," said Mariella, sounding surprised. "I do remember."

Matthias gave her a meaningful look. "I didn't know the half of it."

She laughed, nudging him with her elbow. "I also remember you saying that you would never change your tune on romance."

Matthias gave a reluctant laugh of his own. "Well, I was twelve years old," he pointed out. "What twelve-year-old is interested in romance?"

"I think I already was by that age," grinned Mariella. Her expression turned mournful. "Not that it's done me any good." In a supreme show of sibling solidarity, she disregarded his sweatiness and threaded her arm through his. "I know I tease you, Matthias, and realistically I'll do that until the day I die. But I do understand, you know, better than you think. There isn't as much pressure on me, because I'm not the heir. But I also feel the same struggle. The task of finding someone who loves *me* instead of my status as princess seems impossible."

"And the only thing more impossible would be convincing our parents to let you marry that person, given that their lack of love for your status would be incomprehensible to them," Matthias added.

"Exactly," said Mariella, laughing lightly. "It's a hopeless case for us both, Matthias."

They'd reached his rooms by this time, and Matthias deposited her in the receiving room to mull on their desperate circumstances while he completed a quick wash in his sleeping chamber. He emerged in a more presentable state to find his sister contemplating his new quill, sitting next to a sealed ink pot on his writing desk.

"When's the last time you had a letter from Jacinta?" he asked abruptly, the question slipping out before he had time to call it back. A strange frisson ran through him at the sound. He hadn't said her name in years.

Mariella turned to him, surprised. "Not for a long time. Two, maybe three years. She just stopped responding to my letters. Why do you ask?"

Matthias shrugged, not meeting her eyes as he crossed the room. "I was just wondering. Hagen said something yesterday that made me think of her and her parents. Well, her and her mother, I suppose."

"Yes," said Mariella quietly. "They must miss her father." She bit her lip. "I think about her often. I wish she hadn't stopped writing to me. It makes me worry. I mean, what if she's...you know."

Matthias stared at her blankly. "What if she's what?"

"Dead," said Mariella.

He stared at her. "What? Surely she couldn't be dead!" The thought had never occurred to him, and now that she'd put it in his mind, his insides writhed uncomfortably away from it.

"I don't have any reason to think she is," said Mariella reassuringly. "It's my mind jumping to the worst conclusion. But it's not impossible, is it? Life is hard in the north. And without her father, I think she and her mother must have struggled a great deal."

"Did she say that?" Matthias demanded. "In her letters, back when she used to write?"

Mariella shook her head. "She never complained. She didn't really tell me anything about her life. It was more that I could read things from what she didn't say."

Matthias stared at her, unable to comprehend this concept.

Mariella fidgeted with the feather of the quill. "I sent her a gold coin under the seal in my letter once, but her reply made it seem like she was offended, so I never did it again." She looked troubled. "It wasn't long after that she stopped responding."

"Why do you think she never responded to any of my letters?" Matthias blurted out.

His sister met his eyes, her own full of sympathy. "I have no idea why. I wish you had let me ask her outright in one of my letters."

He shook his head stubbornly. "I'm glad you didn't."

After all, surely a crown prince was allowed some measure of pride. But he did wish he'd thought to ask her for a reason in their brief encounter the day of her father's funeral. There were many things he wished he'd said that day. It had been such a fleeting moment together, and he'd undeniably made a mess of it. Not that she'd been especially expansive, either, but given she was about to bury her father, he felt she could be forgiven for not expressing herself very clearly.

"What did Hagen say that made you think of Jacinta?" Mariella asked curiously.

"His parents worked for the Frossian royal family at their northern retreat," said Matthias. "And of course, given he's a singer, there's songcraft in his blood, just like Jacinta's father had songcraft."

Mariella raised her eyebrows. "That's quite the coincidence."

"His father is dead as well," said Matthias. "I didn't even ask how he died."

"That's terrible," said Mariella sympathetically.

"I went to the funeral." Again Matthias blurted the words out. He had no idea why he was in such a confiding mood. It was as though saying Jacinta's name had opened a floodgate. "Well, not to the funeral itself."

"You went to Hagen's father's funeral?" Mariella asked blankly.

Matthias gave a pained laugh. "No. Jacinta's father."

His sister stared at him. "No you didn't. *I* went to Jacinta's father's funeral. You definitely weren't there. Mother and Father said you couldn't go, remember?"

"Of course I remember," said Matthias irritably. "I disobeyed them. I was taking part in a military training exercise a day's ride north of here at the time. I convinced an officer to cover for me, and I went to Briarford alone."

"And Mother and Father never found out?" Mariella demanded, amazed.

He shook his head. "Not as far as I know."

"Thank goodness for that," his sister said fervently. "Why would you take the risk?"

"I wanted to see Jacinta," said Matthias, his throat tight. "She'd lost her father. I wanted to...I don't know. Be there for her."

She frowned. "So why didn't I see you at the funeral?"

"I didn't go to the ceremony," he said. "I snuck into the manor and stayed there. She came through, I don't know why. I gave her my condolences then."

Mariella leaned toward him, squinting. "Matthias, you're blushing. What did you do in that manor? Did you kiss her?"

He laughed. "Of course not. We were children. And I am most definitely not blushing."

"You were sixteen and taking part in a military training exercise," said Mariella matter-of-factly. "You weren't a child." Her eyes glazed over as she cast her mind back to the time of the funeral. "And neither was Jacinta."

"She thought I was ashamed," said Matthias. "She didn't say it, but I think she was angry that I wouldn't go to the ceremony. I wish I had."

Mariella shook her head. "No way, Matthias. You made the right decision. It was just a funeral. Mother and Father would have been livid. I was here when they got your letter saying you intended to go to the funeral. Something about the way you declared your plans rather than asking permission really bothered them. Father said that if you defied him, he would recall you from the training exercise and hold back your military advancement for two years."

Matthias shrugged. "I know. They said as much in their reply, and that's what stopped me at the time. Such an overreaction to a perceived defiance—I can't imagine why they felt so strongly about it. It was enough to intimidate me when I was sixteen, but I have a different perspective now. What's another two years?"

Mariella snorted a laugh. "Such a wise old man, aren't you? At the ripe old age of twenty."

Matthias shrugged again. "I hadn't seen her for four years, and I haven't seen her in the four years since. She was once my closest friend, and I spent the rest of my childhood trying without success to find another friend I could be myself with, the way I could with her. For all I know, that was the last time I'll ever see her. I wish I'd swallowed my pride and sat beside her at her father's funeral."

Mariella studied him thoughtfully. "I never dreamed you were still harboring such strong feelings on all this. You never told me."

"Well, what's the good of talking?" Matthias said, strapping his everyday sword back to his side. "Mother and Father effectively ended the friendship by cutting Briarford out of our lives, and that's all there is to it. We had no real say in any of it."

Mariella looked as though she was debating whether to say more, but Matthias was finished with the conversation.

"Come on," he said. "Let's find this handsome Frossian singer."

"All right," said Mariella, her smile more tentative than before.

Matthias strode from the room before she could further question him. He wasn't sure why he was deciding to open the lid on issues he'd buried within himself for years. Between the threat of giants to the north, his parents' hints about eligible brides, and his growing duties as crown prince, he had enough on his mind without digging up the past.

Even if his heart apparently hadn't quite let go.

CHAPTER FIVE

Jacinta

Jacinta woke with the dawn, her first awareness the emptiness of her stomach. The meager meal she'd made the previous night from what she'd gleaned in the manor's overgrown kitchen garden had been far from satisfying. And today would likely see them eat the last of the dried meat she had in storage. What would they eat tonight?

She pushed herself out of bed, trying to banish these gloomy thoughts. At least there was still wood she could forage for a fire. Perhaps she'd be lucky and find berries. Or perhaps today someone in town would be willing to give her a meal in exchange for some labor.

"Good morning, Jacinta."

Her mother was already up, stoking the fire, over which a pot of bubbling water hung.

"I found some old tea leaves in the cupboard," the older woman said. "Just the thing on a brisk morning."

"Thanks Mamma," said Jacinta, gratefully receiving the mug her mother offered her. She held it for a moment, letting it warm her hands before taking a sip. It was weak. Her mother was probably trying to eke out the tea leaves.

"Well, it won't be an easy day," her mother said curtly. "But we'll manage, Jacinta. I think I'll head into town and see if I can find any work. You take some time to wake up."

"No, I should come," said Jacinta. Guilt swirled through her at the memory of her last trip into town. How could she have been so careless as to fall afoul of an elf bargain?

"You can follow when you're ready," her mother told her. "But don't rush yourself. The day is long."

Jacinta sensed that her mother wanted to be alone with her thoughts while she walked, and she said no more. She wasn't ready to go anywhere, anyway. She needed to use the outhouse first. Once her mother had left, she made her way across the yard, noting the frost on the ground. Autumn had barely begun. It was only going to get colder.

After shooing a mouse from the outhouse floor, Jacinta made her way in. The bats roosting in the ceiling didn't bother her, and she was quick about her business. It was only after she emerged that she remembered the beans she'd planted the day before.

"I suppose I may as well check if something's grown," she muttered.

She knew most things didn't grow overnight, but after all, they were supposed to be magic beans. She strolled around the outhouse only to stop dead in her tracks at the sight that met her eyes. Something had indeed grown overnight, at a truly impossible rate. A number of shoots—presumably five— emerged from the place where she'd planted the beans. It was difficult to tell the number because they twisted together into one giant beanstalk, thicker than her arms. The stalk had grown along the ground, curling and twisting, but basically stretching in a northward direction. It must have been growing profusely all night, because it disappeared from sight.

Bewildered, Jacinta followed it, stepping carefully over the beanstalk and its various shoots. Who knew if it was poisonous, or otherwise dangerous if touched? She didn't trust that elf Valwynn as far as she could throw her.

The simple hut and the outhouse were soon out of sight, and still the beanstalk continued to make a trail northward. Her curiosity growing by the minute, Jacinta picked up her pace, her eyes searching the distance ahead to try to see where the beanstalk ended. Battlement Wall loomed over her, its silent menace growing ever closer. The sun, rising over the sea far to the east, cast its weak light on the scene, revealing the gently uncurling leaves along the stalk's length. It seemed to still be growing at an unnatural rate.

Jacinta craned her neck to look at the top of the wall, but by now she was too close to see its full height. Soon she would reach the wall, and what would happen then? Would the beanstalk grow up the stone?

Her guess proved wrong. When Jacinta drew to a stop in front of Battlement Wall, the plant continued. But it didn't go up and over. It went through.

As in, straight through. The beanstalk had grown into the stone as if the wall was no impediment. More than that, its passage had somehow carved a hole all around it. Jacinta stood in bemusement, staring into a small tunnel through the stone.

"Do I...do I climb through?" The words were muttered to no one in particular, and no one answered. But the closest tendril of vine shifted slightly, a leaf uncurling before her eyes.

The elf certainly hadn't exaggerated when she'd said the beans were magical. But what had she meant by the claim that they were more valuable than Jacinta's cow? What benefit could Jacinta gain from entering Kjemper? No one *wanted* to go into the giants' land. That was why the Frossians had built Battlement Wall all those generations ago. To keep the giants trapped in their frozen wasteland and create an insurmountable barrier of separation between the enemy races.

But Jacinta couldn't deny that her curiosity was raging. She thought fleetingly of all the childhood games she, Mariella, and Matthias had played, pretending they were sneaking over the wall to fight giants, or defending their homes against the imaginary invading brutes. She thought also of the dilapidated hut she shared with her mother, where no food waited to fill her empty stomach.

If there was ever a time when she'd had nothing to lose, this was it.

Riding the wave of recklessness that washed over her, Jacinta knelt next to the tunnel, finally risking it and touching the vine. Nothing sinister happened. In fact, it felt like an ordinary plant under her touch. She put her knees on either side of it, crawling forward into the hole with the beanstalk under her. It was very dark inside the tunnel, and it went for longer than she expected. Just how thick was Battlement Wall? She was still in total darkness when a tremor shook the ground, sending fear racing through Jacinta as she braced herself against the stone around her and waited for the wall to stop shaking.

It was over quickly, but Jacinta still felt rattled. The closeness and the darkness were doubly unnerving now. Jacinta was just starting to wonder if the tunnel had actually delved underground when she saw a dim circle of light ahead. She increased her speed, eager to breathe fresh air again, even if it was the air of Kjemper.

The circle grew until she could see a glimpse of frozen ground on the other side. A moment later the tunnel abruptly ended, and she poked her head out to cautiously survey the area. Seeing no sign of anyone, she pulled herself from the hole, straightening up and brushing dirt from her gown.

She was in Kjemper.

She could hardly believe it. In spite of living all her life in the shadow of Battlement Wall, she'd never expected to see the land of the giants. Her curious eyes found a landscape similar to the one she'd left behind except, if anything, more barren. The air was cold, and there was plenty of frost still on the ground. She moved forward out of the wall's shadow, seeking whatever warmth the weak sunlight could provide.

To her right, the wall stretched away eastward. She knew from the Vadolisian side of the wall that it continued until it reached the ocean, not far away. With the land between her and the coast so empty on this side of the barrier, she could almost fancy she heard the cry of a gull. But it was probably her imagination.

To her left, the wall continued westward out of sight. Jacinta was interested to see that not far away, a jagged glacier of ice seemed to have formed against this side of the wall. It continued on for some distance. Further into Kjemper to her left, she could see what appeared to be a mountain range of ice. The land of the giants was truly a frozen wasteland.

But not an empty wasteland.

She frowned as she directed her eyes straight ahead of her. She could just make out a structure in the distance. Her frown deepened as she considered it, unable to determine what it was. It didn't look like any building she'd ever seen. It seemed to be a wooden structure, and it rose above the rocky ground like a tower. Was that what giants' dwellings looked like?

Faint sounds carried to her on the wind, impossible to decipher, but sufficient to remind her she needed to be cautious. This land wasn't abandoned. Many giants lived here, and in addition to being enormous, strong, and normally savage, they had a particular aversion to humans.

Jacinta's eyes scanned across the space in front of her, and she realized with surprise that the beanstalk hadn't ended when it emerged from the wall. It was still growing along the ground in a northeasterly direction.

After a moment's internal debate, Jacinta decided to follow it. She'd come this far, and she'd seen enough to be convinced that there was more to the elf's bargain than she'd first assumed. What would she find at the end of this growing trail that would make the beans more valuable than Princess?

The stalk twisted and writhed its way along the hard soil for some distance before it disappeared from Jacinta's view over a small rise in the ground. When she reached the rise and peered cautiously over it, she drew back quickly.

The beanstalk had finally come to a stop. It didn't continue down the other side of the rise, where the ground dipped to a lower point than where Jacinta was standing. But something else was there—this structure was definitely a dwelling. She peeked back over the mound behind which she was crouched, studying the building.

It had looked huge at first glance, but she realized that was only because of the larger size of giants. In fact the building looked like a simple hut, with proportions much the same as her own dwelling. Magnified several times.

Who lived here? And why had the beanstalk brought her to this dwelling? Jacinta examined the plant nervously. Was Valwynn intending that she would steal something equal in value to the cow she'd traded, and fulfill the bargain that way? But that didn't seem right. If Jacinta had to steal her prize, it wasn't exactly being provided by the elf in exchange for Princess. There was too much risk to justify the reward, especially since giants were unlikely to have anything of great value. From everything Jacinta had ever been taught, the giants were even more destitute than the humans of the northern region had become as the land grew more barren.

It was of course entirely possible that she wasn't supposed to go near the dwelling at all. Maybe the plant was leading her to something else, and the building just happened to be nearby.

But a surreptitious search around the end of the plant showed nothing of interest. It seemed to just peter out on hard, unremarkable ground. The only notable feature of the area was the giant dwelling. And although the vines were still gradually growing before her eyes, the stalk wasn't getting closer to the building. It was just thickening, with tendrils reaching out and wrapping themselves around it.

"Nothing to lose, remember?" Jacinta murmured to herself, as her stomach gave another twang of hunger.

Steeling herself, she crept along the vines, up and over the rise. Unfortunately there was no cover on the barren ground between her and the building. But the house was quiet as she approached it. She ducked low and tried to move unobtrusively, her intention to peek in a window if she could get high enough to see into one.

But she was only halfway to the house when a familiar clucking sound disturbed the stillness of the morning. Jacinta froze as a chicken—a regular-sized, unremarkable chicken— came bobbing its way frantically across the yard. Fear raced through her at this sign of life, but it was nothing to the terror she felt at what followed the chicken.

Her first clue that the fowl was being pursued was the thud-thud of the vibrations she felt as two enormous feet shook the ground. A second later, a figure came into view, a figure that looked almost human but at the same time totally foreign.

The giant was at least twice as tall as Jacinta, and her skin was gray and rough, as if she was hewn from stone. She had dark hair pulled tightly back, its flowing waves not unlike the seaweed Jacinta had seen when her parents took her to the seashore once. The giant's limbs were overlong, but the stoutness of her frame prevented her from looking lithe or lanky. She was, in short, enormous and terrifying.

"Blasted chicken, get ee back here now!" the giant roared, her eyes fixed on her quarry as she barreled forward, closing the distance with gigantic strides.

She swept the unfortunate bird into one arm a moment later, the chicken looking absurdly small next to its captor's huge form. It was as the giant paused to growl inarticulately at the bird that she noticed her visitor, standing frozen and terrified in the middle of open ground.

"Eh?" The giant's squarish head swiveled toward Jacinta, her expression startled. "What's this?"

"I..." Jacinta's voice came out as a squeak the first time, and she had to try again. "I mean no harm," she managed, her voice still not sounding familiar at all. "Please, just let me go home."

"But ye're no elf!" the giant cried, her eyes widening further as they raked over Jacinta's body. "Ye're an 'uman! How did ee get here?"

Jacinta said nothing, unsure what answer would be least likely to get her killed.

"Ye've breached the wall, have ee?" The giant's voice was grim now, her yellow eyes narrowing. "A scout, perhaps? We knew war with the 'umans might be coming." She raised the fist of the hand not clutching a chicken in front of her. "Ye'll not be carrying messages back to—"

"No, I'm not a scout!" Jacinta said, her words tumbling over each other in her fear. "I swear, there's no army. I didn't even plan to come here. It wasn't my idea. It was the elf's. She gave me these beans, and they grew into a plant, and it led me to...to your house."

There was a long moment of silence, during which the giant stared at her as though she was mad. Then, slowly, comprehension seemed to trickle into her overlarge head.

"Was this elf perchance called Valwynn?"

Jacinta's mouth fell open in her astonishment. "Yes," she managed, swallowing. "Yes, her name is Valwynn."

The giant let out a sigh so gusty it actually made Jacinta's skirts flap a little. "Shoulda known there'd be trouble. This is what comes of confiding in an elf."

She unclenched her fist, scratching at her head in a weary kind of way.

"Beats me what she expects me to do with ee, though. Why'd she send ee here, eh?"

"I have no idea," said Jacinta faintly. "Is...is she a friend of yours?"

The giant let out a guffaw so shrill, Jacinta actually winced.

"Elves and giants aren't friends. Our kinds hate each other."

Jacinta bit her lip, saying nothing. That's what she'd always been led to believe, but hadn't the giant just spoken of confiding in Valwynn?

"Arr, I guess ee'd better come inside," said the giant. She cast an eye over Jacinta's form again. "Seems stories of the destitution of yer kind are accurate, then. Ee look famished."

Jacinta said nothing, but her stomach chose that moment to growl audibly at this mention of food. She was also rattled by the giant's lack of aggression. She almost sounded...compassionate. That wasn't how giants were supposed to be.

Not that she should complain, Jacinta supposed. It was a welcome relief not to be slaughtered on sight.

"Come on, have a bite," said the giant impatiently, Jacinta's silence seeming to irk her. She jerked her head in a command, then turned and strode into the dwelling.

Jacinta hovered for a moment, perplexed by the whole encounter. Everything she'd ever been taught about giants told her she should be running for her life in the other direction. For all she knew, the giant intended to make a meal *of* her rather than give a meal *to* her. But she didn't hesitate long. No part of her really believed she would turn back now. She was far too fascinated, and, after all, she'd already decided she had very little to lose.

Pushing herself forward, she followed the giant into the house. It was a surreal experience, entering the simple kitchen. It was so much like her own hut, but completely out of proportion. The wooden tabletop was about level with her eyes, and the fireplace was easily large enough for her to stretch out comfortably inside it.

Hopefully that wasn't the direction this encounter was going.

"Sit." The curt command came from the giant, her tone impatient again.

Jacinta did her best to comply. There were only two chairs at the table, and they were so large she had to climb one like a ladder in order to sit on it. Or rather kneel, as was necessary to bring the tabletop within reach.

"Eat."

The giant pushed a plate of half-eaten food toward Jacinta. It had the remains of a loaf that had obviously been the length of her arm and the width of her torso, and a few crumbly pieces of cheese. She was so hungry, she barely cared whether the food might be poisoned. It was hard to imagine the giant would bother with such strategies, when a single punch to Jacinta's head from one of those fists would easily do the job.

"Gar, I don't like this."

The giant turned away, placing the chicken in a small wire coop as Jacinta inhaled the bread. The bird ruffled its white feathers irritably, its red comb wobbling in a disconsolate way. Why the chicken was being kept inside Jacinta couldn't imagine, but it was the least of her concerns.

"I don't want to see yer pitiful state," the giant went on.

"Don't ee go thinking I've got a softness for 'umans, because I don't. I don't care if yer all starving and naked, so long as it's happening over the other side of the wall, and I don't have to see it."

"Fair enough." Jacinta paused to pick a morsel of cheese from her gown. She didn't want to waste a crumb. "I feel much the same about your kind."

"Good." The giant seemed pleased. "Then we're agreed. Now let's get this over with and get ee back where I don't have to look at yer gaunt face."

"Get what over with?" Jacinta asked warily.

"Didn't ee come for information?" the giant demanded.

Jacinta pushed the now-empty plate away, feeling more content than she had in days, in spite of her precarious situation. Perhaps it was that feeling that prompted her to take the approach of total honesty.

"I don't know what I came for. I just followed the stalk that grew from the beans Valwynn gave me. I didn't have a plan for when I got to Kjemper. I didn't plan—or want—to come to Kjemper."

"Then why come at all?" demanded the giant in irritation.

Jacinta shrugged. "Honestly, I had nothing to lose, and my curiosity brought me."

The giant let out a groan, running two broad hands across her face. "The stories are true. 'Umans *are* pathetic."

"Not all of us," said Jacinta, torn between amusement and offense. After holding the giant's gaze for a long and charged moment, she let her shoulders drop. "But I have become a little pathetic, yes."

The giant let out a rumbling chuckle. "One thing I'll say, ye're not what I expected."

"Neither are you," said Jacinta frankly.

"Arr, I'm not normal for my kind," the giant said breezily.

"Most'd prefer to squash ee than look at ee. It's not in our nature to care for other creatures. But I'm the type to take a rodent outside rather than step on it, and ye're in much the same category."

"Thank you," said Jacinta with utmost politeness. "You're very kind."

The giant brought an enormous hand slamming onto the table, palm down. Jacinta jumped as all the dishes rattled.

"No I'm not, and don't let me hear ee say it again!" The giant was almost roaring now. "I'll not have tales spread about me!"

"I apologize," said Jacinta, feeling afraid for the first time since she'd been presented with food. "I didn't meant to insult you."

The giant just studied her through narrowed eyes, her breathing gradually slowing.

"Watch what ee say, that's the only warning I'll give."

Jacinta nodded, swallowing hard. She'd been a fool to let herself relax when she knew so little of the customs of her hostess. She never would have dreamed that being called kind would be considered such an insult to a giant. Clearly it wasn't an attribute that was valued among the reportedly brutal creatures.

At Jacinta's compliance, the giant seemed to set aside her anger.

"Did Valwynn send ee because ye're important?" she asked.

Jacinta shook her head nervously. "I'm not important. I'm no one."

The giant frowned. "Do ee at least have the ear of yer king? The one that's almost as big as a giant, or so they say? The one who took a singer 'uman for his queen then killed Queen Grograna and escaped her castle unscathed?"

It took Jacinta a moment to realize what the giant was talking about.

"You mean King Herleif and Queen Adrienne of Frossen-land," she said. "I'm not from their kingdom. I'm from Vadolis. My king is King Fidelius." She lowered her gaze. "And no, I don't have his ear."

The giant let out a groan so deep, Jacinta thought she heard a window rattle.

"What did Valwynn send me a useless 'uman for, eh? What's the point of ee?"

"What would be my point if I *did* have the ear of my king?" Jacinta asked curiously.

"Well, then ee could carry the information, couldn't ee?" the giant said irritably. "Do ee comprehend the risk I'm taking, speaking with ee? My husband could be home any time, and he'll end me as sure as ee if he knows what I'm up to."

"Where is he?" Jacinta asked nervously. "Is he far away?"

"He's at work, of course." The giant clearly thought the question foolish. "At the mining tower over yonder."

CHAPTER SIX

Jacinta

Jacinta stilled, struggling to make sense of what she'd just heard. "Mining tower?" she repeated. "Are...are there precious metals under the ground in Kjemper?"

The giant guffawed. "Don't be daft, little pipsqueak. We don't mine rock. We mine magic."

Jacinta made to stand, then realized the ground was too far below her to do it easily.

"But...giants can't mine magic. Only elves can do that. Giants aren't supposed to be able to access magic at all."

The giant snorted. "Not supposed to? According to who? Yer kind? Do ee think we answer to yer kind?"

"But even humans don't know how to mine magic," Jacinta insisted. "How could you have figured it out?"

The giant was silent for a long moment, studying Jacinta's face.

"It's clear ee know nothing," she said at last. "And I don't intend to tell ee more than ee need to know. If ye've any sense, ye'll find a way to get yer king's ear. Ye'll tell him that the giant king won't be satisfied with what he has. He won't stop until he's taken what he wants from all of Providore. And if the 'umans are wise, they'll strike before he gathers even more strength."

Jacinta stared at her hostess, feeling the color drain from her face. "The giants intend to declare war on the humans?" she asked.

"Did I say that?" The giant sounded irritated, and Jacinta noticed she kept glancing out the window. "Just take the message."

"But why would you advise us to act against your own king?" Jacinta asked suspiciously.

"He's not my king," growled the giant. "We never had no monarch before Grograna's line. We never needed no monarch. Our kind do best when left to manage ourselves. But her parents were determined to set themselves up as rulers. They managed it, too, through conflict too bloody for yer delicate 'uman ears to handle. Not that they got to enjoy it for long. Less than two decades before their daughter decided it was taking too long to get to her turn, and did away with them. Grograna built on what her parents'd done, too. She used magic to make herself a fancy castle, and got her hands on all the gold ee could dream of. Never mind that accumulating the wealth for herself sent the rest of Kjemper into poverty. I'd love nothing better than to see her son toppled, and I'm not the only one."

The giant's fierce expression melted away as she sighed. "My husband isn't among us, though. He likes his job at the tower. Thinks because he gets a few meager snatches of the gold himself, he's on the inside. But he's being used, same as the rest of them. It's all to fuel the so-called king's greed."

"And you want the human kingdoms to intervene?" Jacinta asked faintly. She didn't relish taking that suggestion to anyone in power.

"Well, I thought it'd be convenient if an outside threat took him down," the giant explained optimistically. "Save us the trouble of doing it." She scowled. "If I could rally my own kind to do it, believe me I would. But we don't rally. That's the whole point. We do best when left to our own devices, not gathered under one leader. Cooperation isn't in our nature." She sighed as she looked at Jacinta again. "I was hoping for that big strong king from Frossenland, but I suppose yer king is a start."

"I think you're trying to trap me somehow," said Jacinta boldly. "To lay a trap for my king perhaps. When you first saw me, you were ready to kill me for fear I was a scout, and now you claim you *want* me to take a message to my king and his armies?"

"I don't want no armies here," said the giant sharply. "I won't see Kjemper overrun with yer kind. It's only our king I want taken down. And that's what's in yer people's interests, too. He's the only one interested in expanding his reach beyond the wall, because he's the only one benefiting from it, as his mother was before him."

"Benefiting how?" Jacinta demanded, but the giant ignored her.

"I thought mayhap yer king could offer to meet peacefully with ours, then pull some trick to kill him when he least expects it. The Frossian king managed to kill Grograna, didn't he?"

Jacinta raised an eyebrow. "I don't think the circumstances of that incident were anything like the ones you just described. That sounds very dishonorable."

The giant let out a snort. "Typical 'uman nonsense. Would ee rather have honor, or life?"

"Both, ideally," Jacinta said mildly.

"Well, ee can't." The giant's voice was dismissive. "Not if ye're in Kjemper."

Before Jacinta could reply, a high-pitched whistling sound cut across their conversation. She looked toward the window, confused, as her hostess let out a hiss.

"My husband's on his way home from the night shift. Ye'd best go." She looked toward the hut's one door and let out a groan. "No time. Hide in here."

Before Jacinta could respond, the giant had grasped her around the middle with both hands, lifting her bodily from the chair. Shushing Jacinta's protests, she opened the door of an enormous cupboard and shoved Jacinta right into it.

"Stay silent and still!" the giant hissed. "If he catches ee here, he'll eat ee as soon as look at ee."

Jacinta barely had time to position herself around the sparse supplies in her hiding place before a loud bang indicated that the door of the hut had been thrown open.

"Where's my breakfast?" the new arrival roared by way of greeting. "Longest night I've had in weeks."

"It might feel long to ee, but ye're home early," said his wife waspishly. "I haven't made it yet. Sit ee down, and I'll cook some eggs."

Jacinta heard a scraping followed by a creaking sound, then a metallic thump. The cupboard door hung somewhat unevenly on its hinges, and Jacinta shifted ever so slightly so she could peer through the crack. It allowed her the tiniest glimpse of the room beyond.

Another giant—even larger than his wife—had settled into the chair Jacinta had just vacated. She gave a shudder at the sight of his angry, gray face. She'd thought the first giant was frightening, but this one looked much meaner. She wondered idly whether, if she became his breakfast, the magic binding her and Valwynn to their bargain would activate and punish the elf somehow. She didn't see what convoluted arguments could claim that getting eaten by a giant provided her with more value than her cow had.

"What's this, then?" The giant's yellow eyes narrowed as they fell on Jacinta's discarded plate. "Have ee had someone here while I've been out?" His suspicious gaze scanned the room as Jacinta pulled her head back from the crack, her heart pounding.

"Course not," said the first giant, sounding irritable. "That's my breakfast. Who've I got to have over, eh? Since ee moved us out to this abandoned corner of Kjemper, not a soul would come near."

"Stop complaining," growled her husband. "The tower here needed more workers, and they were ready to pay more. There's more to do closer to the border, ee know that."

Jacinta pressed her eyes to the crack again, watching in mingled alarm and disgust as the giant's words were punctuated by a yawn that showed far too many of his pointed, uneven teeth. They were almost as yellow as his eyes.

Those same eyes were drooping as the giant leaned his vast head on one elbow. Jacinta kept her gaze carefully on him as she pondered his words. Why was there more to do near the border? What exactly was the purpose of these mining towers? Quite apart from her own imminent danger, the whole situation was deeply alarming.

"Look at ee, ye'll be asleep afore I can cook aught," said the giant's wife from out of Jacinta's view. "Get a few winks while I prepare yer food. I'll wake ee when it's ready."

The giant grumbled a few times, but he clearly didn't have the energy to resist. He pushed himself to his feet with a groan and disappeared from sight. Jacinta held her breath, maintaining her position and trying not to make a sound.

A couple of minutes passed, then she heard a heavy tread cross the room, and a door creak open. A moment later, it clicked quietly shut, and the footsteps returned. Next thing she knew, she was blinking into the light, the giant's gray face filling half her vision.

"Come on," said her hostess in quiet tones. "Out ee get. He's asleep, but he won't stay that way for long on an empty stomach. Get ee off back home, and take my message."

Jacinta had already taken a step toward the door, but she paused. "No one will believe me," she said in a whisper. "I'm not complaining, I'm just telling you the simple truth. My word won't carry weight with anyone, let alone the king. I don't want you to have false expectations of what I can achieve."

The giant was clearly impatient for her to be gone, but she let out a sigh. "All right, then. I suppose I'd better send ee with something to prove ee were here."

She glanced around the room, her eyes settling on the floor next to the recently vacated chair. Following her gaze, Jacinta saw that the giant had dropped a sack when he'd sat down—enormous to her eyes. The drawstring had come loose to reveal a glint of gold.

"Here ee go. He won't miss a few." The giant reached into the bag and took out three golden coins, each the size of Jacinta's palm, and as thick as three of her fingers together. "That should convince yer people ye've been in our land, at least."

"Yes," said Jacinta faintly, staring down at the volume of gold in her hand. "It should. Thank you."

"Stop thanking me," said the giant irritably. "It makes me feel all dirty." She wiped her nose on an already grubby sleeve.

"All right," said Jacinta, feeling a trickle of amusement in spite of her predicament. "Then I suppose I shouldn't thank you for preventing your husband from eating me."

The giant gave a snort she only just stifled in time. "Gullible creature, aren't ee? I spoke to frighten ee into compliance, child. Giants don't eat 'umans any more than 'umans eat elves." Her gaze was suddenly penetrating. "Ee don't, do ee?"

"No," said Jacinta, definitely holding back a laugh now. "We don't eat elves."

The giant nodded. "He would have just squashed ee, and I'll

tell ee to yer face, I wouldn't have stopped him if he'd found ee. It's his house same as it's mine, and if ee prefers to kill rodents rather than put 'em outside, that's his affair. So ye'd best get out of here while ee can."

"I will," said Jacinta quickly. "I'll go straight home."

The giant nodded impatiently, apparently not inclined to say more. Jacinta deposited the gold coins in her pocket, hurrying out the door and toward the hidden vine. She did spare one curious glance over her shoulder toward the mining tower she could see in the distance, but she wasn't so foolhardy as to venture that way to explore. Not now that she had something to lose again.

The coins jangled in her pocket as she cleared the rise and started following the beanstalk back toward the wall. She could hardly believe her luck that the giant had so carelessly given her three. One would be enough to prove she'd been into Kjemper. The others would make the difference between survival and starvation for her and her mother.

The jog back to Battlement Wall felt faster than the journey there. Before she knew it, Jacinta was crawling back into the tunnel, welcoming the close darkness as a friend this time. She had no idea what any giants would make of the vines and the tunnel if they saw them, but at least she was now far enough in that they wouldn't see her. And the tunnel wasn't big enough for a giant to crawl through.

When Jacinta emerged from the other side, she was up and running the moment her feet found the ground. She tore across the barren land, her heart pounding with excitement and relief as her home came into sight. She leaped over the beanstalk, rounding the outhouse and hurrying for the hut, calling out as she went.

"Mamma! Mamma, come and see!"

There was no answer, and it wasn't until Jacinta had flung

the door wide that she remembered her mother had gone into town to look for work. Turning away, she decided she would run straight there. This news couldn't wait.

She'd barely crossed the yard, however, when her mother's familiar form came into view. She looked far too weary for so early in the day, but Jacinta didn't let the sight dishearten her. Her mother would soon perk up when she saw what Jacinta had brought home.

"Jacinta, there you are," said the older woman, catching sight of her daughter. "I thought perhaps I'd missed you on the road somehow. I suppose you've also ascertained that there's no work to be had in Briarford?"

Jacinta shook her head. "I never made it to town, Mamma. I went somewhere else entirely. Look!"

She grabbed hold of her mother's hand, dragging her toward the outhouse.

"If this is about the bats, I've told you, they're doing no one any harm," said her mother. "They'll keep the mosquitoes under control." She paused. "Unless you think we should try to eat them."

"No, no, forget the bats," Jacinta said impatiently. "Something grew from the beans, Mamma. Look!"

The pair came to a stop just behind the outhouse, and Jacinta saw her mother's eyes go wide. Silently, the older woman trailed her gaze along the plant and out of sight.

"Where does it lead?" she asked, dazed.

"Into Kjemper," Jacinta told her. "No, it's true," she said earnestly, as her mother turned startled eyes to her. "It goes all the way to Battlement Wall, then burrows straight through! I followed it."

"You went into Kjemper?" her mother repeated faintly. "Just this morning?"

Jacinta nodded, her words tumbling over each other as she

described the morning's adventure to her mother. She didn't leave out any detail, eager for the other woman's opinions on all she'd seen and heard. They walked as she spoke, and by the end of her tale, they were standing next to the tunnel that disappeared into the darkness of Battlement Wall.

"Where's the tunnel?" her mother asked blankly.

Jacinta frowned at her. "What do you mean? It's right there."

Her mother stared from the beanstalk to Jacinta. "Have I lost my mind, or have you? I see no tunnel."

"You don't?" Jacinta moved toward it, placing her hand into the hole around the vines. "But...it's right here."

Her mother let out a shout, hurrying forward and tugging Jacinta's arm back. She held her daughter's hand up before her face, staring at it in alarm.

"What do *you* see?" Jacinta demanded.

"The vine disappears at the wall," her mother said. "It grows right up to the stone, then just stops. It looked like you stuck your hand into a solid wall, and your hand disappeared in front of my eyes."

Bewildered, Jacinta took her mother's arm, pulling the older woman forward to the wall. She attempted to guide her mother's hand into the hole only to find that while her hand continued, her mother's stopped. The older woman was left with her fingers laid flat against thin air, as if it was the rough stone of Battlement Wall.

"Strange," breathed Jacinta. "I never imagined it was visible—and accessible—only to me." She pondered for a moment. "Must be something in the magic Valwynn put in those beans. I suppose it's safer. This way we won't have curious neighbors wandering into Kjemper when our backs are turned."

Her mother made a scoffing noise in her throat. "When's the last time a neighbor came to pay us a call out here?"

"True," Jacinta agreed absently. She still felt better knowing that the tunnel wasn't open to just any passerby.

"Come on," said the older woman, turning back toward their home. Neither spoke again until they were settled at the table in their kitchen. Jacinta expected her mother to comment on whatever the giant king was up to, but her thoughts were apparently focused closer to home.

"Why did you go in there, Jacinta?" the older woman asked reproachfully. "Why risk your life for idle curiosity? Imagine if the tunnel had closed, and you'd been trapped in there!"

Jacinta shrugged. With a full stomach from the giant's food, and a pocket full of gold, it was difficult to recapture the frame of mind she'd been in when she first saw the beanstalk.

"I guess I figured I had nothing to lose."

"Well. I suppose being squashed by a giant would at least be a quick way to go," her mother said prosaically.

"Precisely." Jacinta let out a laugh.

Her mother eyed her. "I haven't heard a laugh that carefree in years," she commented. "You don't seem any the worse for your misadventure."

"Honestly, Mamma, I feel more alive than I have in ages," Jacinta told her. "It was terrifying while I was in there, but now I'm safely back..." She shook her head. "Well, I'd thought I was done with adventure and excitement. It was almost like a childhood game come to life."

Her mother was silent for a long moment. "Do you think this giant told you the truth? Do you think she was genuine in wanting you to warn our king that the giant king has designs on our kingdom and needs to be stopped?"

"It's impossible to know for sure, of course," Jacinta mused. "And she definitely didn't tell me everything she knew. But she really did seem surprised when I appeared. I don't think this was some kind of plot between her and the elf. I think she was genuine in what she said." She gave a shrug. "Whether her advice is sound is another matter, of course."

"Yes." Her mother drummed her fingers on the table. "What are you going to do with the information?"

Jacinta hesitated, then drew the three enormous coins from her pocket. Her mother's eyebrows rose as Jacinta laid them side by side on the wooden surface.

"When I was there, it all seemed very urgent," said Jacinta slowly. "But now..." She tapped each of the coins in turn. "We could live for a long time off these, if we went about it carefully."

Her mother's expression was inscrutable as she met Jacinta's eyes. "What about the message? This is your chance to visit the capital, like you used to be so desperate to do. You have a valid reason now, and with this gold, you'll easily be able to afford the journey."

Jacinta squirmed a little in her seat. She didn't want to say it aloud, but now she was back in her own world, the idea of traveling to the capital and seeking out the king was more terrifying than the giant had been.

"Don't you think it's a lost cause? King Fidelius won't listen to me."

"Is this about the prince and princess?" her mother asked, ignoring her question. "I thought you'd want to see them again."

Jacinta drooped in her seat. "Honestly, I don't know if I do, Mamma. It's been such a long time, and..." She glanced down at her tattered, dirty gown.

"I understand," her mother said quietly. She hesitated for a moment, then said, "I noticed you stopped asking me to send letters for the princess a couple years ago."

Jacinta shrugged. "There didn't seem anything to gain from continuing to correspond so long after any chance of the friendship continuing had faded. Our lives are so separate now, and so different. I didn't want her to feel obligated to keep showing me kindness, and to be frank, reading letters about her royal life in the city brought me no great pleasure."

"Yes, I figured it was something like that." Her mother was tapping her fingers on the table again, seeming ill-at-ease. "I won't try to force you to do anything, Jacinta. No one can do that. But it does concern me to think that the giant king might be plotting against our kingdom, and no one but us be aware of it."

"Maybe you could take the message to the king," Jacinta suggested, brightening.

Her mother considered for only a moment before shaking her head. "No. The elf didn't choose me, and I didn't see or hear what you did. I can't even get through the wall to confirm it. A second-hand account would be even less convincing. It's already a slim hope that King Fidelius will listen to a word you say."

Her voice had darkened by the end of this speech, and Jacinta frowned. It was time to be forthright.

"Mamma, if I ask you a question, will you answer it honestly?" she asked.

Her mother looked suddenly wary, and after waiting in vain for her to respond, Jacinta pushed on.

"Did the king and queen fire you and father from your positions at the manor?"

Her mother relaxed slightly, leaning back in her chair. Her reaction convinced Jacinta that wasn't the question she'd feared, and it made her wildly curious to know what was.

"No, they didn't," her mother told her. "But they did criticize one aspect of our...performance. And I'll freely admit that your father and I didn't take that well. We made it clear that if our behavior wasn't satisfactory, we'd withdraw from our roles. They certainly didn't try to stop us."

Jacinta's frown only deepened as she remembered how capably her mother had run the household, and how meticulously her father had maintained the grounds. "What aspect of your performance was lacking?"

"That's a matter between those involved," her mother said. "I'd rather not get into it."

Jacinta debated pressing further, but decided against it. They had other things to worry about beyond dredging up old grievances between her parents and their former employers.

"Do you think I should travel to the capital to take the giant's message to King Fidelius?"

Her mother sighed. "I think since the message has been given, someone needs to take it. I won't deny I wish it could be someone other than you." She leaned forward, surprising Jacinta by squeezing her hand. "But it's also true that if anyone deserves the chance to see more of the world beyond this town, it's you, Jacinta."

"Thank you, Mamma," said Jacinta, touched by the tribute from her usually undemonstrative mother. She closed her eyes, drawing a deep breath. She had so many conflicting emotions regarding the idea of going to Vallen, it was hard to sort out what her conscience told her she should do.

Take Matthias and Mariella out of it, she told herself. *What would you think then?*

The answer was clear. If her murky feelings regarding the possibility of seeing her old friends weren't a factor, she would think taking the giant's gold without passing on the message it was supposed to support would be the actions of a thief.

And while she'd been desperate, she'd been hungry, and she'd been bitter...she'd never yet been a thief.

Well, unless you counted the abandoned produce from the manor's kitchen garden.

"I'll do it," she said aloud. "I'll take the message to the king. If I'm made a fool of, well...it is what it is."

"All right." Her mother nodded, communicating neither

approval nor disapproval of this plan. "In that case, there's a great deal to be done. The reason I was coming back here was that I had a thought to go to the next town over. There's a regional market there, and I thought I might find some work assisting on a stall. The timing is perfect. We'd be wise to barter these coins there rather than here, where everyone knows us. I'll take them."

Jacinta nodded, handing two of the coins over. The third she would take to Vallen with her as proof of her claim.

"Will you come to the capital with me?"

Her mother shook her head. "I think I'd best stay here, and keep an eye on that vine. I don't think we should mention any of this to anyone in Briarford. What if you're not the only one who can see the tunnel? What if it's only visible to the young, or those with magical blood in their ancestry, or any number of other possibilities? It could be disastrous to have people sneaking through the wall to try to get coins of their own, or explore Kjemper. And I won't tell anyone in the next town where we're from. Word will inevitably spread regarding the giant coins, and we don't want anyone following us back here to find out more."

Jacinta nodded her agreement. "Do you think these two coins will be enough to get us some laying chickens from the next town? Even a cow? I'd feel more comfortable leaving you if I knew you'd have eggs and milk while I'm gone."

"Yes, I think both are possible," said her mother. "And we'll need to get you a new gown. You can't travel to the castle in that."

Jacinta looked down at her garment, secretly elated. She hadn't thought her mother would consider a new gown worth spending the gold on, but she'd been dreading appearing before her royal former friends in rags.

"Come on." The older woman rose briskly to her feet. "Food

for a three-day journey, provision for me while you're gone, a new gown, a ticket on a public vehicle to the capital...we'll have to be shrewd if we're to get all that. Let's not wait until the market is dying down for the day."

Jacinta stood as well. "Let's hope there are no elves at the market this time," she said dryly.

Her mother gave a wry smile. "I'll handle the coins, shall I? Don't worry, Jacinta. I've never been out-bargained yet. We'll have you on your way to the capital by tomorrow morning."

CHAPTER SEVEN

Matthias

"That was brilliant!" Matthias's face split into a grin as he wiped sweat from his brow. "Can you show me that again, more slowly?"

Hagen lowered his arm, clearly battling his own enjoyment. "Are you sure, Your Highness?" he asked. "I mean, Prince Matthias," he corrected himself hastily, at Matthias's pointed look.

Even after a couple weeks of close proximity, the apprentice singer still hadn't fully accepted that Matthias meant it when he said to drop the title. But he was slowly making progress.

"Of course I'm sure," said Matthias. "How often do you think I get the chance to spar with a singer? The way you combine your songcraft with your hand-to-hand combat is incredible."

Hagen let a grin slip through his respectful demeanor. "I topped my class at combat," he said. "Most singers are more academic in focus, but I like to be active."

"It shows," said a new, bright voice.

Matthias turned in irritation, his expression long-suffering as he studied his sister. "What are you doing here, Mariella?"

"I came to watch you two spar," she said cheerfully. "The

rumor spread throughout the castle that the two of you were going to train in the Academy of Song's training yard rather than the castle's so that Hagen could use magic in the fight, and I knew it would be a show worth watching." She grinned encouragingly at Hagen, although she addressed her brother. "You just got pummeled, Matthias. It was incredibly satisfying to watch."

"Thanks for the support, as always," said Matthias, directing a resigned look toward Hagen. The singer was suppressing a smile.

"Is it my turn now?" Mariella asked innocently.

"Your turn for what?" Matthias gave his face another wipe with his sleeve. "You're interrupting, Mariella. Hagen was just going to demonstrate his magic for me again, with explanations this time."

"He can demonstrate on me." Mariella smiled brightly at both of them. "I want a turn sparring."

Matthias stared at her. Had she lost her mind? "You don't spar. You haven't been trained in combat."

"I'm aware of that," said Mariella pointedly. "Do you think you need to remind me that I'm denied most of the fun you get?"

"I really don't think you'd find fighting as much fun as you imagine," said Matthias, amused.

"You're probably right," said Mariella. "Wielding swords and wearing chainmail doesn't appeal to me at all. But what I just saw Hagen do was much more interesting."

"You can't learn that," Matthias pointed out. "You have to be a singer to use magic."

Mariella sighed. "Yes, I know that. But he didn't just use magic. He used some sleight of hand that *looked* like magic, in order to enhance the effect." She looked at Hagen. "Didn't you?"

His face split in a reluctant smile. "You're very observant, Princess Mariella."

"It's a necessary skill for a princess," she informed him. "I'm expected to be present for everything, and never make any mistakes, but no one tells me anything willingly. I'm not considered worthy of being in the direct line of communication, let alone decision making. So I need to have my eyes and ears open all the time if I have any hope of being across what's happening."

Matthias stared at his sister, surprised by her frank words. It was clear she was in earnest, and not much contemplation was required for him to acknowledge the truth of everything she'd said. She'd never expressed those thoughts to him before, though, and he didn't know what would make her share them with Hagen, a near stranger. A glance at the singer showed that Hagen looked both troubled and thoughtful, his gaze seeming to hide many reflections as he considered Mariella.

The princess had been speaking seriously, but she suddenly flashed a smile. "And when it comes to getting people to behave in a revealing manner around me, I find my most effective strategy is to be flippant and lighthearted. No one thinks you'll listen, or understand even if you did. It's amazing what you see that way." She flicked her hair over her shoulder, her smile impudent as she gestured toward Hagen with her head. "You, for example, are easier to read than you think. You find me interesting. Dare I say it, even fascinating."

The usually stoic Hagen colored visibly, and Matthias felt a wave of pity for him.

"Mariella, leave the poor man alone," he said in exasperation. "Since when are you an expert in human behavior? Besides, everyone's interested in you. You're a princess."

"That's just it," said Mariella brightly, shifting her gaze from Hagen to Matthias in an act of mercy. "Most people don't find me especially interesting. Most people like that I'm a princess but have no interest in me. Their reaction to me doesn't change at all when they spend time with me, because they're not receiving any new information regarding the only aspect of me that caught their attention: my royal status. It's rare to have someone's curiosity captured by who I actually am."

"That's too convoluted for me to keep up with," Matthias complained. "I came here to spar, Mariella, not to have deep conversations about whether our identities can be untangled from our status."

Mariella laughed. "I know. And I came to spar as well." She turned an expectant face to Hagen. "What do you say? Can you teach me some of those maneuvers?"

"Well..." Hagen seemed torn. "I probably could, but I'm not sure if it's appropriate."

"I won't tell if you don't," said Mariella, repeating what she'd said to Matthias in the castle training yard.

Hagen looked uncertainly toward Matthias, who shrugged as if to say, *up to you*, then leaned back against a nearby pillar.

With a deep breath, the singer turned to the princess. "It's about distraction. Or misdirection if you prefer. It's a particularly useful skill for singers in combat, but I'm sure we could adapt the strategies to be relevant to you."

"Why is it particularly useful for singers?" Mariella asked curiously.

"Well, I don't know how much you know about songcraft," Hagen said, "but the role of the words in a song are not as central as most people think. They're very useful for beginners —telling the magic in simple words what you want it to do is the fastest way to get results. But that's just because, as humans, we're taught to use words to direct and define our thoughts. Our thoughts don't actually need words."

"Don't they?" Mariella sounded doubtful, and Hagen smiled.

"Think about it. If someone lived all alone on an island, and never learned any spoken language, they'd still have thoughts, wouldn't they?"

"I suppose," Mariella acknowledged. "But they'd have no way to communicate them to anyone."

"That's not true," said Hagen, shaking his head.

Irrelevantly to the conversation, Matthias acknowledged to himself that Mariella had a point about the way the singer responded to her. He didn't act like he was speaking with a princess. Most people wouldn't directly contradict her like that. But most people also wouldn't take her questions so seriously.

"They would just have to find other ways of communicating," Hagen said. "And there are plenty of ways to communicate without words. It's the same with singing. We can learn to channel the magic through our song without using words. But it takes time to acquire the skill. At the start, it's much easier to just tell the song what to do."

Mariella nodded. "So far I'm with you. But what does that have to do with misdirection?"

Hagen looked approving of her focus. "Advanced combat training includes learning to disassociate the words of your song from the exercise of the magic to the point where you can direct your song to do one thing while your words actually *say* something else entirely."

"Ooh, that's very clever!" Mariella said, impressed. "I can see at once how useful that could be."

Hagen nodded. "I didn't do that to Prince Matthias just now, but the principle is the same. I used misdirection to do one thing with my hands while my magic was performing a different role entirely. That's how I disarmed him that last time."

"Huh." Matthias shook his head slowly. "That makes me feel better. I thought I saw your attack coming, and I thought I countered it effectively. But next thing I knew, I'd lost my weapon."

Hagen nodded. "I made as if to disarm you with my hands,

but I actually used my magic in an unrelated attack. It is absolutely possible for you to learn to defend against what I did, even without magic. But you won't do it while you're focused on trying to defend against the normal combat move you think I'm planning."

Matthias nodded, unfolding his arms as he pushed away from the wall. "This is excellent, Hagen. I had no idea how much you were able to teach me! Show me how to defend against the magical attack you used last time."

"Uh uh uh." Mariella held up a finger, pushing it into Matthias's chest. "You've just had a turn with our new friend and favorite singer. It's my turn."

To Matthias's astonishment, Mariella's slim finger pushed him physically backward with enough force to send him into the pillar he'd just been leaning on. She seemed as taken aback as he was, and it took him a moment to hear past her delighted laugh and catch the low hum of song coming from Hagen.

"Oi!" he told the singer, without any real heat. He couldn't keep the smile from his face. It had been so long since he and Mariella had enjoyed the company of someone their own age who was so willing to be natural with them.

"Sorry," Hagen said in his gruff voice. "It's another kind of misdirection. A singer who looks physically strong using their magic to give extra strength or power to someone whom an enemy would perceive as weaker and less of a threat."

"Hey!" Mariella said. But a moment later, her face relaxed into a grin. "No, you're right, I am weaker. I won't try to deny it." She waggled the temporarily empowered finger in Matthias's face. "But appearances can deceive, so watch yourself, brother dear."

Matthias rolled his eyes, although he was chuckling. "I tremble in fear." He considered his still-smirking sister for a moment, then sprang into action, grabbing her arms and twisting them behind her in a move he hadn't used since they were rough-housing children. He did it gently, so as not to cause any pain, but his grip was as firm as iron around her wrists.

"Hey!" she cried indignantly, aiming a kick backward at him, which he nimbly dodged. She turned appealingly to Hagen. "You see what I'm up against? Can you teach me any move to defend against this?"

The princess spoke lightly, but Hagen didn't laugh or give any other sign of thinking her request was a joke. He ran a hand over his chin as he thoughtfully considered the pair.

"Probably," he said after a moment, giving a decisive nod. His rather severe face relaxed into a smile. "But it won't do much good if I teach it while he's listening."

Brother and sister both laughed at that, Matthias releasing Mariella at last. She responded by ruffling his hair, another childhood gesture that she now had to stand on tiptoes to achieve.

"I like the way you think, Hagen," Mariella informed the singer in a businesslike tone. "It seems I should hire you as a tutor, or possibly just to follow me around and give magical power to my every seemingly innocuous move." She saw that Hagen looked wary and smiled reassuringly at him. "That was a joke. I know you have plenty of your own duties. I'm just saying that with my underestimated position and your raw power, we could be quite a combination."

For the second time in the short conversation, Hagen's neck flushed with color. Matthias thought he looked pleased this time, however.

The sound of approaching footsteps made them all turn to see one of the academy's clerks entering the training area.

"Your Highnesses," the man said, bowing to Matthias and Mariella in turn. "And Trainee Hagen." He nodded his head respectfully to the singer. "I apologize for the interruption. But a messenger from the castle just requested your presence on behalf of the king, Prince Matthias."

"Thank you," said Matthias politely. "I will come at once." The clerk bowed again before hurrying off. As soon as he was gone, Matthias let out a sigh. "Duty calls. Thanks for the training, Hagen. Come and find me when your afternoon sessions with your masters are complete. My father knows I intend to show you the market district this afternoon."

"Thank you, Prince Matthias," said Hagen, dipping his head. "I look forward to it."

Matthias paused, looking inquiringly at his sister.

Mariella shook her head. "I'm not going back to the castle yet. If I've been as clever as I think I have, I won't be missed until luncheon, and I don't intend to cut my morning short."

Matthias nodded, telling himself not to begrudge her the small freedom. He had more duties than his sister, but they came with many benefits she was lacking.

"Well, try not to teach her anything too dangerous," he told Hagen. With a grin, he added, "Dangerous for me, I mean."

Mariella chuckled, but Hagen was harder to read. His gaze passed back and forth between the siblings, leaving Matthias uncertain of his feelings regarding being left alone with the princess.

Leaving them to sort it out, Matthias departed the academy, walking the short distance back to the castle. The two buildings sat side by side, separated only by the castle's extensive grounds.

Matthias had intended to seek his father out in the king's study, but as soon as he entered the castle, a servant directed him to his mother's private rooms instead. Curious, he made his way to the royal wing, wishing he'd had the chance to freshen up since his sparring session with Hagen. His father didn't concern himself with Matthias's attire, but the queen liked her children to be well dressed at all times.

The number of guards at the door told him that his father was inside the suite as well as his mother, and it was with some trepidation that Matthias entered.

"Matthias, excellent." King Fidelius waved his son to a seat. "Let's make this quick, shall we? I have some pressing reports awaiting me."

"No objections from me," said Matthias, greeting his mother respectfully. "Of course, I don't know what *this* is, so my opinion isn't what you'd call well-informed."

"Ah, yes, of course." The king sounded impatient already, but Matthias didn't let it dismay him. It was just his father's way, probably the inevitable result of having so many tasks requiring his attention at all times. "We wanted to discuss your betrothal, Matthias."

Matthias frowned as he took a seat across from his parents. "I thought you said there was no urgency."

"There isn't the least urgency for you to marry," his mother agreed. "Not at your age. But we're of the view that it would be beneficial for you to form a betrothal sooner rather than later. The betrothal can be as long as we choose to make it. But if your choice is made, it will give me time to help prepare the young woman in question for her role as a member of the royal family." She glanced at her husband. "We feel it may also help to settle expectations others may have formed."

"What do you mean?" Matthias asked, his gaze transferring to his father. "Naturally I'd be pleased to stop having every girl in the court making eyes at me anytime I walk past, but I doubt that's your primary concern." He reflected for a moment. "Not to mention that if you think the behavior would stop because of a mere betrothal, not yet formalized into marriage, you don't know much about the young women in question."

"And I have no particular wish to know more of them," the king said dryly. Clearing his throat, he leaned back in his chair.

"You're right, that's not what your mother meant. As you know, I've been requesting practical support from a number of our wealthier noblemen as we prepare for the possibility of invasion by the giants. Some of them have been less than subtle in their determination to bring their daughters to my notice. I won't go as far as to say that they're refusing to help unless I make promises, but..." He sighed. "Let us simply say that I would be glad to have the perceived bargaining chip removed from the equation. Then I think I would face fewer complications in gaining their support."

"Nothing to cheer a man up like being referred to as a bargaining chip," said Matthias glumly.

"It's foolish to speak of your desirability as if it was a hardship," his mother informed him shortly. "I imagine you wouldn't be dancing with delight if you faced the problem of *no one* wanting you."

"No, probably not," Matthias acknowledged, unable to help laughing. "But there's not much romance in the picture you paint."

"I wasn't trying to be either romantic or artistic," said the king. "We're talking of serious matters, Matthias, try to focus."

"Yes, Father," said the prince meekly. "I assure you, I take it seriously." It was only his life they were speaking of, after all.

"Have you given further consideration to my suggestion that Lady Letitia would be a good choice for you?" his mother asked hopefully.

Matthias shifted uncomfortably in his seat, thinking of Lady Letty's shrill giggle and calculating eyes. "I don't know, Mother."

"Her father is a duke, Matthias," the king reminded him. "And with his extensive holdings in the north, he has the capacity to be of enormous assistance."

"I thought the whole point was to *not* use my marriage as a tool to buy your court's support," said Matthias dryly.

"I don't need your marriage to buy the duke's support," said King Fidelius. "He's shown his loyalty. And I would like to reward it."

Matthias let out a breath that was almost a groan. "Father, I wish you would find another way to reward it."

"What's wrong with Lady Letitia?" his mother asked, sounding as offended as if she'd raised the girl herself. "She's well-mannered, of excellent stock, and very beautiful."

Matthias shrugged, unable to muster any enthusiasm. How could he explain to his parents that in addition to feeling that he had no idea who she actually was underneath all that styling, he felt certain he'd never be able to feel truly himself in her presence?

"I suppose she's pretty enough," he said, his voice pained. "She's just so...silly."

"All young girls are silly," said his mother dismissively.

"They're not." Matthias spoke the contradiction too emphatically for politeness. "And saying that is a disservice to all the ones who aren't."

He shook his head, his thoughts flying inevitably to the least silly—and most likable—girl he'd ever known. What was she like as the young woman she'd now be? He supposed it was possible she'd gotten sillier and more superficial as she got older, but it was hard to believe. He studied the queen's face.

"Is that really what you think, Mother?"

"I don't mean any great offense," his mother said placatingly. "They generally grow out of it. But they're taught to think of little else but young men at this age, and is it any wonder it makes them silly?

Matthias frowned, not satisfied. "What about Mariella? She's a young woman now, and she's not silly."

"Mariella is extremely silly," said the king irritably. "In spite of her superior education. So that just goes to show that your mother makes a good point."

Matthias shook his head, his thoughts on his sister's unexpected comments in the academy training yard. "Mariella isn't silly. Far from it. She acts that way sometimes, but that's only because it's the mask you've shown her you expect. Underneath, she's as sharp as a blade."

"I'm not sure that's any better," said the king, seeming impatient with the direction the conversation was taking. "We're not speaking of Mariella, anyway. We're speaking of you, and the duke's daughter."

"Lady Letitia," the queen supplied.

"Yes, her." The king nodded approvingly. "Are you really set against the idea, Matthias?"

Matthias drew in a breath. "I'm not enthusiastic about it."

"Hm." His mother looked disappointed, but she folded her hands in her lap. "Well, we aren't going to push you, Matthias. As you said, there's no burning urgency. But I encourage you to think about it. She's as eligible as anyone else, and she'll mellow with age."

Matthias was saved the necessity of responding when a knock sounded at the door.

"Enter," called the queen.

The door swung open to reveal the castle's steward, who bowed to each of them in turn.

"Your Majesty, I apologize for the interruption. A young woman has arrived at the castle requesting an audience with you. She claims to have information regarding the giants."

All three royals straightened in their seats, and the king narrowed his eyes. "Is she credible?"

"She provided evidence that she'd entered Kjemper," the steward said. "The messenger said it convinced him, but apparently she was reluctant to part with it to anyone but yourself."

The king stood. "I will see her in the small audience hall."

"I'd like to come, Father," said Matthias, standing quickly.

The king nodded. "Certainly. You should keep abreast of any developments regarding the giants."

The queen apparently shared Matthias's curiosity, because the three of them made their way to the room together. There was no throne in the smaller chamber, unlike the grand public audience hall King Fidelius used when he opened his doors to the general public. But there was a slightly raised dais onto which the three royals emerged from an antechamber. Moments after their arrival, the door to the corridor opened, and the steward ushered in a young woman with a simple gown and dark, slightly wavy hair.

"Approach," King Fidelius said, gesturing her forward. "You have information for me?"

"Yes, Your Majesty." Something about the girl's voice made Matthias pause as she ducked her head in an attempted curtsy. "As unbelievable as it must sound, I carry a message for you from a giant."

With the words, she straightened, and Matthias got a good look at her face for the first time. He froze, shock immobilizing him as he took in the high cheekbones, red lips, dark brows, and straight nose.

Features he would know anywhere, regardless of the passage of years. Her eyes flicked to him then quickly back to his father, but the flush of her cheeks betrayed her. Surely she didn't really intend to act like a stranger?

Matthias certainly didn't. He took a half step forward, still grappling with his disbelief at her sudden appearance. His voice was croaky as he spoke the name that had been often in his thoughts but rarely on his lips across the last eight years.

"Jacinta?"

CHAPTER EIGHT

Jacinta

Jacinta swallowed, finding it suddenly hard to breathe, caught as she was in the piercing beam of Matthias's gaze. If she'd thought the prince grown up and handsome when she'd seen him the day of her father's funeral four years before, it was nothing to the man he'd grown into since.

He was tall, his tawny hair appealingly swept back from a strong brow, and his eyes still the same dark blue she remembered. He was lithe, but by no means scrawny. On the contrary, his every move radiated power and confidence. He carried himself with the air of a man who knew he was the prince of a prosperous kingdom.

And she'd do well to remember it, too.

"Jacinta?" The king was visibly startled, his eyes flying between his son and Jacinta before he exchanged a veiled look with his wife. "You're the daughter of the housekeeper and groundskeeper from the manor at Briarford?"

Jacinta cleared her throat, trying to stand straight. She was incredibly weary from the three-day journey, but she was determined to present a respectable picture. "Yes, Your Majesty. But the errand that brought me to the capital has nothing to do with my parents' former roles."

"I'm sure." The king's voice was dry, and Jacinta watched in dismay as his whole demeanor changed. He'd already been every bit as intimidating as she remembered, if not more so. "I take it you didn't see fit to fully identify yourself to my steward. I do not have time to entertain deceitful attempts to get my attention."

Jacinta pursed her lips, holding back the retort she longed to utter. This was the king. She had to tread carefully. But it seemed that her mother had been right that she would be wise not to reveal her former connection to the royal family prior to seeing the king, for fear she would never be given the chance to deliver her message. She hadn't understood it at the time—she still didn't understand it—but clearly her mother had anticipated this reaction. How deep had the conflict between her parents and the monarchs gone?

"Father, what are you talking about?" Matthias didn't share her hesitation to speak plainly. "You're going to accuse her of wasting your time before you've even heard her out? I have no doubt Jacinta came here with good reason." He turned his gaze to her, still seeming dazed. "I can hardly believe it's you. It's been so many years." His face softened slightly. "But you look the same."

Jacinta gave a strained smile, straightening the folds of her skirt uncomfortably. She didn't believe for a moment that she was physically unchanged, and she didn't relish the idea of the prince looking too closely. She'd been pleased with her gown when they'd purchased it from the market, but she'd forgotten just how lavishly the royal family dressed. She looked like exactly what she was—a rustic peasant standing in the presence of exalted people.

"You look different...Your Highness." She added the title

uncertainly. It felt strange on her tongue—they'd never had titles between them before—but she wasn't brave enough to dispense with it in front of the king and queen.

Something shifted in Matthias's face, and it wrenched her heart. Even after all this time, even with everything that stood between them, she was drawn to him like a moth to flame. She had to fight a childish instinct to run to him, throw herself into his arms like she had the day of her father's funeral.

But she wasn't fourteen anymore, and he owed her absolutely nothing. There was nothing between them now but fond childhood memories, and she knew perfectly well that wasn't enough to give her the right to take liberties with the crown prince. She cast her eyes around the room, wishing Mariella would materialize from a corner somewhere. Judging by the king's reaction, this one interview would likely be all the contact she'd have with the royal family. She would have so loved to see Mariella before she left.

"I apologize for the offense I've unwittingly caused, Your Majesty," she said, addressing herself to the king once again. "I didn't mean to be deceitful. The fact that we've met before truly is irrelevant to my message. I stumbled into the land of the giants by a strange chance."

"What?" Matthias took another step forward, alarm crossing his usually cheerful features. "What do you mean *stumbled into*? Don't tell me you've gone into Kjemper?"

Jacinta nodded, not quite meeting his eyes. She couldn't allow herself to be warmed by his evident concern. "I have, although I certainly didn't plan to." She paused, self-conscious. "It's a strange tale, and I fear you won't believe it if I tell it as it happened."

"Of course we will," said Matthias encouragingly. He stepped forward, hesitating for the briefest moment before placing his hand on her arm, making as if to guide her toward a row of chairs pushed against the wall. "Sit down, tell us the whole story."

"Matthias." The king's voice was sharp, and Matthias dropped Jacinta's arm like it was burning.

She barely noticed the confused expression the prince was directing toward his father, too distracted by the sensation left behind from his casual touch. She could almost swear her arm *was* burning. What was wrong with her? They'd once been such close friends, and contact between them had never felt charged or unnatural then. Why was it so unsettling now, when they were near strangers, and neither his proximity nor his opinion should matter to her?

"Don't you intend to hear Jacinta's message, Father?" Matthias challenged, staring between his frowning parents in bewilderment.

The king let out a long breath. "Of course we do. But I'm sure the girl is willing to stand."

"I'm perfectly willing, Your Majesty," said Jacinta in a tone of cool politeness. "My tale is simple, if incredible. It came about as the result of an elf bargain."

"An elf bargain?" Matthias repeated in amazement. At least one of her three listeners was satisfyingly intrigued. "I didn't think elves hung about the north anymore."

"No, generally speaking they're among those who've lost interest in the northern region as it has become increasingly barren of both arable land and magic," Jacinta said, keeping her face carefully expressionless.

Matthias's mouth closed with a snap at her words, and she mentally chastised herself for letting her unjustified bitterness trickle out.

He owes you nothing, she reminded herself. *He did nothing wrong in stopping coming to Briarford.*

"But this elf must have had reasons of her own for being in

Briarford," she went on quickly. "She caught me in a moment of distraction when I took my cow to the market to trade it, and trapped me into exchanging the animal for a handful of magic beans."

"Your cow?" Matthias asked. "Not Princess?"

"Y-yes," said Jacinta, taken aback that he would remember. "Yes, it was her."

"She's stayed with you all this time!" he said in amazement. "I remember you were fond of her. More fond than anyone had any right to be about a cow."

He grinned lopsidedly, the once-familiar expression transforming his face into the approachable companion of Jacinta's childhood and yet simultaneously taking her breath away. It was a confusingly muddled sensation. As she stared back at him, no doubt looking as idiotic and empty-headed as she felt, his expression sobered.

"You must have been sad to part with her."

"I feel we've strayed from the point," interjected King Fidelius disapprovingly.

"Yes, Your Majesty." Jacinta gathered her scattered thoughts. "Having been so foolish as to be tricked into the bargain, I was of course bound by its magic. The elf was unwilling to give me any information regarding the beans she'd been at such pains to pass over to me. I took them home and, although I had no great expectations from them, I planted them in my yard."

"And did they grow into something?" asked Matthias avidly.

She nodded. "They grew overnight into an enormous stalk. It didn't grow upward, but along the ground in a northward direction. When I followed it, I found that it had tunneled right through Battlement Wall and into Kjemper."

"What?" King Fidelius stiffened. "The wall is breached? Do you tell me that giants could be entering our kingdom unchecked at this very moment and you've been wasting time discussing a cow?"

"No, Your Majesty," Jacinta assured him quickly. "The hole isn't big enough for a giant to come through. I barely fit." She hesitated for a moment, wondering if she should tell him that her mother had been unable to see it. But she decided that would only make her tale sound more far-fetched.

"But why did you go through?" Matthias asked, the alarm back on his face. "Surely that was incredibly dangerous!"

"Dangerous and foolish," agreed the king. "What did you have to gain by entering the giants' land?"

Jacinta shrugged. "To tell the truth, Your Majesty, I felt that I didn't know what I had to gain until I'd seen what the vines were leading me to. And it seemed worth finding out, because on this side of the wall I had nothing to lose."

Matthias frowned at her words, his gaze much too shrewd. Deciding not to give him a chance to ask uncomfortable questions, Jacinta pressed on.

"The beanstalk led me to the home of a giant, and I confess the encounter didn't go at all as I would have predicted."

"You spoke with an actual giant?" Matthias's face was white now, but Jacinta kept her voice light and calm.

"I did. Although she did most of the talking. She seemed to know the elf, although she was as bemused as I was as to why the elf had apparently sent me to her."

"She knew the elf?" King Fidelius betrayed the first hint of interest in her story. "Perhaps there's some truth to King Herleif's claim that the giants have elves working with them."

Matthias looked sharply at his father, his face mirroring Jacinta's surprise. "I thought the elves despised giants."

"Most do," the king acknowledged. "And any I've spoken to have vehemently denied that any of their kind would work with giants. But perhaps they've lost touch with their brethren in the northern part of the continent to a greater extent than they've realized."

"They wouldn't be the only ones," said Matthias softly. His gaze passed once again to Jacinta, making her squirm where she stood. She really shouldn't have taken that veiled shot at him before. It had been unwise as well as unjust.

"In any event, the giant asked me to carry a message to my king," she hurried on. "She said that the giant king won't be satisfied until he's taken what he wants from all of Providore, and that the human kingdoms would be wise to strike before he gets any stronger."

"She claims the giant king will invade the human kingdoms?" King Fidelius asked. He frowned as he absently shifted his hand to rest on the hilt of his sword. "It's nothing we haven't been suspecting since King Herleif emerged from Kjemper."

"Actually, Your Majesty," Jacinta interjected hesitantly, "she seemed careful *not* to say that. If anything, she seemed impatient when I talked about invasion. But she didn't want to tell me exactly how the giant king is a threat to us here." She swallowed. "She also spoke of mining towers. Her husband is employed in one."

"Mining towers?" the king asked blankly. "For precious ore?"

"That's what I assumed," said Jacinta. "But she said it was for...well, magic."

"Magic?" The king was scoffing now. "Giants don't mine magic. They don't have the ability either to access it or to manipulate it."

"Unless they had elves working with them," said Matthias slowly.

His father shot him a sharp look. "Elves mine magic from the ground with handheld tools and manipulate it painstakingly into talismans. It's fine craftsmanship requiring finesse and extensive training. It's nothing to do with the type of industry suggested by mining towers."

Matthias raised his eyebrows.

"That's how the elves *we* know mine magic. Those are the methods favored by those who create talismans to sell at the market. It doesn't necessarily mean it's the only way magic can be mined. Every kingdom has prohibited humans from engaging in any magic mining, so we've never explored whether that kind of industry is possible. Perhaps in Kjemper, the same restrictions don't apply."

The king looked unconvinced, and Matthias pressed on.

"Think about it, Father. Jacinta's just said that this giant knew an elf personally. What if these renegade elves, whom the rest claim don't exist, have helped the giants to develop a magic-mining industry? King Herleif claimed that there are elves working with the giants, too. He also claimed that the former giant queen had an unexplainably huge stock of powerful talismans, along with other evidence of magic in her castle."

"I do not think King Herleif fully understood what he saw," said the king dismissively. "His wife is a singer. He no doubt took her perceptions as fact when in reality I believe she was an uneducated peasant who likely had very little understanding of what she witnessed."

Jacinta raised an eyebrow. It wasn't really a surprise that the king had such an attitude toward a peasant girl who'd married a king, but it was a little surprising that he felt it strongly enough to say it in front of her.

"And even if it were true that the giants are somehow mining magic, it would benefit them very little," King Fidelius went on. "We all know how bare of magic the northern region is. There's too little magic in the ground there to substantially change the balance of power." He shook his head. "No, I do not believe the giants have access to vast amounts of magic. The simple proof is that they haven't invaded us and tried to overwhelm our lands with it."

Jacinta frowned. "Perhaps they don't wish to invade us. Perhaps they're happy with their own land."

"Do I take it that Kjemper was a fertile and pleasant land then, rather than the barren wasteland we've believed it to be?" the king asked her coldly.

Jacinta's shoulders slumped under his glare. "No, it was as barren as you imagine." She straightened. "But after all, so is the north of Vadolis, and many of us still choose to live in the homes of our fathers." In the corner of her eye, she saw Matthias shift, but she kept her eyes on the king. "I think they have some pride in their land. When the giant first saw me, she spoke of humans breaching the wall as if it was there to keep us out rather than keep the giants out. And I saw no evidence of a desire to relocate."

"Since you didn't witness it in your one brief visit to the house of an unknown giant on the fringes of their society, it must be impossible," said the king, his voice heavy with irony. "The truth is you know nothing of the state of affairs in the castle at Kjemper."

Matthias was frowning at his father. "She knows something we didn't know. And without her coming all this way to tell us, we still wouldn't."

The king ignored him. "How do we know the giant was telling you the truth? For that matter, how do we know *you* are telling us the truth? Didn't you gain entrance to the castle by claiming to have proof?"

"I do have proof," said Jacinta shortly. She reached into the traveling bag slung over her shoulder and pulled out the last of the coins the giant had provided. "She gave me this so I could prove to other humans that I'd been to Kjemper. Unless you've ever seen a coin like this elsewhere in Providore."

With visible reluctance, the king approached close enough to examine the coin. Jacinta held it out, offering for him to take it, and he did so. She watched as he turned it over in his hand, examining the markings around the edge which suggested the giants had some kind of centralized currency.

"It's enormous," Matthias said, leaning over to look more closely.

"It certainly looks like a coin a giant would use," Queen Bronte said, having also approached for a better look.

"Yes, it does."

The king sounded like he resented the acknowledgment, leaving Jacinta perplexed as to what made him so stubborn regarding her claim. Surely he wanted all the information he could get about any threat from the giants. She was starting to understand why her parents may have had a falling out with their royal former employer. She'd had almost no interaction with him as a child—she'd had no idea he was such an inflexible man.

"It was part of the payment her husband received for his work in the mining tower," she explained. "I think it's just their normal currency, but I got the impression he was being paid well." Not that their dilapidated hut supported that assessment. "I overheard him say that there was more work to do at the towers closer to the border. I'm not sure what he meant by that, but I assume it has something to do with the other giant's comment about their king planning to take what he wants from our side of the wall."

"How did you overhear him?" Matthias asked, his brow creasing. "I assumed you only spoke with the one giant."

"Yes." Jacinta scratched the back of her neck, feeling foolish. "He came home early, and she didn't think he'd let me live if he saw me, so she shoved me into a cupboard."

"This story gets less and less credible," said the king, unimpressed.

"I think you mean more and more dangerous!" Matthias protested. His eyes were genuinely troubled as they rested on her face. "It seems you took a great risk to bring us this information. We're in your debt."

"No such thing," said King Fidelius with a touch of impatience. "If your tale is true, I'm certainly appreciative for the information, vague as it is. But you must acknowledge that you're expecting us to believe a great deal without evidence. If we assume that all you've told us is true, even you cannot guarantee that the giant didn't mislead you. She may have been laying a trap."

"The same possibility occurred to me, Your Majesty," Jacinta acknowledged. "And you're right that I can't prove her to have been genuine." She shrugged. "But I believe her."

"That doesn't convince me," the king said brutally. "I cannot make decisions that affect the kingdom based on nothing but faith in either your honesty or your judgment."

"Father." Matthias was looking at his father like he didn't know him, his disapproval clear.

"It's not personal, Matthias," his father said. "I must be circumspect in whom I trust, because the whole kingdom can bear the cost of my mistakes. You'll understand when you're king."

The logical part of Jacinta's mind acknowledged that his words were perfectly reasonable. She didn't really even blame him for not trusting her. But something about the way the queen's eyes lingered on her made her feel that it *was* personal. Irritation stirred within her toward her mother. Pride be hanged, she shouldn't have sent Jacinta into this situation without giving her the full picture about whatever happened between the two families all those years ago. Clearly it wasn't possible for the monarchs to fully separate the past from the message Jacinta carried.

"I understand, Your Majesty," she said, ready to bring the interview to an end. "I cannot control whether you believe me, or what you do with my information. I've discharged my errand, and that's the end of my role. With your permission, I will take my leave now."

She lowered herself into a bow, surprised to find when she straightened that the king's expression had softened slightly. Perhaps he'd been afraid she intended to linger, claim the friendship of the past as a means to impose on the royals and stay in the castle, or some other liberty. If he suspected her of an ulterior motive in coming, it might help explain his skepticism.

"Wait, child." The king turned the giant coin over once more in his hand. "I withhold final judgment until events can unfold, but I am inclined to believe your tale if only because it is too far-fetched for you to fabricate and expect us to believe."

Jacinta wasn't sure how to respond to this, so stayed silent. The king looked up from the coin at last, meeting her eyes.

"I do not, however, believe that the giants have access to significant amounts of magic. It seems more credible to me that the giant with whom you spoke misled you for her own purposes."

"The giant didn't actually say they have magic, Father," Matthias pointed out. "That's our speculation based on what Jacinta saw and heard, and on King Herleif's experiences."

"She did say that their mining towers are for magic," Jacinta said, her tone apologetic at the contradiction of the one member of her audience inclined to view her favorably.

The king nodded. "Precisely. She clearly manipulated this girl's impressions so as to leave her with the conclusion that the giants had magic. Of course, if they did, it would be a grave threat to us, and one we need to know about. But without any evidence, I must treat it as the merest rumor."

Jacinta held her tongue, trying not to resent the clear snub in being called *this girl* when by this point of the conversation, the king must know her name. After all, there was nothing to be gained by arguing with him. Whether he acted on her report, whether he even believed it, was really none of her concern. She bowed again, intending to take her leave for real this time, but the king spoke once more.

"If, however, you were to return to Kjemper and bring back some evidence to show that the giants have access to magic, it would be a different matter."

Jacinta froze in place, her heart beating frantically in her ears. He wanted her to go back?

"Return to Kjemper?" Matthias repeated, apparently sharing her reaction. He looked aghast. "Father, you can't be serious. You intend to send her into the land of the giants alone?"

"If she can find someone willing to go with her, I won't prevent it," said King Fidelius, his voice unconcerned.

"*I'll* go with her," said Matthias staunchly.

The king's demeanor instantly changed, his response coming in unison with his wife's. "Absolutely not!"

Matthias gave them a look. "So you do acknowledge that it's dangerous, then. How do you justify sending an untrained civilian?"

"I'm not sending her," his father said dismissively. "She's under no obligation to go."

Jacinta set her teeth. His meaning was clear. She was under no obligation to go, but if she didn't bring back more evidence, he would persist in thinking her either a liar or gullible.

"I'll get the evidence," she said, her pride overcoming her better sense.

"Jacinta!" Matthias protested.

But she didn't look at him, not trusting herself as she added, "And I won't endanger anyone else in the process."

The king inclined his head. "It is a matter for you. Should you acquire more concrete evidence, I will receive it."

"Very gracious of you," said Matthias hotly, turning to his father.

Jacinta drew in a breath, the full tension of the confrontation catching up with her now that it was drawing to a close. The king's nod was a clear dismissal.

With a murmured farewell and another attempt at a bow, she turned toward the door. Her eyes lingered for only the briefest moment on Matthias, who was still glaring at his father.

She'd made it most of the way across the room before the prince noticed her departure.

"Jacinta! Wait!"

She turned to see him striding toward her, his expression a mixture of reproach and alarm.

"Surely you're not just going to leave?"

"I...I've passed on my message," she said, her mouth dry under the glare of the monarchs.

"Matthias, come," said the king. "We need to discuss these developments."

"Hold on, Father," said the prince angrily. "I need a minute to speak with Jacinta."

"No, you need to come now," said the king, a dangerous note in his voice. "This young woman has discharged her errand, as she said. We have no cause to inconvenience her by keeping her longer than is necessary."

"Inconvenience her!" Matthias repeated incredulously. "What are you talking about?"

Jacinta had heard enough. In spite of his protests, the prince had stopped at his father's words, and was still far enough away that she could slip out the door without too much fuss. And much as she appreciated the unexpected level of warmth with which Matthias had greeted her, she had no desire to linger in present company. It was clear that the king's dislike of her family went far beyond what she'd understood. Staying where she wasn't welcome would only lead to her own humiliation.

She hurried to the door, finding a young servant awaiting her beyond.

"Can you show me the way out of the castle, please?" she asked, trying to master her tumultuous emotions enough to keep her voice steady.

"Of course, miss," the servant said, turning obligingly to lead the way.

Jacinta followed him, tripping over her feet in her haste to leave the castle. The opulence overwhelmed her as much as the encounter with the three royals. She'd thought the manor house in Briarford grand. It was nothing to the luxury of the castle. No wonder they hadn't continued their visits to the northern estate. The real surprise was that they'd made the trip for so many years.

When they reached the entranceway, Jacinta turned, murmuring her thanks to the servant.

"I...I don't know if I'm supposed to pay you for your trouble," she stammered, only to have the servant wave his hand.

"I wouldn't take coins from someone as pretty as you, miss," he said, with a cheeky wink. "You don't need to pay for assistance, not in the castle. They pay us well enough to manage."

Jacinta smiled faintly, relieved that she wouldn't have to dip into the stash of coins in her pocket. She already wasn't confident she had enough to get her home. The outward journey had cost more than she and her mother had projected.

She would manage. If necessary, she could probably find a

few days' work at a tavern along the route somewhere. Times weren't as desperate in most of Vadolis as they were in the north.

Drawing her cloak about her, Jacinta strode away from the castle. She did her best to push her swirling thoughts down with the reflection that she'd have more than enough time to wallow on the stagecoach home. For as long as possible, she would keep some semblance of her peace of mind by *not* dwelling on those deep blue eyes and their overwhelmingly piercing gaze.

CHAPTER NINE

Matthias

"**M**atthias, stop making yourself ridiculous," the king snapped, his features tight with disapproval.

"I don't feel that I am," Matthias retorted. "And I'm sure if I was, Jacinta would be ready to overlook it." He turned to look at her, only to see empty space and hear a click as the door closed.

"Hang it, why is she in such a hurry to run away?"

"It's to her credit that she doesn't wish to be an imposition," said the king. "There's no reason for us to linger here. We should discuss this matter further."

On the word, he turned and stalked toward the antechamber through which they'd entered. Pausing, he looked back, his glare demanding that Matthias follow.

Matthias looked between his parents and the closed door. He was sorely tempted to disobey and run after Jacinta, but his father's scowl promised he would regret it. Besides which, Jacinta hadn't exactly seemed eager to stay and talk with him. Burning with frustration, he turned away, following his parents out of the audience hall with clipped strides.

He wasn't satisfied, however. The idea of being closeted in

his father's study while Jacinta was within his reach for the first time in four years made him feel like he was tied to a chair. His eyes flitted distractedly around the corridor as he walked, alighting on a familiar head of pale hair.

Hagen.

Matthias slowed his steps, allowing a little bit of distance to form between him and his parents as he signaled to the singer. Hagen changed course, moving quickly to the prince's side in response to the silent summons.

"Hagen, I need your help," said Matthias quietly.

"Of course, Prince Matthias," said Hagen. "Anything I can do."

"Find my sister." Matthias pushed on, refusing to be deterred by the wary expression on Hagen's face. "Tell her that Jacinta just came to the castle and was basically thrown out. She just left. She can't be far! Mariella will find her if she possibly can."

Hagen looked bewildered, but to his credit he didn't waste time seeking clarification. With a reassuring nod, he strode off along the corridor. He seemed certain of his direction, so that was something.

Now buoyed by a tiny bubble of hope, Matthias caught up to his parents in time to enter the king's study in his mother's wake.

"Close the door." The king's tight, clipped words told Matthias that he wasn't happy.

The prince did as he was told, his own expression far from pleasant as he turned to face his parents.

"Why did you treat Jacinta that way?"

"I don't know what you mean," said the king. "I treated her in the same manner I would treat any of my subjects."

"You were openly rude!" Matthias contradicted. "Accusing her of deception, disparaging her...I won't even engage with the childishness of you pretending not to remember her name!"

"Enough!" the king roared, his irritation flaring into anger with alarming speed. In fact, he was angrier than Matthias had ever seen him. "You will not speak to me this way! I am your father and your king. You dare to call me childish? Your every word demonstrates your immaturity. You are not ready to be trusted with the responsibility you must one day bear."

Matthias stared at his father, unable to comprehend the strength of his reaction. They didn't always see eye to eye, but the king wasn't usually so unreasonable.

"I'm not in any hurry to take on the role that's waiting for me," he said with a bite in his voice. "But when I do, I trust I'll treat everyone with respect. You spoke to her as if she was an untrustworthy waif trying to trick you out of gold."

The king made a noise in his throat. "It's not gold I'm worried about."

"Then what?" demanded Matthias. "Why were you so suspicious of her?"

His father drew a long breath, his eyes searching as he looked back at Matthias. Whatever he saw seemed to satisfy him, because his tone became milder.

"It's to your credit that you wish to trust people, Matthias, but those with royal position must be shrewd. Most people will have designs on us, and many of them are very skilled at hiding it. I know that girl was a playmate of sorts during your childhood. But that was many years ago, and the situation is entirely different now. You don't know her at all, and there's no way to tell if she's trustworthy."

"There you go again, pretending you don't know Jacinta's name!" Matthias was far from mollified by this speech. "And she wasn't just a *playmate of sorts*. She was my closest friend for most of my childhood!"

"You're exaggerating," said his mother in a dampening tone. "You only saw her for a month of each year."

Matthias shook his head incredulously. "I forget how little you were both actually involved in our daily activities when we were in Briarford. I spent much more time playing with Jacinta in that one month than I did with all my other so-called friends in Vallen put together during the entire rest of the year. Mariella and I both did." He glared at his parents. "And you're wrong that we don't know if she's trustworthy. Jacinta and I have both changed since we were children, no doubt."

He paused, his thoughts flying to the attractive young woman who'd just catapulted so unexpectedly back into his life. There was no doubt at all that she'd changed outwardly, at least. He gave his head a shake.

"But one look at her was enough for me to know she hasn't changed *that* much. In spite of the years that have passed, I'd trust her much more readily than I'd trust most of the members of your court." He gave his father a challenging look. "If you want to talk about people who have designs on us in every interaction, you need look no further than your own backyard."

"I never claimed that schemes and manipulation were limited to the peasant class," said the king dryly. "And I don't know why we're arguing about these matters in light of the information we've just received. We should be discussing the threat of the giants. If they have access to magic and intend to use it on the kingdoms south of the wall, it's gravely concerning."

"Oh, so now you've decided Jacinta was telling the truth, have you?" Matthias said angrily. "I thought you weren't inclined to trust either her honesty or her judgment."

"I'm not," the king said coldly. "But I would still be wise to consider the ramifications if her tale proves to be true. You seem to be particularly unhappy with me at present, Matthias, but even you can't accuse me of being incautious."

"Is it your idea of cautious to send an untrained eighteen-year-old girl alone into the land of the giants with no resources at her disposal and only vague instructions to gather evidence for you?" Matthias demanded. "That plan seems absurdly foolhardy to me."

"That's because you're not thinking clearly," said the king, lowering himself into the seat behind his desk. "In fact, it's an incredibly cautious plan. This girl—Jacinta," he corrected, at a glare from his son, "is a civilian. Her way into Kjemper was provided by a chance over which we had no control, and which cannot be traced back to us. A trained operative would have information of value to an enemy if caught, and therefore would present a risk for us. She's an ideal spy, because she has a way to enter enemy territory without the crown's assistance or official support, and even if she's captured, it wouldn't pose any threat to the kingdom."

Matthias slammed his hands down on his father's desk, causing both his parents to jump in their seats. "To the kingdom?" His own voice was raised now. "What about the threat to her?"

"As I said." The king articulated every word, his face once again hard and angry. "The matter is in her hands. I haven't required her to enter Kjemper, and I don't intend to. We may well hear no more from her, if she decides not to pursue the matter. She can go back to living her usual, safe life."

"Or we may hear no more from her because she's gotten herself killed trying to convince you to believe her!" Matthias said. "And how do you know her life is safe?"

"Well, if it isn't, I don't know why I'm being criticized for supposedly introducing danger into it," the king pointed out.

Matthias stood upright, pinching the bridge of his nose with frustration. There was no reasoning with his father, it seemed.

"I think your father is right that it's entirely possible we hear no more of this matter," the queen interjected. "Matthias, your time would be much better spent thinking about your own situation."

"Quite right," the king agreed, leaning back in his chair.

Matthias stared between them. "What situation?"

"What we discussed earlier," his mother said. "Your suit with Lady Letitia."

"My suit?" Matthias repeated irritably. "There is no suit. I told you I'm not interested in Lady Letitia." His thoughts weren't collected enough to be articulated, but with the image of Jacinta's slim, tense form before his eyes, he knew with even more certainty than before that pursuing Lady Letty was the last thing he intended to do.

"Well, a prince doesn't serve only his own interests," the queen said sternly. "She's an excellent match, Matthias, and your father has made it clear that formalizing a betrothal soon would be of great assistance to him. You need to take this matter more seriously. If there's no valid objection, I see no reason we can't proceed."

"What do you call valid?" Matthias demanded, outraged. "How about the fact that I don't like her. In fact, I *dis*like her. Is that not valid?"

"Not especially," muttered the king.

"I thought you weren't going to push me," Matthias said with a scowl.

"And I think we've shown you more than enough forbearance in this area," said Queen Bronte calmly.

"It's been an hour!" Matthias protested.

"Matthias, I don't have the time or the energy to argue with you," cut in the king. "Your mother is right. You should take our suggestion of Lady Letitia more seriously."

Matthias deflated. It was clear he wasn't going to win any arguments today, and truthfully he was just relieved to hear his father refer to his mother's pushing as a suggestion. It seemed no one was actually about to force his hand.

"I don't have any desire to argue with you either, Father," he said stiffly. "I think it will be best if I withdraw."

"Yes, do that," said the king, nodding. "We can discuss the matter with the giants more at a later time, after I've had a chance to speak with the Frossian ambassador."

With as respectful a nod as he could muster in his still-irked frame of mind, Matthias took his leave. He hurried toward the part of the building which contained all the royal suites, wondering whether Hagen had located Mariella in time. To his relief, he found the singer hovering near the entrance to the royal wing, clearly waiting for him.

"Hagen!" he called, quickening his pace. "Did you find her?"

The singer gave a curt nod, dropping his voice. "I encountered the princess almost as soon as I left you. I told her your message, and she said to tell you she'd take Jacinta to the pond if she found her."

"Thank you, thank you, thank you," said Matthias. He had to stop himself from hugging—and no doubt alarming—the reserved singer. "Why don't you come with me? I'm less likely to get stopped by anyone if I appear to be on an errand with you." He smiled apologetically. "And I enjoy your company, of course."

Hagen chuckled lightly. "No need to make explanations, Prince Matthias, I'm very ready to help in whatever way I can. Princess Mariella seemed as frantic at receiving the message as you were when giving it. Clearly this person is important to you both."

"She is," said Matthias, grateful that Hagen wasn't someone who always wanted everything explained.

The two of them hurried out a side door of the castle and across an expanse of manicured garden. Matthias spotted some strolling courtiers and ducked behind a hedge to avoid being seen.

"This way," he told Hagen, who increased his strides to keep up.

The singer slowed his pace as they approached a large, central fountain. But Matthias pressed on, his eyes on the park beyond the gardens. The pond was no decorative fountain in a thoroughfare. It was a much more secluded spot. That was why he and Mariella had always favored it as children. It had been one of their little hideaways, back when they had the luxury of hiding from people they didn't want to speak to.

The pair left the garden and continued on into the park. Matthias could barely contain his impatience as they walked into a small copse of trees, but unsurprisingly, the pond was abandoned when they reached it. His interview with his parents had been short, after all.

"Come on Mariella," he muttered to the air. "Don't let me down."

After only a few minutes of tense waiting, during which Hagen stood back at a respectful distance and let Matthias fret in peace, a rustling sound brought Matthias's head snapping up. His heart lurched strangely as two figures came into view, one practically dragging the other by the arm.

"Mariella, you found her!" Matthias ran forward a few steps, then stopped, feeling strangely unsure what to do with his arms and legs.

"Yes, I found her," said Mariella grimly. "A mere stone's throw from the castle, trying to board a public coach heading north!"

Matthias turned reproachful eyes on Jacinta. "You were leaving? Just like that?"

She pulled her arm gently free of Mariella's grip, hugging herself in a gesture of discomfort that made him long to reassure her somehow.

"I…I think it's best."

"You were going to leave without even seeing me?" Mariella demanded. "Jacinta, how could you come to my own castle and not even try to see me?"

Jacinta's shoulders slumped. "I'm sorry," she said, her eyes genuinely apologetic as she met the princess's. "I did want to see you. I was disappointed when you weren't with your parents." She paused visibly before her eyes slid to Matthias. "I was glad you were there, though."

"Were you?" Matthias tried to smile, but the gesture didn't feel natural. "Not as glad as I was, I think."

Jacinta shook her head, not quite meeting his eyes. "That's not true."

"It's been so long, Jacinta." Mariella moved forward, throwing her arms impulsively around her friend. "I'm so happy to see you."

Matthias longed to copy his sister, but he didn't, something holding him back.

Lots of things, actually.

Jacinta relaxed a little under Mariella's approach, returning the other girl's hug. "You too. It feels an eternity since I saw you."

"You stopped answering my letters," said Mariella reproachfully. "Why?"

Jacinta squirmed. "I…I guess I didn't really have much to say."

"That's a pathetic excuse," Mariella informed her brutally. "I had enough to say for the both of us. I was afraid you'd died, Jacinta!"

Matthias expected Jacinta to laugh off the dramatic declaration, but she didn't. She gave a wan smile that he found more alarming than tears would have been.

"Not yet," she said lightly.

"You look...good."

Matthias wanted to groan with his clumsiness. He'd been eager to interject himself, feeling that Mariella was hoarding Jacinta's attention, but he should really have thought of something better to say before opening his mouth. His eyes scanned her willowy form, dark hair falling in loose yet orderly waves onto the shoulders of her simple but attractive gown. At least his unsophisticated words had been accurate.

Apparently Mariella didn't agree. "She doesn't look good." She frowned at Jacinta. "You're skin and bones, Jacinta. Don't you eat anymore?"

Jacinta's face was suddenly shuttered, a guardedness in her expression Matthias couldn't remember ever seeing when they were children.

"I do my best." She turned to Matthias in a businesslike way. "You should really encourage your parents to take my report seriously, Matthias. I think the giant was telling the truth."

"What's this about a giant?" Mariella demanded, but Matthias waved her off.

"I'll explain all that later." His eyes stayed fixed on Jacinta's brown ones. "I'm just glad you've dropped the title. You spoke to me like I was a stranger, Jacinta!"

She gave the same wan smile. "It felt strange, didn't it? But I don't think your parents would have appreciated any informality. And to tell the truth, I wasn't sure whether you would either."

"Why would you think I'd changed so drastically?" Matthias demanded. "What did I do to earn that opinion?"

"Nothing," said Jacinta quickly. "You did nothing."

She'd spoken placatingly, but her words hung heavily in the air for a long and painful moment.

"I'm so happy to have seen you, Mariella, but I really do need to go," Jacinta said. "I asked at the coach house, and that was the last coach heading northward today bar one. I need to get on the next one, or I'll be stranded."

"You won't be stranded," said Mariella staunchly. "You can stay here with us."

"At this pond?" Jacinta asked dryly, the spark of her old dry humor making Matthias smile.

"No." Mariella shot her friend an exasperated look. "At the castle."

Jacinta was shaking her head before the word was fully formed. "I'm confident your parents wouldn't want that," she said.

"That never stopped us from doing things in the past," Matthias pointed out.

She gave him a speaking look. "We're not ten years old anymore."

"I'm well aware of that," he told her calmly. "But I haven't forgotten what our friendship once meant to all of us, even if you have."

"I haven't forgotten anything," said Jacinta, clearly stung. "But things are so different now from how they were then. So much has passed since we were children."

"And we know about none of it," said Mariella unhappily. "Because you wouldn't let us share in it."

"It wasn't my choice to end our friendship," said Jacinta in frustration. "It was out of all our control." She cast an appealing glance between the two royal siblings. She barely seemed to have noticed Hagen, hovering uncertainly in the background. "You have to live your life here, and I have to live mine in Briarford. I need to get home to my mother. This journey is already taking almost a week, and I don't like to leave her alone that long."

"I'm sure she's eager for your return," said Mariella unhappily. "But I want more time with you, Jacinta. And I know Matthias does too." She looked to her brother, who nodded quickly.

"Of course I do. Do you think five minutes is enough to catch up on four years?"

"Eight years, really," said Mariella. "The funeral doesn't really count."

"No," said Jacinta, looking anywhere but at Matthias. "It doesn't, does it?"

His throat felt suddenly tight, the memory of their moment alone in that dusty room filling his mind. He could still feel her held against him, still remember the way her hair had smelled. She was so close now. It would be so easy to step forward and put his arms around her again.

He came back to reality, noting her stiff posture and averted eyes. It wouldn't be easy at all. He doubted she'd let him near her. So much stood between them now, and he didn't pretend to understand half of it. All he knew was that it broke his heart. He'd been sad about it a week ago. Now that he'd seen her again, it was closer to devastating.

"Thank you for coming to find me, Mariella," Jacinta said softly. "It means a great deal to me, honestly. If I find evidence to convince the king of my tale, perhaps I'll be back. If not..." She gave that same weak smile. "Well, if you're ever in Briarford, be sure to drop by."

"But you can't just leave," Mariella complained. "Do you even have a ticket for the coach?"

"No, but I'll buy one," said Jacinta, edging away.

Mariella's gaze was shrewd. "Do you have enough to get you comfortably home?"

"I'll manage," said Jacinta.

"That definitely means no," Mariella said grimly, turning to her brother. "Matthias, give her some coins."

Matthias shook his head regretfully, ignoring Jacinta's sputters of protest. "I wish I could, but I don't carry coins on me."

"Nor do I," said Mariella in dismay.

A discreetly cleared throat made them turn to see Hagen stepping forward. "Please, allow me, miss," he said respectfully, pulling a small pouch from his pocket.

"Thank you, but no," said Jacinta firmly, holding her palms up in a gesture of defense. "I couldn't possibly take money from you."

"Of course you can," said Matthias, taking the pouch and holding it out. "It's very kind of Hagen to loan it, but we'll pay him back and then some."

"That's not necessary, Prince Matthi—"

"Don't be absurd," Matthias cut Hagen's words off shortly. He turned to Jacinta. "It's a small payment for the danger and expense you incurred in bringing your message to my father. Consider it a royal reward."

"I don't want it," said Jacinta, starting to sound desperate. "I really just need to get to the coach house before—"

"If you don't take it, we'll keep arguing with you until you miss the coach," said Mariella crisply. She took the pouch from Matthias's hand and forced it into Jacinta's pocket. "It would be selfish not to take it, Jacinta. It would be like saying you don't care how much we'd be worrying about you."

Against these tactics, Jacinta seemed to run out of defenses. She deflated slightly, inclining her head in thanks to Hagen, then the others. "I'm grateful for your help," she said. "And you don't need to worry about me. I'll be fine. I'm glad to have seen that you're well, too."

Mariella looked as dissatisfied with this farewell as Matthias felt, but Jacinta didn't give them the chance to protest. She was already walking away, clearly on edge in the castle grounds and no doubt eager to reach the coach in time.

Mariella let out a low groan before addressing Hagen. "That really was kind of you, Hagen. Do you know how much was in it, precisely?"

"I do, Your Highness, but it's truly not necessary to—"

"It is," said Mariella emphatically. "I'll see that you're repaid immediately."

Without warning, Matthias's legs surged into motion. He found himself hurrying into the trees, his longer strides catching Jacinta in no time.

"Jacinta." He reached out, grabbing her arm and pulling her to a stop. "At least let me walk you to the coach house."

She shook her head, her voice not quite natural as her eyes rested on the hand that gripped her arm.

"Thank you, but it's not necessary. And to tell the truth, I don't want trouble with your parents."

"Forget about them," said Matthias impatiently. "I don't know what's making them so reactive, but they'll get past it."

"Easy to say about your parents," said Jacinta with a touch of humor. "Not so easy when it's your monarchs."

"You can't truly be thinking of going back into Kjemper alone," Matthias blurted out. "Jacinta, it's far too dangerous."

"I'll be all right," she said, clearly not eager to discuss the topic. "Don't worry about me."

"But I do worry about you." Matthias inched closer. "Don't go alone, Jacinta. I'll come with you. I don't care what my parents say."

"You can't come, Matthias," Jacinta said sharply. "For so many reasons. Not least of which is that I think I'm the only one who can see or access the tunnel."

"What?" Matthias demanded, more alarmed than ever by

this new revelation.

"I know adding details like that makes my story less credible," she said ruefully.

Matthias shook his head. "No, Jacinta, I believe you. Without a doubt. I just don't like it."

"Well, sometimes we have to do things we don't like," said Jacinta, smiling. "Goodbye, Matthias."

"I'm coming to the coach house with you," he said in determination, stepping forward.

"No." Jacinta looked alarmed. "Please don't."

"I want to make sure you're safe," he argued.

"And I appreciate the thought." She looked exasperated. "But it will only hinder me. I assume the residents of the capital know you on sight. I'll be heckled on the coach if you accompany me."

"Heckled?" Matthias felt his brow lowering. "What do you mean? Will you be safe?"

"I'll be safe if you keep your distance." The words burst out of Jacinta with such intensity, Matthias took a step back.

She drew a deep breath, her tone softening. "It's not personal. I don't live in your world, Matthias. It doesn't benefit me to be connected with you. Quite the reverse."

Matthias didn't know what to say. "I certainly don't want to cause you any trouble," he said at last.

"I know." Jacinta's voice was even softer, and for a moment he thought he caught in her eyes a hint of the regret flooding him.

Jacinta had half turned to go, but she hesitated for a moment, then, catching Matthias completely by surprise, she pushed up onto her toes and pressed a light kiss to his cheek.

"Sorry," she said thickly, stepping quickly back. "I'm sorry for the liberty. It really was good to see you again."

And before Matthias could gather his disordered wits, she

was gone, practically running across the park. He lifted a hand slowly to his cheek, his fingertips tentative as they touched the place her lips had been.

"Is she gone?" Mariella emerged from the trees behind him, Hagen in tow.

"Yes," said Matthias, dazed. "She left."

"I can hardly believe she appeared here like this!" Mariella said. "I'm so glad you sent Hagen to find me, Matthias. I would have been devastated to miss her." She frowned. "Not that seeing her brings much pleasure, does it?"

"What do you mean?" Matthias asked, his cheek still tingling. "Seeing her was the best thing that's happened around here in a long time."

Mariella stared at him in disbelief. "Did you not see her, Matthias? Her gown, her thinness, her hopeless eyes. Whatever she says about being fine, all isn't well with her."

Matthias gave his head a slow shake. "I thought she looked beautiful."

His sister made a noise of irritation in her throat. "Of course you did. I didn't say she's not beautiful. I said she's not fine. And I stand by it."

Matthias brought his gaze down to hers at last, his brow creased. "Do you really think she's in trouble? What can we do, Mariella?"

Hagen shifted, surprising Matthias by interjecting. "If you'll forgive me for giving an opinion on someone I don't know..." he started. Both siblings nodded encouragingly, and he continued. "I'm not sure what you expected, but the state of her health— her lean form, and general weariness—is absolutely normal for residents of the northern region of Frossenland. I would imagine that the same is true in Vadolis's north. Particularly bearing in mind that she'd just had a grueling journey to reach the capital. She seemed to me a young woman with many burdens to carry, but it was easy to see at a glance that she has the strength to do it without being crushed."

Matthias considered these words. "Yes," he said softly. "She was always incredibly strong." His hand clenched and unclenched, a feeling of helplessness sweeping over him. "I truly didn't realize things were so bad in the north. It never seemed that way when we were children."

"I think we had very little idea what was going on around us when we were children," said Mariella sadly. "And I believe it has genuinely gotten worse up near the border in the years since then."

"Why did we stop going?" The words burst from Matthias. "If we'd kept going each year, we'd know the true state of things. Maybe we could have helped make things easier. Why does Father seem to care so little about what happens to those in the north?"

"Well, our northern region is very small," said Mariella with a sigh. "Briarford is one of the few towns strongly affected by the increasingly barren state of the land. It's not like Frossenland, where so many people live in the north."

"Or at least used to," interjected Hagen sadly.

"As for why we stopped going to Briarford each year, do you truly not know?" Mariella's eyes were searching. "It's often seemed to me that you didn't, but I wasn't sure if you just wanted to avoid talking about it."

"What do you mean?" Matthias demanded. "Do you know the reason?"

"Of course I do," said Mariella in exasperation. "Even at the time I suspected it, and I was only ten! In the years since I've become more and more certain."

Matthias stared at her. "Well? Don't keep me in suspense!"

"It was because of you," said Mariella matter-of-factly. "You and Jacinta."

"Me and Jacinta what?" Matthias asked, perplexed.

"They didn't like your friendship." Mariella sounded like she was trying to be patient.

"Well, they never exactly encouraged it," Matthias acknowledged. "But from what I remember, they never seemed to care too much. And it wasn't just me who was friends with her. So were you!"

"Yes," Mariella agreed. "And while they didn't love that friendship, it didn't concern them. But yours did."

"But why?" Matthias demanded.

"Isn't it obvious?" Mariella's voice was pained. "You were too fond of her, Matthias. And too open about it. She was your favorite person in the world. Even at the age of twelve, it was obvious how drawn to her you were."

"I still don't understand," said Matthias blankly.

Mariella actually growled. "At this point, I think you're being deliberately obtuse," she complained. "Clearly you're in denial yourself, if you're going to make me spell it out. Matthias, they were worried about you falling in love with her."

Matthias's mouth fell open. "But that's ridiculous!" he said. "We were children. I never dreamed of looking at her in that way. Her or anyone."

Mariella nodded. "You weren't quite there yet at age twelve, but they could see the danger. And I can understand why. Don't forget that by that age *I* was already showing interest in what they would call romantic nonsense. I think they figured it wouldn't be much longer before either you or Jacinta, or both of you, started to have similar thoughts. So they took great care that our contact didn't continue anywhere near your youth or hers. They obviously wanted the connection to stay as an innocent memory of childhood and nothing more."

"That is a ridiculous reason to try to end our friendship," said Matthias angrily.

"Is it so ridiculous?" Mariella asked, her brows pointedly raised.

He frowned down at her, not entirely sure of her meaning. But his thoughts were already flying to the charged encounter he'd had with Jacinta the day of her father's funeral. It was the first time he'd seen her when they were both out of the realm of true childhood, and his reaction to her had been...quite different from their childish connection.

"Are you saying you agree with their actions?" he demanded, irked.

"Not at all." Mariella was calm in the face of his rising ire. "But that's because I don't have the least objection to Jacinta. You have to admit that according to Mother and Father's criteria, she's not at all eligible."

"I don't have to admit anything," muttered Matthias. "And I've a mind to tell them exactly what I think of their interference."

He strode off on the words, giving no sign that he heard his sister calling after him.

"Matthias, think carefully before you do that! Remember it will impact more than just you!"

He didn't break stride, but his sister's words did their work, slowly bringing reason into his anger as he made his way toward the castle. He wasn't sure if she meant that their parents would be stricter with Mariella if he showed signs of rebellion, or that Jacinta would suffer in some way. But by the time he reached his father's study, he'd acknowledged to himself that either option was enough reason for him to hold his tongue. Inside, he still seethed over the way his parents had interfered in his friendship, and turned one of the best parts of his life into one of the most painful, but outwardly he'd regained his equilibrium.

That didn't mean he had nothing to say to them, however.

To his surprise, he discovered that his parents were both still in his father's study, deep in conversation. He had an uncomfortable guess what they'd been talking about, but he kept it to himself.

"Father, I've been thinking," he said. "And I really think I should go to Briarford. I think I should oversee the attempt to—"

"That is absolutely not happening." The king didn't even let him finish. "You're not needed in Briarford. But you can be of service elsewhere, Matthias."

"What do you mean?" he asked.

"Your mother and I have been considering it, and we think you should travel to Frossenland, to discuss today's events with King Herleif."

Matthias's frown deepened in thought. "To talk about the giants?"

The king nodded. "King Herleif knows more about Kjemper than any of us do. He's indicated his desire to work together to address the threat of the giants, and it seems wise to take this matter to him. It's not something I would wish to put in a letter."

Matthias drew a deep breath, reminding himself that he'd never really imagined his parents would let him go to Briarford.

"Very well," he said. "I'll leave in the morning. I want to take Hagen with me."

"Hagen?" his father repeated vaguely. "Ah, the Frossian singer. Yes, that's a good thought, Matthias. He will be helpful to you in his native land." He lowered his eyes to the stack of papers on his desk, apparently ready to move on to the next thing. "I'll leave the details to you."

Matthias strode from the room without a word, his heart pounding and his ears thrumming in his agitation. He took no pleasure from being in charge of the details. If only his parents would allow him the freedom to do as he saw fit in the areas of his life that really mattered.

CHAPTER TEN

Jacinta

As predicted, Jacinta had plenty of time on the three-day journey home to wallow in her thoughts. She was fortunate to make it onto the public coach. She'd only had minutes to spare, and had secured the last available seat. It made the journey uncomfortably crowded, but her main feeling as the vehicle trundled out of Vallen was relief. She couldn't bring herself to be sorry she'd seen her former friends while in the capital, but she also wasn't sorry to be putting space between herself and all the complicated memories they evoked.

She leaned against the edge of the carriage, the conversation with Matthias and Mariella replaying in her mind. It had been years now that she'd thought of them as *former* friends, but they'd given no sign of being reluctant to claim her.

The king and queen, on the other hand...

But Jacinta told herself not to dwell on the humiliation of their reaction. It would only make her task of returning to them with proof all the harder. And she was determined to return. She might be poor and insignificant, but her word meant something. She refused to be considered a liar by her monarchs.

If her determination was strengthened by the fact that returning to Vallen meant she would likely see Matthias and Mariella again, she didn't acknowledge it to herself. She would be very foolish to pin any hopes on a rekindling of their friendship. It warmed her heart to know they weren't ashamed of the old connection, but it changed nothing. Their worlds could not comfortably intersect outside of the blissful bubble that had been those childhood months in Briarford. They might not yet realize that, but Jacinta did.

And it made her parting action all the more inexcusable. Why had she bestowed that chaste kiss on the prince's cheek? What madness had taken hold of her that she'd thought that was a good idea? On some level, she knew the answer. She'd done it because she'd imagined doing so countless times, and she recognized that their hidden rendezvous in the castle park was likely the only time she'd ever be allowed to do it. But that didn't make it any less outrageous.

Needless to say, far too many of the idle hours of travel were spent in contemplation of that foolish parting gesture. The new height of his frame that had required her to push up on her toes, the fact that up so close, the freckles of childhood had been faintly visible across his nose, the look on his face when he realized what she'd done. He'd looked so surprised, and no wonder. What did he think of it now? What did he think of her?

Perhaps it was better not to know. If he thought badly of her after their sudden reconnecting, it would only bring pain. If he thought warmly of her...it would just bring a different kind of pain, given the impediments that stood between them.

Impediments he understood better than he pretended to, she told herself sternly, in an effort to restore reality to her thoughts. He'd chosen not to write, so he must have comprehended the impossibility of a continued friendship better than

Mariella had. Even when he'd escorted Mariella to Jacinta's father's funeral, he'd understood that it wouldn't be wise for him to publicly associate with Jacinta and her family. Painting him as open-hearted and oblivious—and herself as the one who was cold and closed, and being sensible for both of them—was too generous to him. Likely he'd just been so taken aback by her sudden appearance, he'd let the warm memories of their childhood rule him for a short while, and would soon return to the common sense that must tell him as surely as it told her that their friendship was a thing of the past.

It was all as it should be. No one was at fault. But Jacinta's heart was so heavy at the thought, she found herself trying to formulate a plan for her return to Kjemper just to avoid dwelling on the prince and princess.

Thanks to a combination of emotional turmoil and the physical toll of travel, by the time Jacinta reached home, she was unspeakably weary. It was late afternoon of the journey's third day, but given how short her time in Vallen had been, she'd spent almost a week in constant travel. She could barely walk straight as she made her way from the town center to the simple dwelling she shared with her mother.

Jacinta's heart lifted a little when she was met with the clucking of chickens. The pair of brown hens bought at the markets with the giant's gold were still alive, then. Hopefully they were still laying.

Smoke was rising from the hut's chimney, too, and Jacinta crossed the threshold gladly. Even the fact that her mother was there, rather than searching for work in the town, was a pleasant change.

"Jacinta!" The older woman greeted her daughter with warmth, moving to intercept her and take her rucksack. "You're home! You look dead on your feet. Sit. I've got some broth on the fire right now."

"Thanks, Mamma," said Jacinta, sinking obediently into a chair. "I did eat at the last stop, but I'm already famished again."

"I'm relieved to hear it," her mother commented, as she ladled broth into a bowl. "I was worried you wouldn't have enough coins for the journey, but if you still had some to spend on food this afternoon, the travel must not have been as expensive as I thought."

Jacinta shifted uneasily in her chair, staying silent. She felt guilty to hide coins from her mother, but she wasn't ready to disclose the interaction she'd had with Matthias and Mariella. She knew that without the coins they'd given her—or rather, their friend had given her on their behalf—she would have struggled to make it home, and she certainly wouldn't have arrived well-fed.

"So?" her mother prompted, when she'd had a chance to eat some broth. "Did you speak to the king?"

Jacinta nodded, laying her spoon down slowly. "I did. I told him all about the elf, the beanstalk, the giant's warning, everything."

"And?" Her mother's eyes were piercing.

Jacinta shrugged. "It was hard to tell whether he believed me. He wanted me to doubt whether he found me credible, I think."

"Of course he did," her mother said darkly.

"Mamma, what did you fight about?" Jacinta asked abruptly. "I think you did wrong by me to send me to the castle without the full story. The king and queen made it very clear I wasn't welcome."

Her mother bit her lip, looking unsure of herself. It was a rare sight. "I'm sorry, Jacinta. I thought you knew enough to brace yourself for a cold reception. As I said, if it had been possible for someone else to take the message, I would have preferred that. But when it comes to elves and magic, and enchantments only one person can see, it's not wise to manipulate matters too much."

Jacinta frowned, very dissatisfied with this lack of answer. But her mother barreled on before she could press for more.

"Did you see the prince and princess?"

Jacinta paused for a long moment before responding. "Matthias was there when I made the report to the king and queen. And Mariella made a point of greeting me before I left."

"How did that feel?" her mother asked, again watching her closely.

Jacinta just shrugged, returning her attention to her broth. Given her mother wasn't being forthright with her, she felt no guilt at keeping her more personal thoughts to herself.

"Anyway," she said, once she'd emptied the bowl, "the main point is I have to go back to Kjemper. The king won't believe the giants have magic without proof."

"What?" Her mother was on her feet, brow furrowed. "Jacinta, tell me you're not serious. You have nothing to prove to him!"

"That's for me to decide," said Jacinta. "Valwynn had her reasons for sending me in there. If another trip into Kjemper is the cost of convincing our king to act on a real danger, then I'm willing to pay it."

"I don't like it," her mother said.

Jacinta shrugged again. She wasn't a child anymore, and she wasn't asking for permission. Glancing around, she spotted a covered bowl on the table.

"I'm glad to see you've been well provided for while I was gone," she commented. "Is that dough?"

Her mother nodded slowly. "I'm baking bread. The chickens are laying, and I've been able to pick up a little work in the next town over. You don't need to worry about me. It's your own future we should be thinking about."

"I can think about the future once this whole bizarre beanstalk situation is finished," Jacinta told her. "Hopefully it should only be one more trip. But it will have to wait until tomorrow. I'm exhausted."

Turning aside her mother's attempts to discuss the situation further, Jacinta retreated to her bed. She was glad to shrug out of her rumpled traveling gown and into her long, warm nightgown. It was still a couple of hours until sunset, but she went to sleep immediately.

When she stirred, the dim light trickling in under the curtain suggested that it was almost dawn. Jacinta sat up, stretching her limbs and peering around the hut. Her mother was asleep in her own bed, and the embers of the fire were almost spent.

Slipping out of bed, Jacinta grabbed a small loaf from the windowsill where her mother had evidently left them to cool after Jacinta went to sleep. She must have been tired indeed to sleep through the smell of freshly baked bread. As she pocketed the bread, her eyes fell on a small canister sitting beside the loaves. She glanced down at her gray nightgown then, after a moment's hesitation, she tipped out the last of the coins from the royals under her pillow. Feeling guilty at the waste, she filled the pouch with the contents of the canister instead.

In moments, she was outside in the cold air and striding across the yard. She devoured the bread on the way to the outhouse, relishing the rare treat.

When she emerged from the outhouse, she glanced back at the hut. All was quiet and still, and it occurred to her that, given her mother's objections, she might be wise to follow the beanstalk while she was alone. She'd brought nothing with her, but then again, it wasn't as though she had a plan for how to find evidence of magic inside Kjemper. A brief scouting trip might be wise.

Jacinta followed the beanstalk all the way to Battlement Wall, the sun rising steadily on her right as she walked. As the wall drew near, she peered ahead, wondering whether it was possible the tunnel might have disappeared. She had no idea what she'd do then.

But the tunnel was still there and, to her great surprise, so was something else. A small figure with pointed ears and an upright posture. Between the crisp white tunic and the pale, silvery hair, the elf could probably disappear against the snow that would cover the ground soon enough. But standing by Battlement Wall's huge, gray bulk, she was unmistakable.

"Valwynn?" Jacinta hurried forward eagerly. "What are you doing here?"

"Ah, Jacinta." The elf turned, looking pleased at the human's arrival. "There you are. I'm checking on my handiwork, what do you think I'm doing? I see it's done just as it ought." She frowned, the tips of her ears wobbling in disapproval. "But where have you been? The stalk should have grown overnight. It's taken you long enough to show up!"

"It did grow overnight," said Jacinta. "And I went through the tunnel the next morning."

"You did?" The elf's emerald eyes widened in surprise. "Well, then. It's not often I miss something so big. How embarrassing."

Jacinta hid a smile, worried she would offend the elf. "Did you mean for the vines to lead me to the house of that particular giant? She seemed to know you."

"Never you mind what I meant," the elf said curtly. "What did you find?"

"A female giant," said Jacinta. "She gave me a warning for King Fidelius, but it was pretty vague."

"And what are you going to do with it?" Valwynn demanded.

"I've already done it," said Jacinta. "I've been to Vallen and back. The king was...less than convinced. He wants me to bring back more proof."

Valwynn made an irritated noise in her throat. "Typical human idiocy. He really didn't believe you? I thought you were supposed to be friends with the royal family? That's half the reason I chose you."

Jacinta frowned at this unwelcome news. "I told you when I first met you that I'm *not* friends with them."

"Ah, but you were protesting much too strongly." The elf waved a dismissive hand.

Jacinta regarded her through narrowed eyes. "What's the other half of the reason you chose me?"

"Because the people in the markets said that you were the toughest and most determined girl in the village," Valwynn said matter-of-factly. "Not to mention you live conveniently close to Battlement Wall. Lots of little things, really. Not any one big thing." She squinted at Jacinta. "Why, did you think you were special? That you had some hidden importance?"

Jacinta snorted. "Hardly."

"Humans are always thinking that," said Valwynn, sounding faintly disgusted. "And it's rarely true."

Jacinta didn't bother engaging with this very elven perspective on her species. "What was your plan in sending me into Kjemper? Did you want me to see what I saw? Did you intend me to take a warning to King Fidelius?"

"Not answering any of that," said Valwynn.

Jacinta let out a breath. "I suppose you want to make a bargain for the information, do you?"

"No. No bargain," replied Valwynn shortly. "Just not telling you."

Jacinta furrowed her brow, confused. "Then why do all of it? Surely you must have had a reason."

The elf remained silent, and Jacinta started to feel annoyed.

"It seems to me that the whole thing is a waste of my time," she said sternly. "I'm half inclined to abandon it all and not bother with getting more proof. What do I care if King Fidelius believes the giants have magic? What do I care if he takes the so-called threat seriously? I should just go about my life and forget about it."

"Don't do that, girl!"

Valwynn's irritability provided the answer Jacinta had been digging for. She might not be willing to admit it, but the elf clearly wanted information about the giants to reach the human authorities. What information exactly was still unclear. Not to mention why Valwynn would care.

"What I *will* tell you," the elf said with great dignity, "is how this beanstalk works."

"I would like to know that," Jacinta said. "But I'm not bargaining for the information." The elf looked irked, but Jacinta pressed on unapologetically. "The bargain we made last time was my cow in exchange for a lot more than she was worth. It seems to me that the beanstalk doesn't have any great value to me if I don't understand how it works."

The elf sighed. "Your logic is sound," she acknowledged, a touch resentfully. "I suppose you could argue that I owe you the information already." Her little face split in a sudden grin. "Besides, I'm well pleased with our bargain. Ferocity is an undemanding companion."

"Ferocity?" Jacinta repeated blankly.

"The cow," Valwynn told her as if it was obvious.

Jacinta stared at the elf. "You renamed Princess *Ferocity*?" She couldn't imagine a more bizarre name for the docile, slow-moving cow, although she was too polite to say so.

Valwynn didn't share the same impediment. "Princess?" she repeated in disdain. "What a stupid thing to name a cow. I can see she's much better with me."

"I'm very fond of her," said Jacinta, annoyed.

The elf raised one silvery eyebrow. "So fond that you intended to sell her at market to be butchered by one of your neighbors?"

Jacinta closed her mouth, aware that the elf had her there. "I didn't *want* to," she muttered. Her voice grew stronger. "Why are we arguing about this, anyway? You were supposed to be telling me how the beanstalk works."

"Ah yes," said Valwynn, rubbing her hands together in a business-like manner. "Since you've already been through the tunnel, you've obviously discovered the main thing."

"Yes." Jacinta frowned. "Why couldn't my mother see the tunnel, though?"

"Because it's not really there," Valwynn said helpfully.

Jacinta stared at her. "Yes it is. Look." She strode forward, sticking her head into the tunnel, then pulling it back out.

Valwynn gave a chuckle. "It certainly looks strange from my perspective."

"Do you mean even you can't see the tunnel?" Jacinta asked, stunned.

"There is no tunnel," Valwynn repeated. "Not really. The beans carried a form of illusion magic—very strong illusion magic, if I say so myself. The stalk is designed to give the planter a path straight from one point to another. In this case, the position of planting to the giant's residence. The magic carried on the stalk goes through any obstacle, creating the illusion that there's nothing in the way. But the illusion only applies to you, because you're the one who planted it." Her voice turned defensive. "My supply of magic isn't unlimited, after all. To make it a universal illusion would require an exorbitant amount of power."

"But it isn't an illusion," Jacinta protested. "I don't just see a hole, I feel it. I can crawl right through."

Valwynn nodded. "Yes, because the illusion magic is strong enough to affect the matter itself. As far as your senses are concerned—touch as well as sight—this section of Battlement Wall doesn't exist."

"If it affects the matter itself, it's not an illusion," said Jacinta skeptically.

"It relates to the way the magic interacts with its surroundings. You're assuming physical matter isn't susceptible to being affected by illusion magic." The elf was impatient now. "Do you want a lesson in magical theory, or do you want to know how the beanstalk works?"

"I suppose the latter, if I have to choose one," said Jacinta. "But I don't like the sound of this illusion idea. If I was halfway through the wall when the magic failed, what would happen to me?"

"You'd be inside a solid wall," said the elf shortly. "What do you think would happen?"

"*Could* something disrupt the magic keeping the illusion in place?" Jacinta asked, eyeing the tunnel doubtfully.

"Only the destruction of the vine should be able do that," Valwynn said. "It won't live forever, but you shouldn't need to worry about it expiring anytime soon. The greater danger would be someone killing the plant."

"So if a giant found the vines and chopped them while I was inside...?" Jacinta started, but the elf shook her head.

"The magic comes from the roots, where you planted the beans. It would have to be severed from this side."

"That's something, I suppose." Jacinta felt less eager than ever about crawling into the hole.

"So are you going in now?" Valwynn asked, cocking her head to one side and making the tips of her ears quiver. "What's your plan?"

"I don't have one," admitted Jacinta reluctantly. "I suppose to get proof of what's happening, I should go to the mining tower the giant mentioned. But my plan for getting there without being seen isn't what you'd call foolproof."

"I wouldn't hazard much on your chances of going that far unseen," said Valwynn, the dispassionate assessment betraying her knowledge of the area on the other side of the wall. "And even if you did, you likely wouldn't see anything that would give proof. Unless you're secretly a singer, you won't be able to sense the presence or absence of magic."

"I'm not a singer," said Jacinta absently. "My father was, but I didn't inherit it."

The elf nodded sagely. "Yes, it skips a generation or five as often as not. Mayhap your children will be singers."

Jacinta snorted. "I'd have to have children first. Which means I'd have to find someone willing to marry me."

"Ah, an attractive, resourceful young thing like yourself, surely some local farmer will snap you up," said Valwynn optimistically.

"As delightful as the prospect is, even that fate is dependent on me surviving my current adventure," Jacinta pointed out.

"True, true." Valwynn nodded sagely. She made a chivvying motion with her hands. "Off you go, then."

"What...now?" Jacinta was taken aback.

"Isn't that why you're here just after dawn?" the little elf demanded.

"I suppose it is." Jacinta eyed the darkness of the tunnel in distaste. "But going to the mining tower is the only idea I had. If you think that's pointless..."

"What I think is neither here nor there," said the elf. "I've just explained to you that you're the only one able to use the beanstalk to get through the wall. And you certainly won't get your proof from this side."

Jacinta bit her lip. "And you really can't come with me?"

"Did you listen to a word I just said?" Valwynn asked indignantly. "Besides, I never offered to come with you. Never dreamed of it." She scowled. "Now see here, don't go getting the wrong idea. I have my reasons for everything I do, and altruism toward humans isn't one of them. I wouldn't make a bargain that only benefited the other party."

"But it didn't only benefit me," said Jacinta blandly. "You've already gained a fearsome new pet out of it."

"You leave Ferocity out of this," said Valwynn loftily. "She's a companion, not a pet."

Jacinta shook her head, a smile playing around her lips. There was something incredibly humorous about the elf's soft spot toward the cow. "Do you know who you remind me of, with your insistence that you feel no generosity or compassion toward humans, even when your actions suggest the contrary?"

"Who?" Valwynn asked the question warily, as if sensing a trap.

"The giant who lives at the other end of this beanstalk," said Jacinta. "She was very adamant that I not think she have a soft spot for me or any humans. Almost killed me in outrage when I called her *kind*."

"How dare you?" The tips of Valwynn's ears went stiff in her indignation. "Me, have something in common with an oafish, savage giant? You take that back, Jacinta!"

"I don't think I will," said Jacinta, undaunted. It was amazing what boldness a full stomach and a small stash of coins could restore to her. "I meant what I said, and I stand by it."

"I've half a mind to abandon you to your fate," said the elf darkly.

Jacinta raised an eyebrow. "Isn't that what you intended to do anyway? I thought you said you couldn't come through and wouldn't even if you could."

"But I was planning to wait to see how it worked out," said Valwynn generously.

Jacinta grinned. "As for that, you can suit yourself. I'm going in."

CHAPTER ELEVEN

Jacinta

Jacinta turned her back on the elf, crawling into the tunnel with a shudder. The knowledge that she was apparently moving through solid wall that had just been tricked into thinking it was a hole wasn't reassuring. It required a level of trust in Valwynn's magic that she'd rather not hang her life on. But she was determined to prove to the king that she wasn't an attention-seeking liar, and she could see no other way to do it.

When she emerged into the weak light of the early morning, she squinted carefully at her surroundings before dropping from the tunnel. There was no one in sight, and the rise of the ground hid the giant's hut. But in the distance, she could just make out the so-called mining tower.

Jacinta moved carefully toward it, her steps slow and measured. She was pleased to see, as she crossed the barren ground, that there was a light powdering of snow on the rocks. Just as she'd hoped. In spite of being early autumn, it was almost cold enough for snow in Briarford. Kjemper was even colder, so she wasn't surprised to see they'd had a snowfall. It was light enough that rocks poked through everywhere, meaning she could avoid leaving a trail if she was careful. But it still gave the landscape the appearance of a white carpet, which was just what she needed.

Pausing to smooth out the pale gray nightgown she still wore, Jacinta pulled out the pouch. She reached inside it, grabbing a handful of flour and dumping it on her head. It would have been more effective if she'd had a looking glass, but after a few minutes of focused effort, she was fairly confident she'd turned her dark brown hair into a grayish-whitish wig of sorts. Between that and her nightgown, she had at least a slim hope of crossing the frozen landscape without detection.

Gathering her courage, Jacinta started off again, her sights set on the wooden structure in the distance. The sun rose as she walked, her booted feet moving carefully from rocky outcrop to rocky outcrop. At least the giants were unlikely to watch the surrounds closely, having no reason to suspect humans of either the inclination or the ability to cross the wall.

The sounds of industry grew as Jacinta approached. Her giant hostess's husband might work the night shift, but the tower evidently remained in full operation throughout the day as well. It was at least two hours past dawn when she came to a stop behind a nearby hill of icy rock, no more than twenty yards from the tower. A steady grinding sound still filled the air, interspersed with the shouts of harsh voices.

Jacinta peered around the rock, hoping the flour still covered her hair. The little of it she could see remained white. Did she dare go closer? No. The ground was too open, with no cover between her and the huge tower.

Her eyes passed upward, marveling at the size of the structure. No wonder she'd been able to see it from the wall. It rose up into the sky, blotting out the gray of the clouds overhead. She caught sight of shapes—looking almost human in size rather than the giants they were—crossing a walkway on the upper level. Jacinta held as still as she could until they were out of sight again, diving back into the inside of the structure.

Tower wasn't quite the right word, she realized. It was more like a gigantic version of the scaffolding her parents had once helped construct around the manor house in order to necessitate some repairs to the stonework. Much of the mining tower had no solid core. It looked like the lower level was a fully enclosed building, but the section that rose into the sky was only a casing for something long and cylindrical. Something that glinted in the light.

All at once, the grinding sound slowed, and before Jacinta's eyes, the cylinder began to move upward. Squinting around her little hill, she realized it wasn't a smooth cylinder at all. It was a spiral, one that had been spinning, but which was slowing toward a stop as the sound died out.

"It's a drill," she breathed, the words directed at no one in particular. It was so enormous, it hadn't at first occurred to her to consider whether it was a moving tool. As she watched, the drill came to a stop, its movement driven by some force she couldn't see. Through the wooden scaffolding, she caught a glimpse of its tip. Frowning, she shifted around the hill, trying to get a better look through the structure. Something was glowing at the end of the enormous drill, something that must be magical in nature. It looked like a tunnel reaching downward between the drill and the ground, except that it glowed unnaturally, and moved slightly about, like a shifting twister.

A new sound carried to Jacinta's ears now that the grinding of the drill was silenced. She went still, straining her ears to catch what the voice was saying. It was surely too high in pitch for a giant.

"...site inspection is complete," came the voice. "Will report...headquarters...all satisfactory results."

Jacinta frowned at the incomplete message she'd caught.

She shuffled further around the base of the hill, trying to move stealthily as her eyes searched the scaffolding. A gasp escaped her as she caught sight of the speaker. An elf was perched on a mid-level of scaffolding, speaking to a giant standing on top of the solid building below, whose eyes were accordingly at the elf's level.

As she stared, the elf swung his head around, and Jacinta threw herself back behind the mound of icy rock.

"What was that?" The elf's voice was sharper now, and carried more clearly. "Something just moved down there."

The giant gave a deep grunt, his voice louder than the elf's. "Probably a fox."

"Too big for a fox," said the elf suspiciously.

The giant didn't sound concerned. "Musk-ox, then. They wander 'round sometimes. Make for a good lunch for those who've forgotten to bring any."

"I'm not convinced it was a musk-ox," said the elf in distaste. "You should have some of your men search the area."

"Listen 'ere, elf." The giant's voice had a dangerous edge. "I might have to tolerate your audits on my site, but ye're not in charge, see? Don't go thinking ee can give orders."

The elf snapped a reply, but Jacinta didn't catch it. She'd already begun hurrying back the way she came, moving in a straight line so that the mound continued to hide her from sight. She took extra care to leave no tracks, her heart pounding at how close she'd come to being caught. She was far from safe yet.

Once there was enough distance between her and the mining tower, she veered to the left, following the rockier ground where it was easier not to leave a trail. The hut she'd visited on her previous trip into Kjemper loomed into sight, surprising her. She'd gone further east than she'd realized.

She was about to correct her course when she heard voices

behind her. Stiffening, she listened in horror to tones too deep to belong to anything but a giant.

"Arr, I dunno. Boss said it's probably nothing, but we gotta check for signs of any intruder. Just a bit further then we can turn back."

Jacinta's heart leaped into her throat as she looked over her shoulder. The rise of the ground hid the speaker from view, but she couldn't count on it doing so for long. Her eyes strayed to Battlement Wall. It was too far away, and there was very little cover between it and her current position. The hut, on the other hand, was barely visible through a hilly section of land. She could probably reach it without being seen if she was careful.

There was no time to overthink her decision. Jacinta took off, running along a snowless ridge of rock before ducking behind another icy mound. She paused to make sure the giants weren't in view, then repeated the exercise. Soon the hut was before her, and the giants' voices were further away. Jacinta moved forward more slowly, trying to calm her racing pulse. Did she stop where she was, trust that they were about to turn back? Or did she need to find better cover?

The approaching giants' voices decided her. They hadn't stopped yet. Keeping low to the ground, she dashed across the small open space between her and the hut, crouching behind a huge barrel standing empty in the yard.

What she hadn't counted on was the giant herself coming around the other corner of the house. The giant froze, her expression confused as it rested on the human kneeling next to her house, fully exposed from her vantage point. There was no sign of recognition on her face, and all at once Jacinta remembered her floured hair.

"It's me!" Jacinta whispered desperately. "I'm hiding from giants from the mining tower. If they find me, they'll kill me!"

"That doesn't seem like my problem," the giant observed.

Jacinta considered threatening to expose the giant's involvement in communicating with a human king, but on balance decided that blackmail wasn't a wise course.

"I've spoken to my king," she said instead. "I think he might move against your ruler, but not unless I return with proof that there's magic in Kjemper."

The giant had perked up at the first part of this speech, but her face dropped in irritation when Jacinta added the disclaimer.

"The uselessness of 'umans," she muttered. Her gaze traveled in the direction Jacinta had come, and she strode forward. As she passed, Jacinta realized that the white chicken the giant had chased last time was once again clutched in her arms.

"What do ee want?" the giant demanded, presumably speaking to the two strangers who'd been behind Jacinta.

"We're looking for signs of an intruder," grunted a deep voice.

"The only intruders round here are the pair of ee," said the female giant in irritation. "My husband's sleeping from the night shift. If ee wake him, he'll have yer heads."

A few grumbles reached Jacinta's ears, but they were receding. She let out a long breath of relief, resting her head back against the barrel. Her giant champion came back into view, looking far from pleased.

"Would it offend you if I thank you?" Jacinta asked carefully.

"It certainly would." The giant's voice was short. "So ye've been to the tower, have ee? Seen something worth seeing, huh?"

"I'm not entirely sure what I saw," Jacinta said.

The giant just grunted. "If ee have any sense, ee won't return to Kjemper. Just take yer message to yer king and wash yer hands of the whole business."

"I need more than a message," Jacinta reminded her. "I need proof that your king is a threat. And my king won't believe that unless he knows you've all got access to magic." She sighed. "It doesn't matter how convinced I might be. He won't take me at my word."

"More sensible than I expected from an 'uman," commented the giant. "So ee want proof of magic, do ee?" She hesitated for a moment, then thrust the chicken toward Jacinta. "Here. Take this. It's driving me spare anyway. Blasted thing won't stay in its cage."

Jacinta stared at the fowl. "Uhhh..." She searched for the words to say it diplomatically. "I'm not sure that will convince him. Chickens aren't considered magical in the human kingdoms. We have plenty of them in Vadolis."

The giant gave a snort of amusement. "Not like this one, ee don't. Now take it before I change my mind. I'll tell the husband it got away at last. Best not to have it here, really. Daft man thinks he's above punishment, but I don't hold with illegal experiments. No sense in looking for trouble."

Illegal experiments? Jacinta took the bird gingerly, confused by the whole situation. She didn't have much faith in the chicken's ability to provide proof, but she wasn't against acquiring another hen. Food was still scarce enough to make it valuable. She strengthened her hold on it, pressing it against her so that one wing was trapped to her side. She had plenty of experience with chickens.

"Is it laying?" she asked.

The giant gave a guffaw. "Aye, it's laying. Ye'll see. Now get out of here, before I change my mind and squish ee myself."

Jacinta didn't need telling twice. Pausing only to reassure herself that the other giants were out of sight, she tucked the chicken more securely under her arm and ran for the out-of-sight beanstalk. She found it over the nearest rise, and hurried along the green and winding path it made. Judging by the sun—

and the grumbling of Jacinta's stomach—noon had passed. Her mother was likely worrying about her.

When she reached the wall, she felt a weight drop from her shoulders. With any luck, this was the last time she'd make the unnerving passage. Crawling through the tunnel was more diffi-cult with a chicken under one arm, but she managed it without losing the bird. The poor creature seemed relieved to be in the clutches of a less enormous owner. Hopefully it would get on all right with the two hens currently residing in a coop in Jacinta's yard.

Jacinta emerged at last into Vadolisian air, scrambling out of the tunnel with a tangle of limbs and a flutter of feathers.

"What is that?" The high-pitched voice alerted her to the fact that, against her expectations, Valwynn really had waited for her. "Did you bring a *chicken* back with you?"

The elf reached out a hand as Jacinta stood, as if to stroke the chicken's feathers. But Jacinta pulled the bird back.

"Keep your hands to yourself," she said sternly. "You have a bad record when it comes to coveting my livestock."

Valwynn grinned. "It is a fine looking bird," she acknowl-edged. "For a chicken."

The chicken gave a sudden squawk, almost startling Jacinta into dropping it. Instead she tightened her hold, narrowing her eyes suspiciously at the elf. "I suppose if given your way, you'd name it Barbarity or something, wouldn't you?"

"Of course not," said Valwynn, surprised. "It seems a civi-lized type of creature."

The chicken jutted its head out with the abruptness of its kind, its beady eyes bulging as it examined Valwynn.

Jacinta shook her head, unable to fathom the strange ways of either elves or giants. "Well, you can't have it," she informed her companion. "According to the giant, this chicken is my proof for the king."

"Really?" Valwynn was intrigued at this, moving in for a closer look. Given the height difference, she had to stand on tiptoes to get a good look at the chicken in Jacinta's arms. Its head darted around curiously, causing its comb to wobble. "What's special about it?"

"No idea," said Jacinta. "But apparently it lays, so worst case, it'll help feed my mother and me."

"That would be a disappointingly mundane use of it," said Valwynn.

"To you, maybe." Jacinta started toward her home, weariness tugging at her. She felt almost as tired as she had the day before, after her three-day journey. "It should be safe enough in our coop in the meantime."

The words were barely out of her mouth when a familiar rumbling started, and the ground shook beneath their feet. Untroubled, Jacinta stood still and waited for it to pass. It wasn't a very big one.

But apparently it was big enough to displease the little elf, whose brow had become stormy.

"Abominable," Valwynn muttered. She looked up to see Jacinta watching her. "Well, I suppose there's nothing more to see here," said the elf. "I'll be on my way."

"Wait." Jacinta held out her free arm to stop the elf. "Where can I find you if I need you?"

"I'll find you if I consider myself needed," the elf said with dignity. "I don't want any humans barging into my sanctuary, including you."

With the words she trotted off, her nose in the air, clearly having no patience for any argument.

"At least say hi to Prin—Ferocity for me!" Jacinta called after her.

The elf acknowledged the words with a casual wave of her hand, not turning.

Chuckling a little, Jacinta continued on to her home, depositing her new friend inside the spacious coop that had once housed many chickens. The hen seemed delighted to find herself in the company of her own kind, nestling down into the hay within minutes. The other chickens didn't seem in the least ruffled by her arrival.

Bracing herself for a less relaxed reception, Jacinta trudged toward the house and the questions that would inevitably await her.

The next morning dawned cold but clear, and Jacinta once again rose with the sun. Her mother was up this time, and Jacinta couldn't help smiling at the suspicious way the older woman watched her sit up.

"Relax, Mamma, no more sneaking off. I'm hoping to never have to return to Kjemper. I definitely don't have plans to go there today."

Her mother grumbled a little, but didn't actually comment. She'd said all she had to say on Jacinta's return the day before.

"Shall I fetch the eggs for breakfast?" Jacinta asked brightly, slipping out of her nightgown and into a simple dress. "If they've all three laid, we'll have quite a feast."

"Yes, do," her mother said. "I'll start the water boiling."

Jacinta pulled on her boots and traipsed outside, making use of the outhouse before wandering toward the chicken coop.

"Good morning, ladies," she said brightly. She lifted the wooden roof over the coop's nesting area, hunting in the hay. "Excellent work, you two," she told the two brown hens who were pecking around the open section of the coop. "Two beautiful eggs."

She locked eyes with the white chicken from Kjemper, who

was still roosting. "What about you, Barbarity? Got an egg for me? Or have I interrupted you in the act of laying? Most rude of me."

The chicken responded with a sudden and intense squawk, jutting its head out abruptly. Jacinta bit back laughter, surmising that she really had caught the bird mid-lay.

"That sounded painful," she told the chicken sympathetically. "But I promise your efforts won't be in vain. There's a pair of hungry humans around here, you know."

The hen stood, shaking out its wings before strutting off toward the other birds. Jacinta reached into the coop, her hand closing over the egg. To her confusion, it wasn't warm, but cool to the touch.

She lifted it, surprised by its weight, only to drop it in shock when she got a good look. She fished it out again, closing the hutch quickly and staring at the egg in her hand. It appeared to be made of solid gold.

"Well," she said to the yard at large. "It seems I have my proof."

~

"Are you sure about this, Jacinta?"

Jacinta turned, trying to smile reassuringly in the face of her mother's worry.

"Of course I'm sure. I made the journey to Vallen last time without incident. Why would you anticipate a problem now?"

"Without incident, hm?" Her mother looked unconvinced. "Rejection by the king and the heartache of seeing your former friends don't count as incidents?"

Jacinta didn't reply, just lacing her boot more tightly.

"You're really determined to go?" her mother pressed.

"Of course." Jacinta frowned. "The whole reason I went back

into Kjemper was to get proof. Now I have proof, of course I'm going to take it to the king. I've already delayed a week longer than necessary, and I'm perfectly well rested now."

"Oh, rest," her mother said dryly. "Is that the reason you've delayed?"

Jacinta shot her a grin. "Well, the chance to accumulate a few more of those daily nuggets of gold may have been a factor."

Her mother gave a reluctant smile, and Jacinta bumped her gently with a shoulder.

"I'll be less anxious, knowing you have resources while I'm gone. Not to mention it'll help pay my way."

"Yes, I won't deny it will help," her mother said. "And I've been glad to have you here for the extra time. I wish you were staying longer."

"I'll be back before you know it," Jacinta said cheerfully. "But I really must be off now if I'm going to reach the next town in time to use this ticket." She waved the ticket her mother had purchased for her on the public coach, hoping she didn't seem too eager to get away. Little as she wanted to admit it to herself, the prospect of once again seeing Matthias and Mariella was pulling her more strongly than it should have. "Hopefully they won't object to me bringing Barbarity along. Judging by the chaos of the coach last time, I doubt anyone will even notice."

"Jacinta, there's something you should know," her mother said, disregarding her whole speech. "I should have told you last time. You were right that it was unfair of me to send you to the castle without the information."

Jacinta stilled, straightening. "Are you talking about whatever disagreement you had with the king and queen all those years ago?"

Her mother nodded slowly. "It was about you."

"Me?" Jacinta's eyes widened. "What do you mean?"

"They...didn't like your friendship with the prince and

princess," her mother said. "They asked us—no, ordered us—to put an end to it. They wanted us to confine you to the servants' quarters."

Jacinta felt the color drain from her face, discomfort swirling over her at this discovery of her role in the changes in her family's fortune.

"I admit we didn't take it well," her mother went on. "And they didn't take our response well, either. We told them that you'd done nothing wrong and that while we could encourage you to keep your distance, we couldn't promise to prevent contact altogether. Not when the royal children were the ones seeking you out as often as the other way."

"It would have made the visits miserable for all three of us," said Jacinta dully. "We would have spent the whole time trying to sneak out, probably."

"I think that's what the king and queen concluded," her mother agreed. "I believe that's why they ended their visits. It was a much more reliable way to end the connection."

Jacinta ran her hands down either side of her neck, shivering. "It certainly was," she commented.

Her mind flew yet again to her encounter with Matthias in the dusty, abandoned manor. His hesitation at attending the funeral hadn't related to any disgrace attached to her father. It was Jacinta he wasn't supposed to associate with. Had he known?

But Mariella had been allowed to attend. What reason did the king and queen have for being so inconsistent? It must have been Matthias's choice. Just as it was his choice not to attempt to continue the friendship via letter, like Mariella did. Of course, Jacinta hadn't written to him, either. Again, no one was necessarily at fault. But it still hurt.

"Why didn't you tell me at the time?"

Her mother gave her a look. "Because you would have felt all the discomfort and misplaced guilt you're feeling now. Except that would have been a lot harder to carry when you were ten."

"Yes, I suppose it would," Jacinta acknowledged. She frowned at her mother. "But that was eight years ago. You could have told me before now."

"Yes." Her mother hesitated. "And I should have. I'm sorry." She seemed uncertain, and Jacinta's frown grew.

But before she could say a word, the ground began to tremble in a familiar sensation. Both women braced themselves as a matter of course, Jacinta grabbing hold of a clay jar that was perched too close to the edge of the table.

When the tremor passed, she replaced the jar, glancing at the sun. "Is there more to the story, Mamma? Because the coach leaves in an hour."

"Of course." Her mother's voice turned brisk again, and she gave a curt nod. "You should go." She picked Barbarity up from the floor and held her up. "Both of you."

"All right." In spite of the need for haste, Jacinta hovered for a moment, searching her mother's face. It had really seemed for a moment like she was going to say more. "I'll see you in a week, Mamma. Be safe while I'm gone."

"I will," her mother told her gruffly, pulling her in for a quick hug. "You take care of yourself."

Nodding, Jacinta pulled her rucksack over her shoulder and, chicken under one arm, stepped out into the brisk air. She'd told herself this last task would be the end of her involvement in the whole strange affair. But she had a discomfiting feeling that the tangle was only getting messier, and she was very much afraid that she was getting pulled further and further into its center.

CHAPTER TWELVE

Matthias

Matthias pulled his horse up at the top of the rise, admiring the view of Sunniva below him.

"It's a pleasant city, isn't it?"

The rider next to him nodded in agreement, his eyes also scanning the Frossian capital below them. "It is," Hagen agreed. "I've spent much of my life there, and it's pleasant to live in as well as to look at."

"More pleasant than the frozen north?" Matthias joked.

Hagen didn't laugh. His face was hard to read as he swapped his reins from one hand to the other.

"I found it so," he said at last. "But others would disagree."

"I'm sorry," Matthias said, confused by the cool reaction but regretful for the discomfort he'd clearly caused. "I meant no offense."

"I'm not offended, Your Highness," said Hagen quickly, his lapse into the title a sure sign that he was closing off.

"Good." Matthias spoke briskly, eager to change the mood. "Because I need my guide."

"We'll reach the city within half an hour, Your Highness," the expedition's head guard informed him, pulling his horse alongside the prince's. "I've sent a scout ahead, and we're expected."

"Thank you," said Matthias. "I'm looking forward to leaving the road for a while."

"It has been a long two days, hasn't it?" Hagen responded, speaking more naturally. "The journey was faster when I traveled the other way."

Matthias gave a humorless smile. "One of the downsides of traveling with royalty is that everything takes forever." He shook his head. "And this is nothing compared to a family expedition, with my mother in a carriage. This journey would probably take a week."

Hagen smiled, copying Matthias as the prince spurred his horse back into motion. The descent into Sunniva passed quickly, the whole mood of the group lightening as they rode through the city gates, which were flung wide to welcome them. They'd had no impediments on their journey, but the passage around the southern edge of Fross Mountains wasn't the easiest trail. Everyone was ready for a good night's sleep in a real bed.

By the time they rode up to the castle, King Herleif and Queen Adrienne were waiting to receive them. The infant prince was even present, little Prince Eerikki asleep in his mother's arms.

"Welcome, Prince Matthias."

The young king strode forward to grip Matthias's hand before he was even out of the saddle. King Herleif was built on such large lines, he didn't have to look up nearly as far as a normal man to meet Matthias's eyes. He positively dwarfed his petite wife.

Matthias slid out of the saddle, returning the other royal's greeting. "Kind of you to greet us in person," he said cheerfully. "Especially the young crown prince. How old is he now? Four months?"

"Barely two," chuckled King Herleif. "He takes after me, it seems."

Queen Adrienne smiled, her eyes fond as they passed between her son and her husband. "He'll tower over me before I know it."

"Congratulations, Your Majesty," said Matthias, smiling at the queen. "And thank you for receiving us. This is—"

He turned to Hagen, only to break off in surprise as the Frossian king gripped the singer's hand, pulling him in and slapping his back with a thump.

"Hagen! This is a welcome surprise. I only just penned a letter in response to yours this morning. I'll tell the steward not to send it." He shook his head reprovingly. "Why did you sneak off like that? We would have given a proper send off if we'd known you were departing for your apprenticeship so soon."

"That wasn't necessary, Your Majesty," said Hagen, seeming uncomfortable under the attention. "I left the day of the prince's christening, so there were other matters requiring your attention."

"Part of being a king is developing the ability to divide my attention between a dizzying number of causes," King Herleif told him. He turned to see Matthias watching the reunion, and smiled. "I hope Hagen's presence in the castle at Vallen has been beneficial thus far. I didn't expect to see him back so soon."

"He's been invaluable," Matthias said quickly. "Soon enough I won't be able to do without him."

"You exaggerate, Prince Matthias," said Hagen, pained.

"He underrates his importance," King Herleif told Matthias wisely.

The prince nodded. "So it seems. I confess I had no idea the two of you were so well acquainted."

"I did tell you that my parents worked for the royal family up in the north," Hagen said quickly.

Matthias gave him a look, and he smiled in sheepish acknowledgment of how much he'd left out.

"Come inside," Queen Adrienne encouraged them. "We would be delighted for both of you to dine with us, and we can discuss these matters further then. I'm sure you'll wish to settle into your rooms after your journey."

The group reconvened for the evening meal, Prince Eerikki being handed off to a nursemaid just as Matthias and Hagen entered the dining hall. Matthias watched the Frossian queen as she gave quiet instructions to the maid. She looked reluctant to part with her child, and Matthias found himself reflecting that the necessity of doing so was probably a feature of royal life. He'd always considered the convenience of servants to be a benefit of his status, but watching the young mother follow her child from the room with her eyes, it occurred to him that not all might share that view. Did she find it difficult to adjust to the restrictions of marrying into royalty? From what he knew, she was a commoner by birth, and her marriage to King Herleif had come as something of a shock to the whole kingdom.

King Herleif's mother, the Dowager Queen Sylvi, and his sister, Princess Runa, joined them as well. Matthias smiled in a friendly way at the thirteen-year-old, who seemed shy in the presence of strangers. The first course was served, and for a moment, all focus was on the food.

"How do you find the Academy of Song in Vallen?" Queen Adrienne asked Hagen, reminding Matthias that she was a singer as well. "Is it very different from ours?"

"The teaching methods seem to be similar, Your Majesty," Hagen said. "But there is a different culture."

"In what way?" King Herleif asked curiously.

Hagen glanced quickly at Matthias then away. "To generalize, Your Majesty, I would say that they're more formal. But I've had little opportunity to experience life at the academy. As you are aware, I'm based at the royal castle in Vallen, and I spent only a short time there before accompanying Prince Matthias on this visit."

"I didn't give him much choice, poor fellow," Matthias said cheerfully. "I needed someone my own age for company, otherwise the journey would have been too dull to be endured."

Princess Runa giggled at his light words, and Matthias sent her the ghost of a wink. Her face flushed, and she lowered her eyes, still giggling. At an austere look from her mother, she subsided.

"I was glad to accompany you, Prince Matthias," said Hagen, also smiling at the joke.

Matthias nodded, happy to let the conversation flow around him. Princess Runa's reaction had pulled his thoughts in a different direction. He'd been the recipient of enough youthful admiration among his father's court to recognize that the young princess was admiring him. It was a harmless, childish type of admiration, and he was wise enough to think no less of her for it. But it brought his sister's words about Jacinta to mind.

What had she said when he declared that neither he nor Jacinta had ever thought of each other romantically?

You weren't quite there yet at age twelve...by that age I was already showing interest in what they would call romantic nonsense.

To his irritation at the time, Mariella had seemed to think there was some weight in their parents' assumption that given a couple more years, he and Jacinta might have begun to see each other in an altogether different light.

Was it possible she was right? If Princess Runa was old enough at thirteen to be thinking of romance, would Jacinta have had the same reaction to him when they were that age? The thought brought a wry smile to his face. He'd been far from smooth or impressive at thirteen. It was natural for a young teenage princess to feel passing fancy for a twenty-year-old visiting prince. If he was her own age, Princess Runa would likely be uninterested.

And Jacinta had always been too sensible for that kind of thing. She'd scorned the idea that girls were trying to kiss Matthias. It was arrogant of him to think she would have fallen for him if they'd kept going to Briarford.

But then...hadn't she kissed his cheek when they said goodbye? Was that really just the action of a friend who'd missed their time together? Even during their secret encounter four years earlier, she'd responded so differently to him. Nothing about the moment when she threw herself into his arms had been like their childhood interactions.

He was aware that the dowager queen was speaking to Hagen, and could only hope no questions would be directed to him. His thoughts wouldn't be stopped now they'd gone down this path. Because the fact of the matter was, there was no use speculating what would have passed between him and Jacinta if his family had continued going to Briarford each summer. They hadn't continued. And he was inclined to think that if his parents wanted to prevent him ever realizing that Jacinta was an attractive young woman, they'd made a strategic error.

Perhaps if their friendship had continued uninterrupted, Matthias would have always thought of her as a playmate. What had instead happened was that her absence had become an unresolved discomfort in his mind, a constant question. And then she'd exploded back into his life, grown up and attractive and very far from the oblivious child of his memories.

Of course, his parents had hoped for that moment never to come, he thought with a scowl. They'd made their feelings on her reappearance perfectly clear.

"So, Prince Matthias."

The sound of his name brought Matthias out of his reverie, his eyes flying to King Herleif.

"Yes?"

"I understand you wish to speak about the giants?"

"They just arrived, Herleif." Adrienne's voice was gentle, and she laid one slim hand on her husband's much thicker arm. Matthias could see why people called her elfin. Her features really were almost as delicate as those of the miniature creatures. "They may wish to sleep before launching into serious discussions."

Herleif raised an inquiring eyebrow at Matthias. "Is it the type of matter you'd prefer not to discuss over dinner?"

"No, Your Majesty." Matthias inclined his head toward the young queen. "Thank you for your consideration, Queen Adrienne, but there's no reason to delay on my account."

He didn't say so, of course, but he was eager not to draw out his visit unnecessarily. Shifting in his chair, he directed his words to the king.

"We received a report from a civilian who went through Battlement Wall into Kjemper. She carried a warning from a giant she met there."

King Herleif and Queen Adrienne exchanged looks, but neither interrupted.

"It's a strange tale," Matthias went on. "She didn't plan to go through the wall. The whole venture was orchestrated by an elf."

"An elf?" He had King Herleif's full attention. "Did the elf give a reason for sending a human into Kjemper?"

Matthias shook his head. "It seems she didn't give any information at all." With as much detail as he could remember, he recounted Jacinta's tale.

"Our conclusion is that the giants have access to much more magic than we imagined," he said. "Or that this giant wished us to think so, at any rate."

"Is the girl who brought the tale credible?" Queen Adrienne asked thoughtfully.

"Yes." Even Matthias could hear that his response was too quick and too vehement. He moderated his voice. "She wasn't a stranger. She comes from our northern region, and her family worked at the manor where my family used to spend time each summer. We played together as children." He nodded toward Hagen. "Much like you and Hagen would have done, Your Majesty."

The king and the singer looked at each other, King Herleif's eyebrow slightly raised. "We never played together as children. We barely had any contact until we were adults and both living in the capital."

"Oh." Matthias felt suddenly foolish, and hastened to redirect the conversation. "The point is, I trust Jacinta's word."

"In that case," King Herleif said, "I will assume her tale is true. I'm intrigued by the claim that many of the giants would be glad to see their king dethroned."

"Does it seem consistent with what you observed when you were in Kjemper?" Matthias asked.

King Herleif nodded. "Yes, I could certainly believe it. What do you think, Adrienne?"

"It wouldn't surprise me," she agreed. "The old queen lorded it over everyone, and I didn't witness much fondness for her. I think she hoarded all the wealth. Even her own daughter wasn't allowed to have gold of her own."

"I saw more of the castle than you did, and I agree. There was gold everywhere, but it was all Grograna's. Even her son Uroch, the one who's king now, had very little license."

"It sounds like he's followed in his mother's footsteps," Queen Adrienne commented. "It's interesting to learn that with him, the monarchy is only three generations old."

"All the easier to topple," King Herleif commented. His wife gave him a look, and he shrugged. "I'm only thinking strategically." His stoic expression gave way to a swift grin in Matthias's direction, softening his somewhat square face. "I don't make it a habit to plot how to destabilize surrounding monarchies."

Matthias laughed. "I'm ready to defend the honor of my kingdom however necessary while in this hostile land," he said humorously. He eyed the other young royal. It was ironic what form King Herleif had been cursed into because even as a human, he was built like a bear. "Although I fear that if you challenge me to an arm wrestle, Vadolis is doomed."

That sent a chuckle around the table.

"Well, I'm certainly glad to be told about this new informant," King Herleif said, his voice more serious. "Not that I need her testimony to convince me that the giants have access to more magic than is logical in their barren land. I saw evidence of that myself, not that anyone but us seemed to take it seriously."

He exchanged another look with his wife, a shadow of frustration crossing their faces.

"But the idea of mining towers is new information," Queen Adrienne commented. "We both saw structures dotted across Kjemper when we flew over. That must be what they were."

The king frowned. "If so, there are a lot of them. But what would be the point if the land is as bare of magic on the northern side of the wall as it is on the southern side?" He fixed his wife with a piercing look. "You're sure you didn't sense magic in the land?"

She bit her lip. "I didn't say that. I did say that the ground itself felt much like northern Frossenland. When I tried to find magic in it, there wasn't much there. But I found magic from somewhere else, remember? It wasn't quite like pulling power from the ground, or quite like harnessing the torrent released by a powerful talisman. But it was something in between those sensations."

Most of the queen's listeners looked as confused as Matthias felt, but Hagen leaned forward, his expression keen. "That's odd," he said. "I've never encountered anything like that."

"Nor have I before or since," she told him. "Prior to that, my experience of magic was so limited. But I've had much more training since, which has only served to highlight more clearly how unnatural it was. There was magic passing through the area, undoubtedly. But it wasn't seeping naturally from the ground like it does here."

"It's the result of their mining," said Hagen thoughtfully. "It must be. They're mining magic somehow, pulling it in a stream under the ground and up through these towers. You must have intercepted some magic from one of those streams, Your Majesty."

King Herleif frowned. "But where is the magic coming from? Where do these streams originate? The whole northern region is barren of magic."

No one had an immediate answer, and after a moment's reverie, the king straightened.

"I'll need to discuss these matters with some of our experts at the Academy of Song." He looked at Matthias. "Perhaps you'd like to join me."

"I would be honored," Matthias said, inclining his head.

He was glad to be involved, but another part of him was disheartened by the realization that it wasn't likely to be a short visit to Sunniva. He had a sneaking suspicion that his parents had sent him to Frossenland partly in hopes that he'd still be away when Jacinta returned with further proof from Kjemper.

Matthias didn't intend to let that happen. But of course, he was all too aware how little it was in his control.

Matthias's prediction proved accurate. Although King Herleif was very interested in the situation Matthias had reported, unlike the prince, he was a reigning monarch. The question of whether the giants were mining magic was only one of many demands on his time, and he wasn't able to dedicate as much time to their discussions as Matthias had hoped.

Not that they were given the chance to be bored. The royal family were excellent hosts, the dowager queen and young princess stepping in to entertain their Vadolisian guests when the king was occupied with royal business and the queen with her young son. They even hosted a reception, at which Matthias had the dubious pleasure of being overtly pursued by the young ladies of yet another court.

At least the Frossian royal castle was very pleasant. The weather wasn't too cold yet, and he spent much of his spare time wandering the gardens with Hagen.

"Do you really think the giants could be mining magic in large enough volumes to endanger us?" he asked on one such ramble, his mind turning over all their previous discussions.

Hagen frowned. "From the little I know of giants, I would have said no. But if there are elves helping them..."

He trailed off, and Matthias wrinkled his nose in sympathy with King Herleif. "I heard the king is still facing backlash from the local elves. They're convinced he was incorrect to conclude from his visit to Kjemper that elves could be assisting the giants in any way. They're apparently deeply offended he'd suggest it, even after all this time."

"I think it's safe to say that if there are elves helping the giants, they're acting against the usual ways of their kind," Hagen said. "Which means they're a renegade group, and I wouldn't put much stock in the declarations of the rest of the elves."

Matthias nodded, falling silent. All his other thoughts on the topic had already been shared exhaustively.

Hagen cleared his throat. "Your Highness, I've been meaning to apologize to you."

"Apologize?" Matthias looked over, noting the reversion to a formal title. "For what?"

The other man looked uncomfortable. "For concealing from you the connection between King Herleif and myself."

Matthias said nothing, waiting for him to elaborate. He'd been curious about the matter since King Herleif revealed the pair weren't childhood friends, but hadn't liked to press.

"The truth is, I'm not entirely easy with the kindness the king shows me. It's generous of him, but I don't deserve it. I don't have any valid claim to the recognition."

"I imagine whoever selected you for the most prestigious singing apprenticeship would disagree," Matthias said.

Hagen shook his head. "The king's notice has nothing to do with that. The only thing binding us together is the fact that our fathers were murdered by the same person—or rather giant—on the same day."

Matthias came to a stop, unsure how to respond. "I'm sorry," he said. "I didn't realize your father had been murdered."

"By the giant queen," Hagen confirmed. "She was there for King Eerikki and Prince Herleif, but my father was a singer, and he tried to intervene." He sighed. "I think the king feels some guilt over the matter, but he carries no blame. There's no need for him to show me kindness." He grimaced. "Especially since I once tried to kill him, thinking him responsible for the deaths."

"That sounds like quite a tale," Matthias said mildly.

Hagen sighed again. "Not my proudest moment. Suffice it to say, I don't take pleasure from the nature of my connection with the king. Truthfully, all I can think of when he shows me grace is the murder of our two fathers. And the fact that he's managed to move forward with his life only highlights how much I've failed to do the same."

Matthias searched the other man's face, taken completely by surprise by this burst of candor. He'd never dreamed Hagen had such strong emotion buried beneath the stiff discomfort with which he received kindness from royalty. He would have to remember to tread more carefully in future.

"Thank you for explaining it," he said at last, deciding that a more personal response would only embarrass them both. "And I perfectly understand your hesitation to do so earlier."

Hagen gave a curt nod of acknowledgment, and the pair walked on. But Matthias's thoughts remained heavy, swirling between the murder of Hagen's father, the tragic death of Jacinta's, and the complex layers of experience that muddied interactions between royalty and commoners.

Slowly but steadily, King Herleif made time to explore the matter of the giants. It took the better part of two weeks for their discussions to reach a point where Matthias could extricate himself gracefully. By that time, the Frossian king had reached a decision.

"Yes," he told Matthias, on the prince's last day in Sunniva. "When my own advisers were reluctant to accept my conclusions about giants having access to both magic and elves, I didn't see the benefit in pursuing the matter further. But this new source has galvanized me. This issue is serious enough to deserve the attention of all of us. If the girl you mentioned brings back further evidence, it will be all the better. But even without it, I plan to go ahead with the summit. I'll send messages to each of the monarchs asking them to come to Sunniva themselves or send representatives. I want to facilitate a serious discussion about Kjemper and the risk it presents to the rest of Providore." He nodded to Matthias. "I hope you will be willing to return for the summit."

"Of course," Matthias said quickly. "I'd be honored."

"Thank you." The king extended his hand. "I'm grateful for the information you've brought, Matthias, and glad for the opportunity to better get to know you."

"You also," Matthias agreed. "I look forward to further discussion."

He and Hagen rode out of the city early the following morning, having taken their leave of the queen the night before. The pace of the group, with a dozen armed guards surrounding them, felt sluggish. Matthias was frustrated at how long their errand had taken, and eager to get on the road. He knew there was every chance Jacinta had been to Vallen and left again already, but he still held on to hope that he would make it back in time.

And if he'd missed her, perhaps he'd defy his parents and ride to Briarford to see her. The thought was equal parts alarming and exhilarating. If he could really find the courage to take control of his own life, even in the face of his parents' opposition, then anything was possible.

His mind started to spin fantasies about what his life would look like if he could construct whatever future he chose, but he reluctantly cut the thoughts off. Daydreaming would be more likely to bring grief than happiness.

The first day of travel passed smoothly, and they made better progress than Matthias had feared. They stopped for the night at an inn just before the ford over the East River. A couple of hours of solid riding in the morning would carry them across the border into Vadolis.

The river crossing took longer than he'd hoped, but after that they traveled at a good pace along the road that skirted the northern bank of the East River. By late afternoon they left the river, turning north for the short ride into Vallen. The group paused at the point the road turned north, to allow passage of a crowded public coach coming from the east.

Content to be so close to their goal, Matthias and his escorts traveled behind the coach all the way into the city. It came to a stop outside a rambling inn situated in one of the city's main squares. Passengers began to dismount, and Matthias glanced over as they passed. The sight of a young woman climbing out of the coach brought him to a swift stop.

"Jacinta!"

He was too far away for her to hear, but the exclamation made Hagen stop beside him. Realizing that their charge was unmoving in the middle of the cobblestoned road, the guards also came to a halt.

Matthias watched in amazement as Jacinta pressed a coin into the driver's hand, hoisting a rucksack up her shoulder as she turned. What was in the rucksack? Had she found the evidence his father had so ungraciously demanded? His stomach was doing strange flips. He'd hurried back to Vallen in the specific hope of seeing her, yet now that she was in front of him, he couldn't seem to make his limbs move.

As she glanced left, in the direction of the castle, Matthias's eyes slid from her face to the creature clutched under one arm. His sudden awkwardness melted away in a mixture of amusement and bewilderment.

"Hagen," he said to his companion. "Am I seeing things, or is that—"

"A chicken," Hagen supplied helpfully. "It's definitely a chicken."

CHAPTER THIRTEEN

Jacinta

Jacinta tightened her hold on the chicken under her arm. It had been a long and unpleasant journey with the fowl in tow, and she wasn't about to let it escape now she was so close. She was extremely weary after her travels, and it was late enough in the day that she was certainly going to have to stay in the capital overnight. It was tempting to secure a room first, and get a good night's sleep before reporting back to the king.

But she knew that she wouldn't be able to rest until her errand was done. In addition to which, she wasn't sure how a city inn would feel about accommodating a chicken. The sooner she handed Barbarity off to the castle, the better.

She'd barely taken a step when the sound of her name pulled her up.

"Jacinta!"

She turned slowly, her heart picking up speed. She knew that voice. Sure enough, her eyes locked with Matthias, mounted on a beautiful stallion and surrounded by guards. At his urging, his horse trotted toward her, his escort parting to let him through.

Feeling tongue-tied, Jacinta watched as the prince swung himself down from the saddle, leading the horse to her with eager steps. Clearly his warm welcome on her previous visit wasn't the result of a temporary lapse in memory. The thought buoyed her.

"Jacinta, I'm so glad I didn't miss you!" he said, stopping several steps away.

"Hello, Matthias," said Jacinta, wishing she could think of something interesting to say. "Have you been away?"

He nodded. "I just returned from Sunniva, where I met with King Herleif. But what about you?" He frowned. "What are you doing here? I mean..." He gave his head a little shake. "I assume I know why you're in Vallen. But what brings you in at the south gate, in a coach traveling from the east?"

"Oh." Jacinta hoisted her rucksack up her shoulder as Barbarity squirmed in the circle of her arm. "It wasn't the most direct route. This coach made a stop in a town just east of the capital. But it was the cheapest fare."

"Oh," Matthias repeated, seeming unsure how to respond to this practical answer. His eyes dropped to her cargo, a hint of the old, familiar smile softening his features. "I'm a little afraid to ask, but...why do you have a chicken?"

Jacinta grinned. "Believe it or not, Barbarity here is my evidence for your father."

"Barbarity?" Matthias raised an eyebrow. "I have no idea how a chicken could be evidence, but it sounds like I should be alarmed. Is it magically enhanced somehow?"

"It is magically enhanced," said Jacinta. "But not in a way that need concern you. The nickname is a joke...not apt at all."

"I should expect no less from the girl who named her cow Princess," Matthias said with a grin. He turned toward his horse, and Jacinta thought he would remount, but instead he looped his hand more comfortably through the reins. "Were you going straight to the castle?" he asked. "We can walk together."

"I was." Jacinta patted her rumpled hair self-consciously. "Although I'm probably in no state to present myself to royalty."

"I disagree," said Matthias, the courteous words light, but something in his eyes a little too intense to match his tone.

Jacinta nodded a greeting to the pale-haired man who'd dismounted beside the prince.

"We never properly met," she said. "I'm Jacinta."

"Hagen," he said, dipping his head politely. "It's a pleasure to meet you."

Now that she was properly looking at the young man, something about his manner and general demeanor told her that he wasn't a nobleman. Jacinta felt herself relaxing slightly, and her smile grew. She'd seen the easy communication between the pair. Apparently the prince hadn't become *too* aware of his station in the years since their lives had diverged.

"I'm very grateful for your assistance last time I was here," she told Hagen.

"No need to thank me," he said, shaking his head. "The prince and princess insisted on reimbursing me."

"I'm glad," Jacinta said forcefully. She saw Hagen's surprise, and gave a self-conscious laugh as she glanced at Matthias. "That wasn't very polite to them, was it? I only meant that it was a considerable amount of money for those of us not accustomed to royal resources. I would hate to think you were fleeced of your life savings by being in the wrong place at the wrong time."

Hagen smiled. "I would rather think of it as the right place at the right time. There was certainly no question of being fleeced."

"Well, I fully intend to pay the amount back to you, or Mariella, or whoever was out of pocket."

"Absolutely not," said Matthias. "It was payment from the

crown for your services in bringing valuable information. And we'd probably best get going."

He didn't seem altogether pleased at their joking, and Jacinta's heart sank a little. She knew she shouldn't be critical of him. It was natural that he would have become more stiff and serious as he aged and grew into his responsibilities.

Nodding meekly, she turned toward the castle, tightening her hold as Barbarity made an attempt to gain freedom. It wasn't a long walk up the cobblestone streets, but every step felt heavy with the silence between Jacinta and the prince. He'd seemed so pleased to see her, but the closer they drew to his castle, the more the barriers between them reared their heads.

This time she didn't have to argue her case to any guards to gain admittance to the castle. She watched, a little awed, as the series of guards stationed along the entrance to the castle sprang to attention as Matthias passed. The prince acknowledged it with a casual nod, seeming to barely notice. He did, however, notice one of the guards stepping forward to intercept Jacinta.

"No, she's with me," he said breezily, apparently oblivious to the small somersault performed by Jacinta's heart at the words. What was wrong with her?

The guard's eyes traveled to the feathery bundle in Jacinta's arms, his expression perplexed.

"Yes, the chicken, too," Matthias said, the words somehow infused with all the confidence and authority of his royal position. The guard fell back with a bow, and no one else tried to bar their passage.

As they entered the building itself, a servant appeared as if by magic, hovering silently near Matthias, ready to receive orders if needed or disappear into the background if not.

Matthias didn't seem to have observed the servant's approach, but as he pulled off his riding gloves, he glanced around, his eyes showing no surprise as they caught on the young man.

"Ah, good. Where can my parents be found, please?"

"I will discover their whereabouts, Your Highness." With a bow, the servant scurried off.

"It's nice to be home," Matthias commented cheerfully as another servant relieved him of his riding gloves. Again, he barely seemed to notice the transaction, but Jacinta had no doubt the gloves would be right on hand in his chamber when he next wanted them.

Jacinta's discomfort was increasing by the second, and the odd looks she and her chicken were receiving didn't help. She glanced sideways to see Hagen's eyes on her. The Frossian didn't try to hide that he'd been watching her, and his gaze was shrewd. He gave her a reassuring smile, as if to say, *I know it's a lot.*

Jacinta relaxed marginally, feeling grounded by this unspoken thread of connection to the real world that lay beyond the castle walls.

"Come on, you two," Matthias said cheerfully, seeing them stopped behind him.

Jacinta had assumed he would wait in the entranceway for the servant to report back to him, but instead he walked briskly down one of the broad corridors, Jacinta and Hagen trailing behind. Somehow, the servant still knew where to find him.

"His Majesty is inspecting the royal guard, and Her Majesty is in her private rooms," the man told Matthias. "Does Your Highness wish to send a message?"

"Yes, thank you," Matthias said. "Request them to meet me in the white salon. Tell them that Jacinta has returned with information for them." He hesitated. "And have someone notify my sister as well."

At least he spoke courteously to his servants, Jacinta noted.

No barking orders like some of the lesser nobles who'd occasionally been invited to stay in the manor in Briarford. But it was hard not to think of her own home, of traipsing into her one-room hut and being able to see at a glance whether her mother was there or not. They didn't even get separate sleeping spaces.

Hagen shifted beside her at the prince's words, and Jacinta was surprised to see him straightening his travel-creased tunic. She wasn't sure what was behind the self-conscious gesture, but she took note, intrigued to discover what was in his thoughts.

Matthias led them around a corner, glancing back with twitching lips as Barbarity let out a squawk of uncertainty at her new surroundings.

"That looks uncomfortable," he told Jacinta. "Have you been carrying her all the way from Briarford? How did you manage at the inns?"

Jacinta grimaced. "I had to settle for less reputable ones in order to be allowed to keep her in my room," she said. "But we managed."

Matthias didn't look pleased with this information. "Let me carry her for a bit. You must want a break."

Jacinta tightened her grip on the chicken, shaking her head frantically. "I couldn't possibly, Your Highness." Matthias gave her an impatient look, and she amended, "Matthias. I couldn't possibly, Matthias."

"I could carry her for a while, if you like," Hagen offered in a friendly way.

Jacinta smiled at him. "Thank you, that's very kind. But I think I'd better hold on to her, since presenting her to the king and queen is my only justification for being here."

She looked back at Matthias, to see his dark blue eyes passing between her and Hagen, their expression veiled.

"This is the white salon," he said, gesturing to the door

they'd just reached. Hagen walked obediently inside, and Jacinta made to follow. To her surprise, Matthias stopped her with a hand on the arm not clutching Barbarity. "It's not true, you know."

"What's not true?" she asked, annoyed with the breathlessness of her voice. Her mind could focus on little but the touch of his skin on hers, and the intensity of those eyes. He'd never looked at her like that when they were children.

"It's not true that the chicken is your only justification for coming here. You're welcome here at any time. The friendship between us, and Mariella of course, is reason enough."

Jacinta swallowed, at a loss for how to respond. Was he oblivious, or trying to convince himself?

"That's...a kind sentiment, Matthias. But you were here last time I came. We both saw how your parents felt about—"

"This is my home as well as my parents'," Matthias said firmly. "And I'm telling you that you're welcome." His grip tightened on her arm. "Last time I saw you—four years ago, I mean, not last time you came to the castle—I didn't express myself clearly at all. I don't want there to be any doubt this time. Jacinta, I'm glad you've come back into my life. I never wanted you out of it."

Jacinta's mouth had fallen slightly open, her mind struggling to make sense of this declaration. Did he not know that the whole reason his family had stopped coming to Briarford was his parents' determination to end their friendship? Or did he not care what his parents thought?

Well, he was the crown prince, but she was nobody. She didn't have the luxury of not caring what her monarchs thought of her.

"Thank you, Matthias," she said quietly. "I'm glad as well. But..." She gently extricated her arm. "But it doesn't change anything, does it?"

On the words, she entered the salon, leaving Matthias watching her with troubled eyes. Hagen was hovering on the far side of the room. He must have been fully aware of the encounter happening in the corridor, but had chosen to give them space. Just like the servants, he understood the role and manner he needed to adopt around royalty. Jacinta would be wise to do the same. But with Matthias so determined to hold on to it, how could she bring herself to let go of the friendship they'd once shared?

What she needed was a good night's sleep, she told herself, with a shake of her head. It was exhausting being pulled in different directions all the time.

When Matthias followed her into the room, he seated himself in an armchair, his expression hard to read. Perhaps seeing the strain on Jacinta's face, Hagen stepped forward to engage her in light, comfortable conversation. She appreciated it enormously, and they passed several minutes chatting easily about the similarities between Briarford and Toveham, Hagen's childhood home.

Less than ten minutes after they'd reached the room, a whirlwind arrived in the form of the princess.

"Jacinta!" Mariella threw herself around the table to embrace Jacinta. "I'm so glad you've come back, and you weren't eaten by a giant or something!"

Jacinta laughed weakly. "Actually, I have it on good authority that giants don't eat humans any more than humans eat elves."

"Whose authority?" Mariella asked, agog. "That giant's? You really have to tell me all about Kjemper, Jacinta!"

"Well, that's what I'm here for," Jacinta said fairly. "But I think I'd better wait for your parents."

Mariella nodded. "I suppose so." Her eyes slid to the side, her face creasing in a fresh smile. "Hagen! You're back from Frossenland. Good to see you safely returned."

Jacinta glanced at the singer as well, noting that the relaxed demeanor that had put her so at ease was gone. He looked almost as stiff as Matthias now. It wasn't that he seemed uncomfortable. More that he was overly conscious of himself. She knew the feeling.

Following his gaze to Mariella's bright countenance, Jacinta hid a smile. It would be interesting to see how this situation unfolded.

On the thought, she realized she was unlikely to get that chance. Perhaps she could write to Mariella once she'd gone home, like they used to. The princess wasn't usually difficult to draw information from.

"You may have noticed, my darling sister, that I have also returned safely from Frossenland." Matthias's voice was deceptively pleasant, and Mariella grinned.

"Oh, yes, hello Matthias. I suppose you deserve a greeting as well."

Matthias eyed her darkly, but the promising start to sibling banter was interrupted by the arrival of the king and queen. Jacinta and Hagen both leaped to their feet, the prince and princess following more calmly. Two guards escorted the monarchs into the room, placing themselves on either side of the long table. Jacinta saw Matthias giving the pair an impatient look, apparently agreeing with her assessment that the presence of the guards was an entirely unnecessary display.

"Matthias, welcome home," the king told his son. "I'm glad to see you safely returned to us. I trust your time with King Herleif was productive."

"Yes, Father, I believe so," Matthias said. "He is of the view that—"

"We can discuss the matter at a later time," King Fidelius said, looking pointedly at Jacinta.

Matthias didn't try to hide his irritation. "I see no reason to conceal the information from Jacinta, Father. She's the one who brought it to us in the first place."

"Jacinta." Beyond taking them as a prompt to finally look at the newcomer, the king ignored his son's words. "I see you have returned also."

"Yes, Your Majesty," said Jacinta, giving a curtsy her best attempt. "As requested, I have returned with evidence of the giants' access to magic."

"I did make that request, didn't I?" The king seemed irritated with his former self for the lapse in judgment. "However, I am at a loss to understand the report I received which claimed that you entered the city in Prince Matthias's company."

"Not quite, Your Highness," said Jacinta quickly, shifting uncomfortably under the king's heavy-browed gaze. "The prince and Hagen happened to see me arrive in a public coach as they rode past."

"It wasn't some orchestrated connection, Father," Matthias said impatiently. "We ran into her as she said, and escorted her to the castle." He gave his father a challenging look. "Since you're the one who instructed her to return with evidence, I *assumed* you would wish to receive it immediately."

"Indeed I would," said the king promptly. He turned back to Jacinta but paused as a quiet clucking issued from the chair which Jacinta had just vacated. "Is that...a chicken?"

"Yes, Your Majesty," said Jacinta quickly, turning and retrieving the bird.

"You brought a chicken into our castle?" Queen Bronte asked blankly.

"I did, Your Majesty." Jacinta held the bird out. "This is my evidence."

For a long and painful moment, both monarchs stared at Barbarity.

"A...chicken?" the queen said faintly.

Jacinta nodded. "I know it seems absurd. But she's definitely been affected by magic. She—hey!" She broke off to scold the chicken, who'd just taken her by surprise with an abrupt bid for freedom. She dove after it. "Stop that, Barba—ra," she amended quickly, not wanting to make even more of a fool of herself in front of the king and queen.

"You named the chicken Barbara?" Mariella asked, grinning openly at Jacinta's struggle.

Jacinta glanced at Matthias, who was disguising a laugh as a cough. At least he didn't betray the even more ridiculous name she'd told him. Jacinta straightened, her cheeks flushed as she held the chicken out in front of her.

"Anyway," she said, flustered, "if you put her in the royal coop overnight, you'll see what I mean in the morning. She lays eggs of solid gold." With the words, she pulled a golden egg from her pocket and laid it on a table. "She laid this one this morning."

Matthias let out a whistle, moving in for a closer look. "Gold eggs? Well, I think we can all agree that isn't natural."

Jacinta nodded, watching as the queen picked up the egg and examined it.

"And I acquired her in Kjemper. From the same giant who sent the warning last time."

"So you claim," said the king, looking at the bird with distaste. In the background, the queen had sent a guard to summon a servant, who promptly arrived to take charge of Barbarity. "Restrain this chicken somewhere secure," the king ordered the servant. "The bird is not to be harmed. We wish to check her laying in the morning."

"Yes, Your Majesty," said the servant, admirably hiding her inevitable bafflement as she held her hands out to Jacinta.

"Oh, right." Jacinta lifted the bird, embarrassed by the trickle of sentiment she felt. "See you later, then, Barbarity," she murmured. "Look after yourself. Keep laying if you want to avoid the ax."

She looked up to see Matthias on the edge of losing his battle against his laughter, while Mariella mouthed to him, *Barbarity?*

Sending the two of them a dark look, Jacinta surrendered her fowl little friend.

"You claim this chicken is your evidence," the king addressed her. "Assuming the creature does what you say, how do we know it came from Kjemper?"

Jacinta hesitated, not having anticipated the question. "I...I don't know how to prove it," she said. "But where else would she have come from?"

"Wasn't your father a singer?" the king challenged.

Jacinta's face hardened, her tolerance for the king's open suspicions instantly lowering.

"My father was a singer," she confirmed. "And a good man." *Whose reputation you carelessly destroyed.* She added the last words silently, not bold or foolhardy enough to say them aloud. "But he certainly never experimented on chickens. If my mother and I had been keeping gold-laying hens all this time, our lives would have been very different, I can assure you."

Matthias stepped forward, frowning at his parents. But before he could say anything, Hagen cleared his throat, unexpectedly interjecting.

"If I may, Your Majesties." He bowed.

The king studied him in confusion. "And you are...?"

"Hagen, Father," said Mariella impatiently. "Remember?"

The king's face cleared. "Ah yes, the Frossian singer undertaking a royal apprenticeship with us. You have some information to contribute, Hagen?"

"I do, Your Majesty." Hagen dipped his head again. "I thought it might be of relevance that any kind of magical experimentation that changes the natural functions of an animal—indeed, of any living creature—is strictly prohibited by all the kingdoms. It was communicated very clearly at the Academy of Song in Sunniva, and I know your academy teaches the same. I believe that even the elves have prohibitions against it. The consequences are too unpredictable."

The king frowned. "So you consider it unlikely that the chicken was magically affected by a singer or an elf?"

"Highly unlikely, Your Majesty," Hagen said. "Because the area of study has always been forbidden, there has been no opportunity to develop it. I doubt a lone singer attempting it without assistance would have success."

"The giant did say that it was an illegal experiment by her husband," Jacinta interjected. "I don't think it's encouraged even in Kjemper." She paused. "Unless she just meant that it was illegal because he used magic for an unofficial purpose."

"Very well," said the king shortly. "Let us proceed as if the chicken did indeed come from Kjemper, and does indeed lay golden eggs. In that case, it is clear that King Herleif's speculation was correct. The giants must have some source of magic beyond the bare traces produced by the northern ground."

Jacinta noted that her discovery was now attributed to King Herleif, but made no comment.

"Where, then, are the rest of the eggs?"

The challenge in the king's voice told Jacinta there was something behind the question. She met his eye cautiously, unsure what he meant.

"The rest of the eggs?" she asked.

"Does the chicken lay daily?" pressed the king.

"Oh." She thought she understood, and she had to stop herself from squirming. "Yes, she does."

"And how long ago did you acquire this chicken?"

Jacinta drew in a breath. "About a week and a half ago."

"So where are the rest of the eggs the hen has laid in that time?"

"Well, I..." Jacinta found herself glancing at Hagen for help, and he nodded encouragingly. "I've spent them."

"As I suspected," said the king coldly. He exchanged a look with the queen, then pulled something from his robes. "We made inquiries into your claims since your last visit. One of our agents recovered this."

He laid an oversized golden coin onto the table next to the golden egg. It was clearly from Kjemper. Jacinta blinked at it, wondering what the big fuss was.

"You told us that the giant gave you one coin as part of her message," the king challenged. "Yet my agent informs me that this was bartered in the market in the next town over from Briarford, by a woman matching your mother's description."

"Did I say that the giant gave me only one?" Jacinta asked blankly.

"No, you didn't." Matthias was frowning at his father again. "I was present when she told her tale, Father. She didn't say anything like that."

"She allowed us to believe it, which amounts to the same thing," the king said impatiently. "Both with the coins and the golden eggs, she attempted to make her actions look disinterested, while all the time profiting from gold which was intended to be given to the crown. What more evidence do you need of my words, Matthias? Those without status will always have designs on those who possess it."

"I beg your pardon," said Jacinta, unable to be sensible and restrained any longer. Her words were icy with anger. "But I do not have designs on your family. I returned to Kjemper at your request, at great danger to myself. I left some of the eggs with my mother, to provide for her in my absence. The others I used to fund my travel to Vallen, which for someone in my position is a costly exercise. As for last time, it's true that the giant gave me three coins, and that I judged only one to be necessary to accompany the message. The rest were used to support myself and my mother, and to get me to Vallen on that occasion. If you will forgive my bluntness, Your Majesties, it seems you are unaware of the true state of things in the north. It is no exaggeration for me to say that for my mother and myself, those two coins were the difference between life and death."

"Jacinta." Matthias's voice was hoarse, but she couldn't bring herself to look at him. She drew an unsteady breath, her hands shaking in both anger and humiliation. The king had sent agents to verify her tale, and *that* was what they'd focused on?

"If you value my information, Your Majesty, you ought to be glad of it," she added, her words calmer but her voice still hard as steel. "I doubt I would have taken the risk of going through the tunnel in the first place if my life hadn't been in such desperate straits. I felt I had nothing to lose. And although I did use the gold acquired in my unplanned trips in Kjemper for my own support, I didn't intend any deceit in doing so. I would most certainly not have been able to bring you the evidence without those funds."

For a pained moment there was silence, even the king seeming unsure what to say in response to her impassioned words.

"You will be reimbursed for your trouble," he said at last.

"Thank you, Your Majesty, but given the change in circumstances, that's not necessary," said Jacinta stiffly. "If you are satisfied as to my account regarding the chicken, I have further testimony regarding my time in Kjemper." When the king nodded for her to continue, she gave a comprehensive account of what she'd witnessed at the mining tower.

"It certainly sounds like they're mining magic," Queen Bronte commented.

Hagen nodded, his expression very thoughtful, but it was Matthias who spoke. The prince's voice was muted.

"Jacinta's account matches the conclusions King Herleif drew during our discussions. The question remains as to where the magic is coming from, given the whole northern region is barren of it."

"That question I'm afraid I cannot answer," Jacinta said.

"No one expects you to," Matthias assured her gently. "You've provided an incredible amount of information and, as you said, you've done so at your own risk. We're very grateful to you."

The king cleared his throat, apparently not eager for the conversation to continue. "Indeed. Where are you staying? It would be best for you to delay your departure until tomorrow, to allow us to examine what the chicken lays."

"I haven't yet secured accommodation," admitted Jacinta.

"She's staying here, of course," said Mariella fiercely. "She's attended the capital on your own errand, Father. There can surely be no difficulty about accommodating her in the castle."

The king and queen both tensed, clearly unhappy with the suggestion. But Matthias hastened to support his sister.

"It is by far the most sensible solution," he agreed. "I'll arrange for a room to be prepared at once."

Not giving his parents time to disagree, he strode from the room. To call the mood of those remaining awkward would be an understatement. The king and queen were looking anywhere but at Jacinta, and she found herself longing for Barbarity back, just so she had something to do with her hands.

"We will discuss the matter more tomorrow, then," the king said at last. With a nod at his wife, he left the room, the guards moving with him.

When only Mariella and Hagen remained with her, Jacinta let out a long breath. "Well. I'm glad to have that behind me."

"You did very well," said Hagen encouragingly. "It's not easy speaking to royalty, especially about personal matters."

"And especially if they're so blatantly inclined to be disagreeable," said Mariella with a scowl. Her expression softened as she met Jacinta's eye. "You did do well, though. Jacinta, I'm so sorry for what you've been through. I suspected times had been hard for you and your mother, but it seems it was even worse than I feared."

Jacinta shrugged, not eager to discuss it. "We manage."

"Let me take you to your room," said Mariella. "I know what part of the castle it will be in. You'll join us for dinner, of course."

"I don't think that's a good idea," Jacinta said quickly.

"Of course it is."

Mariella's expression was mulish, and Jacinta's alarm grew. How did she make her friend understand that in pushing her parents to include Jacinta where she wasn't welcome, Jacinta would be the one to suffer?

Fortunately, she didn't have to, Hagen coming to her rescue instead.

"I'm sure you're weary after your travels, Jacinta," the singer said kindly. "I eat early with a group of others undertaking various apprenticeships in the castle. You'd be very welcome to join me as my guest."

"Thank you," said Jacinta, relief flooding her. "I would be glad to."

She looked pleadingly at Mariella, who didn't seem happy with this development.

"I don't mean offense," Jacinta said.

Mariella's smile was swift although unconvincing. "Of course not. Come on, I'll get you settled."

With a final grateful smile at Hagen, Jacinta followed the princess into the corridor.

CHAPTER FOURTEEN

Matthias

Matthias strode blindly down the hallway, hardly aware of his surroundings. He couldn't remember the last time he'd been so distressed. Leaving the room had been his only option. Otherwise he might give in to his instinct to pull Jacinta into his arms and protect her from the world, and something told him that would create some problems with his parents.

And possibly with Jacinta.

Two gold coins the difference between life and death? *Jacinta's* life and death? The thought was unendurable. And instead of having compassion for the suffering of their own people, his parents had hurled accusations at her, as if she was a thief.

Matthias ground his teeth together. He'd never felt so angry at his parents in his life. If they tried to turn her out of the castle, they would find that he'd reached his limit. He would fight for her if that was what it took.

Emerging from his haze of distress for long enough to remember his errand, he instructed a servant to request the housekeeper to prepare a room in the wing of the castle used for wealthy and titled guests. He almost hoped his parents would challenge him on the choice of location. He was spoiling for a fight.

Recognizing the state of his mind, he made for the training yard. He could think of no other way to burn off his anger. The group of noblemen's daughters who seemed so often to hang hopefully about the area tried to catch his eye, but he ignored them completely. His heart was in too much turmoil to have the patience for politeness.

"Your Highness." The captain on duty greeted him with a bow. "How can I help you today?"

"I need a hard fight," Matthias said shortly. "Someone who won't let me stop to think."

The senior guard eyed him shrewdly. "I have just the candidate."

He called over a burly soldier, who looked very ready to take on the challenge. After a brief warm up, Matthias had the satisfaction of losing himself to the rhythm of the fight, his mind blank as his body responded out of instinct to the constant attacks. Fueled by his restless energy, he gave a good account of himself, letting up after half an hour with the compliments of his opponent.

As soon as the fight ceased, Matthias's mind flew straight back to Jacinta's situation. He was tempted to seek another bout, but it was almost the dinner hour, and he needed time to clean himself up. He assumed that Mariella would have orchestrated for Jacinta to join the family at the meal, and he didn't want to present himself to her sweaty and disheveled.

Having completed a quick wash, he made his way to the family's private dining hall, only to be redirected to the dining hall they used when they had guests. Heartened by this unexpected sign of respect for Jacinta, he hurried that way, straightening his sword belt.

When he entered the dining hall, however, there was no sign

of Jacinta. His father was seated at one end of the large table, with his mother at the other. On his father's left sat a stony-faced Mariella, beside a middle-aged couple. And across from the princess, a young woman Matthias recognized all too well.

"Matthias." The queen smiled welcomingly at him. "There you are. We'd almost despaired of you."

"I didn't realize I was keeping so many waiting," said Matthias, with the barest layer of courtesy.

"Yes, isn't it delightful?" Queen Bronte said serenely. "The duke has just returned from a visit to his northern holdings, and he and Her Grace have honored us with their company to tell us about the state of affairs in the north." She smiled innocently at him. "And their daughter, of course. You know Lady Letitia, Matthias."

"I do."

Matthias was unable to muster any enthusiasm, but he did his best to send her a polite smile. To his irritation, he realized that she'd been strategically placed next to his empty chair. He walked across the room, taking his seat across from Mariella with stiff movements.

"We're delighted you and your family could join us, Your Grace," the king said to the duke, as servants appeared with the first course.

"As are we, Your Majesty." The duke looked well pleased, his gaze passing to his daughter.

"Indeed," Lady Letty said on cue. "We are most honored."

Matthias felt his jaw twitch, and his eyes found his sister's. *Where's Jacinta?* he mouthed.

Mariella's face reflected his own irritation. "Eating with the apprentices. As Hagen's guest." She didn't look any more pleased about it than Matthias felt.

"What's that, my dear?" the queen asked, a definite warning in her tone.
in her tone.

"Nothing, Mother," said Mariella, picking at her food.

She didn't try to engage Lady Letty in conversation, a fact Matthias couldn't help feeling aggrieved about. They were a similar age, after all, and had moved in the same circles all their lives. His sister could at least try to rescue him. But she clearly had troubles of her own on her mind.

The meal passed at a glacial pace, Matthias still too distressed to be good company. What were Jacinta and Hagen talking about? Was she feeling rejected, or glad to escape the royals? Honestly, given her reception by his parents, he couldn't blame her if she felt the latter.

"I'm not letting her slip away first thing," he said abruptly, his voice low as he directed the comment to Mariella. "Not this time."

"Neither am I," she assured him, ignoring the conversation going on between their father and the duke. "I'll be at her door at the crack of dawn if I have to."

Matthias nodded, appeased. It was probably better for her to do that than him, after all.

"In short, Your Majesty, I'm very well pleased with how I found my estate," the duke finished, his hand resting in satisfaction on his portly belly.

"I'm delighted to hear it, Your Grace," the king said, taking a sip of his wine. "You weren't troubled by the tremors we've been hearing about?"

The duke shrugged. "We did feel a few during our visit. But they were minor, and not disruptive that I could see."

"How far north do your holdings go, Your Grace?" Mariella asked blandly.

"A bit more than halfway between the capital and Battlement Wall," the duke said. "So, well to the north."

Matthias raised an eyebrow. "That's not as far north as I'd

supposed. It strikes me as concerning that the tremors are felt even there, even if they are minor."

"I don't think it need concern you, Your Highness," the duke told him indulgently. "I daresay they're no stronger up near the wall than they are on my land. You know what northern folk are like. Rustics, most of them, unable to resist spinning a yarn."

Mariella's face was like flint, and Matthias felt the same way. "Indeed?" he asked, with cold politeness. "That hasn't been my experience."

"Eh?" The duke squinted at him. "Your experience, Your Highness?"

"You forget, Father," said Lady Letty smoothly. She'd given up on her doomed efforts to catch Matthias's attention, and had joined the general conversation. "The royal family used to spend a month in Briarford each summer." She gave the prince a dazzling smile. "And were sorely missed in Vallen during their absence."

"Ah yes, you're quite right, Letty," said the duke. "I'd forgotten." He shook his head. "If you'll forgive me for saying so, Your Highness, childhood memories are always rosier than the truth. Likely you don't remember just how primitively the northerners live."

"Well said," Queen Bronte agreed. "It's natural to remember childhood with more fondness than events deserve, I think."

"If the northerners live primitively, isn't it evidence of the poverty and desperation you claim is absent from the northern lands?" Mariella asked blandly.

"Mariella." The queen's voice was reproving, but the duke didn't seem troubled.

"Not at all, Princess, although your concern is natural. I shouldn't have brought up these unpleasant topics in such delicate company." He nodded at his daughter. "My Letty is the same. She doesn't like to speak of the suffering of those less fortunate. She has a great deal of sensibility, you understand, and it distresses her."

Lady Letty nodded sagely, apparently either unaware or unconcerned by the dark look the princess was giving her.

"Indeed?"

Matthias would have liked to applaud the perfect frosty politeness with which his sister uttered the words. Instead, he contented himself with shifting ever so slightly in his chair to put more distance between himself and the duke's daughter.

"Oh yes," said Lady Letty. "It's not a pleasant topic for anyone, is it? Suffering and misery. But Father assures me it's no such thing. Most of those who claim destitution exaggerate in order to take advantage of those of us with tender hearts."

"Tender hearts," Mariella said, still speaking in the same expressionless tone. "Yes."

"Quite right." The duke nodded. "As I said, I've just spent a substantial visit in the north. I have a singer on staff, and he claims that magic is less plentiful than it used to be, but there's still more than enough for him to perform his usual functions. And the land is perfectly arable. I see no cause for concern."

"Your holdings aren't in the true north, though, Your Grace," said Matthias, irked to see his father nodding his agreement of these claims. "I believe the situation near the wall has truly deteriorated in recent years."

"Perhaps so, Your Highness." The duke remained imperturbable. "But if we're speaking of the area immediately south of Battlement Wall, it's a small region which never had much to recommend it. Anyone who *chooses* to live in the wall's shadow brings hardship on themselves, surely."

Anger boiled up in Matthias, all the hotter for its impotence. There was nothing he could do to fight this willful denial of the plight of people like Jacinta. At least not at this dinner. When he was king, perhaps. But that felt so distant as to be meaningless.

And even then, he didn't know how he'd fix it. He couldn't keep providing coins to every northerner, like he'd done for Jacinta. How could he show those of his people who loved their northern home that the crown saw their hardship and cared about them? If only he could find some way to combat the growing barrenness of the region, as King Ryker of Teren had found a strategy to help alleviate the dangerously rapid growth of magic in the Forest of Ilgal. There must be an opposite solution for their troubles.

The meal was a nightmare that seemed like it would never end, but eventually they were released. Disregarding politeness, Matthias declined his mother's suggestion that he take Lady Letitia for a walk through the castle gardens, claiming exhaustion after his travels. He took his leave of the guests, ignoring the disgruntled look on Lady Letty's face. Mariella followed his lead, hurrying to join him as he slipped into the corridor.

"I'm going to find Jacinta," she said. Her clipped tone communicated her feelings about the interview they'd just endured, without the need for words.

"We can go together," said Matthias.

The siblings hurried along the corridor, Mariella taking the lead. Apparently she knew where the apprentices ate, which Matthias had to admit he didn't. Their arrival caused all the apprentices to rise hastily to their feet, conversation dying down immediately.

"I'm sorry to interrupt your meal," said Mariella lightly. "We're looking for Hagen."

"He just left, Your Highnesses," said a young female apprentice. "But I believe he's coming back."

Mariella frowned in confusion, but before she could ask more, a firm tread in the corridor made them both turn.

"Hagen!" Mariella moved to meet the Frossian as he approached. "Where did you go? Where's Jacinta?"

"I've just seen her to her room, Princess Mariella." Hagen looked surprised as his eyes flicked between the two royals. "Is all well?"

"Not really." Matthias scowled. "Why did Jacinta retire so early?"

"Well, I shouldn't speak for her..." Hagen started. Seeing their faces, he added, "I believe she was overwhelmed, Prince Matthias. All of this," he gestured at the castle around them, "is a lot for someone in her position."

"You seem to understand her very well," said Mariella, the words coming out suspicious.

"We have enough in common for me to empathize with her," Hagen said. He still looked uncertain as he studied the princess's face. "Have I erred in some way?"

Matthias let out a breath. "Of course not," he said quietly. "Thank you for looking out for her when we were prevented from doing so."

"It was my pleasure." Hagen inclined his head.

Seems like it. Matthias managed to stop himself from uttering the ungenerous words aloud.

"She won't be asleep yet," said Mariella suddenly. "I'm going to go see her."

She hurried off down the corridor. Matthias wished he had the freedom to do the same, but he knew it wasn't possible in his case. He would have to wait until morning. At least he could trust his sister to make sure Jacinta didn't slip off.

He didn't blame Mariella for being upset. She hadn't been present to see the way their parents had received Jacinta on her previous visit. Although Matthias had told her about it, it would be different seeing it for herself.

"It can't have been an easy day for Jacinta." Hagen's hesitant voice broke into Matthias's thoughts.

"Yes," he said curtly. "I know."

Hagen cleared his throat, and Matthias glanced at him, trying to curb his irritation. None of this was the singer's fault.

"If you have something to say, you can speak freely, Hagen."

Hagen nodded, but it was still another long moment before he spoke.

"You've traveled to the Frossian royal castle in my company, Prince Matthias," he said, surprising Matthias with the direction of the conversation. "So you've seen the relationship I have with King Herleif." He took a moment to gather his thoughts. "I mean this with no malice whatsoever. I have a very high regard for my king, both as a ruler and as a man. But at times I have reflected that the kindness and attention he shows me is for his own benefit rather than mine. Not that he would intend it that way," he added quickly. "He truly acts from a generous heart. But while it may provide a balm to his own feelings, well..." He shrugged. "You say I can speak freely, so I'll do so. You witnessed yourself the discomfort I feel over the unearned recognition."

Matthias frowned, not pretending to misunderstand his friend. "You think I should leave Jacinta alone? That trying to elevate her in my parents' eyes might make me feel good, but will only do her harm?"

"I didn't say that, Prince Matthias," said Hagen calmly. "It merely occurred to me that given my own experiences, I may have a unique perspective to offer."

And, inclining his head once more in a gesture of respect, he turned and strode into the apprentices' dining hall, leaving Matthias to his less than pleasant thoughts.

CHAPTER FIFTEEN

Jacinta

Jacinta woke with the dawn, her first sensation one of luxurious comfort. When had her bed ever felt like this?

"Oh good, you're awake!"

The cheerful voice brought Jacinta's eyes snapping open. She sat up to see Mariella perched on a chest at the end of her bed, apparently having been watching Jacinta sleep.

"Mariella!" she squeaked. "That's terrifying. How long have you been there?"

"Oh, I don't know," Mariella said, hopping up and moving to the curtains. "Half an hour, maybe?" She pulled the curtains back, causing weak light to filter into the room. "It seems I was right to think I'd need to come hideously early."

"But why?" Jacinta demanded, pulling the covers self-consciously around her. "Why are you watching me sleep like a crazy person?"

"That's no way to speak to a princess," said Mariella, turning back to her with a grin. "And you know why. So you couldn't sneak off while I slept."

"I'm not at liberty to sneak off," Jacinta informed her

through a yawn. "I'm supposed to wait for Barbarity to lay an egg, remember?"

"Jacinta, *why* have you named that chicken Barbarity?" Mariella watched her friend sliding her legs around to get out of the large bed and pointed. "There are slippers laid out for you, look."

Jacinta was taken aback at the discovery, but she slipped her feet into them nonetheless. "It's just a little joke with the elf who got me into this whole mess. She renamed Princess *Ferocity*, so I thought the chicken should have a name to match."

"If you say so." Mariella had drifted to a wardrobe and was rifling through it. "Without time to make new gowns, it was slim pickings among the gowns left at the castle by various guests over the years. Sadly you're too tall and elegant to fit into mine."

"Elegant?" Jacinta let out a snort that was anything but. "If you say so."

"I do." Mariella pulled out a vine green gown and held it up, squinting. "Yes, this will be a good color for you."

"I don't need to borrow a gown," said Jacinta quickly. "The one I was wearing yesterday will be fine."

"No, it won't," said Mariella uncompromisingly. "Impressions are important. Besides, I've sent it away to be washed, so you can't wear it anyway."

Jacinta let out a soft groan. "I'll feel foolish in borrowed finery."

Mariella didn't seem troubled by this information. "Maybe so, but you'll *look* fabulous. Come on, I'll help you get into it."

Jacinta frowned at the princess. "Surely this isn't part of a princess's role. Shouldn't servants be getting you dressed rather than you dressing the guests?"

"If you're saying you'd rather have a servant helping you than me, I'm deeply offended," Mariella scolded. "Now stop being difficult and come here."

Jacinta submitted meekly, unable to help laughing at the martial light in her friend's eye. "You haven't become any less ferocious with age," she informed the princess.

Mariella grinned. "Trust me, being fierce is a necessity in my station. You just have to find the right ways to hide it cleverly."

"It does seem like a lot of pressure."

Jacinta glanced around the opulent room as she pulled off her nightgown. It was more luxurious than she could have imagined prior to her arrival at the castle. Far larger and more grand than any room at the manor. And it was a guest room, not even the suite of a member of the royal family!

"Do you miss it?" she asked. "The carefree summers in Briarford?"

"More than you can possibly imagine," said Mariella fervently. "Matthias and I both begged our parents to continue the visits. For years we would try. But they wouldn't be moved."

She raised the gown meaningfully, and Jacinta allowed her friend to slip the garment over her head. She found herself unable to meet Mariella's eyes, guilt lancing through her.

"I'm sorry about that."

"What do you mean?" Mariella tugged the gown down, revealing her creased brow and questioning eyes. "Why are you sorry? It's not your fault."

Jacinta drew a deep breath. "It is, though. I didn't know it until recently, but my mother told me. The reason your parents stopped coming is because they disapproved of our friendship. And when they directed my parents to keep us separated, my parents weren't very cooperative."

"Is that how your mother said it?" Mariella asked, studying her friend thoughtfully. After a moment, she gave her head a little shake before kneeling to pull the gown into position. "I know about that," she said patiently. "And that certainly doesn't make it your fault."

Jacinta wasn't entirely convinced, but she didn't argue as Mariella laced up her gown.

"There." The princess looked her over in satisfaction. "You look much more presentable."

Considering her reflection in the looking glass, Jacinta had to agree. Her cheeks were still hollow, and her eyes tired, but she looked much more elegant than she had when she'd stumbled into the room the night before, with her hair a mess, in a ruffled gown that smelled of chicken feathers.

"I'll just brush your hair for you, then we can go and check on that chicken." Mariella advanced on her with a brush. "What time do they usually lay?"

"I can brush my own hair," Jacinta told her, pulling the brush from her friend's grip. "And it varies. But she usually lays early. I wouldn't be surprised if there's already a golden egg waiting. But I don't think we should go and check."

"Why not?" Mariella asked, watching as Jacinta tamed her hair with her eyes on her reflection.

"Because I don't want to be accused of planting the egg," Jacinta said. "It's best if we let someone official find it."

"Oh." Mariella frowned. "You're probably right." She peered out the window at the growing light. "Well, let's just go to breakfast, then. My family will be shocked to see me there." She grinned. "I'm not usually an early riser. Most days I have my breakfast brought to my room a couple of hours after my family have eaten."

Jacinta gave a polite smile, unsure how to answer this revelation. It sounded delightfully indulgent, and she supposed if she had the luxury, she'd do the same. But she didn't have the luxury. Most days her rumbling stomach woke her before the sun, and the labor of trying to secure food for the day began immediately. It made it hard to respond naturally to Mariella's confidence.

"I don't think I should join the royal family for breakfast," she said. "I can eat with the apprentices again. Hagen told me I'd be welcome."

"He did, did he?" Mariella's tone was no longer light. "Quite the blossoming friendship there, it seems."

Jacinta shrugged. "He was very kind yesterday. But of course I don't really know him."

Mariella nodded, her expression disapproving. Jacinta couldn't help feeling deflated. If even the apprentice singer was too exalted a person for Jacinta to befriend, what was she supposed to do with herself in the castle?

"You should definitely eat with my family," Mariella said firmly. "It will be convenient for you to be on hand when the report about the chicken is brought to my father."

Jacinta gave in, but her misgivings didn't decrease. She walked a step behind Mariella as they left the room and made their way down the cold stone corridors. Whatever the princess might want to believe regarding her old friend, Jacinta knew she wasn't welcome in the royal family's inner circle. And she wasn't an oblivious child anymore, who could remain unaware of any disapproval from the king and queen. She was an adult, fully alive to their feelings about her. Being pushed into their company could only bring her discomfort.

Jacinta's eyes wandered around her as they turned down another corridor. The tapestries hung along the passage were intricate and eye-catching, many beautiful colors giving life to the cold, stone hallway. One tapestry showed a field full of wheat stalks, another the stately mountain faces of Fross Mountains. Still another showed a grand city on a river. Vallen, no doubt. It was an ode to their kingdom, and she found it beautiful.

Beautiful and decadent.

Just like the stained glass on the nearest window, casting soft colors on the rich carpet that lined the floor. A decorative urn stood on a plinth in an alcove just past the window, and peering at it as she passed, Jacinta realized it was lined with gold.

She folded her hands nervously in her skirts, feeling faintly alarmed by the grandeur around her. What if she were to trip and damage a tapestry? Or knock over an urn? Any one of the items in reach was worth more than she could ever hope to repay.

"Here we are," Mariella said happily, unaware of Jacinta's inner turmoil. She pointed ahead to a door flanked by guards.

Jacinta patted her hair self-consciously, hoping that her nerves weren't too obvious. How would the king and queen react to her appearance?

"Good morning!" Mariella practically sang the words as she pushed the door open, obviously relishing her family's surprise at her appearance. "I've risen with the sun today."

"Mariella." Queen Bronte spoke mildly. "This is certainly a surprise." Her eyes slid past her daughter on the words, and she tensed slightly as she caught sight of Jacinta hovering behind the princess.

Jacinta half-expected to be scolded, but for a moment, the queen said nothing. Her eyes were very thoughtful as they passed over the newcomer's figure. It was all Jacinta could do not to fidget. Would the queen recognize the gown? Perhaps accuse her—yet again—of stealing?

The sound of a scraping chair brought Jacinta's eyes flying to the man sitting to the queen's right. Matthias's gaze was fixed on Jacinta as he stood abruptly, and she felt her cheeks heating. There was nothing critical in his expression that she could see. Apparently a fancy gown made everyone look at her differently.

"Jacinta!" Matthias strode around the table, his smile warm. "I'm so glad you could join us."

Jacinta cleared her throat. "Princess Mariella requested me

to accompany her," she said, her eyes flicking to the king. "But I don't wish to intrude."

King Fidelius gave his daughter a hard look, which Mariella didn't seem in the least intimidated by.

"Yes, I thought you would wish to have Jacinta close at hand when the chicken lays, Father. Since you wished to speak to her further when that happens."

"Mm." After a moment's consideration, the king inclined his head slightly in Jacinta's direction. "It is a worthwhile thought."

Matthias obviously considered that permission enough, because he laid a hand on Jacinta's elbow, steering her toward an empty seat right across from his own.

"Are you sure *you* aren't magical?" he asked Jacinta humorously. "Getting Mariella out of bed and to the breakfast table at this hour is quite a feat."

The princess stuck her tongue out at him as she sank into a seat next to Jacinta.

"Ooh, this is a much nicer spread than I usually have in my room," she said, her eyes eager as they examined the fare.

Jacinta's gaze followed the princess's, hunger gnawing at her stomach at the sight of so much food. Dazed, she took in the platters of fruit, the still-steaming bread rolls, the cooked eggs and sausages, and the tureen of porridge. Mariella was already ladling food onto her plate, but Jacinta couldn't seem to make her limbs move. Was this what the royal family had for breakfast every morning? All she could think of was her mother, waking alone in their hut so far away. What was she eating for breakfast this morning? An egg from the chickens, and some warm milk from the cow, if she was lucky. A lump rose in Jacinta's throat.

"Are you all right, Jacinta?"

Matthias's soft voice brought her back to her surroundings. She hadn't even noticed herself doing it, but she had her arms wrapped around her torso. She lowered them quickly, nodding as she reached for a bread roll. There was even a dish of butter.

"Did you sleep well?" Matthias asked in his friendly way.

Jacinta thought of the luxuriously soft mattress and the fire that had kept her room warm all night.

"Very well, thank you," she said politely. "After two nights on the road, it was a very welcome respite."

Matthias nodded, but no one else jumped in to aid the conversation. Not that Jacinta minded. She was more than happy to focus on her food. She contented herself with two bread rolls and a modest bowl of porridge, after which she felt more full than she could remember being in a long time.

She was just finishing her porridge when a servant entered the room and approached the king, her face flushed and excited.

"Your Majesty." The woman curtsied. "You wished to be informed as soon as the chicken laid an egg."

"Ah yes." King Fidelius fixed her with a stare. "And?"

"It did, Your Majesty. It laid an egg, but it's not any normal egg. It seems to be made of solid gold!"

Jacinta laid down her spoon, watching the king in antic-ipation.

"Thank you. Tell them to keep the chicken separated from the others." He dismissed the servant, waiting until the woman had left the room before turning to Jacinta. "Well."

"It seems you have your proof, Father," said Matthias. "I trust you're satisfied?"

"It is a sobering conclusion," the king said, his eyes still on Jacinta. "But it seems I must truly consider the possibility that the giants have magic."

"Just as King Herleif claimed," Matthias agreed. He bit his lip. "I've been thinking about it, Father, and this is even more concerning than what King Herleif witnessed. At least what he saw was in the castle in Kjemper. But the giant who gave Jacinta that chicken was no royalty. If even an average giant working in a remote outpost could access enough magic to pull off an experiment like this..."

He trailed off, and his father nodded heavily in response. "The same thought has occurred to me," he said. "And it's a troubling one." His gaze passed to Jacinta. "I will arrange for you to speak with my chief intelligence officer this morning. I wish you to describe to him in as much detail as you can remember everything you saw within Kjemper."

"Yes, Your Majesty," said Jacinta.

"I'll accompany her," said Matthias quickly. "I would like to hear the account myself."

"You've already heard the account, Matthias," said Queen Bronte. "And you're not at liberty to attend the meeting this morning. I've arranged for you to go riding with Lady Letitia."

Jacinta didn't know who Lady Letitia was, but judging by Matthias's reaction, this news wasn't welcome.

"What?" The prince turned to his mother in indignation. "What do you mean you've arranged it for me?"

There was no compromise in the queen's gaze. "If you hadn't run out of the meal last night too quickly for politeness, you would have been able to organize it for yourself, Matthias."

"Why does Matthias have to go riding with Lady Letty?" Mariella demanded, her eyes narrowed suspiciously.

"Lady Letitia is the prime candidate for his future wife, that's why," said Queen Bronte shortly.

For some reason, Matthias's eyes darted to Jacinta on these words. She felt her face heating, and lowered her gaze quickly to her empty bowl.

"Matthias marry Lady Letty?" Mariella gasped, her horrified tone so exaggerated as to be comical. "Mother, no! You can't reward her type of scheming tactics! She'd become even more insufferable."

"That is no way to speak of a lady, Mariella," said the king sharply. "This is not a matter for you."

"But surely you don't want to marry Lady Letty!" Mariella appealed to her brother.

"Of course I don't," he said gruffly. He turned to the queen. "Mother, can't I go riding with her another time? It seems too much to ask Jacinta to be interrogated by the chief intelligence officer without support."

"Certainly not," said the queen. "You will keep your engagements, Matthias. If Jacinta is afraid to be interviewed, it is for her to say so."

"I'm not in the least afraid, Your Majesty," said Jacinta, raising her head again. "Or in need of company. I am ready to speak with the officer at his convenience."

"Excellent," said the king. "I will send for him immediately. I'm sure you wish to return to your home."

"No." Mariella's voice held as much steel as either of her parents'. "She's not going home today. Jacinta is an old friend, Father, and we haven't had the chance to spend time together in years. Not to mention she has important information for the kingdom. It's not practical to send her off immediately only to perhaps have to call her back." Her face set in uncompromising lines. "I'm determined that she'll stay at least until the Autumn Gala."

The king and queen both looked far from pleased with this suggestion, but Matthias's face lit up at the idea.

"The Autumn Gala?" Jacinta repeated cautiously.

"It's a ball," said Mariella, turning to face her friend with dancing eyes. "People come from all over to attend it."

"Members of the court come from all over to attend it," corrected the queen.

"And you can come as my guest," Mariella continued blithely, choosing not to hear her mother. "It's always great fun."

"I...I don't feel it's my place," said Jacinta faintly, unable to help stealing a glance at the king and queen. They were exchanging a look, their expressions wary.

"Nonsense, of course it is." Matthias was beaming at her. "Like Mariella said, you're an old friend."

The king cleared his throat. "We can discuss that matter more at a later time. For now, I'll have a servant lead you to an interview room, and will summon the officer." He gave his son a pointed look. "And you have a ride to prepare for."

Matthias's face fell, but Jacinta didn't stay to hear any further argument. She rose hastily, following a servant from the room as indicated.

She'd been perfectly able to recognize that the king's main focus was getting her out of the room, so it didn't surprise her that she had an hour to wait before the intelligence officer came to find her. She'd expected an intimidating force, but the officer was relaxed and patient. He listened with great focus as she recounted every little detail she could remember about her strange adventures. It was actually a great relief to tell her story to someone who was listening closely, without prejudice or personal feelings affecting the matter.

When she was released, she made her way to the gardens, feeling the need for fresh air. She'd just done a lap around the fountain when she caught sight of a pale-haired figure striding toward her.

"Hagen." She waved at the singer, smiling in genuine pleasure at the sight of a friendly face.

"How are you, Jacinta?" The Frossian returned her smile, his gaze sympathetic. "Still standing? Haven't been knocked off your feet by it all?"

"Not yet," she said ruefully. "It's certainly overwhelming, isn't it?"

"It is," Hagen agreed. "But you do get used to it after a while."

"I'm not sure I'll be around long enough for that to happen," said Jacinta. She gave her head a little shake. "Although if Mariella has her way, I'll be around a little while yet. She wants me to stay for the Autumn Gala." She peered up at him. "Have you heard of it?"

Hagen nodded. "Oh yes. I've received an invite, earning me the envy and resentment of many. Most apprentices don't get that honor, but apprentices in songcraft have a different status. Too elevated to be considered servants, not titled like the court..."

"Existing in a strange in-between state," Jacinta finished for him. "That must be uncomfortable."

"It is at times," he acknowledged. He shot her a swift smile. "But I am looking forward to the gala."

Jacinta smiled vaguely, unable to say the same.

"I came looking for you because it's the lunch hour," Hagen went on. "Would you like to eat with the apprentices again?"

She nodded gratefully, happy to have a strategy to escape being dragged to the royal family's meal again. They'd barely made it halfway across the yard, however, when the prince's tall figure appeared at the nearest castle entrance.

"Jacinta!"

His eyes passed between the pair of them, his expression mirroring Mariella's earlier disapproval. It was disheartening that neither sibling seemed comfortable with her friendship with Hagen. Perhaps the singer sensed it, because he moved into the castle, leaving the two of them to their conversation.

"How was your ride?" she asked Matthias politely.

He grimaced. "Tedious. But thankfully it's over. Where are you off to? I came looking for you for lunch."

"Hagen's kindly offered for me to eat with the apprentices," said Jacinta. She could see he was going to protest, and she hurried to add, "It really is the simplest way, Matthias. It's kind of you and Mariella to want to treat me like we're still children and playmates, but your parents are obviously as uncomfortable about it now as they were then. Why put us all through the awkwardness?"

"Because to me, our friendship is worth it," said Matthias quietly. His eyes were so sad, she longed to lean up and smooth the crease from his brow. "Is it not worth it to you?"

Jacinta's heart twisted at his expression. Of course she was touched by his willingness to pursue their friendship. But it was based on impossibilities, and lies he was telling even himself. His instincts knew it, even if his heart refused to acknowledge it. Just as they had at her father's funeral, and in the years he declined to write like his sister was doing. It occurred to her that his excess of enthusiasm now might even be prompted by misguided guilt over those occasions. He hadn't been wrong to distance himself then, in order to protect himself from all the ways their friendship might cost him. Was she really expected not to protect herself now?

"You're asking too much of me, Matthias," she said, her voice coming out choked. "Please don't ask more of me than you'd be willing to pay yourself."

With the words, she swept past him, relieved to find Hagen still waiting. If only she could erase the look on Matthias's face from her mind.

The prince didn't seek her out for the rest of the day, and Jacinta told herself it was a good thing. Mariella came and found her in the afternoon, and the two spent a couple of hours in contented conversation. With the princess, it almost felt like they'd picked up where they left off. For some reason, it seemed to be impossible to achieve the same thing with the prince.

Somewhat to Jacinta's surprise, the king and queen didn't

insist that she leave the castle, or forbid her from attending the Autumn Gala. It seemed she was to be accommodated until then. Perhaps it helped her case that she continued to eat with Hagen and the apprentices, and didn't intrude on the royal family. She didn't see King Fidelius or Queen Bronte, so had only her speculation to suggest that they were happy with the arrangement. Matthias and Mariella, however, both showed the same disapproval anytime they sought Jacinta out only to find her in Hagen's company.

Jacinta did wonder uneasily if she should take their displeasure more seriously, but the Frossian singer's friendship was a lifesaver for her. Both Matthias and Mariella spent time with her where they could, but they had duties that occupied them much of the time. Especially Matthias. During much of the following days, Jacinta was at a loose end, painfully aware that she had no true justification for her presence in the castle. She gathered from comments made by Matthias that action was being taken regarding her evidence of magic in Kjemper, but she wasn't included in that process at all.

Of course, Hagen had responsibilities that occupied him as well. But during meal times and other rest times, he made himself available to help Jacinta navigate the unfamiliar world of the castle.

It was certainly a beautiful place. In some of her leisure hours, Jacinta wandered the corridors, admiring the splendor around her. Sometimes, she passed Matthias on these travels, striding down the corridor with purpose, usually flanked by guards. Whenever he caught sight of her, he'd stop to greet her, looking like he wished he could linger, but never doing so. As much as she appreciated the gesture, Jacinta wasn't trying to catch his eye. Her favorite encounters were when she managed to evade his notice, and could watch him unseen as he went about his business.

It didn't take much observation to see that he was capable, confident, and well-respected. And as much as it put him further out of her reach, it made her happy to see it. He'd grown so much since their childhood summers together. He'd grown into his role as crown prince, and she had no doubt he'd one day grow admirably into his role as king. She surprised herself with her desire to witness it, and her sorrow that she was unlikely to have the chance. He was certainly captivating to watch.

And she wasn't the only one who thought so. More than once, she observed other young women trailing him, these ones much better dressed and more polished than she was. Not that their behavior conveyed much grace. They were as silly as children when the prince was involved. Jacinta remembered Mariella teasing Matthias about the phenomenon during their last summer in Briarford. It was astounding to discover the behavior hadn't improved much in the eight years since. How in the world had the poor man endured it all these years?

The group had a definite ringleader whom Jacinta learned, both from her own observations and from conversations with Mariella, to recognize as Lady Letitia. The young noblewoman had a certain air about her, a kind of smug triumph. For some reason it made Jacinta feel ill to witness it. Like all the girls, she would simper and smile when the prince was present, but as soon as he was gone, her manner became much less appealing. Jacinta was inclined to agree with Mariella's view on the situation. It was hard to imagine Matthias being happy with a woman like that for his wife.

Not that it was any of Jacinta's business, of course.

On one occasion, the day before the much-anticipated gala, Jacinta was returning to her room after breakfast with the apprentices when the familiar group of young women passed by her. They had an air of great excitement, even more marked than their usual manner after an encounter with the prince. And after passing Jacinta, they hurried down a corridor she hadn't yet explored.

Curious, Jacinta redirected her steps, following them at a discreet distance. They turned into a walkway with open windows along it, the draft catching Jacinta by surprise. The group of girls clustered at one of the windows, giggling to one another. Peering over their heads as she walked past, Jacinta couldn't see what had their attention. The windows seemed to look onto a strip of garden, beyond which she could see stone pillars. The clang of metal sounded faintly from the other side of the plants, accompanied by the occasional shout.

More intrigued than ever, Jacinta stepped through an open doorway, following a path that wound through the garden strip. She emerged between the pillars she'd caught a glimpse of, and drew up short.

She was standing at the edge of a square, dirt yard, full of men either engaged in what appeared to be training drills, or undertaking fights in pairs. Many of them were shirtless, although most of those still fully clothed wore the uniform she'd come to recognize as that of the royal guard.

Before Jacinta could do more than come to an abrupt stop, a sudden cheer made her jump. She looked over to see one half of the closest pair of fighters disarming his opponent with a neat maneuver. The fight had attracted a number of observers, whose reaction suggested the favorite had won.

The disarmed man acknowledged his loss with a grin, and the victor turned, also smiling, to accept water from a squire. His lighthearted expression froze on his face as he caught sight of Jacinta, however, and she felt a similar paralysis creep over her.

Matthias.

"Jacinta?" The prince took several strides forward, stopping short when he was still some paces away. He didn't seem to know what to say, a sensation with which Jacinta could sympathize.

Without her permission, her gaze flicked quickly down to his bare chest, then back up. She'd thought many times since reconnecting with the prince that he'd changed a great deal since they were children.

She hadn't known the half of it.

Face burning, her gaze shifted to the group behind Matthias, all of whom were now watching her with expressions ranging from astonishment to hilarity. Then she glanced backward at the garden shielding the training yard from the view of the castle corridor, where the young noblewomen currently lurked.

"I'm not supposed to be here, am I?" Her voice was pained as she at last forced herself to meet Matthias's eyes.

To her surprise, he showed none of the embarrassment she felt. On the contrary, he seemed amused.

"Probably not," he said. "But Mariella does it shamelessly, so you're in good company. And it's a pity, because this is one of the most interesting places in the castle."

"It does look interesting," Jacinta agreed, casting another look over the various activities. "Is it the training yard for the royal guard?"

"That's right," said Matthias. The same squire who'd given him water materialized at his side, offering him a dry cloth. Matthias took it with a word of thanks, mopping his face. "You're not finding me at my best," he said, still sounding more tickled than bothered.

It occurred to Jacinta that he must be aware that he had nothing to be self-conscious about in displaying his muscled, athletic torso.

"Actually, you gave an excellent account of yourself in that fight," she said, trying not to watch—or show any hint of disappointment—as he donned his tunic. "That was a neat move."

"Thanks."

Matthias's grin resurfaced. He was practically bouncing on the balls of his feet at the compliment, his demeanor so reminiscent of his childhood self that Jacinta couldn't help smiling.

"Do you always win?" she asked innocently.

"Not always." His grin inched closer to a smirk. "But most of the time."

"Hm." Jacinta cast another look over the assembled guards, many of whom were built like bears, and all of whom showed evidence of extensive training in their movements. "Then I think they must be letting you win, because of you being a prince."

"Oi!" Matthias made a grab at her braid, in a move so familiar from their childhood antics that Jacinta instinctively dodged it. But the prince had remembered himself in time, withdrawing his hand before it could actually make contact. "You take that back," he said, more mildly.

Jacinta grinned at him. "I won't."

He narrowed his eyes. "Do I have to fight another duel to prove myself to you?"

Jacinta snorted. "Against me? That wouldn't prove much. I'm scrawnier than I used to be."

Matthias let out a shout of laughter. "No, not against you. I meant against one of the guards. You can pick whichever one you like."

She raised an eyebrow. "You're that confident you can beat any of them?"

"No." Matthias's smile was disarming. "But I'm confident I won't disgrace myself, and if I lose, all the better. You'll have to admit you were wrong."

She couldn't help laughing at that. "I'll pass. You really don't need to prove anything to me."

"If you say so." Matthias's gaze was suddenly a little too penetrating. "And I wouldn't describe you as scrawny, by the way."

Jacinta dropped her eyes, unable to hold his any longer. To her relief, when Matthias spoke again, his voice was more natural.

"What brings you here? Were you looking for me?"

"Don't overrate your importance, *Your Highness*," she told him crisply, secretly delighted to see him grin at the teasing. "I wandered in here by accident, it was nothing to do with you." She paused, glancing at the barely visible castle corridor. "Actually, now I think about it, you probably were the cause, weren't you? I didn't realize. I followed a group of very silly noblewomen, curious to see what had them all excited."

Matthias groaned, his eyes scanning the gardens as he shifted to be partially behind a pillar. "They are silly, aren't they?"

Jacinta nodded. "You should be used to it by now. Haven't they been doing this since you were twelve?"

Matthias grimaced. "No one would have been impressed watching me fight when I was twelve, I promise you."

"I know," said Jacinta, nodding sagely. "You were all arms and legs, and far too easy to sneak up on. I used to tell you that you wouldn't last five minutes in a fight with a *real* giant."

Matthias's laugh rang out again. "Your memory is much too sharp, Jacinta," he told her sternly.

Jacinta's smile became more strained, the words hanging between them. There was too much truth to the jest. Both of them had memories too accurate to allow them to discount everything that stood between them.

"Well, since I apparently shouldn't be here, I'd better take off before gossip spreads."

"I hate to tell you this, but gossip will have already spread by now," Matthias informed her. "But I wouldn't let it worry you."

Jacinta frowned. Easy for the prince to say. Did he really forget so easily how tenuous her position in the castle was? But maybe he was right, she told herself. One more day and she'd be leaving, without expectation of ever returning. What did it matter?

That thought made her want to do something more reckless than speaking with the prince in the training yard, but she restrained the impulse.

"You are staying for the Autumn Gala, aren't you?" Matthias's eyes were suddenly intent.

Jacinta smiled. "I don't think I have any choice in the matter. Mariella is very determined."

"Good." Matthias relaxed. "I hope to see you before then, but my schedule seems to suddenly be very full." He scowled, as if suspecting foul play in the change in his routine.

Jacinta wouldn't be at all surprised if the king and queen were trying to keep their son busy enough not to have time for the unwanted guest. Or Matthias was cautious enough to want to limit his time with her but didn't want to admit it. After all, from what she'd observed, the prince's duties hadn't been demanding enough to prevent him from taking regular rides with Lady Letty.

She banished the ungenerous thought, reassuring him with a smile. "No need to worry about me. I'll be well taken care of until tomorrow evening. And I'll see you at the gala."

With the words, she turned away and hurried back to the main part of the castle. She barely saw where she was going, too busy trying unsuccessfully to decipher the look in the prince's eyes as they'd parted.

CHAPTER SIXTEEN

Jacinta

Jacinta turned in front of the looking glass, trying not to let Mariella's hovering unnerve her as she took stock of herself.

"Well?" the princess demanded impatiently. "What do you think?"

"I think…" Jacinta ran a hand down the deep blue fabric of her full skirt, the top layer soft and sheer beneath her fingers. "I think I look like I'm playing the part of someone else."

She looked up, letting a grin escape at last.

"I like the part, though."

"Good." Mariella looked satisfied. "And you're not playing a part. This is you, Jacinta. You deserve all of it." She nodded decisively. "And it suits you."

"I don't know how you figure any of that," said Jacinta. "But I'm not arguing. Where did the dress come from again?" She examined one long sleeve, appreciating the warmth of the fitted garment. "Are you sure I'm allowed to wear it?"

"Of course you are," the princess said impatiently. "It's an old gown I had altered to fit you. You can consider it yours." She gave her friend another critical look. "The color suits you much better than it did me."

Jacinta turned back and forth, secretly thrilled with the way the full skirts swished around her. She agreed that it was a good color on her. But she couldn't get past the feeling that she was dressing up as someone else. The Princess Jacinta she'd played in her childhood games with the royals, perhaps.

Well, she thought recklessly, why not? Why not play a part for the night? Tomorrow she'd be on a public coach back to Briarford. She may as well make the most of the one gala she'd be likely to attend.

Mariella was very regretful about not being able to escort Jacinta to the ballroom, but Jacinta was happy not to enter in the conspicuous presence of the princess. She knew where to go and was content to make her way there alone at the appointed time.

When she entered the ballroom, she couldn't hold in a gasp of childish delight. The space was breathtaking, thousands of candles glinting from chandeliers and brackets along the walls. Tables laden with food lined one side of the huge space, and swathes of colorful fabric were draped down the walls. Jacinta quickly realized she'd been foolish to take the commencing time literally, however. Hardly anyone was there, and she felt awkward moving about the mostly empty space. She eyed the food longingly, but no one else was eating yet, so she didn't approach the tables.

Finding a corner to wait in, she watched as the room slowly filled. When half an hour had elapsed, the space seemed full of swishing skirts and cheerful chatter. The group of Matthias's admirers swept past her, Lady Letty giving her a measuring look.

"Who's she?" whispered one of the noblewoman's companions audibly.

"Haven't you seen her hanging about the castle?" Lady Letty didn't attempt to lower her own voice. "She's some country peasant who attended the castle with a message, and has been refusing to leave ever since. Very poor taste."

Jacinta felt her lip curl. Was she supposed to be cowed by these tactics? The noblewoman's pettiness exposed Lady Letty herself, not Jacinta.

"I heard she actually went into the training yard when the prince was training yesterday," said another girl. "My brother told me. She was *ogling* him when he was fighting. Made quite a scene."

This time the barbed words succeeded in bringing a flush to Jacinta's cheeks. She was painfully conscious of having erred on that occasion. The fact that the glances being thrown at her were more jealous than genuinely offended did nothing to soften her mortification.

Even if watching Matthias fight had been *almost* worth it.

"Poor dear," said Lady Letty with weakly disguised vindictiveness. "I daresay she didn't know any better, being a rustic."

Jacinta held her head high, pretending she couldn't hear the comments clearly aimed at her. Thankfully, she didn't have to endure any more. At that moment, a herald stepped onto the raised dais at one end of the ballroom, clearing his throat importantly before announcing the royal family.

Like everyone else, Jacinta watched with interest as the king, queen, prince, and princess entered the ballroom. They were all resplendent in their finery. Crowns of varying magnificence decorated each royal head, and Mariella's gown seemed to fill the room with its splendor.

But Jacinta's eyes were drawn to Matthias. An understated golden circlet glinted in his tawny hair, giving him an especially dignified air. He wore a deep red doublet with golden lacing, the chest decorated with a number of military honors that meant nothing to her. His breeches were mostly covered by almost knee-high black boots that gleamed in the candlelight. And across his chest he wore a sash of the same deep blue as her gown.

As Jacinta watched, Matthias scanned the room. His eyes skated over the nearby group of noblewomen, who were excitedly discussing his appearance, and landed on Jacinta. She felt her heart pick up speed as the prince's face lit up in recognition. Was she the one he'd been searching the room for? She couldn't help a surge of satisfaction at the disgruntled way Lady Letty cleared her throat, even if she was a little ashamed by the smug edge to it.

Into the hush that had fallen over the room at the royals' arrival, the king spoke words of welcome that Jacinta barely heard. They seemed to be the signal for people to start eating food, however, and there was instant movement toward the tables once the king stopped speaking.

Jacinta didn't join it. Her eyes were locked on Matthias, who was still watching her with flattering focus. Her breath caught in her throat as he strode across the room, making straight for her.

"Jacinta," he said, when he stood right in front of her. His eyes flicked over her gown. "You look...beautiful."

The simple praise brought another flush to Jacinta's cheeks, this one much more pleasant.

"So do you," she said breathlessly.

A swift smile of amusement lit Matthias's face, making it easy to ignore the derisive sounds from the nearby group at her bumbling words. It helped that the prince didn't seem to even notice the young noblewomen.

"Thank you," Matthias said somberly. "I must say, I'm not told that nearly often enough. Mariella gets told she's beautiful all the time—you can't imagine how left out I feel."

Jacinta laughed, punching him lightly on the arm in a

playful move that drew a collective gasp from their little audience.

"You know what I meant," she said, pulling her hand back quickly. "You look very," she waved a hand vaguely, "fancy." Feeling suddenly reckless, she added, "And handsome."

Matthias's smile warmed at her last words, and he shifted slightly closer.

"That means a great deal coming from you," he said. "You've never been a flatterer. I don't think you have it in you."

Jacinta smiled. "Flattery isn't required in this case. You've grown into your role just as impressively as I always knew you would, Matthias."

His eyes searched hers as he tried to decipher these earnest words. Perhaps he'd caught the tiny hint of sadness in her voice. His behavior was that of her familiar Matthias, but his appearance was a stark reminder of how unapproachable he really was.

"The dancing is about to open," Matthias blurted out. He kept his expression impassive. "I'm under strict instructions from my mother regarding the opening dance. But will you save one for me afterward?"

Jacinta blinked in surprise. "That's kind of you to ask," she said carefully.

"I'm not being kind," said Matthias bluntly. "I'm asking you to dance because I want to dance with you."

Jacinta bit her lip. "Matthias, I don't know how to dance. All I know are the simple country dances we used to do as children."

He studied her face for another moment before his own features creased in a smile. "I'll take that as a yes."

Before she could respond, he'd swept away, striding to the group clustered nearby.

"Lady Letitia," he said formally, holding out his arm. "Would you do me the honor of the first dance?"

Lady Letty batted her eyelashes in a way Jacinta found nauseating. She took the prince's arm with every appearance of bashfulness, although she wasn't above throwing a gloating look back at Jacinta as the prince led her away. Jacinta just shook her head. She would have thought the noblewoman would be humiliated rather than triumphant to learn that the prince was dancing with her solely out of obligation. But she had no idea how the social struggles of the elite worked. Perhaps obligation was enough to satisfy the titled girl.

Not wishing to witness their interactions, Jacinta's eyes scanned the room. She saw the queen watching her and let her eyes skate quickly past. The monarch's expression hadn't been what she'd call friendly. Mariella's magnificent gown drew her eyes next. The princess was standing with Hagen, her posture communicating impatient expectation to Jacinta's eye.

As she watched, the princess said something to the singer, who smiled mechanically and gave a short response. Mariella still seemed to be waiting for something, but a moment later, an impeccably arrayed man approached her, and bowed over her hand.

Her shoulders slumping in defeat, Mariella accepted the offered dance, throwing a disgruntled glance over her shoulder at the Frossian as she did so.

Intrigued, Jacinta moved closer, edging around the room until she stood by Hagen's side.

"Good evening."

He turned, smiling when he saw her. "Jacinta! Good evening. I didn't notice you here."

"I came too early," she said. "I've been hanging back waiting for the excitement to start." She followed his gaze to where it now rested, back on Mariella. "Why didn't you ask Mariella to dance?"

"The princess?" Hagen's tone of surprise would make anyone think he'd gone weeks without seeing Mariella, rather than speaking with her moments before. "I couldn't ask her to dance. It would be incredibly presumptuous of me."

Jacinta considered his words. She could see his point, but she wasn't satisfied. "Did *she* ask *you*?"

Hagen looked even more startled. "Of course not."

"Hm." Jacinta's eyes found Mariella and her partner among the dancers, noting the elegance with which the pair moved across the floor. "Yes she did. Take my word for it."

Hagen looked bewildered, but he didn't argue. He didn't seem inclined to pursue the conversation at all.

"How about you?" he asked, after a minute's silence. His voice had reverted to its usual kind tone. "Would you like to dance?"

Jacinta smiled. "Thank you for the offer, but I don't know how to do this dance."

"It's easier than it looks," Hagen said. "We learned it at the academy. If you follow my lead, we can make a passable effort."

Jacinta looked at him uncertainly, then gave a reckless grin. "Oh, all right. Why not?" She had nothing to lose with Hagen, after all.

Taking her by the hand, Hagen led her to the edge of the mass of moving people. They chose a spot near the back corner of the room, far from the royals' graceful maneuvering. Laughing and stumbling, they did their best to move through the steps, Jacinta surprising herself by how much she enjoyed it. Hagen's hand was cool and steady in hers as he guided her, and his light good humor kept her from taking herself too seriously. She felt a surge of gratitude toward the singer. He'd been a good friend to her. Safe and predictable. Nothing felt too risky with him. The stakes were low, and that was just the refreshing influence she needed in the quagmire that was the castle.

"Thank you," she said, when the music paused and couples moved off the floor. "That wasn't so bad."

Hagen chuckled. "High praise. Come on. Let's get some food."

Nodding, Jacinta followed him to the nearest table, helping herself to a glass of something cool and sweet. Dancing was surprisingly tiring.

She'd barely taken a bite of her food when a tall figure appeared in front of her. Matthias held himself tensely compared to their last conversation, his expression wearing the disapproval that had made her uncomfortable on other occasions.

"Jacinta, I thought you said you didn't know that dance."

"I don't." Jacinta grinned at Hagen. "But Hagen helped me muddle my way through."

"Hm." The prince turned to the singer. "Very considerate of you. You may wish to be mindful of the impression you give, however."

Jacinta felt her face flush at this reference to her standing. Hagen was following the prince's pointed gaze to someone across the room, but Jacinta didn't look to see who was judging them.

"Yes, Your Highness." The Frossian was stiff now, not meeting Jacinta's eye.

"Can you spare a dance for me as well?"

It took Jacinta a moment to realize Matthias was speaking to her. She placed her food back on the table, her hands suddenly shaking.

"Are you sure it's the best idea?" she asked, unable to keep an edge from her voice. After all, if it would hurt Hagen's reputation to dance with her, wouldn't it hurt the prince's more?

"Yes, I am," said Matthias, apparently unperturbed. "In fact, it's the best idea I've had all night." He held his hand out.

Jacinta was eyeing it uncertainly when the music started up, and all her wariness fell away. "I remember this song!" she cried. "Mariella used to bully one of her minders to play it, and we'd romp to it around the manor."

A smile bloomed on Matthias's face, banishing the imperious manner of earlier. "I requested it specifically. Now let's see if you still remember the steps."

"Of course I do," said Jacinta indignantly. "It's you who'll have to keep up with me."

"I don't doubt it," grinned Matthias, his hand closing over hers.

It didn't feel at all like Hagen's. It was warm, its grip as strong as his draw was undeniable. Jacinta felt vividly aware of the contact, her fingers tingling under his. She surrendered herself to the feeling, letting him pull her out into the group of dancers already lining up. She could see bewilderment on some faces, and guessed that country dances like this one didn't usually get played at formal balls in the castle. But it didn't dampen her excitement. It only made Matthias's gesture more meaningful.

Her skirts swished around her as she and Matthias lined up. She knew the smallest pang of sadness that this wasn't one of the dances where he would be holding her close the whole time, but immediately told herself off for the foolish thought. She didn't know those dances, and while she could muddle her way through with Hagen, too many eyes would be on the prince and his partner. Including those of the monarchs. A lively country dance was much less dangerous.

The next moment she was swept away by the music, and all other considerations were lost in the joy of the movements, and the happy memories they evoked. She passed Mariella in the line, looking as bright and delighted as she felt, and her heart swelled. She'd tried to tell herself she didn't care that the friendship had faded, but she couldn't deny the joy she felt in knowing that all they'd shared wasn't lost.

Then the dance brought her and Matthias back together, his warm hands on her waist and his dark, intense, blue eyes reminding her that some things couldn't just be picked up where they'd left off.

When the music ended, she stepped back at once, thanking Matthias for the dance without quite meeting his eyes. She tried to pull away, but Matthias held her hand for a moment longer than the dance required.

"I meant what I said before." His voice was soft and low, and Jacinta felt compelled to look into his eyes. They bored into hers with an intensity that made it hard to breathe. "You look beautiful."

"I feel like I'm playacting." The confession slipped out before she could stop it.

Matthias shook his head. "You're not playacting. You look very much yourself." A sudden smile quirked his lips. "You look like Princess Jacinta."

Her breath caught a little at this reference to their childhood game. The old joke felt much more loaded now, here, in this ballroom in his castle. With an effort, she forced herself to smile in return.

"You certainly don't look like my servant."

Someone claimed Matthias's attention at that moment, and Jacinta took the opportunity to slip away. She hurried into the throng, eager to find a quiet corner in which to compose herself. Snatching a goblet from the tray of a passing servant, she made her way around the edge of the room until she reached a large potted plant. From behind it, she could still watch the couples lining up for the next dance, but she needn't fear being disturbed.

She watched for some time from her vantage point, noting that no more country dances were played. Her eyes rarely left Matthias, who certainly didn't lack for partners. He seemed ill-at-ease though, his eyes regularly sweeping the room. Was she conceited to wonder if he was looking for her? Mariella was also in high demand, her true feelings about each of her partners impossible to read beneath the overly cheerful front she presented to them all. It looked exhausting.

Speaking of which, Jacinta was starting to flag, the rush of energy that had overtaken her when she danced with Matthias fading quickly. She wasn't used to events like this one, and she felt overwhelmed and out of place. She was just starting to wonder whether she could leave the ballroom, or whether it was rude to go so early, when an imperious voice caught her ears.

"The prince requested it, did he?"

Jacinta peered through the leaves of the plant, unease shooting through her as she realized that King Fidelius had drifted in front of where she hid. She didn't want to be caught eavesdropping, but she didn't see how she could leave without being seen. As she hovered, indecisive, the king gave a curt command.

"Tell the prince I wish to speak with him. Immediately."

Jacinta swallowed as a servant scurried off into the crowd. Another song had just finished, and Matthias was conspicuous in the middle of the dancers. The servant approached and bowed low. After a conversation Jacinta couldn't hear, the prince strode toward her position, his expression veiled.

"Is all well, Father?" His mild tone didn't deceive her. She held as motionless as possible, desperate not to be seen.

"Matthias, I understand that you've requested another country dance."

"Yes, Father." Matthias's voice was devoid of emotion. "I thought it would be a welcome change."

"You *thought*," his father corrected, "that you would make a spectacle of yourself again. But once in an evening is quite enough."

"Honestly, Father, all this fuss over a dance," said Matthias impatiently. "I doubt anyone even thought anything of it."

"You're mistaken," said the king shortly. "Your mother informs me the matter has been the subject of gossip for the entire evening. You made a fool of yourself and of Lady Letitia."

"Lady Letty has nothing to do with this," Matthias said, his voice becoming sharp for the first time. "I've made no promises there, Father. I did as I was told and opened the dancing with her. My obligations are met."

"Your obligations are only just beginning," the king said in irritation. "And you are not filling me with confidence that you understand them. This is not merely a role, Matthias. It is your life you must give in service to our kingdom. I don't care how fond your childhood memories of this girl are, it's time to let her go."

Jacinta barely dared to breathe, horror washing over her at the topic of the conversation she'd so unluckily become privy to. She was the one causing tension between Matthias and his parents. Her fist opened and closed nervously over her skirts. No doubt the king thought her scheming for Matthias's crown.

She wasn't the only one to be upset by the king's words. Matthias's voice was stiff and his frame taut as he replied.

"I disagree."

The prince wasn't looking at his father, his eyes fixed determinedly on a point over the king's shoulder. To Jacinta's alarm, Matthias's blank stare sharpened as his gaze obviously found its way through her shielding leaves. His mouth fell open in a moment of genuine horror before he snapped it shut and returned his gaze to his father.

"It's your ball, Father," he said. "If you don't like the music

I've requested, give your own orders to the musicians. They'll follow your instructions. Let's not make a scene in the middle of the ballroom."

"Very well." The king spoke tightly. "But we will discuss this matter further, Matthias."

"As you wish, Father." The prince's impatience seemed so obvious to Jacinta, she was nervous the king would figure out the cause. But a moment later, King Fidelius was striding away, and Jacinta let out a long breath.

"Jacinta." Matthias was staring through the plant, not approaching. "I...I don't know what to say."

She swallowed, checking that the king wasn't watching before sliding out of her alcove.

"There's no need to say anything, Matthias. I...I have to go."

"No." His hand shot out and took hold of her arm, his grip strong. "Please let me explain, Jacinta. Please don't be angry with me."

"There's nothing to explain," she said desperately, her emotions threatening to overwhelm her. "And I'm not angry with you."

"If you're not angry, then why do you keep running away?" Matthias demanded.

"To protect myself! And you!" The words burst out of Jacinta. "Matthias, why are you so determined not to see what's obvious? Friendship between us will only bring us both pain."

Matthias loosened his grip, his expression troubled. "I never wanted to cause you pain, Jacinta."

"I know," she told him, tears pricking her eyes. "I know you didn't. None of this is your fault. I admit, I used to feel bitter that you stopped coming to Briarford, and that you didn't come to my father's funeral, even though you came so close in order to escort Mariella." Matthias's face twisted, and she hurried on.

"But I always knew deep down that it wasn't reasonable to

feel bitterness. And now I can see that more clearly than ever. Matthias." She raised her eyes to his. "I didn't understand the pressures you face here, I can acknowledge that. But I also didn't comprehend the...the luxury of your life. It's a world away from mine. Even now, my mother is barely scraping by. How can I stay here and keep gorging myself on all this?" She waved a hand toward the closest food table. "I just don't know how to reconcile it."

Matthias's face was troubled, and for a moment he seemed unsure what to say.

"I'm sorry," he said. "I...I don't know how to reconcile it either."

"You have nothing to be sorry for," said Jacinta. "You haven't done anything except what a prince is supposed to do. But it's all just..." She raised her hands helplessly. "Too much for me." She shook her head. "Your parents are right. And my mother was right too, when she discouraged me from trying to keep contact. There are reasons why friendship between people of our classes isn't wise or practical."

"I don't believe that."

Matthias's answer was quick but not impulsive. She couldn't deny his earnestness. It sent a pang through her heart. More than anything, she wished things could be different, could be the way he seemed to believe they were. But they weren't, and she couldn't afford to risk her heart. He was still who he was, and she was...no one.

"I'm sorry, Matthias," she said frankly. "I never wanted to hurt you either, but even if you're determined to face the pain our friendship would bring, you have to give me the right to protect myself."

Again Matthias's answer was swift, his voice low and throbbing this time. "To me, you're worth the pain."

Jacinta's eyes pricked once more, a lump rising in her throat.

Unable to bear the look on his face, she turned away, hurrying toward the door. She was so distracted, she ran right into a full-skirted figure whose arms shot out to stop her progress.

"Jacinta! You're not really leaving?"

"Mariella." Jacinta winced at the look on her friend's face. "Did you hear all that?"

"I did." The princess's features crinkled with distress. "Jacinta, he's trying his best."

"I know he is," said Jacinta, unable to bear going through it all again. "I don't blame him, I just..."

"He didn't escort me to the funeral."

Jacinta blinked at Mariella's abrupt words. "What?"

"Matthias didn't come to the funeral with me. Our parents forbade him to go, and he snuck out and went anyway. I didn't even know he was there. He was risking more than you comprehend, and he did it because he wanted to be there for you."

"I..." Jacinta put a hand to her head, overwhelmed by it all. What was she supposed to do with that information? "I have to go, Mariella."

With a swish of her skirts, she brushed past her friend, refusing to look back toward Matthias as she went. The clock struck nine as she stumbled from the ballroom, and a sudden idea occurred to her. The overnight public coach would leave in half an hour. It would be tight—she wouldn't even have time to change—but she could make it. She'd only promised to stay as long as the Autumn Gala, and she'd done that now. There was nothing keeping her in the capital.

Longing rose up in her for the simplicity and familiarity of home, and she didn't give herself time to think about it. Practically running to her room, she threw her few belongings into her rucksack and bolted from the castle. She just had to hope that her fancy attire wouldn't make her a target for thieves on the long journey northward.

CHAPTER SEVENTEEN

Jacinta

Jacinta pushed her way through the door of her familiar hut, weary beyond words but relieved to be home. The journey had felt unending, and she'd had plenty of time to regret her hasty departure. She hadn't realized when grabbing her rucksack that some overly helpful servant had hung her own laundered gowns in the wardrobe along with her borrowed ones. She'd had nothing to change into, and had been forced to travel all the way back to Briarford in her ballgown.

Hopefully Mariella had meant it when she said Jacinta could consider the dress hers.

"Jacinta!" Her mother rose quickly from beside the fire, her eyes widening at the sight of her daughter's disheveled finery. "I didn't expect you back this evening!"

"I sort of ran away," Jacinta admitted miserably. "Mamma, it was just...all too much."

"Come here," her mother said, her voice gentler than usual. "Take my seat by the fire while you tell me about it. You must be freezing."

"I am."

Jacinta sank gladly into the chair, holding her hands out to the blaze. It had gotten colder the further north she went. It wasn't even winter yet, and there was already a light snow on the ground in Briarford. The capital had been so much warmer. A pang of guilt went through her at the wistful thought. Briarford was her home, she reminded herself. Not Vallen. No matter how pleasant and luxurious it might be.

She looked up to find her mother watching her expectantly. "Now what happened to bring you back like this? And where did you get that gown?"

Jacinta ran her hands down her sadly crumpled skirts. "Mariella gave it to me. She talked me into staying for the Autumn Gala. It was beautiful, Mamma. Like a fairy tale I'll never forget. But...it wasn't real. At least not for me. I got overwhelmed, and I left straight from the ball. I caught the overnight coach out of the capital."

Her mother tutted as she prepared her some tea, bustling about in a way that told Jacinta she was more concerned than she wanted to let on.

"Such impulsive reactions, Jacinta," she scolded. "It would have been much more sensible to wait for the morning."

"Yes, probably," Jacinta sighed. "But I just couldn't face another goodbye. And there was no reason I had to stay. I delivered my message—and the chicken—and I stayed for the gala like I promised Mariella. It was time for me to come home to you, Mamma."

Her mother's face softened a little as she handed Jacinta the steaming mug. "Well, I'm very glad to see you, of course. When you wrote to say you'd been invited to stay for a bit longer, I half expected that you'd never want to come home."

Jacinta made a noise of protest which the older woman waved off.

"I wouldn't have blamed you. It's natural enough."

Jacinta leaned back in the chair, closing her eyes. "None of it is natural, Mamma. It's a strange other world. And although the prince and princess were kind, plenty of others made it clear I didn't belong." She shifted into a more comfortable position. "Not that I needed anyone to tell me what I already knew."

Her mother was silent for a long moment, and Jacinta let out another sigh. It was as though a great emptiness yawned inside her, but it was a comforting emptiness, somehow. It was familiar, like the simple hut. She knew what was expected of her in Briarford, and more importantly, she was sensible enough to have no unrealistic expectations of life. That was the key difference. In Vallen, she'd felt like she was constantly fighting with the part of her threatening to develop foolish expectations. Here there was no risk of that.

"What about the giants?"

Already half-asleep, Jacinta forced her eyes open. "The giants? I don't know. King Fidelius wasn't exactly eager to share his plans with me. I don't think I'll be called upon to play any further role."

"Well, that's a relief," said her mother firmly. Taking charge of the situation, she coaxed Jacinta to eat some food, then chivvied her to bed.

Once again in the dubious comfort of a much harder bed than she'd slept in at the castle, Jacinta was only too happy to surrender to the oblivion of sleep.

When she woke, dawn had long since passed, but her mother was still in the hut. Jacinta yawned, pushing herself to a sitting position as she surveyed the small space.

"You're here, Mamma. What time is it?"

"I can afford to spend the morning here with you rather than looking for work in town," her mother assured her. "I want to hear more about what happened."

Jacinta shivered as she slipped her feet into her boots. The fire was lit, but the cold still crept in from the walls.

"There's not much to tell, Mamma."

"I don't believe that for a moment." Her mother's voice was dry. She searched Jacinta's face. "You said the prince and princess were kind?"

Jacinta's shoulders slumped as she shuffled closer to the fire. "They were. They wanted to believe that we could pick up where we left off, I think. But they were only fooling themselves." She paused. "If that."

"If that?" her mother pressed.

Jacinta sighed. "It's nothing. They truly were welcoming. But...they didn't exactly encourage me to mingle in their circles. One other person befriended me—an apprentice singer. And both the prince and princess disapproved of any friendship between us. They didn't say as much, but it was clear."

"Sounds like they saw you more as a plaything than a real person," her mother said darkly. "They didn't want to share."

Jacinta squirmed. The same thought had occurred to her, but she hated to think it of her old friends. "I don't know if that's true. I think it's more likely they could see from the outside the inappropriateness of the friendship, but couldn't see it from the inside, regarding our own connection." She gave a twisted smile. "But they can see it, really. At least, Matthias can." She hesitated. "I never told you this, Mamma...but he was here in Briarford the day of Pappa's funeral. I saw him at the manor. But he wouldn't come to the funeral."

She paused, thinking of what Mariella had told her about that day. It seemed Matthias had taken a great risk to be there at all. And yet...

"Ugh." She ran her hands through her hair in frustration. "I don't know what to think. Matthias seemed willing to defy his parents for me when I was in Vallen. But he wasn't willing to at the funeral. And he wasn't willing to all those years when Mariella wrote to me and he didn't." She groaned. "What am I saying, anyway? Why *should* he take a risk for me? I don't expect it."

She didn't add it aloud, but her confusion continued to swirl at the thought of how Matthias had acted and spoken in the capital. She might not expect it of him, but he seemed to expect it of himself. Which made his lack of contact over the last eight years all the more bewildering.

"Jacinta..."

Her mother's voice was reluctant, and Jacinta thought for sure the older woman would try to redirect her mind from any thought of friendship with the royal family. But when she looked up, fully prepared to assure her it was unnecessary, the look in her mother's eyes made her pause.

"What is it?"

Her mother bit her lip. "There's something I kept from you. I told myself it was for the best, but it's been eating away at me since you first went to Vallen. I'm surprised you didn't discover it while you were there. I promised myself I'd tell you when you came back."

"Tell me what?" Jacinta demanded, uneasy.

For an uncomfortable moment, her mother just looked at her. Then she stood, walking over to a cupboard and retrieving a sturdy little box Jacinta knew she used to store personal items. Jacinta watched in confusion as her mother took out a small bundle of letters.

"He did write, Jacinta. For the first couple of years the letters from the princess had sealed envelopes inside them. From what you've said, I'm guessing he had to hide his correspondence that way to prevent his parents forbidding it. But I...well, I didn't think it was wise for you to fill your head with dreams about a prince. I opened each of the letters before giving it to you, and took his out."

Jacinta just stared at her mother, too shocked to even feel anger at this revelation.

"I never read them," her mother assured her. "They're still sealed. I just didn't like the idea of him writing to you. Even the princess made me uncomfortable, but...less so."

Taking a deep breath, she held the bundle out to Jacinta.

"I'm sorry, Jacinta. I should have told you before now."

Jacinta took the letters with numb fingers, a horrible feeling of betrayal prickling at her. So all along, when she'd thought Matthias didn't bother to write, he'd thought she was just ignoring his letters? Why hadn't he said anything about them when she'd been in Vallen? Was that why he'd seemed at times so uncertain, so hesitant? That reaction was probably explained by her cold behavior, actually. Behavior that would have seemed entirely consistent with what he thought he knew.

"I can't believe you did this," she whispered, lifting one of the letters and turning it over in her hand. It was clearly addressed to her, in a firm, neat script nothing like Mariella's looping one. "I can't believe you lied to me."

"I didn't lie," her mother said quickly. "I just—"

"Mamma." Jacinta cut off the empty denial, her expression making it clear that she wasn't interested in hearing excuses.

Her mother fell silent, at least having the decency to look ashamed. "I'm sorry," she repeated.

Jacinta didn't answer, seizing a knife from the table and opening a letter at random.

Jacinta,

It's me again. I rode a new horse today, the wildest one I've ever saddled. She almost threw me! She's a spitfire, but I can already tell we're going to be firm friends. Father says that if I work on my horsemanship, I can take part in the military parade at the end of the season. Wouldn't that be amazing? I wish you could be here to see it. You'd probably laugh at me, riding among all those big, strong soldiers and thinking myself quite something. It would probably do me good. Everyone here is too afraid to tell me what they really think. I know it sounds like it would be nice, but it actually gets exhausting very quickly. Not like the way it is in Briarford.

Jacinta, I wish you would write back. Are you angry with me? I'm sorry we didn't come this summer. Mariella and I begged Mother and Father to bring us, but they refused. I haven't given up, though. I'm going to keep pestering them until they let us come and visit. Maybe next summer.

Please write back. I want to know how you are. I miss...well, everything. How it used to be.

She tore her eyes from the paper, unable to bear reading more. How many times had he begged her to reply? How many times had she seemed to callously ignore him while responding to his sister?

She knew she would be angry with her mother later, but she was still too hurt for the anger to make itself felt. Her own parents, just like Matthias's, had intervened in a friendship that had once been so precious to both of them. They'd taken it upon themselves to pick and choose which of the royal siblings she could be friends with, to add more barriers between her and Matthias, as though the ones that already existed weren't plenty to contend with.

Against her better judgment, she glanced back down at the page. *Please write back.* The words seared her eyes. *I miss...well, everything.* Tears blurred her vision, escaping her control and running down her cheeks.

"Jacinta, I'm sure you think I was terrible to do it, but this is why I didn't give you the letters," her mother said, a hint of pleading in her voice. "I didn't want you to cry over him. I wanted to protect you from feeling this pain. There's nothing for you in the royals' world. The king and queen made that very clear. Nothing but pain."

"That wasn't your choice to make." Jacinta's voice was hollow.

"You were only ten years old," her mother said defiantly. "It was my choice to make."

"I'm not ten years old now." Jacinta stood suddenly. "And I haven't been for a long time. You didn't protect me from pain, Mamma. You just chose what type of pain you wanted me to experience. And I maintain that it wasn't your choice."

She drew a breath.

"I don't want to fight with you. I need some space to clear my head."

Without another word, she strode from the hut, the letters still clutched in her hand. She spent the rest of the morning wandering the deserted land between their hut and the wall, reading over Matthias's letters, sometimes crying, sometimes too weary to feel much. By the time she returned home, her head was clearer. She'd expected her mother to be out, but she was waiting, and her expression told Jacinta she wasn't going to try to defend herself.

"I don't agree with what you did," Jacinta said abruptly. "But I still don't want to fight with you about it."

"I'm not fighting," her mother said quietly.

Jacinta nodded, taking a moment to collect herself. "Whatever my feelings about all of it, I've realized that it makes very little difference. I used to wish Matthias would write, but I never really held it against him that he didn't. The truth is, whether he did or not, it doesn't change the barriers between us. The biggest impact is that you made me appear fickle and petty in my silence. And although that stings, I can swallow my pride and deal with it."

"It was never my intention to make you look bad," said her mother.

Jacinta just shook her head, unable to face getting into it. The other thought, that she couldn't bring herself to say aloud, was that her silence had caused Matthias pain. Prior to her time in Vallen, she would have thought it presumptuous to think he would be hurt by her lack of response. But his manner while she was in the capital, and the contents of his letters, made it undeniable. Only, she couldn't throw that in her mother's face, because she couldn't bear speaking of it. Not yet. Maybe never.

"I've been thinking it all through," she went on, "and the long and the short of it is that it's all in the past, either way. It's time to put this whole chapter behind me. I've delivered my message and my evidence to the king, I've fulfilled any obligation to the elf or the giant or the crown. I need to look to my own future now."

"Very well." Her mother seemed subdued, but thankfully she didn't protest Jacinta's decree that they weren't going to speak further about it.

"I do have one question," Jacinta said. "Do you think I should destroy the beanstalk?"

Her mother frowned. "I'm not sure. It seems unwise to take an irrevocable step like that without consulting the king, or the elf, or somebody."

"Then I'll just leave it," said Jacinta firmly. "I'm certainly not traveling back to Vallen to consult with the king about it." She tapped her pocket, where the small pile of letters was concealed. She wasn't sure she trusted her mother enough to leave them in the hut. "I think I'll go check on the beanstalk now. Make sure nothing's changed."

Her mother didn't try to stop her as she once again left, swiping some bread on her way out. Whatever her current feelings toward her mother, it did lighten her heart to see that food appeared to be plentiful in the little hut.

Jacinta made her way along the length of the vine, devouring the bread as she went. She'd been so caught in her thoughts all morning, she'd barely noticed her hunger. From what she could see, the beanstalk was unchanged, still green and thick in spite of the snow around it.

When she reached Battlement Wall, the tunnel was still there, a little more obscured by the leaves of the vine than before, but still passable. Not that she intended to crawl through it.

The real surprise wasn't the beanstalk, however. It was the diminutive figure perched calmly on top of it, deeply engrossed in her task.

"Valwynn?" Jacinta demanded, her mouth falling open as she examined what the elf was holding. "Are you...knitting?"

"Ah, Jacinta," the little elf said in approval. "At last. Took you long enough to check on the tunnel."

Jacinta blinked at her.

"And I assume your other question was rhetorical, since you can clearly see that I'm knitting."

"Is that a bonnet?" Jacinta demanded, not really thinking through the politeness of her next words. "It looks too big."

"Well, it's not for me, is it?" Valwynn said irritably. "It's for Ferocity. The nights are getting very cold."

Jacinta just stared, trying to think of a response to the information that the elf was knitting a bonnet for her old cow, and coming up completely blank.

"How did you know I'd be here?" she asked faintly, deciding

to abandon the topic altogether. "How did you even know I was back from Vallen?"

"Since my embarrassing oversight the first time you went, I've been keeping a closer eye on things," Valwynn informed her. "And by things, I mean you."

"Oh." Jacinta was taken aback by this information. "Well, there's not much to report. I gave the chicken to the king. I think she's being examined by experts from the Academy of Song, but I wasn't privy to the details."

"Yes, yes, very well." Valwynn waved one knitting needle carelessly. "But what's the king going to do about the giants?"

Jacinta shrugged. "I don't know. No one told me, and I didn't ask."

The elf groaned. "Of course you didn't. Useless human." She chuntered angrily to herself for a moment as she finished her row, then stabbed the needle into the yarn. "So you've washed your hands of the affair, have you?"

"There's nothing more for me to do," said Jacinta defensively. "I don't know why I should be involved further."

"Because you're my link to information, that's why," said Valwynn indignantly. She studied Jacinta for a moment, then let out a breath. "You look pale and drawn. You've had an ordeal, have you?"

Jacinta opened her mouth, unsure what to say, but the elf mercifully waved her down.

"No, no, don't give me the details, I don't care, and I don't want to know." She eyed the human. "But I'm not convinced your part in all this is done, so I don't intend to let you slip through my net just yet."

"You make that sound so ominous," Jacinta complained.

"As long as you don't cross me, you have nothing to worry about," the elf said airily.

"That's not reassuring!" protested Jacinta.

"It should be." Valwynn looked her over. "All right, then. I'll be off. But I'll be keeping an eye out."

Without another word, the elf shoved her knitting back into a bag and hopped down off the beanstalk. Jacinta watched in bemusement as the visitor strolled away toward the west. She couldn't decide if elves were just strange in general, or if Valwynn was an oddity among her kind.

In any event, there didn't seem to be anything for Jacinta to do about any of it. Valwynn might think her part wasn't over, but from where Jacinta stood, it seemed to be. She didn't intend to put herself forward again, and she couldn't imagine King Fidelius seeking her out when he was clearly eager for her to disappear from his children's lives.

With all that in mind, she tried her best to put the whole affair from her thoughts. Times were easier than they had been, but supplies weren't plentiful enough for her and her mother to sit around all day. They picked up what work they could in Briarford and the next town over, cleaning, helping set up market stalls, one night serving in a tavern. They weren't at the point of desperation anymore—they didn't wake wondering what they'd eat each night. But they continued to work hard to ensure they had food not just for the day, but for the days to come.

Two weeks passed slowly. There should have been more than enough to do to keep Jacinta's mind occupied, but somehow she still found it hard to keep her thoughts from dwelling on her time in Vallen. Or more particularly, on the people she'd spent that time with. And, guilty as she felt when she thought of the good friend Mariella had been to her, it wasn't the princess who occupied her thoughts.

But she'd be foolish to dwell on Matthias, and she knew it. It was impossible to help wondering whether he was thinking of her, but she tried to shut those thoughts down quickly. As the past had shown, there were many considerations that would keep him from pursuing thoughts of her when she wasn't right in front of him.

Although that wasn't entirely just, she reminded herself. Not since she'd learned about the letters. It was a constant battle not to give in to the urge to reread those letters over and over. Her mother had been wrong to withhold them, but she was right about the pain they'd bring.

By the time two weeks had passed, Jacinta might not have fully succeeded in putting Matthias from her mind, but she had at least settled back into the routine of life in Briarford. The beautiful ballgown was laid away in the trunk under her bed, not likely to be called upon again. Unsurprisingly, winter had crept in early, and snow now dusted the ground throughout the town. The nights were bitterly cold, and the days not much better. Jacinta and her mother were preparing to settle in for the harsh winter months, their stores much more comfortable than they had been the winter before.

At least, they thought they were preparing to settle in. Jacinta was crossing the yard one blustery afternoon, her arms full of firewood she'd just split, when she received a shock. A carriage rumbled into their yard, its wheels crunching on the icy ground. The very presence of visitors was surprising enough, but that wasn't what made Jacinta freeze. The carriage was fit for royalty, with a fancy crest emblazoned on the side. It wasn't the royal crest of Vallen, but it looked equally as grand.

As she watched, dumbfounded, the vehicle came to a stop. She expected some exalted person to descend, but no one did. Instead, the carriage driver peered at her through the scarf muffling his face.

"Are you Miss Jacinta?" he asked.

"I...yes." Jacinta almost dropped the bundle of wood in her amazement.

The man brightened. "Excellent. I've come to collect you."

"To collect me?" Jacinta repeated. "For what?"

"For the summit," the driver said, seeming perplexed. "The one King Herleif is hosting in Sunniva to discuss the giants. His Majesty has specifically requested your attendance."

For a moment, Jacinta could only stare. "Me? King Herleif of Frossenland wants me to attend his summit?"

The servant nodded enthusiastically. "That's right. And we've cut it a little close if we're to have you back in time for the commencement. I don't mean to rush you, miss, but do you need long to prepare?"

"No." The answer came from behind Jacinta, and she turned to see her mother crossing the yard. "She doesn't need long."

"But...Mamma..." Jacinta trailed off helplessly.

Her mother gave a tight shake of the head. "When a king summons you, Jacinta, you don't dilly-dally."

Out of the corner of her eye, Jacinta caught the driver nodding approval of this principle, but she wasn't convinced.

"What about you?" she demanded. "How will you manage without me?"

The driver cleared his throat. "His Majesty is aware that you live with your mother, miss. In recognition of the hardship your absence may cause her, he has sent this. With his thanks."

He fished a pouch out from a compartment underneath his seat. It jingled promisingly as he leaned down to hand it to Jacinta's mother. Jacinta half expected her mother to refuse out of pride, but the older woman took it with a nod. Apparently it was only Vadolis's king she had an issue with.

"I am grateful for His Majesty's generosity. And we'll have Jacinta ready to leave shortly."

She chivvied her still-protesting daughter into the house. Jacinta's arguments fell on deaf ears as her mother bustled about, packing supplies into a large traveling bag.

"When else will you get a chance to see Sunniva?" her mother pointed out, as she retrieved the ballgown from under Jacinta's bed. "Just in case," she said, folding it carefully into the bag along with a number of lesser gowns.

The whole exercise took less than half an hour, and before Jacinta could quite understand what was happening, she was being ushered into the carriage.

The driver was very solicitous, settling her with a blanket around her legs. It was all surreal, and a far cry from her experiences of traveling to meet with her own country's royal family. As they rattled out of town, Jacinta settled back against the comfortable seat, reflecting that with this level of luxury, she wasn't at all averse to a solitary journey of several days.

But it wasn't to be. They'd just cleared Briarford itself when the carriage pulled to a halt. Pressing her face against the window, Jacinta saw why. A small figure was planted confidently in the middle of the road, barring passage.

"Yes, that's good, thank you," said a familiar, high-pitched voice. "I'll just hop in here."

"Valwynn?" Jacinta demanded, staring as the elf marched up to the carriage door.

"Are you going to let me in?" Valwynn demanded of the bemused carriage driver.

"I, uh...my orders relate only to this young woman," he said helplessly.

"Jacinta knows all about it," said Valwynn airily. "I should be at the summit."

"She is very closely involved in all this," Jacinta said. "I don't object to her riding with me."

"Well..." The driver hesitated, clearly wavering. "If you're sure."

"It's decided," Valwynn said briskly, nodding at the door. "Now come on."

"I can open it." Jacinta swung the door open, her tone scolding. "No need for him to get down."

"Hmph." The elf clambered in, not seeming pleased. "Not proper process," she muttered.

"How are you here?" Jacinta demanded, as the carriage started back into motion. "How did you even know I was leaving?"

"Don't you listen to a word, girl?" Valwynn asked. "I told you I would be keeping an eye on you. I gather we're going to Sunniva?"

Jacinta nodded. "King Herleif has called some kind of a summit, I believe. To address the situation with the giants."

Valwynn let out a sigh as she leaned back against the cushioned seat. "Very good. It's time the humans did something about all this." She gestured vaguely out the window at the frozen landscape. Her voice grew more determined. "And it's time I stopped hiding from my regrets and actually did something about them."

Jacinta stared at her. She was desperately curious to know the nature of Valwynn's regrets, but she didn't get the sense the elf would welcome questions. Far from encouraging conversation, Valwynn looked like she was settling in for a snooze.

"Oh, I almost forgot," the elf said, coming back to life suddenly. "I brought this for you. You'll disgrace our region if you go to a royal summit all in peasant clothes."

Jacinta watched in astonishment as the elf pulled her old mink muffler out of a rucksack she'd deposited on the seat beside her.

"How did you get this?" Jacinta breathed, taking the offered garment.

"Bought it at the markets the same day I met you," Valwynn said, sounding pleased with herself. "Thought it might come in handy."

"Are you proposing a trade for it?" Jacinta asked uncertainly.

The elf had already shut her eyes, leaning back against the seat again. "No. Think of it as a gift freely given. Didn't I tell you I'm looking to scrub out my regrets? I may as well practice a little generosity. Heaven knows I need the preparation to endure days closed up with a group of self-important humans."

With the words, she folded her arms over her chest, her posture making it clear she didn't want further conversation. Murmuring her thanks, Jacinta sat back in her own seat, her throat tight with emotion as she ran her hands over the muffler Matthias had once given her.

There would certainly be benefits to being as un-sentimental as the little elf. She wasn't sure what to expect from King Herleif's summit, but she had a feeling a clear head would serve her better than muddled emotions.

CHAPTER EIGHTEEN

Matthias

Matthias glanced at his nearest companion as his horse crested a hill, bringing Sunniva into sight.

"We're almost there. I hope it was worth it, Mariella."

"Oh, it definitely was," his sister said brightly. "So that's Sunniva! I never thought I'd get the chance to visit. Hagen, your home is beautiful."

"Thank you," said the singer from Matthias's other side. "I'm fond of it."

"You know, you're not expected," Matthias reminded his sister.

"I'm sure King Herleif and Queen Adrienne will be delighted to welcome the princess," Hagen said mildly.

Matthias sighed. "Probably. But our parents won't be equally delighted when we arrive home, that's all I'm saying. They're going to be absolutely livid that Mariella snuck off to join the delegation."

"I didn't sneak off," Mariella said. "I brought a maid."

Matthias gave her a look, but she just laughed, the sound light and tinkling.

"Matthias, I know they'll be angry. And I'll deal with it when we get home. But if you think I went through all that only to spend the trip moping and nervous, you're mad. I fully intend to enjoy the experience." She glanced behind her, toward their own, distant kingdom. "Besides, they would have discovered I was gone within hours. I did leave a note, you know. They've had three days to send someone after me to drag me home, and they obviously decided not to do that."

"Of course not," said Matthias. "However angry they are, they wouldn't want to publicly humiliate you. That would publicly humiliate them," he added matter-of-factly. "They know you'll be safe in this formal delegation, surrounded by guards. They'll act like it was always the plan for you to accompany us, and then let you have it when we get home." He considered it, then added glumly, "Me too, probably."

"Well, that's a price I'm willing to pay," Mariella said, the cheeky note to her voice suggesting she was speaking not just of her own inevitable punishment. Her words turned wheedling. "Come on, Matthias, surely you don't begrudge me this one adventure? I'm never allowed to go anywhere the way you are. Our old trips to Briarford were all the travel I've ever done."

He sighed, unable to withstand this appeal. "Of course I don't begrudge it. I'm just worried about you, Mariella. Father is going to be furious."

Hagen looked between them, seeming a little concerned himself. But he'd so far declined to join in with any of Matthias's warnings to his sister, or in fact to criticize the princess in any way.

"Forget about Father," said Mariella flippantly. "I'm very curious to hear what King Herleif has to say at this summit. You said he's gathered royalty from all over the continent, right?"

Matthias nodded. "He said he'd invited representatives of each crown. I don't know if they'll all be royals."

"I hope they are," said Mariella. "It will be exciting to all be together!"

"Hoping to catch a prince, Princess?" Hagen quipped. Matthias threw him a glance. Over the course of their journey, he'd had ample time to notice that the singer was becoming very casual with Mariella.

"Thankfully they're all taken," said Mariella, ever cheerful. "Not a single kingdom in Providore has an unmarried prince now. Except Vadolis, of course," she added as an afterthought. She grinned at Matthias. "You're falling behind, brother."

He rolled his eyes. "You sound like Mother. Next you'll be trying to pressure me to propose to Lady Letty."

Mariella shuddered. "That I'll never do. I don't want her as a sister, thank you very much."

"Well, I certainly don't want her as a wife," Matthias said shortly.

They'd reached the bottom of the hill now, leaving a straight stretch of road between them and the gate of the capital. He urged his horse forward, eager for a change in topic.

"Come on. They'll be waiting for us."

Sure enough, King Herleif and Queen Adrienne were once again waiting. They didn't bat an eyelid at the discovery that the Vadolisian princess had joined the group, the young queen just murmuring a quiet word to a woman who looked like the housekeeper. She hurried away, and Matthias had no doubt a suitable room would be prepared in no time.

"Your arrival is timely," King Herleif told them, as a steady stream of servants carried their belongings inside. "Almost everyone is here now, and the summit will begin tomorrow morning."

Matthias nodded, pleased to hear that they would get straight to the point.

"But tonight," Queen Adrienne interjected, "we can relax.

We are delighted for the opportunity to host all our guests at a private dinner."

"Just the representatives," King Herleif agreed cheerfully. "Which obviously includes you, Hagen. We decided to keep it small, thus incurring the displeasure of my court, most of whom want maximum opportunity to rub shoulders with the visiting royalty."

"But incurring our gratitude," smiled Matthias.

"We figure you all have plenty of fawning courtiers to deal with at home," King Herleif said matter-of-factly. "We'll let you settle in, and look forward to speaking further at dinner."

By the time the group had been shown to their rooms and freshened up, there was little time left before dinner. Matthias, Mariella, and Hagen made their way toward the appointed dining hall, the princess's steps especially bouncy.

"In a good mood, are we?" Matthias asked her.

"I'm curious to see who's come," Mariella told him. "Aren't you?"

"I am, actually. I wonder if any of the monarchs have attended in person, or if they've all sent representatives like Father did."

His question was soon answered. When they entered the dining hall and saw a group of only ten others seated at a modest-sized table, all belonging to their own generation, Matthias's spirits lifted. In spite of the high rank of those present, the gathering felt much more relaxed than he'd expected.

"Ah, the Vadolisians," said King Herleif, greeting them warmly. "Take your seats, and let me introduce everyone. Some you'll know, Prince Matthias and Princess Mariella, but Hagen will appreciate the introduction."

"Yes, Your Majesty," said the singer, looking a little over-whelmed.

Matthias reflected that his assessment of the gathering as relaxed was probably a relative matter.

"Your Majesties, Your Highnesses, Demetrius," King Herleif said, smiling at the group. "Let me present Crown Prince Matthias of Vadolis, Princess Mariella of Vadolis, and Hagen, current holder of the prestigious exchange position as a Frossian singing apprentice in the Vadolisian court."

Matthias nodded to everyone. He didn't know who the untitled Demetrius was, but he supposed he would soon find out. He realized with surprise that he knew the identity of one of the other attendees, even though he'd never met her before. Queen Bianca was something of a legend. For one thing, the young ruler of the island kingdom of Selvana—which had only recently re-established contact with the mainland—was a singer. In addition, she would stand out in any crowd thanks to the contrast between her dark skin and her snow-white hair— the result of exposure to wild magic as an infant.

As others had told Matthias, the effect was mesmerizing. And the young queen held herself with a quiet grace, her smile open and friendly as she looked at the newcomers. No one would guess that she alone of the gathered guests wore the responsibility of a ruling monarch. He could see why Prince Farrin of Medulle had fallen for her when stranded on the island of Selvana.

No wonder King Herleif had referred to Majesties as well as Highnesses. It was remarkable that the pair were present— Matthias had never expected a Selvanan representative at this summit.

"My wife, Queen Adrienne, you all already know," King Herleif was saying, nodding at the other singer queen at the table. "And next to her is Crown Prince Otto of Teren, and his wife, Princess Gisela."

Otto waved cheerfully to Matthias with the arm that wasn't

around his wife's shoulders. Matthias had been happy for the Terenan prince when he'd heard of his marriage to a Terenan girl from the Forest of Ilgal. Otto was only one year older than Matthias, and although they hadn't had much opportunity to spend time with one another, they had always been friendly. Matthias had even been invited by Otto's family to visit Terenford a few years back, although he'd suspected at the time that the invitation had more to do with the queen's hope that he might form a marriage alliance with Otto's stepsister, Princess Rosa. It was a scheme neither she nor Matthias had been excited about.

Speaking of Princess Rosa...

"And Princess Rosa," King Herleif continued, his gaze passing to the dark-haired young woman beside Gisela, "not just a princess of Teren any longer, since her marriage to Crown Prince Emmett of Medulle."

Princess Rosa gave Matthias a broad grin, looking very comfortable beside her Medullan husband. There was a rueful hint to Matthias's answering smile. Apparently her objection hadn't been to the concept of a foreign prince, just to him specifically. Not that he bore any grudge. He'd never felt the smallest need to look outside Vadolis—or within royal circles—for a bride.

"Prince Matthias, Princess Mariella, Hagen." Prince Emmett nodded to them all, his voice low and solemn. The elder Medullan prince had always been more serious than his younger brother, according to rumor. "We are delighted you could all join us."

"Indeed we are," King Herleif agreed. "Next to Prince Emmett we have Prince Farrin of Medulle—forgive me, now King Farrin of Selvana, and Queen Bianca." The Frossian king looked very well pleased with this introduction. "We are honored and frankly amazed that they were able to join us. It was pure luck that they were visiting Medulle at the time the Medullan king and queen received my communication, and pure generosity that they decided to accompany Prince Emmett and Princess Rosa."

"We felt Selvana should be represented," Queen Bianca said in a soft voice that nevertheless carried the confidence of a monarch. "We may seem distant from the giants, but we take an interest." She glanced at her brother-in-law. "Particularly after what Emmett told us, that a very similar thing occurred in the Forest of Ilgal, within Teren's borders, as happened in Selvana."

She must have seen their confusion, because she added, "In both instances, rogue elves admitted to working with someone outside their own forest, but were either unable or unwilling to identify whom, even after their scheme was dismantled. It was impossible not to wonder if the mysterious outside party might be the same in both instances, in which case whatever's going on here on the mainland is of relevance to Selvana as well."

Matthias nodded thoughtfully. He still didn't fully under-stand, but no doubt it would be further explained at the summit.

"Very wise of you," King Herleif said approvingly. "And our last guests are likely unknown to all of you. Princess Estelle represents Korallid."

"The mermaid empire?" Mariella gasped, her eyes widening as they settled on the young, fair-haired woman sitting beside Queen Bianca.

"Precisely," said King Herleif. "Princess Estelle is the youngest daughter of Emperor Aefic. And her husband, Demetrius, has also been so kind as to join us."

Matthias and his companions fumbled through greetings, all of them too polite to comment on the fact that the princess was very clearly human. Although, looking closely, Matthias could see streaks of turquoise in her hair that were definitely not normal for a human. And her husband's dark amber hair was also not a color he often saw. Interesting that he had no title. The man held himself like a guard, not a royal.

"They serve as Korallidian ambassadors to the Medullan court," King Herleif explained. "They also traveled with Prince Emmett and Princess Rosa."

"We brought quite a crowd," Princess Rosa said cheerfully.

"We did as well," Prince Otto added. "King Herleif didn't mention them, but the summit will also be attended by representatives of the Imperator, the chief elf in Ilgal. His granddaughter and heir came, with quite a posse. They elected not to attend dinner, however."

"Yes, I was getting to them," said King Herleif goodnaturedly. "And we're also expecting one more party. But in their absence, we can certainly make a start on this excellent food."

The words acted as a prompt, and servants appeared at the guests' elbows, each carrying a steaming bowl or overflowing platter. The evening passed quickly, conversation flowing freely between the young royals. It was rare indeed to have a gathering of so many of Matthias's peers, and he thoroughly enjoyed it. It was certainly a sign of King Herleif's influence on the continent that the other three mainland kingdoms had sent their crown princes, not to mention the attendance of the Selvanan monarchs.

Matthias noticed that Hagen sat next to Demetrius, the two untitled members of the gathering falling into easy conversation. He wouldn't blame the apprentice singer for feeling overwhelmed, and he didn't try to draw Hagen into interactions with the royals. It was the sort of thing he wouldn't have even thought about a few short months ago. His friendship with Hagen had certainly given him insight into the position of a commoner among royals. If only he'd had that insight early enough not to cause Jacinta unnecessary discomfort.

And his thoughts were back on Jacinta.

He still wondered regularly whether he should have thrown caution to the wind and ridden after her the day following the Autumn Gala. He'd been distressed enough by the discovery of her hasty departure that he'd strongly considered it. But she'd given no indication that she wanted that.

Still, it was hard to accept that if he didn't do something about it, he might never see her again. He couldn't let that happen.

Matthias sighed. There was nothing to be gained from further descent into the endless cycle of thoughts he'd been stuck in since Jacinta left Vallen. He needed to focus on the present.

Everyone retired to bed early, worn out by their various journeys. For his part, Matthias slept dreamlessly and woke eager for the summit to begin. Breakfast had been brought to his room, and he was told that a servant would be ready to show him to the meeting room at his convenience. He wolfed down some toast and hurried into the corridor, ready to hear what King Herleif had to say.

The servant led him along a few short corridors and into a pleasant room dominated by a large, square table. Matthias nodded to the servant before turning to face the few attendees already gathered. His eyes scanned over the Selvanan and Medullan representatives before pausing curiously on several elves. The diminutive creatures must have had cushions piled on their chairs, because they sat high enough to rest their arms on the table. Most of them looked young—at least by elven standards—but the one on the end had the pale, silvery hair of old age. Matthias's head was half inclined in greeting when his eyes caught the human figure sitting on the other side of the last elf, and he froze.

Jacinta.

CHAPTER NINETEEN

Matthias

Matthias stood rooted to the spot as his mind caught up with what his eyes were seeing. Jacinta was here.

Her face was pink as she returned his gaze. Rising to her feet, she smiled tentatively in greeting. Was she the final party King Herleif had mentioned?

Matthias stepped forward, navigating around the table to meet Jacinta.

"You're here," he said, feeling stupid at the unnecessary observation.

"Yes." Jacinta ducked her head. "King Herleif was kind enough to send me a carriage."

"I'm glad," said Matthias. His eyes strayed down to the mink muffler around her neck, and he stilled. "That's..." He trailed off, his hand reaching out without thought until his fingers brushed the soft fur. Memories swirled through him as he raised his eyes to hers, bringing a myriad of emotions with them.

"You remember." Jacinta's voice was quiet, and for a moment, Matthias forgot there was anyone else in the room.

"Of course I remember," he said. "I haven't forgotten any of it. Not a single moment."

Before Jacinta could reply, the door opened, and the Frossian king entered.

"Ah, Prince Matthias," said King Herleif. "Good morning. I see you've met the elven representatives from the Forest of Ilgal. This is Asivah, heir of the Imperator, and her companions." His eyes held a hint of humor as they rested on the silver-haired elf. "And our other elven guest, Valwynn. She arrived late last night with Jacinta." His gaze lingered on how close Matthias was standing, taking in the prince's dazed expression. "Who is, I believe, known to you."

"Yes," said Matthias, pulling himself together. He stepped back, trying to speak more normally as he smiled at Jacinta. "I'm very glad to see you again, Jacinta."

"No need to tell me I wasn't invited or expected," the elf Valwynn interjected comfortably. "I'm well aware of it, Your Majesty. But I should be at this summit, that's all I have to say. Jacinta certainly wouldn't be here if it weren't for me."

"That's true," Jacinta said, looking like she was trying not to smile as she resumed her seat. "Whether it's true that it's all you have to say, I will decline to comment."

"Insolent young snip," said the elf, not seeming especially bothered. Her eyes moved to the door as another royal arrived, and Matthias didn't miss the recognition that flashed through them.

"Valwynn?!" Queen Adrienne was clearly astonished. It seemed that while her husband may have seen the new arrivals the night before, she hadn't.

"Yes, hello, Adrienne," said the elf, eyeing her. "You look well. Had a child, I heard."

"I...yes."

"Adrienne? You know Valwynn?" King Herleif looked at his

wife in bewilderment. The pair exchanged a glance full of unspoken meaning, some understanding causing the king's eyebrows to shoot up.

"I see," he murmured. "Interesting."

This exchange was naturally intriguing, but Matthias had no chance to ask any questions. Mariella and Hagen chose that moment to enter—their arrival suspiciously synchronized—and Mariella squealed with delight to see Jacinta. Beating Matthias to it, she seated herself beside their fellow Vadolisian, leaving him to sink into a chair across the table. There was no further opportunity for casual conversation with Jacinta. The room quickly filled with the rest of the visiting royals, and King Herleif wasted no time in getting underway.

"Thank you all for assembling here," he said. "We've done our welcomes and greetings last night, so I'll get straight to business. As you all know, the purpose of this summit is to discuss the situation with the giants. Some of you may not yet have met Jacinta, who hails from Briarford in Vadolis's far north, and her companion, Valwynn the elf."

Jacinta smiled in a strained way around the table.

"I believe you're all aware of the fact that Jacinta has been into Kjemper," King Herleif continued. "With the assistance of magic refined by Valwynn, she passed through the wall and explored the giants' land firsthand."

He nodded to her. "Would you be willing to share with this group what you've already shared with your king?"

Jacinta nodded, and Matthias was filled with admiration at her poise as she rose to her feet. Clearly and without embellishment, she repeated her account of her dealings with the giant on her first visit to Kjemper, and what she'd witnessed on her second.

"Thank you, Jacinta," said King Herleif courteously, as she sat. "You've shown great courage in putting your own safety at risk to bring this information back from Kjemper." He looked at the rest of the group. "I have discussed these matters at length with my advisors, and Jacinta's information leads us to believe that, contrary to our prior assumptions, the giants have access to vast stores of magic."

From various nods around the table, Matthias gathered that none of this information was new to anyone. The Frossian king's eyes rested on the elves from Ilgal as he continued, all of them watching him with expressionless faces.

"Based on what Jacinta witnessed, our best guess is that the giants are, in fact, mining magic with the help of elves."

"Preposterous," muttered one of the elves. But the one called Asivah, heir of the Imperator, held up a hand to silence him.

"We, of all elves, are not in a position to declare anything impossible," she contradicted. "We will hear King Herleif out with open minds."

"Yes, Heir," the elf muttered, subsiding.

"We know few details," King Herleif acknowledged. "But in my view, the fact that a giant explicitly told Jacinta that the human kingdoms would be wise to try to unseat the giant king is something I do not feel comfortable to simply ignore."

"I agree," said Matthias. "Our shared border with Kjemper is small compared to Frossenland's. But the risk of invasion by the giants is still a matter that weighs heavily on our minds in Vadolis." He nodded to King Herleif. "It has done since your return, Your Majesty. Jacinta's news only highlights the danger."

"Invasion." The quiet, scoffing voice came from Valwynn, who seemed to be addressing herself to Jacinta rather than the group. "Can humans think of nothing but military matters?"

Jacinta made a shushing motion, obviously not eager for the elf to bring attention to them. But Hagen, seated next to Mariella, leaned around the Vadolisian princess to study the elf.

"Do you imply that the danger from the giant king isn't a

military invasion?" the singer asked. "Are you saying he threatens us with something else?"

"I'm not saying anything," said Valwynn with dignity. "Merely commenting on the human condition." She examined Hagen, her tone tinged with approval. "But I will say that it's no surprise that the royals are the least likely to be paying attention to what's actually important."

"Thank you," said Matthias dryly.

Jacinta sighed. "She's been like this all the way here. Muttering dark asides but not actually *saying* anything useful. It was a long journey."

This casual criticism caused the elves from Ilgal to look at Jacinta askance, but Valwynn herself didn't seem troubled. Clearly she and Jacinta had an easy understanding by this point.

"In any event," King Herleif said with the air of a man trying to regain control of the conversation, "gaining more information will be difficult. As many of you know, both Adrienne and myself have crossed Battlement Wall into Kjemper. We did so by means of using a significant volume of magic to control the wind and carry us up and over. Since hearing the report from Vadolis, I've had agents investigate the wall, with the assistance of some of our top singers. It appears that crossing over the wall that way is no longer possible. At least not clandestinely. Since Grograna's death, the giants have placed some kind of magical barrier along the top of the wall, and it would require a significant magical assault to overcome it. That would be likely to draw attention, and I'm not eager to mount an overt attack against Kjemper based on rumors they may attack us."

"Nor are we," Prince Otto said, murmurs from around the room echoing the sentiment. The Terenan prince frowned thoughtfully at his wife. "It hardly needs to be added that the new magical protection on the wall supports the conclusion that the giants have a great deal of magic."

Princess Gisela glanced at the elves from Ilgal. "What did you make of the towers Jacinta described, Asivah? Do you think they're for mining?"

The young female elf leaned forward, placing her elbows on the table and steepling her fingers. "The untitled human girl's account seems conclusive. If it is accurate, and she is being truthful, then we must conclude that the giants are mining magic from the ground."

"But I thought Kjemper's ground was as barren of magic as northern Frossenland's," said King Farrin, frowning. "I thought that was how magic worked. The more barren the land, the less magic it produces. The more lush the land, the more magic pours out of it. Isn't that why Selvana's jungle is overrun with wild magic while the northern wastes of Providore are...well, magical wastes as well?"

"That's always been my understanding," Queen Adrienne said. "It's what they teach at the academy here. And it's supported by my experience when I lived in northern Frossenland. There was very little magic in the ground."

"Humans."

Valwynn's mutter once again broke into the conversation, and this time, Matthias noted Asivah looking pointedly at the older elf. Valwynn obviously saw it as well, because she raised an eyebrow in Asivah's direction.

"Do you have something to say, forest-dweller?"

One of Asivah's companions let out a hiss. "You should show more respect to our Imperator's heir."

"The Imperator is your leader," said Valwynn dismissively. "Not mine. I don't hail from Ilgal. And from my dealings with those who do, I don't have a very good opinion of you forest elves."

"I beg your pardon?"

It took Matthias a moment to realize that one of the elves

had stood. He must have put his feet on his chair rather than the cushions on which he'd been sitting, because his height wasn't increased by a significant amount.

"I'm sure you heard what I said," Valwynn responded dismissively.

"Friends, let's keep cool heads," said King Herleif, his voice no less commanding for its calming tone. "You must surely be aware that not all of us understand the unspoken causes of your frustration with one another."

"She understands," muttered one of the other Ilgal elves. "And you shouldn't have invited her here to bandy our kind's secrets about."

"Don't blame the human king, I invited myself," said Valwynn. "And your talk of secrets exposes you for a fool. What nonsense is that? Just because elves don't choose to communicate freely doesn't give us ownership of any information."

"I am inclined to agree with you." Asivah's voice cut in, her calm tone a stark contrast to the heated exchange. "I believe we have reached a stage in Providore's development where it would be to the benefit of all to communicate more clearly about the state of the land."

"Providore's development?" repeated Prince Emmett. "A curious choice of words."

"We elves are more connected with the land than humans," Asivah said matter-of-factly. "We don't just mine the magic—we identify it. We find it, and steward it, and that gives us a greater sense of how the land is faring. And Providore is ailing. It has been for some time. I have exchanged views often with my grandfather about how to respond."

"*Thank* you," said Valwynn, her tone and impatient gesture more irritated than grateful, in spite of her words. "Finally, someone says it."

"Someone says what?" Princess Rosa asked, sounding alarmed. "What does it mean that Providore is ailing?"

She'd directed her question to Valwynn, but the older elf remained silent. When it became clear she wasn't going to answer, Asivah once again spoke, her gaze shrewd as it rested on Valwynn.

"It seems to me that she speaks of the human understanding that the volume of magic produced by the ground is directly related to the fertility of the land. Elves do not share this belief. But I note that the Vadolisian elf does not say so."

"I'm not Vadolisian," Valwynn said. "I come from Frossenland originally."

"You make no reply to my other speculation," Asivah observed, sounding satisfied. "You can't speak, can you? You're bound by a bargain of some kind."

Valwynn sniffed, folding her arms over her chest and leaning back in her chair.

"A bargain?" Jacinta's eyes flew between Asivah and Valwynn. "A bargain with whom? The giants?"

A rustle went through the other elves, some of them narrowing their eyes at Valwynn. She met their stares unflinchingly.

"I suspect she is unable to say without triggering the bargain's magic," said Asivah. "Although of course I'm only speculating."

"Hang on..." Hagen once again spoke, apparently too caught up in the elves' revelations to worry about being surrounded by such high-ranking company. "Forget bargains and giants for a moment. I want to understand what you mean about the volume of magic not being tied to the fertility of the land. How can that be? Why then are the Selvanan jungle and the Forest of Ilgal so overrun by magic?"

Asivah's eyes drifted to Prince Otto. "You should be able to answer that."

"I should?" The Terenan prince blinked, his expression apologetic. "I can't, I'm afraid."

"You've figured it out, you just don't realize you have yet," Asivah told him. She spared a glance for Queen Bianca and King Farrin. "I suppose you figured it out first, didn't you? Teren just copied you." She nodded at Prince Otto. "What task are your people undertaking in Ilgal even now?"

"They're...trying to clear some of the magic," said Prince Otto. "A group of singers is drawing it from the ground and releasing it, as much as they can. They're moving very slowly through the forest, but we think in time it will make a difference."

"The same is happening in Selvana," confirmed Queen Bianca.

"You're saying singers are the key?" Hagen leaned forward, clearly fascinated. "That the absence of singers makes the magic worse?"

"Elves remove magic directly from the ground when we mine it," Asivah said. "But we do nothing to tame the flow of magic that emanates up from the soil. If there's no one to manipulate it, of course it will swell beyond manageable levels."

Queen Bianca was clearly just as riveted. "Is that why the magic went wild in Selvana? Because the island was uninhabited by humans for so long?"

"And the humans who settled there didn't try very hard to tame the magic," King Farrin pointed out. "When they realized it was so dangerous, they moved into the trees. There was no singing until you came along."

"But..." Princess Rosa frowned. "There have always been singers in Ilgal. Why would the magic there have been growing so wild in recent years?"

"There haven't been that many singers in Ilgal recently," her stepbrother, Prince Otto, contradicted.

"He's right," Princess Gisela chimed in. Matthias remembered that she was from Ilgal herself. "The forest has never been as heavily populated as the plains. And it's become more and more common for singers to leave Ilgal for the capital or elsewhere, sometimes as soon as their ability is discovered."

"And we know now that those who stayed were being gathered up and prevented from singing," Prince Otto said. He shook his head slowly. "The timing makes sense. The rapid increase in the pace at which the magic was growing wild matches the disappearance of the singers."

King Farrin nodded. "In both Selvana and Ilgal, the human response to the crisis has just made it worse, because the more the humans withdrew—the singers along with them—the worse the problem became. It's a perpetual cycle."

"So does that mean that even after we've lifted some of the excess magic, the only way to maintain a manageable level is to convince more singers to live in the forest?" Prince Otto asked.

"It sounds like it," said King Herleif thoughtfully, when none of the elves responded. His eyes rested on his wife. "I confess, I'm more interested in what this new perspective means for the northern wastes. If all climates should produce the same basic volume of magic, why is the north so sparse of it? By that logic, you would imagine there were too many singers there, draining the land, in order for it to be as it is. But that's not the case. It's never been as well populated as the southern region. And although singers are born there just like anywhere else—Adrienne and Hagen providing proof of this—they're not what I'd call plentiful. How then do you explain the barrenness of magic?"

"It is not my responsibility to explain anything," said Asivah, the tips of her pointed ears stiffening as she raised one fine eyebrow.

Valwynn let out an audible sigh, but said nothing.

"The mining." It was Jacinta's quiet voice that broke the silence, her eyes on the elf beside her. "It's because of the mining, isn't it? And is that what causes the tremors as well? Is that why they've been growing steadily worse for years?"

"Wait." Hagen's eyes widened as they rested on Jacinta's face. "Are you suggesting that the giants' mining activities can reach under the wall? That they can drain magic not just from their land, but from northern Frossenland and northern Vadolis?"

"Surely that's not possible," Matthias said, alarmed.

"Why not?" Jacinta asked, her face pale. "The wall doesn't continue under the ground, does it? And it's not a magical barrier. Or at least, it wasn't until recently. We don't understand the mechanics of their mining. How can we be sure it's not reaching into our own lands?"

"That's what you meant," Matthias realized, his words addressed to Valwynn. "That the risk to our kingdoms from the giant king isn't one of military invasion. This is the real attack against us. And he can do it without ever leaving Kjemper."

He exchanged a look with Mariella. "We've been focusing on the wrong kind of defense."

"As have we," said King Herleif grimly.

"You're a smart girl, Jacinta," Valwynn said approvingly. "I knew I picked you for a reason." She nodded at Hagen. "That singer also has a good head on his shoulders. I thought the royals would need help figuring it out."

"Is that what you were bound by a bargain not to disclose?" Jacinta demanded. "That the giants are mining the magic out from under us? Will they eventually drain all of Providore if we don't do anything to stop them?"

"If she's bound by a bargain, she can't confirm any of that," said Asivah.

"But there are things I can say." Valwynn rose to her feet on her chair, her ears quivering. "Contrition is not common among my kind, and not comfortable for us."

"I think you'll find it's not comfortable for humans either," Adrienne pointed out.

Valwynn raised a small, slender hand. "Whatever. My point is, I have been experiencing regret for some time for my part in...events. I have attempted to erase that regret through my interactions with both Adrienne and Jacinta. But it's not enough. Now you've all reached the conclusions you have, I hope it will be. It's not just about the effect on the human kingdoms. To me, that issue is peripheral at best. It's about the land itself. As Asivah said, as an elf, I am connected to the land. I care about it. And it's not supposed to be this way. Magic is supposed to be spread evenly, the way it emerges by nature. It's not natural or healthy for it to be stripped from one region or heavily concentrated in another. The whole continent suffers for it." She narrowed her eyes at Asivah and her companions. "A truth I believe the elves of Ilgal have forgotten."

There was a moment of silence, then Asivah also stood. "You are right," she said, inclining her head courteously to the older elf. "But not completely. Not all of Ilgal's elves have forgotten it. I do not ask you to confirm it, because I suspect you cannot. But I presume from your talk of regret and your disdain for your forest-dwelling brethren that you became caught up in the plot orchestrated by my cousin Lonik. I think there can now remain no doubt that the party with whom he communicated and plotted outside the forest was the giants. He must have orchestrated the mining industry that has allowed the giants to steal magic from northern Providore. A region the welfare of which, I confess, we have little interest in."

The elf drew a deep breath. "I regret my cousin's actions, as does my grandfather. I regret the disrepute he has brought to our family and our people. We are ashamed that one of our kin would conspire with giants."

"He did not represent our leader or our people," protested one of the other elves. "And he has paid the price."

"Indeed," Asivah said. "But we have been unable to say with confidence that all of his conspirators have been found and stopped. I suspect now that there may be a number of them still sheltering inside Kjemper, out of our reach."

"Not out of Jacinta's reach."

Everyone turned to look at Valwynn, who was once again seated, leaning back in her chair.

Matthias frowned. "I think Jacinta has assumed more than enough risk through your schemes," he said, not caring that he wasn't being very polite to the elderly elf. "The threat from the giant king and his mining activities isn't her problem to solve."

"Certainly not," agreed King Herleif briskly. "But it is a problem we must consider very carefully. We cannot afford to let Providore be drained of magic. And that's not even considering the danger we would all be in if the giants used that magic aggressively. If King Uroch of the giants is causing us harm—causing our very land harm—without ever breaching the wall, we cannot simply leave him be. Friends," he looked somberly around the table, "we have much to discuss."

CHAPTER TWENTY

Jacinta

"What do you think, Jacinta?" Mariella appealed to her friend. "Briarford isn't too far from the coast. Is sending spies by sea a viable option?"

Jacinta leaned back against the cushioned carriage, forcing herself yet again not to look out the window for Matthias and Hagen. She still couldn't decide if it had been kind of the princess to share the carriage with Jacinta rather than riding as she'd probably prefer, or unkind of both the prince and princess to insist that she return to Vallen with them rather than just going home.

"I don't know, Mariella. I think the Vadolisian mariners would agree with the Frossian ones who advised King Herleif that the waters are too dangerous. I've never heard of anyone sailing north from Briarford. Only south. The waters to the north are what sailors call a ships' graveyard."

The carriage went over a bump in the road, causing Mariella to fall back against the cushions as well. She sighed. "If we can't go over the wall clandestinely, and we can't sail around it safely..."

"It leaves only my tunnel," Jacinta finished dully. "Which no one but me can access."

"No one expects you to go back into Kjemper, Jacinta," Mariella said quickly. "You've done more than enough." She glanced out the window as a mounted figure came into view, and Jacinta allowed herself to follow the princess's gaze. "Matthias won't allow it," Mariella finished.

Jacinta pulled her eyes from the prince's upright form, wishing Mariella's words didn't send an unsettling thrill down her spine. Her thoughts flew to their departure that morning. The air had been crisp, and she'd worn her mink muffler. Her cheeks heated as she remembered the way Matthias's eyes had softened at the sight of it. He hadn't been lying when he said he remembered everything.

It was probably for the best that he didn't know she'd sold it and only gotten it back thanks to Valwynn.

With a sigh, Jacinta pulled her mind back to the conversation at hand. As heartening as it was to know that Matthias wanted to shield her from danger, she didn't share Mariella's confidence that Matthias would somehow prevent the king from sending her into Kjemper. The prince had shown before now that he lacked either the willingness or the power to defy his father where she was concerned.

"This is more pleasant than the ride over," Mariella said, wriggling into a more comfortable position. "Don't tell the boys, but much as I like riding, I was exhausted by the time we reached Sunniva."

Jacinta smiled. "The boys? You sound like you're talking about your brothers, but last I checked, you only have one."

Mariella waved a hand toward the window. "Matthias and Hagen. Look at them, they're as chummy as brothers these days." Her expression became veiled. "But Hagen is most definitely *not* my brother."

"Hm." Jacinta hid a smile as she studied her friend.

It seemed to her that Mariella was trying to avoid looking out the window for Hagen as much as Jacinta was trying to prevent her eyes from searching for Matthias. It was a depressing thought, because it meant her attempts at nonchalance were probably as futile as her friend's.

"Well, it's a more pleasant journey for me as well," she said, deciding not to tease Mariella. She would be wise not to start something she couldn't finish. "Valwynn wasn't a bad traveling companion, but you're much better at conversation."

"I'm surprised she decided to stay in Sunniva," commented Mariella.

"Apparently she wanted to catch up with Queen Adrienne," said Jacinta. "She never even told me she knew the Frossian queen." She smiled. "Although, from the way she addresses her, I think she's forgotten that she's a queen now. Anyway, she says she's done what she set out to do, now that all the kingdoms are aware of what's happening, and feels no more obligation to be involved."

"How pleasant it must be to have full control over where your obligations begin and end," said Mariella dryly.

Jacinta nodded her agreement. "I wouldn't place much reliance on Valywnn's declaration, though. She's become accustomed to interfering. I doubt she'll be able to stay out of it altogether." Her mind drifted back to the summit, during which Valwynn had found plenty to say in spite of the restrictions placed on her by whatever bargain she was involved in with the giants. "Do you think all the monarchs will share the conclusions reached by their representatives?"

Mariella nodded confidently. "I do. Everyone, including Father, will be unwilling to act openly against King Uroch or the giants. No one wants to declare war with Kjemper."

"At least everyone at the summit seemed to feel that if the

giants attacked Frossenland or Vadolis, their kingdoms would come to our aid," Jacinta said.

"Yes, that's a relief if true," Mariella agreed. "And they all said that they'd give resources to any covert efforts to bring down King Uroch."

"And destroy his castle," Jacinta reminded her. "I wonder if King Herleif and Queen Adrienne are right that dethroning the king and destroying the building would be enough to end the monarchy."

Mariella shrugged. "They've both been to the giant capital. They know better than anyone. They seemed to think that without the wealth and pomp of the castle and its contents, a prospective new ruler would have to start from scratch in establishing himself."

"Yes." Jacinta considered the matter thoughtfully. "And if the giant who sent the message with me is right, they would be unlikely to get much support from the other giants."

"Kill the king, destroy the castle," Mariella summarized. She grinned. "Not asking much, are they?"

Jacinta smiled absently, her thoughts still on the distant frozen land she'd now visited twice. For a moment there was silence in the carriage, then Mariella shifted uncomfortably.

"Jacinta, there's something I should tell you. About when we get home." She grimaced. "I wasn't supposed to be on this trip. I sort of...snuck off. And I fully expect my parents to be in a rage with me when we arrive. So just...brace yourself, I guess."

Jacinta stared at her friend in dismay. "How much trouble will you be in?"

Mariella sighed. "Impossible to know. But I don't think it will be pretty."

"Was it worth it?" Jacinta asked curiously.

Mariella's answer was immediate and certain. "Absolutely. I'll take the consequences."

Jacinta had to admire her friend's courage. She also had to tell herself, as her eyes strayed to the carriage window, not to make unflattering comparisons. She'd seen for herself in her time in Vallen. The crown prince and heir had pressures on him that even his sister didn't face.

The journey passed too quickly. Jacinta found the days on the road almost idyllic in her new company. The summit faded behind them—the threat of the giants with it—and the specter of the king and queen's reaction to everything was out of reach ahead. There were servants and guards with them, but nothing like the constant intensity and formality of the court. For a few happy days, Jacinta, Mariella, Matthias, and Hagen enjoyed something almost like normalcy.

Of course, they were traveling at the crown's expense, so there were no public coaches or noisy taverns full of drunken locals. They stayed at pleasant inns, enjoying meals together and talking by the fire in private parlors late into the night. The setting was entirely different, but the feel of their interactions reminded Jacinta of their easy childhood adventures together. And Hagen was a welcome addition, the four of them naturally falling into various pairings at different times, with no odd one out. Jacinta would have been happy if the journey could have lasted a month.

But of course, it couldn't. Even moving at an easy pace, it took less than four days to travel from Sunniva to the Vadolisian capital. All too soon, the road peeled away from East River, making straight for the city's large southern gate.

Jacinta's nerves grew as they rode through the city and eventually into the castle courtyard. She was miserably conscious of the fact that she wasn't expected, and was unlikely to be welcome. A message had clearly gone ahead of them, because when the group alighted, the king and queen were waiting for them. And Jacinta didn't miss the anger that flared in King

Fidelius's eyes when she stepped out of the carriage behind Mariella.

"I should have known who put you up to this, Mariella," the king said, his voice low and angry.

The princess looked between her father and Jacinta, her bemusement turning to indignation. "What are you talking about, Father? Jacinta had no idea what I was up to. None of us even knew she'd be at the summit until we arrived in Sunniva!"

"Keep your voice down." The king's words were low and clipped. "We will discuss this matter more in private."

He and the queen turned toward the building, Mariella following with a defiant toss of the head. Jacinta hovered, uncertain, until she felt someone approach behind her. She looked around to see Matthias. His eyes were on his sister's retreating back, and he looked concerned, but his words were for her.

"I think it might be best for you to lie low for a bit, Jacinta. I wish I could look after you, but I don't want to abandon Mariella."

"Of course you should go with her," Jacinta said quickly. "I'll be fine."

Matthias hovered for another moment, looking unconvinced, until a firm step behind him made them both turn.

"I can make sure Jacinta's looked after," Hagen said reassuringly. "We'll manage, won't we, Jacinta?" He spoke pleasantly, but his brow was creased in concern as well, no doubt for Mariella.

"Of course we will," Jacinta agreed.

Matthias looked between them, once again showing that discomfort he always displayed when the singer was friendly to Jacinta. But after a moment, he gave a curt nod, striding into the castle after his family without a backward glance.

Jacinta pulled her gaze from his back, trying to smile up at

Hagen. "I can't say I envy either of them a place in that conversation."

"Nor do I," Hagen agreed. "Let's find ourselves somewhere quiet to wait."

Jacinta was grateful for his company in the hours that followed, especially since unlike her, he lived at the castle and had spaces he could occupy unobtrusively. But she was even more grateful for the fact that he didn't press her for conversation. It was clear that he had as much on his mind as she did, and both were content to wait mainly in companionable silence.

By the time she'd eaten dinner in the apprentices' dining hall, Jacinta was starting to wonder whether Matthias and Mariella had decided not to seek them out to tell them what had happened. Surely they couldn't still be closeted with the king and queen? Her question was answered when a servant wended his way through the dining hall toward them.

"Is all well?" Hagen asked the man.

"Excuse me," the servant said. "But my message is for her." He nodded at Jacinta, whose heart skipped a beat.

"Me?" she asked nervously.

"Yes, miss," the servant said. "The king has specifically requested your attendance."

Jacinta looked at Hagen in dismay. The singer was frowning, his eyes fixed on the servant.

"Are the prince and princess with His Majesty?"

"I believe so," said the servant.

Hagen gave a decisive nod. "We'll both come."

The servant looked uncertain, but Hagen clearly wasn't asking for permission. He stood, offering Jacinta a hand. She let him pull her up, her thoughts edging toward panic. If the king was asking for her by name, it couldn't be good news.

They made their way through the castle in the servant's wake, eventually ushered into a small meeting room. The scene inside was tense, to say the least. Mariella was seated at a table, looking defiant, and Matthias was pacing the room, his fists clenched. When Jacinta and Hagen entered, he froze, casting a furious glance at his father.

"Father, I object in the strongest terms to—"

"Your objection has been noted," the king said in a cool voice. His eyes were unforgiving as they rested on Jacinta. If he'd even seen Hagen, he gave no sign of it. "Come in, Jacinta."

She did so, her hands clenched nervously in her skirts. "You called for me, Your Majesty?"

"I did," he replied. "I have received a briefing on the summit from the prince and princess. I understand that the mutual decision of those present was to pursue covert methods of defeating the giant king, and, if possible, destroying his castle."

"Yes, Your Majesty," said Jacinta warily.

He nodded. "I have considered the matter and decided what measures Vadolis will take. I intend to send you through the tunnel you've traversed before. Your main object is to gather information on the state of matters in King Uroch's castle."

Jacinta could feel her face drain of color, but she told herself sternly to stop being foolish. This instruction came as no great surprise to her.

"That's an absurd plan, Father," Matthias interjected. "Jacinta isn't trained or equipped for a mission like that. You'd be sending her to her death!"

"I see no need for these dramatics," the king said dismissively. "She has successfully breached the wall on two previous occasions."

"That was different," Matthias protested. "You want her to travel all the way to the capital!"

"It is true that the entrance point into Kjemper is not near the capital, Your Majesty," Jacinta said. "From what King Herleif and Queen Adrienne said about its location, I suspect it would be several days' travel."

"Through hostile enemy territory!" Matthias added.

"We will naturally send you with provisions," the king told Jacinta.

"Father, what right do you have to order her to her death?" Matthias's fists were clenched so tightly, his knuckles were white. Jacinta couldn't remember ever seeing him so worked up.

"I am her king," King Fidelius said, his own voice rising to match his son's. "I have every right." He turned to Jacinta. "Your previous trip into Kjemper was undertaken in response to a request. This time I will send you as an official agent of the crown. Will you accept the directive?"

Jacinta's eyes flew to Matthias. He was shaking his head, his emotions barely contained. But what choice did she have? She had nothing to gain from defying her king. How could Matthias expect it of her, when he didn't do it himself, and the king was his own father?"

"Yes, Your Majesty," she said miserably. "I have no great faith in my ability to achieve anything of use in Kjemper. But I recognize that I'm the only one who can pass through the tunnel. I will do as my king commands."

"Good," King Fidelius said shortly. "At least someone in this room still has respect for the crown." He cast a dark glance at his son. "You should leave as soon as possible, Jacinta. The sooner you gather information, the sooner those intending to answer my other call can do so."

"Your other call?" Jacinta asked, bewildered. In her peripheral vision, she saw Mariella toss her head, but it was Matthias who answered.

"Father wants to punish Mariella for coming to Vallen," said Matthias tartly.

"Nonsense." The queen's voice was sharp. "Your Father's

plan is an excellent response to the outcome of the summit. And the reward offered is an appropriate and time-honored way to motivate private citizens to undertake important work with high risk and otherwise low reward."

Matthias scoffed. "You want to put an end to Mariella's antics once and for all," he contradicted. "Or at least, make them not your problem."

Jacinta exchanged a look with Hagen. "We don't know what you're talking about," she said to Matthias.

The prince drew in a controlled breath. "Father is issuing a call through back channels. It won't be publicly announced, but word will spread quickly enough. Any man who kills King Uroch will be awarded Mariella's hand in marriage."

Out of consideration, Jacinta forced herself not to respond to the impulse to look to Hagen for his reaction. But out of the corner of her eye she could still tell that he'd gone completely still at the prince's words. As for Mariella, she folded her arms, her face set in belligerent lines. For her part, Jacinta had no idea what to say.

"Never mind me," said Mariella. "Jacinta, Matthias is right. The command for you to enter Kjemper alone yet again is ridiculous. You absolutely don't have to do this."

"Thank you for your concern," said Jacinta quietly. "But I think I do. It's not just the royal order," she added quickly, seeing both Matthias and Mariella about to protest. "The information that came to light at the summit changes things. I don't want to see Providore drained of magic, or see the giants empowered to take control. And if I'm the only one who can get into Kjemper without raising a fuss, how can I do nothing?"

"A noble sentiment," said the king curtly. "So it's decided. You will stay at the castle tonight, while provisions are prepared. Tomorrow, a carriage will take you north."

"And I will accompany you," said Mariella decisively.

"You certainly will not." There was no compromise in the king's voice. "You will be under strict watch after your antics in Sunniva, Mariella. You're not going anywhere."

The princess scowled, but said nothing. Jacinta could see that she was plotting how to get around the restriction, but personally, she wouldn't bet against King Fidelius. Not given his current humor.

"But I will." Matthias's face was as hard as flint. "If the crown is to send Jacinta on this dangerous mission, I will see it done."

"You can't get through the tunnel, Matthias," the queen reminded him.

"But I can get to Briarford," Matthias said. "I'm going, and that's final."

"Need I remind you who is king here?" King Fidelius growled. "You are not to leave Vallen, Matthias, or I'll—"

"You'll what?" Matthias interrupted, bolder against his father than Jacinta had ever seen him. "Disinherit me? I respect your position as king, Father, but it's time you respected mine as well. I'm the heir to your throne, and I'm a grown man. It's well past time for you stop controlling my every movement. I can't force Jacinta to disregard an order I consider highly inappropriate, but I can force myself to overcome my own childish reluctance to exert my better sense when I disagree with you."

The king's jaw worked furiously for a moment, and Jacinta sensed that it would benefit no one for her to witness the coming argument.

"I will withdraw to rest and prepare for the journey," she said quickly.

"A room is being prepared for you," the queen said, inclining her head. Jacinta thought she saw a hint of approval in the older woman's eyes at Jacinta's evident desire to give the family privacy.

Jacinta and Hagen lost no time in vacating the room, Jacinta's mind whirling too much to even properly thank Hagen for his support. He seemed lost in his own thoughts as well, peeling off as a servant directed Jacinta to a room. A much simpler room than the one she'd previously occupied, she noted. Not that it bothered her.

She slept fitfully, her dreams full of frozen plains and angry giants. When she woke, the weak sunlight of early morning slanted through the curtains. She dressed quickly, guessing that the king would have prepared everything for an early departure.

She wasn't wrong. By the time she'd wolfed down some food in the apprentices' hall, Hagen was wending his way through the crowd toward her, a rucksack over his shoulder.

"Are you ready to go, Jacinta?" he asked.

She nodded, abandoning her food and standing. "Are you coming?"

He nodded. "The prince requested that I accompany him, and of course I'm very happy to do so."

The anxiety sitting on his brow made the words seem half-hearted. It seemed Mariella wasn't coming, then. She followed Hagen to the courtyard, where the princess waited, looking disconsolate.

"Be careful, Jacinta," Mariella said, embracing her friend. "Don't get yourself killed on Father's whim."

"I don't plan to," said Jacinta lightly. She saw Mariella's eyes stray to Hagen, and moved away to give the pair some space.

Matthias was standing nearby, looking confident and in control and incredibly handsome in his traveling gear. It seemed he'd won the day against his father's objections, then. Jacinta's heart swelled with pride in him for finally taking a stand. There was no denying he was even more attractive in this moment than she'd already found him.

"Jacinta."

The cool voice came not from the prince, but from the king, who appeared at Jacinta's elbow.

"Your Majesty." She attempted to dip into a curtsy.

"Your provisions for the journey into Kjemper have been packed into the carriage," he said.

"Thank you," she replied, feeling awkward.

"I wish you all safety and success on your mission," King Fidelius said. He stepped back. "I will await a full report upon your return."

Jacinta nodded, trying to fight down the nervous lump that rose in her throat.

"And...my instructions are merely to gather information, yes?" she said.

"That's right." The king surprised her with a wry smile. "Don't worry. No one expects you to assassinate the giant king."

Jacinta nodded, curtsying again as the king turned away. A servant came to invite her to climb into the carriage, and before she knew it, both Matthias and Hagen had followed her in. The prince must have said his goodbyes before she arrived.

"You're not riding?" she asked the pair.

"Not this time," said Matthias, as the carriage began to move. "We'll stay with you." He bit his lip. "I wish we could come with you through the wall, Jacinta."

"I don't," she said emphatically. She saw that Matthias looked a little wounded, and she smiled. "I don't want the safety of the crown prince in my hands."

"Who says my safety would be in your hands and not the other way around?" Matthias asked, his affronted tone making her smile more widely. When he spoke like that, he reminded her so much of the boyish prince of her childhood memories.

The carriage moved steadily northward with its escort of guards, no one speaking much until they'd left the city. Once they were on the open road, however, Matthias turned to Jacinta with purpose.

"I have something for you."

"Oh?" Jacinta told her foolish heart to stop beating at double speed. It was unlikely to be a romantic gesture with Hagen there.

"It's a talisman," said Matthias. "For you to take into Kjemper."

Hagen leaned forward with interest as Matthias pulled a pouch from his pocket. "It's small, if it fits in there. I haven't actually seen it yet. I'm glad to see you acquired it successfully, though."

Matthias gave a humorless smile. "Very delicately worded," he told his friend, before turning to Jacinta. "What Hagen means is that I stole it. And my father won't be happy when he discovers it. But you don't need to worry. He'll be angry at me, not you."

Jacinta couldn't see any reason why the king's anger need be limited to only one of them, but she didn't say so.

"Why did you steal it, Matthias? That seems like a terrible idea."

"No," said Matthias belligerently. "What's a terrible idea is sending you alone into Kjemper without even offering magical assistance."

"What kind of magical assistance are we talking about?" she asked doubtfully.

Matthias tossed the pouch up once, catching it in the palm of his hand before tossing it onto her lap. "The kind crafted by the most skilled Vadolisian elves as part of a covert initiative between our military and our Academy of Song."

"Military?" said Jacinta in alarm. "Matthias, even with magical assistance, I can't attack anyone. At least, I can't do so and win. Especially against giants."

"Do you think I'd ask that of you?" Matthias demanded indignantly. "This might have been developed by the military, but its function has nothing to do with taking life. It's designed to remove physical barriers—in this case, specifically stone. It contains a significant amount of magic. It's not enough to bring down the vastness of Battlement Wall, of course. But if you find yourself unable to return to your tunnel, it should be capable of breaching Battlement Wall with a large enough hole to get you back through."

Jacinta stared at the pouch. "If your father has access to such an object," she said, "wouldn't it be better to use that to get someone more qualified than me through the wall in the first place?"

The prince shook his head. "You forget that our aim is to be covert. This...wouldn't be. I'm advised that the resultant destruction would likely be dramatic."

"What does it do to the stone?" Jacinta asked dubiously.

"Reduces it to ash," Matthias said simply. "At least, that's what it's supposed to do." He grimaced. "To be perfectly frank, its full effect is unknown. It hasn't yet been tested, so I don't know how much stone it would destroy. But it contains a lot of magic."

"And is therefore extremely valuable," interjected Hagen. "So my recommendation would be to use it only in the direst of circumstances."

Matthias nodded his agreement.

"I understand," said Jacinta, receiving the pouch. She felt nervous to have an object stolen from the crown, but she couldn't see what she would gain by refusing it at this point. She tipped out the contents to see an oblong object, like a marble in texture, but considerably bigger and more oval.

"And be careful not to let it touch rock," Hagen reminded her. "The magic will activate as soon as it does. If you accidentally touch it to a random boulder, it'll destroy that rock, and any others directly touching it, and all that power will be wasted."

Jacinta nodded, returning the talisman to the pouch and stowing the whole thing in her pocket.

The journey passed more quickly in the comfort of a private carriage, but it lacked the cheerful feel of the trip from Sunniva. Matthias was trying not to show it, but he was still deeply disapproving of her mission, and clearly terrified of the outcome. His demeanor made Jacinta feel more and more like she was riding to her doom. The closer they got to Briarford, the more agitated the prince became, and the more he withdrew. As always, Hagen stepped in and made an effort to keep Jacinta relaxed with his friendly conversation, and as always, Matthias seemed to resent it.

When they at last reached Briarford, all their nerves were frayed. The servants went ahead to attempt to make the manor inhabitable—Matthias had insisted on staying there, and refused to lodge in the nearest inn, a town over—but Jacinta requested that the carriage go straight to her home. She knew her mother would be wondering why it had taken her so long to return from Sunniva.

"Will we be welcome?" Matthias asked tentatively, as the carriage came to a stop in Jacinta's bare yard.

Jacinta nodded, nerves suddenly overcoming her. It was partly from embarrassment at what Matthias would think of her simple home. But also, truth be told, she had no idea how her mother would receive the prince.

"Of course you're welcome," she said, aware that the words were unconvincing. "But...there's something I probably need to tell you." She felt her face color.

"I'll step out," said Hagen quickly, with the sensitivity Jacinta had come to appreciate in him. He pushed the door of the carriage open, descending onto the frozen ground.

Jacinta found herself unable to look Matthias in the eye. Although they'd been together a great deal in Sunniva and on the two journeys, they'd never had time alone. Mariella had always been there, or Hagen, or any number of servants and guards. She'd used the lack of privacy as an excuse for not telling Matthias before now. But it was time.

She drew in a breath, forcing herself to look up at the prince. He looked concerned, his eyes intense as they rested on her face.

"I should have said this earlier, but I didn't know how to bring it up. I'm sorry I never replied to any of your letters."

CHAPTER TWENTY-ONE

Jacinta

Jacinta watched as surprise flickered across Matthias's face. She had the sense that the letters were a mystery he'd given up on solving.

"I always wondered," he said softly. "But I know I had no right to assume that—"

"No." Jacinta cut him off with a shake of her head. "That's not true. We were good friends, and you wrote to me. You had every right to expect that I would reply. The truth is that I didn't receive the letters. I only learned about them very recently." She dropped her eyes, unable to bear his unwavering scrutiny. "My mother didn't think it was wise for me to correspond with you. She removed your letters before giving me the ones from Mariella. She only confessed to me after my last trip to Vallen. I thought…"

"You thought that unlike Mariella, I didn't care enough about you to write to you," Matthias finished steadily.

Her eyes were still lowered, but Jacinta caught his movement as he leaned forward. The next thing she knew, his hand was on her chin, its cool pressure gently lifting her face to his. Her skin felt numb where he touched it, like none of this could be real.

"I hope you know now how wrong you were to believe I didn't care," Matthias said, his eyes holding her in thrall. "I'm sorry you thought I'd forgotten you." A frown creased his forehead, and he dropped his hand. "Why didn't you write to me, or ask Mariella?"

Jacinta swallowed, able to breathe again. "I was too proud," she admitted ruefully. "And too upset you weren't coming back. And too uncertain of where we all stood given..." She gestured vaguely. "Everything."

Matthias leaned back against the seat of the carriage. "I wouldn't have understood that then," he admitted. "But I think I'm starting to now."

Jacinta tried to smile, but the gesture felt strained. Try as she might to tell herself that it was good for Matthias to finally understand the barriers between them, she couldn't seem to make her heart believe it.

"Come on," she said. "In spite of her deception, I'm eager to see my mother. And Hagen will be wondering what's become of us."

"Yes," said Matthias, his expression changing as usual at the mention of the Frossian singer. "We should go."

Jacinta led the way out of the carriage and across the frozen yard, Hagen joining them from where he'd been waiting a respectful distance away. Her mother was predictably flustered by the appearance of the prince and a stranger in her humble dwelling. Matthias, Jacinta was grateful to see, treated her mother with friendly courtesy, giving no indication of his knowledge of the wrong she'd done him all those years ago. Jacinta could see the guilt in the older woman's eyes when they rested on Matthias, though. It surprised her that her mother seemed to assume Jacinta had told the prince about it. Even she hadn't been sure she was going to do it.

Another reaction Jacinta couldn't help noticing was

Matthias's as he looked about the small, simple space. Nothing in word or manner revealed anything but pleasure at being there, but she caught the lingering distress in his eyes when he thought he was unobserved.

She understood why. The servants' quarters at the manor hadn't been fancy, but her current home was very different. She shouldn't have brought him here. But he'd been so determined to come.

Jacinta's mother was clearly unhappy to discover her daughter was to go through the wall again, but she said little while their guests were present. When a servant arrived to collect Matthias and Hagen and take them to the manor, they had a hasty discussion and agreed that they would reconvene in the morning before Jacinta approached Battlement Wall.

"I hope to have something for you in the morning," Hagen said, when Jacinta walked them into the yard. "I've been working on it. It's not quite there yet, but I'll stay up as long as it takes."

"Thank you," said Jacinta, surprised. "I'll be grateful for any help." She noticed Matthias watching them rather than listening to the servant who was trying to speak to him, and she stepped back. "I'll see you in the morning."

Hagen nodded. "Don't you stay up all night," he told her firmly. "Get as much sleep as you can."

"I will," she assured him.

With a final nod, he rejoined Matthias, and the two of them left with the servant. Hesitantly, Jacinta walked back into her house.

"Well." The abrupt change in her mother's manner was almost comical. "That was...something."

"I probably shouldn't have sprung them on you like that," Jacinta said wearily. "But I'm so little in control of my life these days, I've learned to just go along with it."

"Never mind me," said her mother crisply. "Jacinta, is the king really sending you into Kjemper for official espionage?"

"Something like that," said Jacinta, sinking into a chair.

"He's punishing us." Her mother tapped a fist on the table in a tense movement. "Even after all these years, he's still punishing us."

"Maybe," said Jacinta. "Or maybe he's just trying to use his only way into the giants' land. I don't know, and I don't see that it makes much difference." She gave a wry smile. "Matthias and Mariella assure me I don't have to go."

"They're right," her mother said emphatically.

Jacinta gave her a look. "They're right that I can just ignore a royal order?"

Her mother grunted. "They're right that you *shouldn't* have to go."

"Well, we both know those things aren't the same," said Jacinta. "Do we have some food, Mamma? I should get an early night."

"Yes, of course." Her mother bustled into motion. "You sit and rest, I'll get dinner started."

Instead of sitting in the chair her mother indicated, Jacinta moved to her bed. After a moment's careful thought, she pulled out the small sewing kit she kept in the nearby cupboard for repairs, and set to work on her most practical gown.

"What are you doing?" her mother asked, baffled.

Jacinta grimaced, thinking of Matthias's defiance in the carriage. He might not fear the consequences of his theft, but she did on his behalf. "Don't ask," she told her mother. "Better not to know."

With a sigh, her mother shrugged, turning away as Jacinta continued unpicking one section of the hem of her chosen gown. Checking that her mother was occupied with the food, she slipped the pouch from her pocket and poured out the oblong marble object. It was beautiful in the firelight, but somehow also deadly. Or was that just because she knew it was capable of great destruction?

Remembering Hagen's warning about not letting the talisman touch stone by accident, Jacinta took extra care in placing it into the open hem and sewing the fabric closed around it. It was the most secure and undetectable hiding place she could think of.

She stitched and restitched the area, determined for it to be secure enough not to be dislodged by whatever scrambling she might do in her quest to reach the giants' capital. She could only hope it would be able to stay safely in its hiding place all the way back so she could return it to the prince. With any luck, she'd be able to exit Kjemper through her tunnel and would have no need to blow a hole in Battlement Wall.

Her task done, Jacinta hurried through a simple meal. Half because of genuine exhaustion, and half to avoid further discussion with her mother over the ordeal to come, she went to bed with the sun. She would need all the energy she could get for what the new day would bring.

For the first time in a long time, Jacinta woke to the clucking of the chickens.

"I wonder how Barbarity is getting on at the castle," she muttered to no one in particular.

"What's that?"

Jacinta sat up, her gaze landing on her mother, who was stoking the fire. "Nothing," she said quickly.

"Your escorts are already outside," her mother said. "I'm making tea for them all."

"What?" Jacinta pulled back the curtain a tiny bit, alarmed

to see that Matthias, Hagen, and a motley group of guards and servants were indeed waiting in the yard. "Did I oversleep?"

"Not really," her mother said. "For some reason, they all arrived at the crack of dawn." She cast Jacinta a glance. "I think that prince of yours was worried you'd try to sneak off to the wall without them all."

Jacinta grimaced, performing a speedy wash and change. At least she didn't have time to get nervous waiting, she reflected, as she pulled on her modified gown and her sturdiest boots. After a moment's hesitation, she donned the muffler as well. It was cold enough south of the wall. It would be even colder to the north.

"I was going to pack you a rucksack, but I've been informed that the crown is providing you with plentiful provisions," her mother said.

Jacinta nodded. "So I've been told." She followed her mother outside, juggling their half dozen earthen cups for the tea to be poured into.

"Jacinta!" Matthias's face lit up at the sight of her, causing Jacinta's heart to jump pleasantly. "Good morning."

"Good morning," she said. She handed the empty cups to the pair of servants who hurried forward to receive them, then cast her eyes over the prince. He looked tired. "You don't look like you got much sleep," she said.

Matthias just grunted. "How are you feeling this morning?" He lowered his voice. "You know, it's not too late for you to decide not to do this."

Jacinta looked pointedly at the crowd gathered in her yard. "It really is. I'm not changing my mind now."

"So where's this beanstalk?" The head guard of the group moved toward them, clearly impatient to see his mission through.

"It's this way," said Jacinta.

She moved across the yard, the group swarming to follow. Matthias walked on one side of her, and Hagen took up a position on the other. Even her mother had joined the procession. The feeling that she was walking to her doom intensified, but she forced it down. She was being melodramatic.

Murmurs of interest passed around the group when the beanstalk came into view, turning to full exclamations when they reached the point where it disappeared into the wall.

"It's closed up!" said a servant, eyeing what must look like solid wall in dismay. She looked disappointed that the spectacle might not occur after all.

Jacinta shook her head. "It's the same as always. I can see a tunnel around the vine. It passes right through."

"Can you really crawl through this invisible tunnel?" a guard asked doubtfully.

"I can," said Jacinta.

"Have you made your personal preparations?" the head guard asked.

Jacinta shrugged. "I don't really have any to make."

The grizzled man gave a nod. "Your provisions are all prepared, and they'll be loaded into a rucksack now." He glanced around the barren patch of land. "We will set up a camp here to await your return."

Jacinta barely had time to nod nervously before she felt a light touch on her arm. "Can I speak to you privately for a moment, Jacinta?"

She looked up at Hagen, surprised. The Frossian singer was as calm and collected as usual.

"Of course," she said.

"Over here, then." Hagen took her arm, leading her across the frozen ground toward a small stand of scraggly trees nearby.

Jacinta couldn't stop herself glancing back at Matthias, who was unable to hide his tension as he watched them. But once

Hagen led her into the trees, she couldn't see the rest of the group anymore, Matthias included.

"Sorry about the secrecy," Hagen said matter-of-factly. "I'm not really sure if I was allowed to make this without supervision, or if I'm allowed to give it to you. But this is it. The thing I said I'd have ready for you this morning."

Jacinta stared down at the necklace in his outstretched hand. The chain was simple and coarse, but the smooth, round disc that formed the pendant appeared to be made of gold.

"Hagen, this looks expensive," she said, distressed.

He shook his head. "The necklace itself isn't much. The only reason I used gold is because it's a good conductor of magic. I've put as much magic as I could muster into it. It's probably the most powerful thing I've ever made."

Jacinta could sense the touch of pride in the apprentice's voice, and she smiled as naturally as she could manage.

"It was kind of you to waste so much effort on me," she said. "What does it do?"

"It wasn't a waste," Hagen contradicted politely. "For the sake of our friendship as well as your mission, I was glad to do it. It's a concealment talisman. The magic is simple in purpose. I put all the effort into the quantity, and didn't want to waste power on crafting anything sophisticated. Hopefully that means it will be potent enough to last until you return. When you wear it around your neck, it will conceal you from all observers. You, your clothes, anything you're carrying."

"Hagen, that's brilliant!" said Jacinta, her enthusiasm real this time. "This will help enormously. I can't thank you enough." She took the offered necklace, impulsively leaning forward to hug the Frossian around the middle.

A cleared throat made her pull back quickly.

"It seems I intrude."

Jacinta's eyes flew to Matthias, standing a few paces behind

Hagen. She hadn't seen him approach through the sparse trees. The prince looked as uncomfortable as she felt, but he didn't seem inclined to withdraw and restore the privacy he apparently thought she and Hagen were seeking.

"Matthias, I...we just...Hagen gave me this!" she blurted out, holding up the necklace.

Matthias stared at it with an unreadable expression for a long and painful moment. Then Hagen, still calm and matter-of-fact, rescued the situation.

"It's a talisman I ordered from an elf back in Vallen," he explained. "I've spent the last several days activating it with my own magic. It should conceal Jacinta from any observing eyes while she's in Kjemper."

"Oh." Matthias blinked. "That's...an excellent idea, Hagen. Why didn't you mention it?"

"I wanted to be sure I could finish it in time," the singer shrugged. He flashed a rare grin. "And I suppose I had pride in my project. I wanted to reveal it only once it was finished." He glanced at the necklace. "Although I suppose neither of you can feel the full effect, can you?"

"I suppose not," said Matthias, his voice still slightly wooden.

Hagen glanced between them, then coughed discreetly. "I'll check how the provisioning is going." With his usual tact, he withdrew through the trees, leaving Jacinta and Matthias alone.

The strained silence was broken by the prince. "A concealment talisman really is a good idea," he said gruffly.

Jacinta nodded, fiddling with the necklace for a moment, then stowing it in a pocket. "It was kind of Hagen. Both to think of it, and to expend what I imagine must have been considerable energy and resources making it. I'm very grateful to him."

"Understandably." Matthias was trying to speak politely, but Jacinta could tell the words cost him effort. "Now I think of it, he has seemed very tired for days past. This morning I could barely rouse him from sleep when it was time to leave, which isn't like him."

Jacinta swallowed, nodding again. She couldn't seem to find anything to say. Not with how close Matthias was standing in the small space between the trees, and all the unspoken thoughts brimming in his eyes.

"You and Hagen get along well," Matthias said, the words falling abruptly into the silence.

"Yes," said Jacinta.

She waited for him to elaborate, but he said nothing. All of a sudden, frustration rose up in her. It was too much. She was on the point of a potentially fatal adventure she didn't want, and her nerves were already frayed to breaking point. And now Matthias was going to make cryptic comments and pull her into whatever he was thinking without even being willing to acknowledge it aloud?

"What of it?" she said testily. "So what if Hagen and I have become friends? Why does that bother you and Mariella so much? You're quick to claim you always wanted to continue our friendship in spite of me being a peasant, aren't you?"

Matthias took a small step back, his brow furrowed in obvious confusion. "I don't recall ever calling you a peasant, Jacinta," he said. "I've never thought of you that way."

"But that's what I am, isn't it?" Jacinta demanded. "That's why your parents hate the very idea of my friendship with their royal children, and always will! Don't pretend you don't see the barriers between us."

Matthias suddenly shifted forward again, reclaiming the ground he'd ceded and then some. Jacinta's breath caught in her throat as she found herself looking up at him, his face inches from hers.

"I was never unaware that others had placed barriers

between us, Jacinta," he said, his voice lower now. "I've always known that, better than you can imagine. But I don't see the barriers. I never have."

"You claim that," said Jacinta, unwilling to back down in spite of her breathlessness. "But both you and Mariella still disapprove of my friendship with Hagen. Neither of you can hide it. How can you claim not to think our status separates us when you're uncomfortable with even an apprentice singer stooping to befriend me?"

"What?" Matthias demanded incredulously. "You can't possibly think that, Jacinta. I know I've been strange about your connection with Hagen, but it was nothing to do with you being beneath him!"

"What, then?" Jacinta demanded, tears pricking at her eyes. She blinked them angrily away, annoyed with her own overly stretched emotions. "Why would you disapprove?"

"Because I'm jealous!" Matthias burst out. Suddenly his hands were on her upper arms, his grip tight with everything he'd been holding in. "Every time you smile at him, or run from me and my crown to him as a safer haven, it kills me!"

"Jealous?" Jacinta's throat was dry, and she couldn't seem to look away from his stormy gaze. He'd seen and understood more about her friendship with Hagen than she'd imagined. "Even if you mean what you say about us, that's foolish," she argued. "A person can have more than one friend."

"Friend?" Matthias's grip tightened, his irritated expression so like his boyhood self it was endearing, even in the heat of the moment. "Jacinta, can you truly be this oblivious?" He shook his head. "You have no idea how much of my life I spend being careful of every word, every look. But I'm never careful with you —I can't seem to manage it! If I gave half the signals I've given to you to any girl in the court—"

He cut himself off, closing his eyes and drawing in a deep

breath. Released from his gaze, Jacinta felt herself breathe as well.

"I'm not criticizing you," Matthias said, his eyes opening slowly and his voice more sincere than annoyed now. "You've never been like those other girls, and I've always loved you for it."

Jacinta's breath caught at the word, but Matthias wasn't finished.

"But it's truly hard to believe you could actually be this unaware of how I feel about you, Jacinta. Have I really hidden it so well?"

She lowered her eyes, her heart beating with uncomfortable speed. "I...I've wondered at times," she admitted. "But it seemed too presumptuous to even suspect it."

"No," said Matthias. "No talk of presumption."

The forceful words were softened by the way his hands slid from her upper arms to her shoulders, his fingers tentative as they moved up her neck, cupping her face. A trail of blazing heat followed his touch, making it hard for Jacinta to concentrate on all her arguments for why they should protect themselves by keeping their distance.

"Not between us," Matthias murmured. "We've never presumed or pretended." He drew a deep breath as he searched her eyes. "At least, we never used to. And it's time for me to stop trying to be anything but candid with you. Jacinta, I want so much more than friendship from you. I've loved you all my life. The nature of that love has changed since we were children, but it's a change that was inevitable. Even my own parents recognized that, well before I did. No distance or years could remove you from my heart. I don't believe anything ever will."

"Matthias."

Jacinta's whisper was anguished, unspeakable joy mingling with despair at his confession. She'd tried very weakly to deny it to herself, but all her feeble attempts were swept away by the fire in his eyes. His words forced her to acknowledge that his love was what she wanted most desperately in all the world.

It was cruel of life to dangle such a prize in front of her when she could never claim it.

"Say something, Jacinta," Matthias begged. "Put me out of my misery one way or the other. Don't hold back for the sake of my feelings. If there's no chance you could ever love me, I'd rather know at once."

"Matthias," Jacinta protested. "You are the best and truest man I've ever known. How could I not love you? How could I not want this?"

But it's impossible. The rest of the thought remained unspoken. A light had sprung into Matthias's eyes at her words, and he hadn't waited to hear more. Before Jacinta could blink, one of his arms had slid down to her waist, and he'd pulled her against him.

All arguments of the barriers between them fled. It never occurred to her to pull away as his lips crushed against hers. Putting distance between them was the last thing she wanted to do.

She could have sworn the sad, barren copse blazed with dancing lights as Matthias kissed her, her own lips eager against his in response. One of her hands had somehow found its way to his chest, the other sliding around to his back and clutching his thick cloak like a lifeline as the prince deepened the kiss.

Jacinta felt like her whole life had led to this moment, as though for one minute of delirious happiness, everything was finally right, finally exactly as it should be. She was in Matthias's arms, holding nothing back from him, fully seen and loved in spite of everything.

And then reality reasserted itself, and she broke the kiss,

gasping for air. "Your timing," she murmured, dazed, "isn't amazing."

Matthias groaned, his lips suddenly pressed against her forehead in a caress that felt just as intimate as the one they'd just shared.

"Jacinta, please don't do this," he whispered, his voice ragged and hoarse. "I can't bear to let you disappear through that wall. How will I stand it, waiting helplessly here while you risk your life, with no way of knowing if you're even alive?"

Jacinta drew in a shuddering breath, pulling fully back from him at last. "The same way I'll bear whatever I find on the other side," she said frankly. "We don't have a choice, Matthias. I don't have a choice."

"Yes, you do," Matthias said earnestly. His eyes begged her to listen. "You could choose to stay with me. To be with me instead of alone and in danger."

Jacinta smiled sadly, lifting one hand to lay it on his cheek. His skin was scratchy. Apparently he'd been in such haste to reach her that morning and make sure she didn't sneak through the wall before dawn, he'd neglected to shave.

"If I truly had that option, I wouldn't hesitate," she told him. "But however we feel, I think we both know we're deluding ourselves to think it's a future we can actually grasp."

"I don't accept that," said Matthias fiercely. But he had no more chance to argue his case.

"Your Highness?"

The gruff voice preceded the figure of the prince's head guard by only moments, barely giving Jacinta time to draw back out of Matthias's reach. She resisted the urge to pat self-consciously at her hair, knowing it would only make her look more suspicious. Hopefully her cheeks weren't as red as they felt. At least she would very soon be out of reach of any repercussions of being caught embracing the prince. There wasn't much even the king could do to her once she was north of Battlement Wall.

"What is it?" Matthias asked, the words as close to a snap as Jacinta had ever heard from him.

"You've been away from the main group too long, Prince Matthias," said the guard chidingly. "And the provisions have been prepared." His eyes passed to Jacinta. "Are you ready, miss?"

She drew a steadying breath, refusing to let her eyes stray to where Matthias's gaze was burning a hole in the side of her head.

"Yes," she said evenly. "I'm ready."

CHAPTER TWENTY-TWO

Jacinta

Jacinta completed the walk back to the wall in a daze. Half of her mind was convinced she was in a vivid dream, but the other half knew that Matthias's kiss was the most real thing she'd ever experienced.

Her mission into Kjemper felt distant and unimportant, and even in her mind's fog, she recognized that was dangerous. She needed her wits to be sharp. It was time to pull herself together.

"You ready?" Hagen asked, his voice full of its habitual kindness as he stepped up to meet her.

She nodded. "As much as I'll ever be."

"Here, miss." A servant handed Jacinta a bulging rucksack.

She eyed it doubtfully. Just how heavy was it going to be? "You're sure the talisman will conceal that too?" she muttered to Hagen.

"As long as you're wearing the rucksack." The confidence in the singer's words calmed Jacinta, and she straightened her back.

"All right, then." She looked around for her mother, the older woman materializing instantly at her side.

"Be safe," said her mother gruffly, embracing Jacinta briefly but fiercely. "Or as safe as you can be in there."

"Yes." Matthias's voice sent a shiver down Jacinta's spine that was far from unpleasant. She'd had no idea he was so close behind her. "Come back to us in one piece."

The words had all the authority of a royal order, but when Jacinta turned to face him, his eyes pleaded with her with as much vulnerability as any man sending the woman he loved into danger.

The woman he loved. That thought was going to take a while to settle.

Jacinta could think of nothing to say, only managing a small nod. She felt as uncertain and helpless as Matthias looked. None of them knew what was coming.

"All right, then," she said to no one in particular. "Time to go." She hefted the rucksack over her shoulder and walked forward with swift steps. When she reached the tunnel, she gave one glance back. Better to just get it over with.

Leaning down, she crawled into the hole. Her movements felt awkward, hampered by the large rucksack, and she was forced almost to slither on her stomach to fit through this time. It wasn't ideal that so many people—some very exalted—were witnessing this maneuver. But she realized that once she was fully inside the tunnel, they would see nothing but solid wall. In moments, there was silence, the murmurs of the onlookers deadened by the wall that she couldn't see or feel, but that her mind knew was still there.

Jacinta kept moving forward, a reckless part of her relieved to be out of the human world and away from watching eyes. But when she emerged into the frigid wasteland of Kjemper, any enthusiasm leaked away. She glanced back at the tunnel, wondering fleetingly if she'd ever see her home again before banishing such morbid thoughts. She might have a longer journey through the giants' land this time, but she was also much better equipped than on her previous visits.

With that thought in mind, she pulled Hagen's necklace out of her pocket and placed it around her neck. She could still see the testing hand she held out in front of her face. Hopefully that just meant the enchantment didn't include the wearer, not that it wasn't working.

Jacinta cast a glance around her, noting where the beanstalk snaked off northward toward the home of the first giant she'd met. But she didn't follow it this time. Based on King Herleif's account, she needed to head west for a long way before she'd reach Kjemper's capital. He'd said it wasn't far north of Battlement Wall, so she'd decided her surest course would be to follow the wall until she caught sight of the city, so as not to risk getting lost.

She set off at a brisk walk, glad that the rocky ground wasn't buried in snow. There was a light layer of powder, and here and there she saw larger drifts, but she shouldn't leave distinct tracks the way she would in proper snow.

The day passed slowly and miserably. It was cold and monotonous, walking alongside the wall for hour upon hour, stopping only to eat sparingly of the rations. Not that there was any lack. Whatever his feelings about her personally, King Fidelius hadn't skimped on the supplies. There was plenty of dried meat, enough bread to keep her full for as long as bread would last, a whole wheel of cheese, numerous apples, two large wineskins full of water—which helped explain the rucksack's weight—and more. There was also rope, a miniature metal pot, a thin dagger in a scabbard, which Jacinta strapped on at the first stop, and a packet wrapped in wax paper which turned out to contain a flint and kindling.

But Jacinta had no confidence that she would complete the journey as quickly as planned, and she didn't want to take any chance of running out of supplies. Besides which, she was used to surviving on small quantities of food. So she ate only enough to satiate her hunger and tucked the rest back into the rucksack.

The best that could be said for the day was that she didn't encounter any giants. She did catch sight of a few more mining towers, but they were all well in the distance, and at no point did she feel that her concealment talisman would be put to the test.

Tired though she was, she would have liked to have kept walking until dark, to cover as much ground as possible. But when she saw a sheltered-looking cave a couple of hours before sundown, she didn't think she could afford to pass up the opportunity. What if she kept going and found herself wandering in the frozen darkness, with no shelter overnight? It was too big a risk.

As well as providing shelter from the weather, the cave helped hide any evidence of her fire. But she still felt nervous as she eventually settled down to sleep alongside the modest blaze. She was so weary on her feet, even the insufficient bed created by her cloak was appealing. She couldn't keep going without sleep. But she would be so vulnerable with no one to watch over her.

Nevertheless, the night passed without incident. Jacinta did her best to conceal the evidence of her fire, but she knew her efforts wouldn't stand up to close scrutiny. After a quick meal, she set off again. Encouraged by the fact that she still hadn't seen any giants, and mindful that the talisman may have a limited lifespan, Jacinta took off Hagen's necklace.

The day passed much the same as the one before. The worst of the monotony was that she had far too much time to think about what had passed between her and Matthias. With little else to occupy her mind, it was impossible not to dwell on the feel of his arms around her, and the gentle way he'd cupped her face. She couldn't decide if his declaration made her own feelings easier or harder to bear. Harder, probably, given none of it did anything to make their ultimate separation less inevitable. What would Mariella say when she heard about what had happened? She'd probably squeal delightedly, as in denial as her brother about the impossibility of Jacinta ever being part of their world.

Jacinta's mind strayed to the way the princess's eyes often lingered on Hagen, and the war she'd seen in the apprentice singer's eyes between the warmth the princess seemed to evoke in him and the cautious distance that was necessary to survival on the fringes of royal society. Mariella might be in denial, but Hagen wasn't. And Jacinta couldn't see a happy outcome for her friends' situation any more than for her own.

By the fourth day of walking, even Matthias's kiss couldn't distract Jacinta from her immediate circumstances anymore. She was cold to her very bones, and more tired than she could remember being in her life. The ground was hard and icy, and more than once she slipped and fell. Even Battlement Wall itself was covered in ice, the formation hiding the rock underneath. It was as though a mountain range had developed against the wall over the generations, but made of ice rather than rock. It emanated cold, requiring Jacinta to travel a little further from the wall than she'd like.

And the cold was far from her only concern. Her body ached from the endless walking, from the uncomfortable nights in dubious shelter, and from the constant weight of the rucksack on her shoulders. At least the bag was getting lighter as she made her way through the provisions, she reflected dryly. Not that she was running out. She'd conserved plenty. She'd also been able to use the metal pot to melt snow over her fire, so her water skins were refilled.

The afternoon was advancing, and she was just starting to think about finding shelter, when she saw it. As she walked, she kept looking northward, hoping to catch a glimpse of the capital, and at last her searching was rewarded. A distant glint caught her eye, like glass reflecting the orange light of the afternoon sun. Could it be the city? Had she finally come far enough west?

Nervously, Jacinta slipped Hagen's necklace back on, tucking it beneath her gown. She hoisted her rucksack over her bruised shoulders and changed direction. As she trekked northward, the ground became even more frozen. She couldn't sense magic like a singer, but the very barrenness of the terrain told her there must be none to be found in the ground itself.

Although, she reminded herself, that was apparently a false assumption. If the elf princess Asivah was to be believed, humans were wrong to think that the fertility or barrenness of the land affected how much magic it produced. That situation had been created by the movement of human singers. If the magic of this land was as sparse as the vegetation, it was because of the giants' mining activities, not because of the climate.

Still, the land felt empty in every way to Jacinta. As the light faded, and the glinting spot on the horizon grew into a dark mass of stone, she could only hope the concealment enchantment would work, given the city wouldn't be as empty.

By the time darkness fell, the city was spread out before her. She'd expected to see more giants than she had. She'd spotted a few from a distance, making their way along the main road that wound around toward the city from the west, their lumbering forms enormous and their gray skin blending unsettlingly with the rocky landscape around them. But generally speaking, the road was deserted enough that she soon decided she could risk walking on it.

Her progress became much faster, but she still didn't reach the capital in time to pass through the huge stone gates before they were closed for the night. Perhaps it was for the best. She would prefer to brave the city during daylight.

Circling back, Jacinta retraced her steps along the now silent road, starting to feel anxious about finding shelter. Fortunately for her, there were a few dilapidated buildings scattered across the barren ground not far from the city. A tentative search of the closest one showed it was long since abandoned. No doubt its inhabitants had moved within the relative safety and comfort of the city's wall. Made for giants, the structure was high-ceilinged and drafty, but she was able to find a passable shelter in what appeared to have once been a small storage space. She didn't dare light a fire so close to the capital, and consequently slept little. But the storage space was so enclosed, it provided considerable shelter from the elements, and with the talisman still around her neck, she had little fear of detection.

When the sun finally rose, Jacinta forced herself out of her hiding place, stumbling on her frozen toes. Peeking out of the building, she saw a pair of giants emerging from the city gates which now stood open. But the road was far from busy. It didn't seem that many giants came and went from the capital. She remembered the words of the first giant she'd met. There was clearly some truth to the suggestion that the giants didn't naturally take to the idea of centralized leadership. Jacinta wondered how many lived in or frequented the capital, and how many preferred to live independently in the far-flung corners of Kjemper.

Jacinta rejoined the road, moving cautiously as she approached the city. The first test of Hagen's magic came when she reached the gates. Now that they stood wide open, they were manned by a pair of giants, and Jacinta held her breath as she stared up at their vast forms. The guards looked bored, their spears held loosely in enormous hands, and their square gray heads swiveling only occasionally to check the empty landscape. One of them picked at uneven, razor-like, yellow teeth with a dirty fingernail. Neither gave any sign of having seen her.

Breathing a silent thanks to the absent Hagen, Jacinta walked between the guards and into the city. She had no idea how she would have managed a stealthy entrance without the Frossian's magic, and she could only be grateful she hadn't needed to formulate a plan.

The streets were almost as empty as the road outside. Perhaps giants weren't early risers, but Jacinta also had the impression that many of the dwellings she passed were deserted. Was this further evidence that more giants than the one she'd spoken to were losing faith in the leadership of their new king? Had they already started to abandon the capital city prized by the king's mother, and move back toward whatever clans and solitary living their kind had once preferred? Jacinta locked these observations away, aware that it was exactly the sort of information she was supposed to be gathering. Hopefully the task of the human monarchs in destabilizing the aggressive giant king would be easier than she'd feared. If some brave warrior—no doubt motivated by a desire to marry poor Mariella —could take out the giant king, perhaps the whole plot against the human lands and their magic would crumble, and all the giants would scatter back to the relative peace of their own in-fighting.

It was a heartening thought that the goal might be achievable, but it still seemed a long way off to Jacinta. That wasn't her problem, though. All she had to do was observe and gather information. And thanks to Hagen's magic, the task was looking to be much easier than she'd feared. She'd already made it to the capital, which had been half her challenge. Now she just needed to get into the castle.

The castle wasn't hard to find. It was enormous, even in proportion to the giant-sized buildings that made up the rest of the city. It rose from the center of the capital, the main road leading straight to it. In spite of her dislike of all it stood for, Jacinta had to admit it was an impressive—even beautiful— sight. Similar to Battlement Wall, the spires and stonework of the castle were coated in ice, so that it glowed crisply in the early morning light. The ice didn't look like a naturally forming glacier, like at the wall, however. It was perfectly molded to the shape of the castle, and Jacinta had to assume it was held there by magic. Whatever the strategy, it achieved its purpose of drawing her eyes irresistibly. As the city began to wake, she had to remind herself to keep her focus on the street before her, so as to leave a wide berth between her invisible form and any passing giants. She would have to be more careful within the castle.

The thought occurred to her, as she crossed the dark stone courtyard in front of the building, that she would be done for if the castle held magical protections intended to identify intruders. But based on what she'd been told of the giant ruler, she was optimistic that the magic at work in his castle had probably been directed to showy rather than practical purposes.

The main door of the castle was five times as tall as Jacinta, and manned by four heavily armed giants. Their chainmail glinted menacingly in the light, and the spears they carried would leave a hole the size of a boulder in Jacinta's middle if one ran her through. Once again holding her breath, she crept soundlessly forward, her hands clutching the straps of her rucksack and her elbows tucked in. Every movement of her feet seemed deafening in her ears, but none of the guards gave any sign of hearing her. One of them was complaining idly to another about the early morning, and they looked as bored as the ones on the city gate. They certainly showed none of the sharp-eyed dedication Jacinta had observed in King Fidelius's personal guards. Her thoughts straying back to Matthias, Jacinta could only be glad that the members of the Vadolisian royal guard were more conscientious than their giant counterparts.

Stop it, she told herself. She couldn't afford to get distracted thinking about the prince. She had more than enough to occupy her. She crept across the castle's entranceway, her nerves growing as a servant bustled past with arms full of linen. She would have to be very careful not to get knocked into. Backing into an alcove, she took a moment to get her bearings. She remembered King Herleif describing the overwhelming amount of gold in the castle's decor. Gaudy, Queen Adrienne had called it. They'd said that every tapestry, every ornament, was golden.

Jacinta frowned. Something had obviously changed in the two years that had passed since then. She couldn't see any sign of gold. Moving cautiously forward once the coast was clear, she made her way down a quiet corridor, everything confirming her first impression. Not only was there no gold or other costly decorations, but everywhere she saw evidence that ornaments had been removed and not replaced. It seemed King Uroch had fallen on harder times than his mother.

She pulled into an unadorned alcove as a pair of servants passed, the two giant men talking between themselves.

"His High and Mightiness is in a foul mood today," one commented, his voice coarse and not even lowered. "Many more days like this, and I'm quitting and going back west. Sick of the nonsense."

The other grunted in agreement. "Shoulda left when that puny human king killed Grograna," he agreed, his voice also rough, but lacking the distinctive accent of the giant from near Jacinta's part of the wall. These giants must hail from a different region of Kjemper. "Wasn't much to be fond of in old Groggy, but at least she seemed to know what she was doing. Didn't let herself be bossed around by a bunch of elves."

He spat on the ground with the word, the other giant giving

an angry mutter as they passed out of hearing range. Jacinta stayed where she was for a moment, her eyebrows raised. The open lack of respect was more extreme than she'd imagined. Things were clearly not going well for Uroch if his own servants spoke of him that way in his own castle. And why did these giants feel their king was being controlled by the elves he was working with? It didn't seem the royals' cooperation with the miniature species had won them any favor in the eyes of their people.

Jacinta began to move again, wandering aimlessly through the building. When she found herself having to dodge giants too frequently, she would change course, seeking a quieter part of the castle. When her stomach began to ache, she found a storeroom in which to crouch and quickly eat some cheese and dried meat. She was nervous the whole time her rucksack was off her back, aware that it wouldn't be covered by Hagen's enchantment unless she was wearing it. But no one disturbed her hiding place.

When the afternoon was wearing into evening, she'd discovered little else of interest, other than confirming the castle's lack of costly furnishings and the general dissatisfaction of its inhabitants. Even the more finely dressed giants who passed, clearly upper-class members of the society rather than servants, didn't seem very happy.

Jacinta was just wondering what to do for the night when one such group passed the empty parlor where she was sheltering. Their disgruntled voices wafted through to her.

"Another night with no dinner. He calls himself a king, wants us to be his court. Grograna at least used to know how to treat the ones she expected to obey her."

"Uroch isn't hosting dinner tonight?" The answering voice sounded indignant.

A scoffing noise met the question. "Oh, he's hosting dinner.

Just not for us. He prefers the company of his smaller friends, apparently."

Angry muttering greeted this announcement, and Jacinta's ears pricked up. Uroch was dining with the elves? That would be a meeting worth eavesdropping on. She had to find out where it was happening.

CHAPTER TWENTY-THREE

Jacinta

Jacinta emerged from her hiding place, moving in the opposite direction from the group of giants, given they apparently weren't invited to the dinner she was hoping to locate. It took her another hour of wandering, but eventually she encountered a promising stream of servants. The platters of steaming food they were carrying made her nostrils twitch, but her stomach was the least of her priorities. She would have to be very careful if she was going to navigate a dining hall full of guests and servants without being detected. Especially if there were elves present who, in her experience, were much sharper-witted than giants.

The servants were amassing in an antechamber, clearly awaiting an order to serve the food. Jacinta had to hang well back from the action to avoid bumping into anyone. Soft music drifted through a doorway, surprising her with its gentle melody. It sounded out of place in the setting. In spite of all the attempts at grandeur, the giant castle lacked the gentility of the human ones Jacinta had visited.

When the servants began to file into the room, Jacinta pressed herself back against the wall. She winced as the buckle of her rucksack clanked into the stone, emitting a small noise. Thankfully the sound was lost in the bustle of the servants' activity, but it was enough to set Jacinta's nerves on edge. She noticed that the door to the dining hall was opening without the servants touching it, suggesting magic was at work.

Foolish, unnecessary magic, she reflected. Perhaps it made the king's feasts run more smoothly, or impressed his guests. But it wasn't as though it was difficult to prop the door open with a normal doorstop. She'd never seen any enchantment that luxurious at work in the castle in Vallen, but she knew from things Matthias had told her when they were children that the castle's security included the use of magic. Clearly the giant king's priorities were different from those of his human counterparts.

When the stream of servants had died down, Jacinta approached the door tentatively, dismayed when it didn't open. She didn't know if it was because she wasn't a giant, or didn't have food, but she didn't like the idea of pushing it open and strolling in. She would have to wait for a better opportunity.

Fortunately it wasn't long before servants began to gather with the next course. Jacinta was ready this time. Standing right by the enormous door, she darted through when the first servant approached, sidling along the wall to get out of the way before stopping to get her bearings.

She'd entered a dining hall which, while huge to her eyes, she recognized wasn't large for its purpose. The several giants seated around the huge stone table filled only a third of it. The other members of the group, although doing nothing to make the room seem more crowded, occupied almost half of the chairs.

Jacinta studied the elves curiously, entertained by the bizarre contrast between their superior and stately expressions and the fact that they were perched on teetering towers of cushions like children at an adults' table. Of course, next to the giants, the miniature elves were much smaller than a child to an adult.

Well, if any elves had lingering doubt that some of their kind could have stooped to working with giants, her account should put it to rest.

King Uroch was obvious, seated at the head of the table. Unlike the rest of the giants who wore gray, he was dressed in a golden tunic, and had a glittering crown on his head. His expression was smug, although Jacinta saw no sign on the faces of any of his companions that they were enjoying the honor of dining with him.

As Jacinta's eyes traveled around the rest of the room, she noted the well-dressed giant woman seated at an enormous harp in one corner. So that was where the music was coming from. The player seemed skilled on the instrument, her eyes closed and her expression serene as she manipulated the strings. The melody was so soothing that Jacinta inched toward that section of the room, although she reminded herself sternly not to let it lull her. She needed her wits about her. At least the sound of the harp would be a good cover for any accidental noise she might make.

"This chicken is dry." The petulant voice rose above the clinking of silverware, and Jacinta's eyes sought the speaker.

Her eyebrows went up at the sight of a female giant seated halfway down the table from King Uroch, her expression sour and her arms folded over her chest. It wasn't the childish posture that took Jacinta aback. It was the giant's size. Her features were definitely those of an adult, but she wasn't much more than half the size of the other giants. Only the presence of the elves stopped her from looking completely out of place.

"Shut your trap, Mundia," said King Uroch irritably. "If you don't like the food I serve you, you can leave."

Mundia. Ah. This must be Princess Mundia, the younger

sister of King Uroch whom the deceased Queen Grograna had wished to marry off to King Herleif of Frossenland. In a twisted way, Jacinta could see the logic. A human husband—even one as large as King Herleif—would be dwarfed by the undersized giant. And she would be a queen, albeit a queen among humans.

Princess Mundia scowled, but said no more. Apparently she was no happier with her brother's rule than the rest of the castle's inhabitants.

"Enough stalling." King Uroch turned to the elf closest to him. "I brought you here to make a report, not to eat all my food in silence like you're too good for me."

"We are too good for you." There was no apology in the high-pitched voice of the elf who spoke. "And it brings us no pleasure to eat your food. You would do well to remember that we do not report to you. We are equal partners in this venture."

The giant king gave a snort that made a few of the elves wince in distaste. "Equal partners, are you? Whatever you tell yourself. Now, I wasn't satisfied with the last account I was sent. I don't want any more excuses about disruptions caused by losing your leader from Ilgal. I don't care about that. If there's a problem, it's up to you to fix it. And my people report that all you do is complain that the ground is dry and do nothing to fix it."

"We do not have control over the state of the ground, and it is not our responsibility to address it." The tips of the elf's pointed ears quivered in his indignation.

"Not in your control?" Uroch said angrily. "You're the ones who set up the mining machines, aren't you?"

"At which time we warned you not to over-mine the area," another elf shot back. "It is your own fault you did not listen. You and your mother."

Jacinta jumped as the giant king slammed a massive fist onto the table, causing everyone's plates to rattle.

"I am king here. You will not speak to me that way!"

"Getting angry changes nothing," the first elf said coolly. "I don't know what you expect us to do. We cannot force more magic into the ground. We've already helped you extend the reach of the mining operation further south than we originally agreed."

"But the land south of the wall is as barren and useless as this land!" raged Uroch. "Don't play stupid with me. You know what I want. The Forest of Ilgal is a huge and untapped source of magic."

"Ilgal is not part of the deal," another elf said swiftly. "And it's too far from the towers' reach."

"That's what you said about northern Frossenland and Vadolis, and you changed your tune on that," sneered Uroch. "Don't think I'm fooled by your lies. You *will* extend the technology of the mining towers to reach Ilgal, or you'll pay the consequences!"

"We are not afraid of you." The head elf made as if to stand, then seemed to remember his precarious perch and settled for glaring at the giant king instead.

"How dare you defy me?" roared Uroch. "I have given you so much gold, my own treasuries are near empty! I demand more magic! That's our deal!"

"That is not our deal," spat the elf. "We don't want more gold."

"Everyone wants more gold." Uroch had returned to scoffing. "You pretend you've helped us mine magic out of generosity?"

"Of course not," the elf snapped. "You know we have our own reasons for wanting the human kingdoms weakened. Our aims were stated clearly from the beginning, with terms the giants agreed to. And Ilgal was never on the table. Our only priority in this venture is to *protect* Ilgal, and in due course, expand its territory outward. Letting you giants get your filthy paws on Ilgal is the opposite of what we want."

Jacinta's eyes widened at the brazenness of the elf's purpose. The cooperation between the two non-human species was more established and more dangerous than they'd even imagined. More monarchs than her own would be eager to hear the information she was gaining. Now she just had to find a way to safely get it home.

"How dare you?" Uroch growled, his gray face livid with anger as he glared down at his guest.

"How dare *you* demand anything of us?" the elf retorted. "We are not your servants, and you can't afford to alienate us. You need us for the continued operation of your mining towers. As we told the queen, if you want more magic than the immediate region can provide, you should focus on building a fleet of ships to get the mining equipment to Selvana. If you want unlimited magic, that island is a treasure trove."

"My mother is dead," said Uroch, showing no sign of any emotion beyond his anger. "I am not her, and the plans you made with her have no hold on me. She discussed the idea of harvesting Selvana before Ilgal became so rich in magic. It's a much closer target."

"You will not touch Ilgal!" Even the elf was almost shouting now, his emerald eyes shooting sparks.

Uroch rose to his feet, the other giants hastening to follow. The giant king strode around the table, fury on his face as he reached toward the elf. A bang went around the room, and the giant pulled his hand back with a cry of pain.

"Do you think we come into your territory unprotected?" one of the elves cried. "If you try to touch any of us again, you will learn just how little of our skill with talismans you've yet seen."

"How dare you bring magic here to use against me?" Uroch

roared. Curling his huge, meaty hands into fists, he swept the elves' plates from the table with a shattering crash.

The music petered out, the harp player as distracted by the conflict as everyone else in the room.

Jacinta inched backward nervously, eager to be out of the dining hall before further violence erupted. If the whole room was thrown into chaos, it would be harder to avoid being knocked or trampled. A glance at the doorway showed that it was clogged with servants who were unashamedly watching the scene unfold. Their unbothered demeanor suggested that a royal loss of temper wasn't an unusual event in the castle at Kjemper.

Nervous to see her escape route blocked, Jacinta whirled around, looking for another way out. But in addition to straying much closer to the now-silent harp than she'd realized, she'd also misjudged her own girth, forgetting to account for the bulging rucksack she wore. The bag caught on the strings of the enormous, giant-sized harp, and to her dismay, the instrument broke into a high, frantic strumming.

Jacinta whirled, instinctively grabbing at the strings to try to still the sound. But that was a mistake. As soon as her fingers closed over the harp, two things happened. First, its strumming increased in volume and pitch to what was almost a scream, and second, it shrank in her hand. The huge standing harp disappeared, leaving Jacinta staring at a human-sized hand-held lyre clutched in her grip.

Presumably Hagen's enchantment now stretched to the harp, but that concealment did her little good.

"My harp!" the player screeched into the confused silence caused by the harp's outburst. She leaped up from her chair. "Someone's stealing it!"

Jacinta jumped backward as the giant made a grab toward where the harp could still be heard. She didn't know what to do.

If she held the instrument, the sound would give her away. If she dropped it, she would reveal her location. And the only way out was still fully blocked.

"What are you talking about?" growled Uroch to the harp player. "No one cares about your harp."

"I care!" the female giant shouted angrily. "I don't trust any of you, so before coming to the castle, I paid an elf to help me enchant it to warn me if someone else tries to grab it."

"You dare to speak to your king that way?" Uroch demanded, affronted.

"You're not listening to me!" the harp player cried, frustrated. "Someone's grabbed it right from under my nose, and whoever it is, they must be invisible. Someone's been listening in!"

That created an uproar.

"You brought spies?" Uroch demanded, as Jacinta's panic began to rise. With the hand not clutching the lyre, she fumbled for the thin blade still strapped to her waist.

"We don't need spies," the main elf said impatiently. "If someone's concealed, it's not one of ours." He barked an order to one of his companions, who hastily withdrew what looked like a large, golden coin, but much slimmer.

"This will counteract any concealment magic," the elf said, as he snapped the coin in a swift motion.

To Jacinta's horror, a rushing sound rose up her body and toward the ceiling, and every eye in the room suddenly fixed on her. Hagen's talisman had been incapacitated.

"A HUMAN!" The cry went up from multiple giants, while the elves stared at her in shock, their emerald eyes narrowing rapidly into suspicion.

She darted for the door, in spite of having no plan for how to get through the throng of eavesdropping servants. Not that it mattered. She didn't get far across the room before one of the giants seized her around the middle, yanking her upward so she was lifted bodily from the floor.

Jacinta raised the feeble blade, but all it did was enrage the giant further. With his free hand, he flicked it from her hand, his other fist tightening around her middle.

"Who are you?" he roared in her face. "Who do you work for?"

"I'm no one," Jacinta gasped out, glad she carried nothing to tie her to the Vadolisian royals. "A thief."

"You think you can steal from me?" King Uroch strode forward, fury on his face.

"Don't be a fool," spat the head elf. "She's clearly a spy, not a common thief."

But Uroch wasn't listening. "Give her to me!" he cried, making a snatch at her.

The other giant was slow to release Jacinta, and she cried out as she was wrenched painfully from one huge fist to another. In the kerfuffle, she heard her gown rip along the seam somewhere, no doubt worn thin by the nights of rough sleeping. Panic threatened to overwhelm her, but she fought it down, knowing that even her sharpest wits may not be enough to keep her alive.

"I'll take that." The shrill voice of the harp player interrupted the king's growls, as the female giant strode forward to where Jacinta had dropped the lyre when she was grabbed. "No idea why you think she's not a thief when she clearly tried to steal this."

"That's not your harp," said the giant who'd first grabbed Jacinta. "It's tiny."

"Of course it's my harp," said the female giant irritably. "It had to be enchanted to change form for me. Expensive magic it was, too, to get it to keep its musical properties."

"You've been playing a *human* instrument in my castle all this time?" Uroch demanded, outraged.

"What choice did I have?" the musician snapped. "Do you think our kind make anything this sophisticated?"

Jacinta's mind whirled while the giants argued, trying to figure out how to use their distraction to her advantage. But Uroch held her too tightly to allow her to get free.

"Is this an important argument to have right now?" one of the elves said impatiently. "We need to deal with the spy. She's heard things we don't want repeated."

"She can't talk if she's dead," said the giant king indifferently.

Tightening his hold still further, he drew Jacinta back. Her mind had barely caught up with the stone wall speeding toward her face when a shrill cry arose from the elves, and the giant's hand slowed instinctively. He was too late to avoid pushing Jacinta into the wall, but the force of the impact wasn't enough to be fatal, as he'd no doubt initially intended.

Even so, it was a brutal blow. Stars burst before Jacinta's eyes, and pain erupted at every point of impact with the wall. In a daze, she felt herself slide down the stone and crumple on the floor. Uroch must have let her go, thinking she had no strength to try to escape.

He was right.

"What is it now?" she heard Uroch demand through the fog in her mind. "You can't possibly want to spare her life. She's a *human*."

"Don't kill her before we find out who sent her," came the reply, in the high-pitched voice of an elf.

Jacinta's sluggish thoughts came together. There was no point hoping for escape. She had no options left. They would try their best to get information from her, and then they would kill her. She could only hope she would be strong enough not to say anything that could cause problems for King Fidelius, or King Herleif, or any of the others. She'd never get to tell them what she'd heard. She'd never get to see Matthias again.

Tears pricked her eyes at that last realization, and she pushed all thought of Matthias aside. She wouldn't spend her last moments mooning. If only there was something she could do to actually make her death worthwhile. If only she was a warrior like the ones who would vie for Mariella's hand, and could have a hope of killing Uroch. She was close enough to reach him, after all. But he was enormous, and she was unarmed, and untrained in fighting.

She shifted painfully, and something cool touched the skin of her leg. For a moment Jacinta was confused, and then she remembered the ripping sound she'd heard, and she drew in a sharp breath. The destructive talisman from King Fidelius's royal treasury was at least partly exposed.

Her circumstances were desperate enough that if she could use it to get through Battlement Wall, she would. But she'd never have the chance. She'd never even make it out of this castle.

The castle. An idea trickled into Jacinta's bruised mind. She had no hope of killing Uroch. But there was another goal King Herleif had mentioned at the summit. He'd seemed to think that destroying the giant's castle would be almost as big a blow to the fledgling monarchy as killing the king. And Matthias had said that the talisman was designed to destroy stone—to reduce it to ash. Hagen had told her to be careful, because all it would take would be for the talisman to touch rock, and it would destroy not only the rock it made contact with, but any others touching it.

Was it possible that there was enough power in the talisman to destroy Uroch's castle?

Jacinta didn't stop to think it through. However little she

could really predict the outcome, using the talisman to damage the castle was her best—and only—chance of striking a blow against the giants' schemes for Providore. And since she was about to die anyway, she really had nothing to fear from the destruction she was about to cause.

Moving slowly, she shifted her arm beneath her crumpled form, her hand questing in her skirts until it found the bulge where she'd sewn in the talisman. As she'd sensed, the oblong marble was partially exposed. Her fingers closed around it, tugging it the rest of the way out of the ripped seam.

"Hey, what's she doing?" The shrill voice belonged to an elf. "She's reaching for something—someone grab her!"

Jacinta's hand shot out, her movements no longer cautious. Squeezing her eyes shut, she slammed her palm against the stone wall behind her, the talisman wedged between her skin and the rock.

Screams rent the air as the wall gave way under her touch. Jacinta forced her eyes open, almost letting out a scream herself at the sight that met her eyes. The stone of the wall was gone, her hand now suspended in midair amid an endlessly falling shower of ash.

It wasn't just cascading from the wall she leaned on, either. Hagen hadn't exaggerated when he'd said that there was a great deal of power in the talisman. Spreading out from the point of Jacinta's touch, there was a river of ash flowing up through the solid stone, branching out and spreading as block after block disintegrated. The walls gave way, and Jacinta braced herself along with the rest of the room as huge blocks of masonry fell from the ceiling above.

But nothing hit her, and there were no crashes as she'd expected. Peering upward, Jacinta realized that the stones had turned to ash long before they'd reached the ground. She was forced to close her eyes again, coughing and gagging as ash filled the air. The gaggle of servants in the doorway were fleeing, but all of the elves and most of the giants at the table were sheltering in place. Jacinta curled into a ball, covering her face as best she could and listening numbly to the cries and screams reaching her ears from more and more distant parts of the castle.

In minutes, all motion ceased. She shook her aching limbs gingerly, a thick layer of ash falling from her with every movement. When she opened her eyes, it was to see a truly unbelievable sight.

Uroch's castle was gone.

At least, the structure itself was gone. The footprints of the rooms were still there, laid bare to the cold night air, with furniture intact, everything sitting on top of a thick layer of ash that used to be the stone floor, and under a thick layer of ash that represented the walls and ceiling. There was broken glass and splintered wood everywhere, where windows and frames had fallen free as the walls around them disintegrated. A few sad half-walls were standing here and there, apparently not properly connected to the rest of the stone for whatever reason. But for all intents and purposes, the talisman had destroyed the entire castle.

As for its inhabitants, everything had been thrown into chaos. Those who'd been sheltering were emerging, and Jacinta could already see some beginning to loot the gold and other valuables left exposed. She doubted there would be much of either Uroch's wealth or his authority come morning.

"YOU FILTHY LITTLE HUMAN!" Uroch's scream of rage made Jacinta jump, and she forced herself to her feet to face him. She didn't want to die cowering in the ash. "I'LL KILL YOU FOR THIS!"

His face was contorted in fury, and Jacinta knew she was facing her final moments. But when the giant reached for her, another bang went around the room, and for the second time that evening, he pulled his hand back with a cry of pain.

"Wait!" One of the elves was speaking, the tips of his ears quivering as he glared murderously at Jacinta. "You can't kill her yet!"

"I AM KING HERE!" Uroch screamed, still beside himself. "I WILL KILL WHOEVER I WISH TO KILL!"

"A king with no castle."

Jacinta didn't bother trying to identify which giant had spoken. She was too focused on the elf who'd saved her life, although she knew he hadn't acted for her sake. Like everyone else in the room, the creature looked comical in the dim light, coated as he was in ash.

"You can kill her in due course," the elf snapped. "But it's more imperative than ever that we find out who sent her. She got past Battlement Wall carrying a talisman with enough destructive power to bring down your entire castle! We need to know where she got in."

"He's right, King Uroch," said an older giant, breathing heavily as he glared at Jacinta. "We need to know how she got into Kjemper."

"Fine," snapped Uroch, seizing Jacinta and raising her to the level of his eyes as easily as if she were a rag doll. "Show me your rat hole, and *then* I'll kill you. I'll do it so slowly you'll know exactly what's happening to you. I'll grind your bones into bread to make my supper."

"But first..." prompted one of the elves, his tone suggesting both boredom and distaste at this display of savagery.

"But first you'll show me exactly how and where you breached the wall my ancestors built to keep you scum out," breathed Uroch, his terrifying yellow eyes boring into Jacinta's. "And if you know what's good for you, you'll do it now."

CHAPTER TWENTY-FOUR

Matthias

Matthias paced across the barren ground, his fingers flicking against the hilt of his sword in a rhythmic gesture that did nothing to calm his anxiety.

"Are you all right, Your Highness?" The calm voice of Hagen broke into Matthias's thoughts.

"A week and a half, Hagen," he said by way of reply. "It's been a week and a half of standing here waiting. I don't know how much more of this I can take."

"I know it hasn't been easy," said the singer sympathetically. "But we knew it would take at least this long for Jacinta to reach the capital and return. Even if all is going smoothly, we can't expect her back any earlier than this."

Matthias groaned. "Even if all is going smoothly. You know as well as I do how unlikely that is."

"I think you underestimate her," said Hagen mildly. "She's careful and clever. And the talisman I gave her should hide her from unfriendly eyes."

"Have I thanked you sufficiently for doing that?" Matthias asked.

"Repeatedly."

The hint of amusement in Hagen's voice told the prince that however much he cared about Jacinta as a friend, the singer was far from crippled by anxiety the way Matthias was. Had he really ever seen the Frossian as a threat? Of course Jacinta hadn't fallen for Hagen. She loved *him*, as some part of him had known, deep down, that she must. There'd been something there since they were children. How could she not feel it too?

The knowledge that she loved him brought Matthias little comfort given Jacinta's whereabouts. Or rather, his total lack of information about her whereabouts. All he knew was that she'd gone through the wall and hadn't come back.

"I know logically that it's no cause for concern that she's not back yet," he admitted to Hagen. "But I also know that we've reached the point now where she could return at any time. What if she doesn't? What if days go by...or weeks? And I'm standing here, with no way to even know if she's still alive, let alone help her?"

"I have no answer for that," said Hagen gravely, the honest response more grounding than soothing lies would have been. "I'm very aware of the same possibility, and I have no idea how we would proceed."

"One thing is for certain," said Matthias fiercely. "I'm not giving up and going back to Vallen without information, no matter how long we've been waiting."

"Nor am I," Hagen agreed.

"Your Highness." The greeting came from an approaching servant, and both men turned.

"Yes, what is it?" Matthias asked, aware his voice was coming out terse.

"A royal messenger from Frossenland has just arrived, riding a couple of hours ahead of King Herleif. Apparently he's bringing a party, and the messenger wishes to know if they can be accommodated in the manor."

"King Herleif is coming here?" Matthias asked, distracted from his gnawing worry for the first time in days. "Yes, of course they can stay at the manor. I'll meet them there. A couple of hours, you said?"

"Yes, Your Highness," nodded the servant, already withdrawing to begin the proper preparations.

Matthias looked at Hagen. "They must have heard about Jacinta going through the wall, don't you think?"

The singer nodded. "I can't imagine what else would bring them to Briarford."

Their questions were answered soon after, when several carriages bearing the Frossian royal crest pulled into the manor's carriageway.

"King Herleif," Matthias greeted the huge form that descended from the carriage. "You're very welcome." He watched in surprise as two other figures followed, each of the three considerably smaller than the last. "Queen Adrienne." He nodded his head to the young queen, searching his memory for the name of the couple's companion. "And Valwynn. Welcome."

"I've lived in these parts for years," said the elf with a touch of irritation. "And I've never seen you here during that time, Your Highness. No need to welcome me to my own home."

"My apologies," said Matthias, astonished to recognize the flicker inside him as humor. It seemed the change in company was good for his shattered nerves.

"I, on the other hand, am very grateful to be welcomed," said King Herleif dryly. The glance he sent toward the elf suggested he hadn't found the journey especially enjoyable. "And to be out of that carriage."

"Carriages just aren't built for your frame, Herleif," said Queen Adrienne. "You really should commission larger ones."

"Nonsense, I'm fine," said the king impatiently. His voice

turned grim as he looked Matthias over. "By the state of you, I'm guessing Jacinta hasn't returned."

Matthias felt himself physically deflate. "No," he acknowledged. "She's been gone a week and a half, and we've heard nothing."

"And she really went in all alone?" Queen Adrienne asked, troubled.

"I'm afraid so." Matthias's words were tight and clipped.

"It's a bad business." King Herleif sounded far from impressed. "I must say, when we all agreed to explore unofficial ways to target the giant king, I didn't expect this. Sending a civilian—a young woman, untrained and alone—into Kjemper—"

"Believe me," Matthias interrupted stiffly, "I argued vehemently against it."

"Hm." King Herleif eyed him. "I have no doubt." He ran a hand through his pale hair. "Well, we came as soon as we heard. And we've brought a few of our strongest singers to see if we can help." He nodded to Hagen. "I see you've brought one of the best, as well. Hagen, some of your old instructors will be pleased to see you here."

"Hagen's been invaluable," said Matthias quickly. "He gave Jacinta a talisman containing potent concealment magic."

"Good lad," said King Herleif approvingly. "I'd expect no less."

Hagen ducked his head, looking pleased with the curt praise. "I wish I could have done more, Your Majesty. Once she passed through the wall, she was out of reach of all of our help."

"Yes, well, we'll see what we can do now we have some more force behind us," King Herleif said. "I sent a message to King Fidelius when we passed north of Vallen, informing him that I was on my way to Briarford with some singers for backup. I'd be surprised if we didn't see him here within the day. Probably with singers of his own, if I know anything of how his mind works."

"My father is coming here?" Matthias asked, not at all pleased with this turn of events.

"Humans always think force is the answer," said Valwynn impatiently. "But no mass of people will help Jacinta if you can't get them past the wall. My contribution is far more likely to be of use."

"What contribution is that?" Matthias asked hopefully. He would take any assistance he could get.

"She feels guilty for her hand in sending Jacinta into so much danger," King Herleif answered for the elf. "Since she personally chose Jacinta to be the only one affected by the illusion magic that tricks her body into being able to go through the wall."

"Don't speak for me," Valwynn retorted indignantly. "I never said I felt guilty."

"Then why have you spent the whole journey working on a talisman to extend the illusion charm?" the king asked, unrepentant.

The elf ignored him, turning to Matthias. "I think I told you at the summit that the beans Jacinta planted carried an excessively powerful illusion magic that tricks her mind and body into thinking there's a hole through the wall. For all other purposes, the hole isn't there, and there's nothing I can do about that. But now that I'm here, if I can get the talisman I've been working on to interact properly with the vine, it might be able to extend the illusion magic to whoever is carrying the talisman."

"You mean they could go through the tunnel too?" Matthias asked eagerly. "Can I have it? When you're finished, I mean? I could pay you plenty of gold for it."

"You?" The elf eyed him skeptically. "I'll have to think about it."

Matthias bit his lip, barely containing his impatience as the group was led into the manor by a helpful servant.

"Prince Matthias." Hagen's voice was low and concerned in his ear. "I don't think you should be going through that wall."

"Who then?" Matthias asked shortly.

"Well, a singer, perhaps," said Hagen. "One trained in fighting?"

"A singer working for my father's guard?" Matthias suggested. He shook his head. "I know what their orders would be, and it's not good enough. Jacinta's safety is all I care about, and no one is as committed to that cause as I am." He paused. "Except her mother, I imagine, and I don't think any of us intend to send her through the wall."

Hagen said no more, apparently having no argument against this point, but his face showed Matthias that he was still troubled. The prince didn't care. He finally had the hint of something he could actually do, and he knew his purpose now. Getting hold of that talisman was his only priority.

The rest of the day passed interminably, with no sign of Jacinta returning. After inspecting the beanstalk, the Frossian royals rested in the manor. Valwynn, meanwhile, spent the afternoon tinkering away near the plant with her talisman and elvish tools, snapping at anyone who approached to leave her alone. Even when everyone else retired to bed, she kept working. Matthias had no doubt that King Herleif was right, and she was motivated by her guilt over Jacinta's fate. At the summit, she'd shown herself to be more prone to a conscience than many elves.

The next morning crawled by, with no change. Matthias's anxiety, temporarily held at bay by the arrival of the Frossian group, returned in full force. By the time another royal messenger arrived, this one wearing a Vadolisian uniform, his nerves were frayed to breaking point. He watched the messenger ride into the manor's yard, three others behind him.

"Prince Matthias." The messenger dismounted as soon as he saw Matthias, bowing low. "I come with a message from His Majesty. He will be arriving within the hour. Princess Mariella is with him, as she wished to view the beanstalk. His Majesty has instructed that you prepare for departure this afternoon. He wishes you to escort the princess back to Vallen, and he will take over supervision of the site here."

Anger flared in Matthias, but he held it in. There was nothing to be gained from arguing with the messenger. It wasn't the man's fault, and it wasn't as though he had the power to change the king's mind. Matthias had no intention of following his father's instructions, but he thanked the rider for the message, nonetheless. His eyes fell on the other new arrivals, and he realized with a start that he recognized one of them.

There was no time to lose, then.

As soon as the men had disappeared inside, Matthias left the manor, hurrying toward the site of the beanstalk. There was no opportunity to make preparations, at least not unobserved. But he had his cloak on, and his sword at his side. What more did he need?

Hagen materialized beside him as he walked, demonstrating to Matthias that he'd once again underestimated the singer's powers of observation.

"Is all well, Your Highness?" Hagen asked.

"No." Matthias's voice was grim. "My father will be here soon, and he thinks he can send me home. I have to get that talisman from Valwynn before he arrives, or he'll convince her to give it to that man I just saw."

"What man?" Hagen asked, bewildered.

"He's the head of Father's intelligence network," said

Matthias. "A real spy. That's who Father would choose to send in through the wall at this point, I have no doubt."

"And that's bad?" Hagen pressed.

"Yes," said Matthias emphatically. "He's highly capable, and extremely loyal to my father. Which is essential in his role, of course. But his priorities will be my father's priorities—protecting Vadolis from being exposed or connected in any way to whatever's going on. Not protecting Jacinta."

"From the perspective of matters of state, that's not entirely unreasonable," Hagen pointed out.

"If the circumstances were different, I'd agree with you," said Matthias. "But Father is the one who ordered Jacinta into Kjemper, without adequate training or protection. He is responsible for her safety, and I don't know what kind of ruler doesn't take that responsibility seriously."

"Also a fair point," Hagen conceded. "So what are you going to do? The elf won't give you the talisman for free."

"I know that," said Matthias. "I suppose I'll just have to pay what she wants."

They passed quickly through the town, emerging into the now-familiar yard of Jacinta's home. Predictably, they found the elf at the beanstalk, although she wasn't working. She was sitting back, squinting at an egg-shaped rock in her hand. As Matthias watched, she gave a satisfied nod.

"Have you finished it?" he asked eagerly.

The elf looked up, seeming faintly irritated by the interruption. "Yes, I've finished it. What's it to you?"

"Can I use it?" Matthias asked urgently. "Please?"

"In exchange for what?" Valwynn's words seemed more reflex than considered thought.

"I don't know how to answer that, because I don't know what you want," Matthias said candidly.

The little elf sighed, glancing up the vast expanse of the

nearby wall. "I want all this to be over," she said. "I want to be free to leave the frozen wasteland of the north once and for all."

"Vallen is a pleasant city," said Matthias quickly. "I could help you relocate there. The crown could gift you a fine house."

She eyed him. "Big enough for me to bring my cow?"

"Err..." Matthias blinked at her. "Yes. Certainly."

"Hm." Valwynn considered it for a moment. "Could you promise me that if I live in the capital, the crown won't ever bother me for either information or assistance?"

"Yes," said Matthias promptly. His father might not like him entering the agreement on his behalf, but once he understood it had occurred, he wouldn't breach it. No one wanted to activate the magic associated with elf bargains.

"All right," said Valwynn wearily. "Your promise holds whether or not you're successful on the other side of the wall, you know."

"I understand," said Matthias. "I'm willing to enter an agreement on those terms."

"Very well," said Valwynn. She handed over the talisman with the air of one glad to be rid of something. "Put it in your pocket. As long as it's on your person, it should work."

Matthias took it eagerly, his hand closing over the oddly warm, egg-shaped stone. He glanced up at the wall and let out a gasp.

"I can see it! The tunnel!"

"Did you think the talisman wouldn't work?" Valwynn asked, amused. "You were daft to make the bargain if so."

Matthias didn't bother to answer. He turned to Hagen. "If I don't return by the time my father arrives, please tell him what occurred." He nodded at the elf. "Including my promises to Valwynn. He'll see them honored."

"Matthias, I don't think this is a good idea." Hagen didn't

even seem to realize he'd dropped the prince's title in his concern. "You'll be alone over there, and—"

"No more than Jacinta has been," said Matthias curtly. "I'm just going to scope it out, Hagen. If I can't find anything nearby, I'll come back to properly provision. But I know my father, and if I don't go now, I may not have the chance."

Hagen said no more, although he didn't look convinced. Matthias didn't stay to argue. Slipping the talisman into his pocket, he strode toward Battlement Wall. Crawling through the tunnel was a strange experience, but not difficult. The opening was plenty large enough for his frame.

When he emerged onto the other side, he scoured the landscape cautiously before crawling out. He could see no one. The beanstalk continued due north, and Matthias followed it far enough to catch a glimpse of the dwelling Jacinta had mentioned. It didn't seem likely he'd find her there, so he doubled back to the wall. Knowing she'd planned to head west to the capital, he did the same, keeping close to the stone and shivering in its shadow. How long had Jacinta walked alone like this, cold and afraid?

Matthias hadn't gone far when he heard the unmistakable sound of voices. Angry voices. Looking around, he spotted a rocky outcrop not far to the north. He darted toward it, trying to step on rocks rather than fresh snow so as not to leave a clear trail. He'd barely concealed himself when the voices became clear.

"This is ridiculous! We've been walking for days! We'll be at the coast soon. We must have gone past wherever she got in."

Matthias's blood seemed to freeze. They had to be talking about Jacinta. Had she been caught, then?

"We haven't." The answering voice was much too high and shrill for a giant. It was surely an elf. "If you wanted this to be faster, you should have gotten her to talk. Our magic is effective in tracking, but it's slow, especially when the tracks aren't fresh. But the trail is definitely still there."

"It's not my fault if she won't talk," responded the giant indignantly.

Matthias hardly dared to hope, but it sounded very much like Jacinta was alive. Unable to bear the suspense any longer, he edged sideways until he could peer around the rock.

The sight before him almost made him cry out. A group of giants, one wearing a gaudy golden crown, were lumbering along in the shadow of the wall. Scurrying around their feet were several elves, one of them holding a thin metal instrument that was pointed at the ground. But none of these figures were what captured Matthias's attention. It was the solitary human in the group, bound at the hands and feet, looking dirty and bruised and very much the worse for wear as she hobbled along, tugged roughly onward by a rope held by one of the giants.

Jacinta.

The relief Matthias felt at seeing her alive was quickly replaced by rage at the state of her. How dare they mistreat her like that? How dare his father expose her to this danger?

"Wait." The elf holding the metal instrument stopped abruptly, holding up one slim white hand. The tips of his ears wobbled as he looked around him. He was directly level with Matthias now. "There's another set of tracks, I think also human. These ones are very fresh. They go that way."

Matthias knew he was exposed, and he found he didn't even care. Brandishing his sword before him, he strode out from behind the clump of rock, letting his anger fuel him.

He saw the moment Jacinta's eyes fell on him, her face contorting in horror. The sight did nothing to calm his emotions. So she'd hoped to die alone to protect everyone else, had she? Not if he had anything to say about it.

"Let her go, you savage monsters," he said, his voice not wavering in the slightest.

For a long moment, the giants and elves just stared at him. Then the giant king burst into laughter, his fellows following suit.

"Wait!" An elf's high voice rose above their mirth. "I recognize him. He's one of the Vadolisian royals."

"That's right," said Matthias steadily. "And I have the might of my crown behind me. Unhand her if you want to live."

"Matthias, no," Jacinta moaned, the anguish on her face tugging at his heart.

As for the rest of the group, again his words were met with guffaws from the giants, and again the elves cautioned their companions.

"If he's royal, he might have power you don't know about," one of them said. She scowled at Matthias. "We've learned to be a little more cautious since the stunt with the castle. Don't think to catch us out again."

She pulled an object from her hand, not unlike the instrument being used to track Jacinta's trail, although this one was larger and more rounded.

"Yes!" she cried triumphantly, as she pointed it at him. "It senses magic. Check the pocket of his cloak, just there." Her finger unerringly found the place where the egg-shaped rock was stored. "I think he has a talisman."

One of the giants lumbered forward, and Matthias took up a fighting stance. He managed to get in a few good slices to the creature's forearm, causing the giant to pause. But as soon as one of his fellows joined, it was over quickly. The two of them were just too big and too strong. They seized Matthias between them, wresting his sword from him and carrying him back to the rest of the group.

"Here it is!" one cried triumphantly, his massive hand

ripping Matthias's cloak as he fished in the pocket for the stone. "Funny thing, innit? Looks like an egg." He gave Matthias a shake that made his teeth rattle. "What does this do then, eh?"

Matthias just glared at him, still too angry and defiant to even feel afraid.

"I'll take that." The giant with the crown—presumably King Uroch—snatched the egg from his disgruntled-looking fellow.

"Oi!" The first giant let go of Matthias, making a grab at it. "I found it, it's mine!"

Matthias took full use of his suddenly freed arm, plunging one hand under his cloak and drawing out a small blade from his belt. He slashed at the hand of the one giant still holding him, causing the creature to let out a bellow and drop Matthias.

The prince hit the ground hard, but he was up the next moment, diving for Jacinta. With two swift strokes of his blade, he freed her hands and feet.

"RUN!" he shouted at her.

He practically shoved her forward, sprinting after her through the chaos of the group. Distracted by the conflict between the king and one of the others, the giants had been slow to respond to his movements. But he and Jacinta had barely cleared the group when the cry rang out.

"Oi, she's getting away!"

Matthias turned to face the giants, shouting to Jacinta to keep moving.

"Matthias!" she screamed.

"Father's on his way with half the Academy of Song," Matthias shouted, the words tumbling over each other in his haste. "Don't argue, just go! Get help!"

He didn't turn to see if she was obeying, all his focus on the giant who'd lunged toward them. Matthias darted to meet him, plunging his small blade straight into the giant's outstretched hand. With a howl, the creature pulled back, Matthias only just managing to wrench his dagger free in time. He could only hope Jacinta was running quickly as he took up a stance in an effort to delay the giants as much as he could.

"Never mind the girl, if he's really the Vadolisian prince he's much more important," screeched one of the elves.

"NO!" The giant king emerged from the throng, stowing the egg-shaped talisman in his pocket. Clearly he'd won the tussle over the magical item. "She destroyed my castle! I vowed to kill her, and I will!"

Pushing aside his astonishment at how much Jacinta had apparently achieved in her short visit to Kjemper, Matthias leaped in front of King Uroch. The giant swept him aside like a rag doll, gripped in a fury that filled Matthias with fear for Jacinta. Picking himself up from the ground, he searched the frozen landscape, relieved to see they'd come further back to the east than he'd realized. They weren't far from where the beanstalk emerged.

Relief turned to alarm as he caught sight of a giant hurrying toward Jacinta from the opposite direction. He called out a warning, but the giant was already turning away from Jacinta, toward the larger group. Her attention was probably caught by Uroch, who was thundering toward them. Even as Matthias watched, Jacinta dove toward Battlement Wall, disappearing into a seemingly solid patch of stone.

CHAPTER TWENTY-FIVE

Jacinta

Jacinta's heart was in her throat as she threw herself toward the wall. Everything in her screamed not to leave Matthias behind, but she knew he was right that the best thing for her to do was get help. He'd managed to get in, so they must have found a way through the wall. If the king was there, with lots of singers, they'd have a much better chance of saving Matthias than she did on her own. And there wasn't a moment to lose.

She was almost to the beanstalk when the giant who lived nearby appeared over the next rise. She must have heard the commotion. Jacinta skidded to a halt, her breath coming in pants.

"Please!" she gasped. "Help him! Don't let them kill him! We're trying to bring down your so-called king like you want, but we need help! If you can just keep him alive until—"

"Go," said the giant curtly. "Even out here, we've heard what you did in the capital. It sounds like we're halfway there. I won't waste the opportunity."

A roar interrupted their conversation, and Jacinta looked back to see Uroch almost upon them.

Jacinta didn't wait to hear more. She threw herself into the tunnel, knowing she'd be safe from the giant king the moment she entered the stone.

Or so she thought. To her horror, she'd barely made it a third of the way through when she heard another roar much too close. Looking back, she saw Uroch forcing his huge form into the tunnel behind her. Panic drove Jacinta forward at twice the speed, her movements hampered in the small space. The tunnel must be bigger for Uroch, because it looked like half his body was submerged in stone, but he kept moving forward.

"I'll kill you!" The giant's growl chased her through the enclosed space. "You and anyone who helped you! I'll wreak destruction on your pathetic human village!"

Jacinta threw herself forward, crawling on her belly as the light at the end of the tunnel grew. What had she done? She thought she was escaping, not letting Uroch loose on Briarford. She couldn't let him get through.

He was almost on her heels when she yanked herself free of the stone, falling to the ground amid screams and cries. The giant's roar echoed ominously out, showing he was seconds from emerging.

Jacinta ignored the watching crowd, sprinting to the closest guard. "Your sword!" she screamed. "I need your sword!"

"Give it to her!" cried a feminine voice Jacinta didn't immediately recognize.

Bemused, the man handed it over, and Jacinta whirled toward the beanstalk. She remembered what Valwynn had told her, all those weeks ago, that destroying the vine from this side of the wall would restore the stone in every way.

Without pausing to think it through, she began to hack away at the vine, just as Uroch's head emerged through the hole. He gave a roar of savage delight at the sight of the throng of humans awaiting him.

"I'll kill you all!" he declared, his eyes falling on Jacinta. "Starting with you!"

She ignored the threat, fully focused on her task. The beanstalk was almost severed. She could see Uroch wriggling forward just as she brought the sword down one last time, the blade slicing cleanly through the plant.

At once, the beanstalk shriveled up, the plant curling in on itself as it turned brown and dry. The effect on the wall was instantaneous. The tunnel shrank into nothing before Jacinta's eyes, leaving the giant's head sticking grotesquely out of solid wall.

Uroch had time for one disbelieving screech of horror before something even stranger happened. As the rock closed around him, his gray skin became grayer, his form hardening and changing. To Jacinta's astonishment, the giant's head changed in a matter of moments to nothing more than the stone that surrounded it.

She'd barely had time to take in this bizarre fact when there was a loud cracking sound. Before the hushed crowd, Uroch's head—now fully made of stone—broke off from the smooth wall and fell, rolling a few paces to land at Jacinta's feet.

She stared down at it for a loaded moment, sword in hand and chest heaving. Then cries and screams erupted all around her. She turned, just managing to make out King Fidelius and Queen Bronte standing alongside the huge figure of King Herleif and the much more petite one of Queen Adrienne, when she was engulfed by eager arms, and her face was filled with an explosion of hair.

"Jacinta! You're alive!"

"Mariella?" Jacinta returned her friend's embrace, dazed. "What are you doing here?"

"I couldn't stand waiting in Vallen, not knowing what was happening!" said Mariella. "It was torture. When Father said he was coming, Mother and I convinced him to bring us along." She looked around anxiously. "But where's Matthias? Hagen said he went through the wall—but how is that possible?"

"I don't know how it's possible, but it's true," said Jacinta, her momentary shock giving way and the urgency of Matthias's plight coming back to her. "He's just over the wall, and the giants have him!" Tears pricked her eyes as she remembered how he hadn't hesitated to dive into danger to free her. "He told me to run for help. He said he thought your father might be here with singers."

"The prince is in the hands of the giants?" King Fidelius's furious voice sent a shiver down Jacinta's spine. Her reaction came less from fear of her own fate than from the true fear she could see in his eyes as he strode toward her. It wasn't a royal reaction—it was a very personal fear, and one she shared to the depths of her soul.

"I don't know why he put himself in danger," she said, her voice unsteady. "I almost despaired when I saw him. But there is one giant there who I think might help him. And now that their king is...gone..." She looked down at the stone head of King Uroch lying lifeless on the barren ground.

"That was their king?" King Fidelius stared down at the grotesque sight as well, his eyes lingering on the crown now permanently attached to the giant's head. Like everything else, it had turned to stone.

"Wow, Jacinta." Mariella's eyes were wide, but Jacinta didn't have time to think about the enormity of what she'd done.

"Matthias," she said desperately, looking to the king. "Is there a way to help him?"

"Orders have already been given," said King Fidelius curtly.

Jacinta looked behind him to see a group of men and women wearing the uniform of the Academy of Song being gathered by the king's personal guard. Hagen was among them, and King Herleif was directing others in an unfamiliar uniform to join them. As Jacinta watched, the king's head guard broke off from the group, coming toward them with a gray-haired singer in tow.

"We've assessed the magical protection on the wall, Your Majesty," the singer reported promptly. "Although we could probably remove it with the help of our Frossian brethren, it would take considerable time."

"We don't have the luxury of time," King Fidelius rapped out. "My son is on the other side of that wall in enemy hands, without aid."

"Yes, Your Majesty." The singer bowed. "For that reason, our recommendation is that we select an individual and put our efforts into shielding him or her from the enchantment. There are risks, but with our number, we should be able to provide a shield of sufficient strength. A few of us would save our strength to summon wind to send the volunteer up and over the wall, traveling through the giants' protections with the help of the shield."

"Just as Adrienne once cleared the wall."

Jacinta had been too focused on the report to notice King Herleif and his wife approaching.

"Summoning the winds isn't complex magic," agreed Queen Adrienne. "At least, not for singers as experienced as these. I imagine anyone selected from this group could do it."

The Vadolisian singer nodded. "But we wouldn't have the volunteer do it. That person—we recommend a singer—should save his or her strength for whatever might be found on the other side."

"Who do you recommend?" King Fidelius asked.

The man glanced back at the group. "Hagen!" he called. As Hagen made his way toward them, the older man went on. "I know he's only an apprentice, Your Majesty, but in terms of magic, his strength is impressive. And perhaps more importantly, so is his physical strength."

He gestured at the others in the group, many of whom were gray-haired.

"We selected our most powerful and experienced singers from the Academy of Song, as you instructed. But most of us are no longer young, and not fighters."

Hagen reached their group, and Jacinta noticed Mariella shifting subtly, so that she stood alongside him.

"For what it's worth, I endorse your selection," said King Herleif. "I agree that there's no one more capable than Hagen, and I can also vouch for his character. I consider him a close personal friend."

"Do you indeed?" King Fidelius seemed taken aback. "I wasn't aware there was such a strong personal connection between Hagen and yourself, Your Majesty."

"Absolutely," said King Herleif staunchly.

Hagen's face looked hot, and he opened his mouth, no doubt to disclaim. He shut it with a grunt, however, as Mariella stomped hard on his foot. Her eyes had lit up at the Frossian king's words.

"Are you willing to undertake the task, Hagen?" King Fidelius asked gravely.

"I am, Your Majesty," said Hagen. "I swear to do all in my power to secure Prince Matthias's safety."

"And you understand the risks?" the king pressed.

Hagen nodded. "It would be an honor to trade my life for His Highness's if the situation required."

"Let's trust it won't come to that," said Mariella, not looking quite as pleased with this answer as her father clearly was. She turned to Hagen, her next words a royal order. "Come back safely. Both of you."

"Yes, Your Highness."

The corner of Hagen's mouth twitched ever so slightly, but Jacinta was too sick with her own worry to get caught up in Mariella and Hagen's situation. If Matthias died because of rescuing her, she would never forgive herself.

Nor would the king and queen, she imagined.

"Let's not delay, then," chimed in Queen Bronte, her voice carrying the same anxiety Jacinta felt. "It sounds like every minute might be crucial."

"Indeed." The representative of the Academy of Song bustled into motion, herding Hagen back toward the rest of the singers.

Jacinta and the royals watched tensely as the group converged on the apprentice, their voices raised in a melodious chorus. Some also pulled out talismans, although Jacinta was too far away to grasp their purpose. The process was faster than she'd expected. In only a few minutes, other singers stepped forward. One of the royal guards unbuckled his own sword belt and handed it to Hagen. The second group of singers waited only until he'd strapped it on to raise their voices in turn.

At once, a fierce wind whipped up around the cleared space, causing everyone to raise their arms instinctively to cover their faces. When Jacinta looked up again, Hagen was already soaring upward at a dizzying speed. He looked unfazed by it all, his usual stoic self as he flew through the air. She heard Mariella let out a breath of relief as his now miniature figure cleared the top of the wall, meaning he'd successfully passed the giants' enchantments.

But the next moment the tension of all the watchers returned as he passed out of sight and into the unknown dangers of Kjemper, leaving them with nothing to do but wait.

CHAPTER TWENTY-SIX

Matthias

Fear clawed at Matthias's throat as he watched Uroch dive into the wall after Jacinta. How had he been such a fool as to forget that since Uroch had taken the talisman from him, he'd be able to enter the tunnel?

Matthias darted forward, but he'd only gone two steps when strong hands seized him, lifting him bodily from the ground.

"Where do you think you're going?" taunted one of the other giants, apparently only too pleased to take over control now that the king was out of sight. "If you think you're escaping through the rathole alive as well, you can think again."

"Have a care," said one of the elves sharply. "If he's the Vadolisian king's heir, you can't just kill him without consequences. You'll put yourselves at war with the human kingdom. With several of them, probably."

"Let them come," scoffed the giant. "Our wall's kept them out for generations. Do you think we're afraid of them now?"

"Don't be a fool," hissed the elf. "Open war benefits no one. Don't imagine we'd stand with you in that circumstance."

Matthias struggled desperately against the giant's grip, his only thought to reach Jacinta. He was the one who'd told her to run, and he was the one who'd given Uroch the ability to follow her, however unknowingly. Would she make it through the wall in time? Or had he sent her to her death?

Before he could get too lost in his panic, the giant he'd seen approach Jacinta strode into his field of vision.

"What's going on 'ere?" she demanded, planting her feet wide and crossing her arms. "Who do ee all think ee are to cause a ruckus in my backyard?"

"Stay out of this, wench," said the giant gripping Matthias, shaking his burden for emphasis. Matthias winced as his head spun.

"Mind who ee call wench," she growled. "Who's the 'uman ee've got?"

"He's the Vadolisian prince, not that any of you are smart enough to care about what that means," said one of the elves crisply. "Maybe you can talk sense into them."

"Impossible," the newcomer said scornfully. "Talking ain't no use with block'eads like these. Only one thing they understand." She pounded one fist meaningfully against her other palm.

"Show some respect, you rustic peasant," growled one of the other giants.

"Oho, think ye're pretty grand, do ee?" the female giant scoffed. "Moving to the capital and lording it up in the castle like some fool 'uman. If you think that'll gain ee the respect of yer own kind, ee can think again."

"How dare you call me a human?" the giant said, outraged.

"Put down the one ye're holding, and we'll see who's 'uman and who's giant between us," the newcomer said gamely.

Before they could actually come to blows, however, a distraction arrived in the form of a sudden, violent wind. Giants and elves alike raised their arms instinctively, and Matthias would have done the same if his arms were free.

"That's not a natural wind!" cried one of the elves.

The warning wasn't necessary for Matthias. His eyes had already caught the figure descending from over the top of the wall only a short distance away. His heart leaped as he recognized Hagen. There was no one he'd rather have standing beside him in a tight corner like this. And hopefully he'd have news of whether Jacinta made it through the wall.

"Another human!" one of the giants complained. He glared at the elves. "I thought the wall was supposed to be secure now."

The elf raised a haughty eyebrow, watching Hagen touch ground nearby. "It is secure against most humans. Only a singer of considerable power could get past it."

"Singer, is he?" The giant holding Matthias let out a growl.

"Yes, I'm a singer," said Hagen, his voice raised as he strode toward them with sword in hand. "And I suggest you release Prince Matthias before I show you exactly what that means."

Matthias had to admire the apprentice's courage. Hopefully he wasn't about to get his friend killed.

"You know King Uroch's orders after what happened to old Groggy," one of the giants said. "We kill singers on sight. Let's rip him up."

"King Uroch is dead." Hagen's words brought an instant pause to the giants' advance. "He was slain attempting to get through the wall. His head lies at the feet of two human kings."

"Uroch's dead?" repeated the giantess who'd been speaking in Matthias's defense. The savage glee in her eyes was unnerving. "Well, that's a relief, isn't it?"

"You're bold to say as much," said a giant from the back, although Matthias noticed he wasn't exactly weeping at the news.

The female giant snorted. "Am I? I've yet to learn of anyone who loved 'im. Or 'is mother." She nodded at the elves. "After all, he's the one who let this lot run wild in our land."

"Watch yourself," said one of the elves angrily.

"No, ee watch yerself," the giant retorted promptly. "Do ee think I don't know that ye've been exploiting us?" She appealed to the other giants. "Giants don't need a king. We've never needed a king. We do just fine for ourselves."

"Not like the king ever did anything for us," muttered another giant.

"And," the female giant went on, "we sure as winter don't need a pack of filthy little elves running around OUR kingdom telling us what to do."

Grumblings passed around the group of giants, many throwing dark looks at their miniature companions. Matthias noticed the elves shifting uncomfortably.

"I say we give 'em twenty-four hours to get out of Kjemper, and kill any left at the end of it," the female giant went on relentlessly. "It's time to take back control of our own lives. Kings and castles and bargains with elves is all 'uman nonsense. We don't want or need any of that 'ere." She glowered at the giant still holding Matthias. "Now put that 'uman down, ee look ridiculous standing there clutching 'im like a child's toy."

The giant dropped Matthias, chastened under the maternal glare of the newcomer. Matthias hit the ground hard, wincing but scrambling quickly to his feet. The giants were all looking thoughtfully from the speaker to the elves, who'd drawn together into a huddle. He could almost believe the female giant had her fellows under an enchantment, so effectively had she halted them in their tracks. Clearly she knew how to communicate with her own kind in a way he never would.

Matthias started to move surreptitiously toward Hagen, but the movement caught the eye of a giant near the back.

"Oi!" The stranger's huge form lunged forward, his hand reaching for Matthias. "Don't just let him wander off. If he's the prince, he might be useful."

The giant's fingers barely brushed Matthias before a low, powerful song burst out of Hagen, and the giant found himself forced back by a mighty gust of wind.

"*Time for us to go.*" Hagen sang the words, not breaking concentration as he continued to create a barrier of wind between Matthias and the giants.

"Yes, get out of here," agreed the female giant, leaning into the wind to speak to Matthias. "We don't want or need yer kind on our side of the wall. I'll deal with this lot." She jerked her head toward the rest of the giants, then lowered her voice. "It's over, little prince, and you can tell the girl as much. Tell her not to come back here. The so-called king is dead and his castle lies in ruins. It's the work of a moment to turn my kind against the elves—cooperating with their likes isn't our way—and the rest of 'em can't operate the mining towers without the elves. If ee leave us alone, we'll leave ee alone. I'd be glad if our kinds never met again. Now go!"

Matthias needed no more prompting. He dove toward Hagen and seized hold of the arm his friend held out. Hagen stopped singing for a moment, his voice apologetic.

"I'm going to have to wrap you up like a child, Your Highness. And just hope that my shield will protect you from the enchantments on the wall as well."

None of that made much sense to Matthias, but he swallowed his pride and didn't object when Hagen wrapped his muscled arms around Matthias's form. The next moment, Hagen's voice once again rang out, even louder this time, as the wind whipped up into a frenzy. The ground fell steeply away as the pair shot into the air, rising alongside the wall at a speed that made Matthias's stomach protest. In moments, they'd popped up and over the stone, and the wind began to lower in intensity, their descent slowing with it.

Matthias barely had time to glimpse the astonishing size of

the crowd awaiting them before his feet hit the ground with a thud that rattled his bones. Hagen stepped away at once as cries of shock and delight greeted them.

But Matthias didn't have attention to spare for any of those calling out to him—not even his family. His eyes sought one figure in the chaos, and his racing heart didn't still until he caught sight of her, upright and safe next to a withered tangle of vines.

Jacinta was all right. He could breathe again.

His eyes passed from Jacinta's pale face to the huge stone head sitting at her feet. He blinked twice, then his gaze traveled back up to meet hers. The tumult of emotions he felt was reflected in her eyes as well, and before he knew it, he was moving, running toward her, completely disregarding their audience.

"Matthias."

Her whisper was choked as he reached her, and he didn't pause. He pulled her into his arms, his breath coming in gasps as the unbearable tension of the last week and a half released at last. She melted into him, burying her face in his chest and clinging onto him with hands that trembled slightly.

"Matthias." His father's sharp voice drew Matthias reluctantly from the moment. "Have a mind to where you are."

"I know where I am, Father," Matthias said calmly. "I'm exactly where I should be."

He wasn't in the least chastened by his father's rebuke, but he pulled back a little, more mindful of Jacinta's dignity than his own. His gaze didn't waver as he met his parents' eyes.

"I know you have your own ideas regarding my marriage, but I have only one. The same one I've had all my life, well before I knew it, and I won't change my mind. It took almost losing her to show me how cowardly I'd been in failing to be honest and unyielding in telling you what I want before now. I want to marry Jacinta, if she'll have me."

"Matthias." Jacinta's whisper of protest caused him to look down.

"Only if it's what *you* want, Jacinta," he said evenly. "I know it's a great deal to ask. But I know with all my heart that you're up to the task. And I would pay any price for a future with you. Which is only relevant if you want to marry me, of course."

She swallowed visibly. "Matthias, I want to marry you more than anything in the world," she said softly. "But you know it's impossible."

"Nonsense," he said staunchly. "It's not only possible, it's the only possible course I can see." He looked at his father again, his gaze entreating him to understand even while his voice made it clear he wasn't asking for permission. "I know it wasn't the same for you, but the summers we spent here in Briarford were the happiest of my memory. I've spent my whole life since searching for the warmth and safety and wholeness I felt in those months, in my friendship with Jacinta."

"What you're describing is the carefree delight of child-hood," said his father impatiently. "It's a phantom, not a reality."

"With respect, Father, you're wrong," said Matthias. "Although I'd begun to think the same, that the *rightness* that always felt lacking was a relic of childhood, something I couldn't find or feel as an adult." He looked down at Jacinta, his gaze softening. "But I was wrong. It wasn't about my age. It was about her. I found it again as soon as she re-entered my life. In the adult version of Jacinta, my adult self has found something much better and much deeper than any childhood fancy. And I'm simply unwilling to let go of it."

"Matthias, that was quite desperately romantic," declared Mariella, moving to stand beside her parents. "And very well said. You and Jacinta are and always have been the perfect match, and I couldn't be more delighted than to see you together again." She smiled serenely at her parents. "And of course there can be no objection from you, Mother and Father. Not after the promise Father made. I know you are a man and king who always keeps your word."

"What promise?" King Fidelius said, visibly agitated.

"You said that any man who kills King Uroch will be awarded the princess's hand in marriage. So surely we can all assume that any *woman* who performs the same feat will be awarded the *prince's* hand in marriage." She gestured to Uroch's stone head at Jacinta's feet, a hint of distaste crossing her cheerful features. "And as we all witnessed, Jacinta claimed the reward."

There was a moment of stunned silence as everyone present grappled with this perspective.

"Stars above, Mariella, you're perfectly right," said Matthias brightly. "Good observation." He looked hopefully at Jacinta, and his heart swelled as she straightened.

"I did indeed kill the giant king, Your Majesty, as you saw," she said, looking the king in the eye. "I did so with the sole aim of protecting my kingdom. I also, with the assistance of a talisman provided by the prince, destroyed King Uroch's castle. It lies now in utter ruin." She gave the king a slightly wobbly curtsy. "It would be the greatest honor of my life to claim the reward you have offered."

King Fidelius didn't seem to know how to respond, but King Herleif apparently had no such problem.

"You are most undeniably due great honor for these feats, Jacinta," the Frossian king said soberly. "Frossenland wishes to honor the mighty giant-slayer who has single-handedly elimi-nated an enemy who threatened all of Providore. If, for what-ever reason, Vadolis does not wish to offer you the position promised, you would be most welcome to take up a position of great honor and influence in my court in Sunniva."

"Hold on." King Fidelius held up a hand, looking harried. "I didn't say she wasn't to be offered the position promised."

Matthias saw Queen Adrienne's lips twitch, but he didn't mind in the least that his father was being manipulated. He felt nothing but gratitude for the fact that he had powerful allies willing to assist in overcoming his parents' most unjust prejudice against Jacinta.

"Yes, Your Majesty," said King Herleif mildly. "But Jacinta may wish to know her options before making any decisions about her future."

"Thank you for your incredible kindness, Your Majesty," Jacinta said to the Frossian king. "But I'm Vadolisian. My kingdom has my loyalty forever. Regardless of my future with Matthias, I have no wish to leave this land."

"Well said." King Fidelius nodded approvingly, casting a sidelong look at King Herleif.

"Then it's all settled," said Matthias brightly. He turned to Jacinta, placing one hand under her chin and tilting her face up to his. "I feel like I proposed to my father instead of to you. Are you sure you'll have me?"

"Since the moment we found each other again, Matthias," Jacinta said, her eyes sparkling as they met his, "the only thing I've been sure of is that come what may, I would never have anyone but you."

Matthias had heard enough. Disregarding the audience, he leaned down and sealed the promise with a kiss. He would have liked the moment to be longer—and more private—but Mariella's voice once again rang out, this time in a cheer.

"This is the perfect ending to Jacinta's ghastly adventure in Kjemper," the princess declared excitedly.

Matthias looked up to see his sister smiling brightly at

Valwynn.

"And none of it would have happened if you hadn't chosen Jacinta to trick into buying your magic beans. None of us could have orchestrated it better if we've tried. I must say, I think it was very romantic of you to go to such lengths to throw Matthias and Jacinta back together after all these years."

"What?" the elf protested, looking revolted. "I did no such thing. I don't care about some human romance. I just wanted to stop what that great oaf was up to." She tilted her chin toward Uroch's stone head. Her expression became more approving as she looked Jacinta over. "And I'll say this for you, you did an adequate job of that."

"Adequate?" Matthias repeated indignantly.

"Yes, adequate," said Valwynn. She eyed him. "And don't think I've forgotten your promises, prince."

"Promises?" King Fidelius asked sharply. Matthias almost felt sorry for his father. He'd never seen the king look so aware of how completely he'd lost control of the situation.

"Nothing grievous, Father," he said, putting an arm around Jacinta and contentedly pulling her close. "She wishes to relocate to Vallen." He paused. "With her cow."

Jacinta let out a laugh, leaning into him with a trusting gesture that made his heart feel like bursting.

"Of course the cow has to come. I really think that's your greatest gain in all of this, Valwynn."

The elf considered the matter, the tips of her ears wobbling slightly as she leaned her head to one side.

"Yes," she said serenely. "I think you're right. Perhaps I'm growing soft from spending too much time with humans, but there's something to be said for gaining a companion with whom you can be entirely comfortable."

"Yes." Matthias's eyes laughed down into Jacinta's as he pulled her close once again. "There certainly is."

Jacinta

"**I** pronounce you man and wife."

The solemn words sent a thrill up Jacinta's spine, too intense to just be called joy. There was so much mixed up in this step, so much that was changing forever.

Her eyes remained riveted on Matthias's, the fierce happiness she saw there calming her nerves. Whatever challenges were coming, they would face them together. And that thought made her feel as strong as a warrior and as powerful as a singer.

She was so caught up in the moment that she'd almost forgotten what came next. Then Matthias leaned toward her, and an even more delicious thrill went through her as he pressed a chaste kiss to her lips.

"I love you, my wife," he murmured, as he pulled away.

Moisture pricked at Jacinta's eyes. After all the bittersweet memories they'd shared—after the years' worth of memories they'd been prevented from sharing—she could hardly believe they'd made it to this place. A place where no one ever had the right to part them again.

Together they turned to face the cheering crowd that filled the huge throne room. It was all a little overwhelming, but with

Matthias's hand firm in hers, Jacinta knew no qualms. Queen Bronte was dabbing at her eyes, and even King Fidelius looked less severe than usual. Matthias and Jacinta had both exerted every effort they possessed over the past six months to warm the king to his son's betrothal, and although it may never be an uncomplicated relationship, Jacinta had hopes that it would never again be antagonistic.

Mariella, standing behind her parents, showed no mixed feelings about the union. She was positively glowing with delight as she applauded the newlyweds, her eyes darting frequently to Hagen, who stood across the aisle, in a place of honor with the most senior members of the Academy of Song.

Jacinta and Matthias weren't the only ones who'd been working hard to influence King Fidelius in the months since the giants' threat was neutralized. Whether he'd intended it, Jacinta couldn't tell, but she was inclined to think that King Herleif had done as much for the other couple as he had for Matthias and herself the day Uroch was killed. The Frossian king's public acknowledgment of Hagen as a close personal friend, combined with the loyalty Hagen had shown the Vadolisian crown in his willingness to sacrifice his life for Matthias's, had made a notable difference in the way King Fidelius interacted with the apprentice.

Not that Hagen would be an apprentice much longer. He was almost fully qualified, and quite separately from his suit with Mariella, he was being heavily courted by the Vadolisian Academy of Song to take up a position in Vallen rather than returning to Frossenland.

All in all, Hagen was in a strong position. He didn't quite have the option Matthias had taken—to boldly declare his determination to marry the woman he loved regardless of what the king and queen thought about it—but to Jacinta's eye, he was handling the situation with tactful persistence. She had high hopes for her friends, that another royal wedding would follow before too many more months passed. And what a joy it would be to her to live her days in Vallen, with not only Matthias at her side, but Mariella and Hagen close as well. Their children would be cousins, and would play together every day, not just in long-anticipated summers.

Speaking of summer…it had just begun, and the outdoor courtyard into which the crowd poured for the post-ceremony celebration was flooded with glorious light. Jacinta closed her eyes and raised her face to the sun, soaking in the warmth. In spite of the love she felt for her hometown—in spite of the signs Briarford was already seeing that the end of the magic mining would mean an improvement in the state of the land—she wasn't sorry to be living further south.

Matthias hovered delightfully close to her side as they received congratulations from a seemingly endless stream of well-wishers. Jacinta had been embarrassed to learn that her fame as a "mighty giant slayer" had spread throughout the land, but she had to acknowledge that it was a relief to see that almost everyone greeted the union of their supposed-savior and the prince with delight.

The few exceptions, in the form of a couple of openly disgruntled young ladies of the court, didn't bother Jacinta. From what she'd seen of Lady Letty in her time in Vallen, Jacinta really thought she might deserve the label of savior, if her reappearance in Matthias's life had saved him from that proposed marriage.

The most distinguished guests they received in the line were Crown Prince Otto and Princess Gisela of Teren. Jacinta greeted the Terenans warmly, pleased to see them again. And once she and Matthias were at liberty, they made a point of seeking the other royal couple out for the chance to properly talk.

"Congratulations again," said Prince Otto, as he slapped a

hand onto Matthias's shoulder. "I don't doubt for a moment that you'll be very happy together."

"That's our plan," said Matthias cheerfully. "It'll be easier now that we don't have a crazed giant king threatening to reach across the wall and drain the life from our land."

"True," agreed Otto with a laugh. "It's certainly a relief. That reminds me, I bring the greetings and best wishes of both Emmett and Rosa, and Bianca and Farrin. Emmett and Rosa had hoped to come, but the doctors have advised against travel this late in her pregnancy." He chuckled, shaking his head at his absent stepsister. "Apparently she said she feels perfectly mobile and everyone should stop making a fuss just because it's twins, and was ready to defy medical advice and come anyway. Emmett had to talk her down."

"She's certainly indomitable," grinned Matthias.

"Always has been," agreed Otto comfortably. "I can't imagine motherhood will slow her down, even if she is having twins. My guess is she'll egg them on to be as unstoppable as she is, and heaven help Medulle is all I say."

Gisela laughed as well. "She'll keep life exciting, which is a good thing for everyone. Emmett, at least, seems to enjoy the adventure."

"Oh yes, speaking of Emmett," said Otto. "He had a letter from his brother in Selvana for us to bring to your father, as well as a message for you both. In addition to congratulations on your marriage, Queen Bianca particularly wished to convey that Selvana is very grateful that through your actions in Kjemper, you removed a threat to Selvana that they didn't even know they were facing." He inclined his head to Jacinta with a smile. "And I want to express precisely the same sentiment on behalf of Teren, in regards to the Forest of Ilgal. We might wish to ease the overgrown magic a little, but we certainly don't want the forest drained of all magic by giants with mining towers."

"How are the reclaiming efforts going?" Matthias asked curiously.

"Well," said Otto, clearly pleased. "In both Ilgal and Selvana, they're what I'd call slow but steady. Oh, and while we're on the topic of Ilgal, Asivah recently sent word with an update about the elves who worked with the giants. As you know, they posted sentries at the border of the forest to try to catch any elves who slipped through King Herleif's guards at Battlement Wall. The Imperator's sentries caught a number of elves trying to sneak back into Ilgal after fleeing Kjemper. Of course no one can ever be certain they got every single one, but Asivah says they're now confident that Lonik's old ring is dismantled, and there's no more orchestrated threat arising from elves and giants working together."

Matthias nodded soberly. "That certainly aligns with what Father's agents have discovered." He glanced around and lowered his voice. "Some of our intelligence agents have been into Kjemper, using the strategy for getting over the wall that Hagen used when he came after me. They report that the towers have been dismantled, and mostly stripped for parts by looters. The capital is still heavily populated, but there's been no move to rebuild the castle. Its ruins were of course also thoroughly looted. I imagine Uroch's gold and other valuables are spread widely among the population now. It seems the giants have by and large returned to the free-for-all lifestyle that is apparently more in their nature."

"So they'll survive in that frozen wasteland, even without all the magic the elves were helping them get?" Gisela asked curiously.

Matthias shrugged. "Giants have lived in Kjemper for generation upon generation, long before the recent monarchy arose and got involved with the elves. The climate hasn't been an insurmountable barrier before." He glanced at Jacinta. "In fact, every indication is that they like the climate, and have no wish to leave their land. Even Uroch wasn't trying to actually move south. Jacinta and I both overheard things in Kjemper that suggested that Battlement Wall wasn't built by Frossians of generations past in order to keep the giants at bay, like we've been led to believe. There's reason to think it was built by the giants, to keep *us* out. Most of them just want to be left alone, and I think we're all on board with that idea."

Otto gave a low whistle. "I suppose that solves the mystery of how the Frossians constructed such an enormous wall, all while supposedly fighting off advancing giants. I'd heard that the details were lost to history. Apparently more so than we realized." He shrugged. "Well, if the giants actually *want* to be confined to their frozen wastes, I can't imagine any of the other kingdoms disagreeing with Vadolis on being content to leave them be."

"Besides which," Jacinta chimed in, "we expect that in time their land will become less barren. Just as we expect regarding northern Vadolis and northern Frossenland. The absence of magic in the ground itself was never natural, and its effect on the land was gradual but significant." She laughed. "Don't get me wrong, I'm sure the north will always be cold, but it won't be so bare."

"Well, that's good news for many." Gisela smiled at Jacinta, perhaps noticing how little the other woman had contributed to the conversation, then directed her words to the two princes. "But now I think you two need to stop talking of business at a wedding. This is supposed to be a celebration!"

"You're absolutely right," said Otto, smiling apologetically at Jacinta.

"Indeed you are," agreed Matthias promptly. "But talk of the improvement in the state of the north isn't just business for us, you know. It's personal. We hope to enjoy the benefits ourselves.

Mother's family has given us the manor in Briarford as a wedding gift. We intend to reclaim it from its disrepair and visit it regularly, when we need a break from court life."

Jacinta smiled fondly, dwelling for a moment on all her daydreams of sharing such trips with Mariella and her family in future. It was fitting that the manor which had been a haven for all of them in childhood could serve the same role now they were reunited as adults.

"It was the most thoughtful of gifts," she said. "I couldn't imagine saying goodbye to Briarford forever. And we'll be able to monitor the improvements to the state of the land up there."

"It sounds wonderful," Gisela said warmly. Otto made a comment to Matthias, and the Terenan princess shifted closer to Jacinta. "How are you holding up?"

She glanced meaningfully at the extravagant celebrations around them, and understanding shot through Jacinta. Gisela was also a commoner, one who'd grown up in poverty and isolation, and must have felt as out of her depth as Jacinta did when thrown by love into royal status. Jacinta felt her whole body relax. The realization that someone understood all the complexities of what she was feeling was more comforting than words could ever express.

She let her eyes roam over the crowd, taking in the titled dignitaries and the dazzling displays of wealth. Her gaze settled on her mother, standing nearby with goblet in hand. Hagen had engaged the older woman in conversation, bless his kind heart. But her attention was clearly never far from her daughter, because as Jacinta watched her, she looked up and met her eye, smiling in a bracing kind of way.

Jacinta returned the smile, grateful to have her mother near, but very conscious of the complexity of the older woman's situation. Jacinta knew she had very mixed emotions about relocating to Vallen and living in part on the generosity of the royal family. But she hoped that in time her mother would settle into her new life and find peace with both the good and bad of their past and the unexpected direction of their future.

"It's...a lot," she said, turning back to Gisela and giving an honest answer. "It's all a bit overwhelming at times." She glanced at Matthias, deep in lively conversation with Prince Otto, and felt herself relax further. "But it's worth it."

"Well said." Gisela smiled, her gaze lingering on her own husband. "My feelings exactly." Her eyes were full of understanding as they returned to Jacinta. "And it does get easier as you get used to it. I promise."

"Well, that's reassuring." Jacinta grinned. "When I'm drowning, I'll write to you for advice and sympathy."

"Do," Gisela said emphatically. "And we would be thrilled to host you both in Terenford when things have settled down enough to allow you to travel."

Jacinta was about to respond when an angry lowing noise sounded across the packed space. Everyone turned in bewilderment, and Jacinta let out a groan as she caught sight of the culprit.

"Is that...a cow?" Otto asked, perplexed.

Matthias directed a long-suffering look toward Jacinta. "Did Valwynn really bring Princess to the wedding?"

"Not Princess," Jacinta corrected him, watching across the courtyard as the cow advanced, staring down a richly dressed courtier who appeared to have offended Valwynn in some way. "Her name is Ferocity now, remember?"

"I think I'm starting to see why," Matthias commented, his eyes also on the white cow as it lowered its head and butted the shocked courtier. "Do you think we should intervene?"

"I try to avoid intervening when it comes to Valwynn," said Jacinta prosaically. "It never has much effect, and it only irritates her." Her lips twitched as she saw Valwynn call the cow off, much as one might do a guard dog. "Seems she has it under control."

"I hope I don't live to regret agreeing to not only help her move to Vallen but to essentially leave her to her own devices," said Matthias, the humor in his voice inconsistent with true regret. "If she shows a tendency to hang around the castle, I suppose she and her beloved cow will keep life interesting."

"I don't think you need to worry," Jacinta reassured him with a smile. "She doesn't want to be in the center of royal life. Much like the giants, I think she prefers to be left alone." Her smile broadened into a grin. "With her cow. I asked her to come today particularly, which is why she made the effort. I confess, I didn't expect her to bring Ferocity, though."

"I've had a fair bit to do with elves in recent times," Otto commented. "And I must say, I've never known one to have a pet before."

"Yes, Valwynn is an unusual creature," Jacinta said. "I've given up trying to figure her out."

"Well, I'm grateful to her," Matthias said. "Whether she intended it or not, she did me a huge favor when she chose to sell her beans to you." He paused, adding after a moment's reflection, "And when she helped defeat the threat from the giants, I suppose."

Jacinta chuckled. "Yes, that too."

It wasn't until hours later, when almost all the guests had finally trickled away, that the newlyweds found themselves with a moment for genuinely private conversation.

"Still standing, my lovely wife?" Matthias asked, putting an arm around her.

Jacinta leaned against him. It was incredibly endearing how determined he was to work in the word "wife" at every opportunity.

"For the moment," she said. "But my feet will give out soon, I imagine."

Matthias grinned, a cheeky twinkle in his eye as his arm tightened around her. "Is that my cue to sweep you off your feet and into my arms, and carry you over the threshold to our rooms?"

Jacinta blushed, even as she laughed too. "I'm not sure that would be the most dignified exit from our wedding reception."

"I suppose not," Matthias agreed reluctantly, casting a disgruntled look at the lingering guests. "But I know these people. They won't leave until they're all but pushed out the door."

Jacinta snuggled her head closer into his shoulder. "Well, you've already dazzled me with your kindness, true heart, and strength of character, husband of mine. You'll just have to impress me even further with your patience."

Matthias's voice was low, throbbing with sincerity as he laid his face against her hair. "I've waited all my life for you, Princess Jacinta. I would have waited eight more years if I had to. You're worth every minute."

Jacinta's heart swelled as she felt him press a kiss on her hair, sending warmth through her. She would have to add heart-meltingly romantic to his list of attributes. The reality that she was now truly Princess Jacinta hadn't fully sunk in yet. She wondered at times if it ever would.

But the other, much more important reality—that she would spend the rest of her life at Matthias's side—felt more real and more right than anything had ever felt in her life. Even as children, some part of them had known it. And now, through a painful and very twisty road, they'd found their way back to the beginning. Back to where they started. Forward to where their new life was just beginning.

And this time, neither one of them would let anyone or anything part them ever again.

NOTE FROM THE AUTHOR

Thank you for reading *Song of Vines*. I hope you enjoyed returning to the world of Providore. I would be so grateful if you would consider leaving a review on Amazon—it would really make a difference!

This sixth book brings *The Singer Tales* officially to an end. But if you're not finished with adventures on the continent of Providore, have no fear—and come check out *Island of Secrets and Sacrifice*! This short novel, although part of the multi-author series *Sacrificed Hearts*, actually takes place in the same world as *The Singer Tales*, a few years after *Song of Vines*. It features a grown up Haiden (Gisela's brother from *Song of Trails*). As always, you'll find more adventure, fantasy, mystery, and hard-won happily ever afters!

Join up to my mailing list at deborahgracewhite.com to be kept up to date on new releases, specials, and giveaways, such as bonus chapters. You'll receive some great freebies, too, including

An Expectation of Magic, a novella which is a prequel to my completed YA fantasy series *The Vazula Chronicles*.

Plus, you'll receive *Dragon's Sight*, an 8,000 word prequel to my completed YA fantasy trilogy *The Kyona Chronicles*.

Again, thanks for entering the world of Providore! I hope to see you back again.

ALSO BY DEBORAH GRACE WHITE

The Kyona Chronicles: YA Fantasy

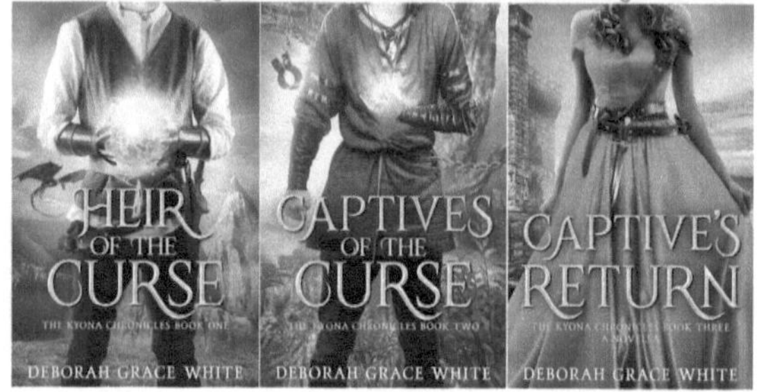

The Kyona Legacy: YA Fantasy

The Vazula Chronicles: YA Fantasy

The Kingdom Tales: Fairy Tale Retellings

The Singer Tales: Fairy Tale Retellings

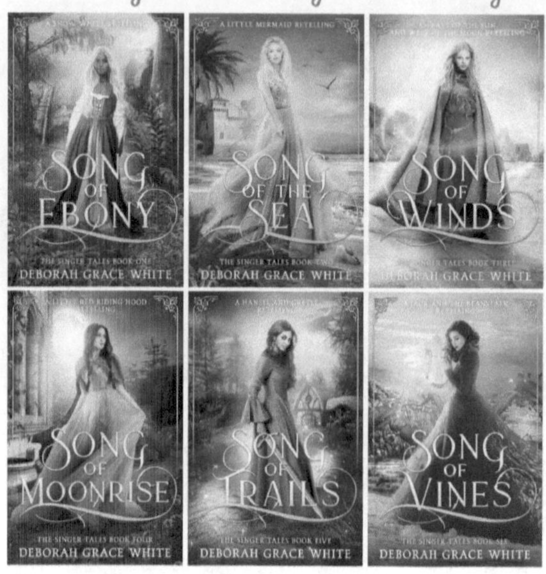

The Unlucky Prince: Fairy Tale Retelling
(Once Upon a Prince Multi-Author Series)

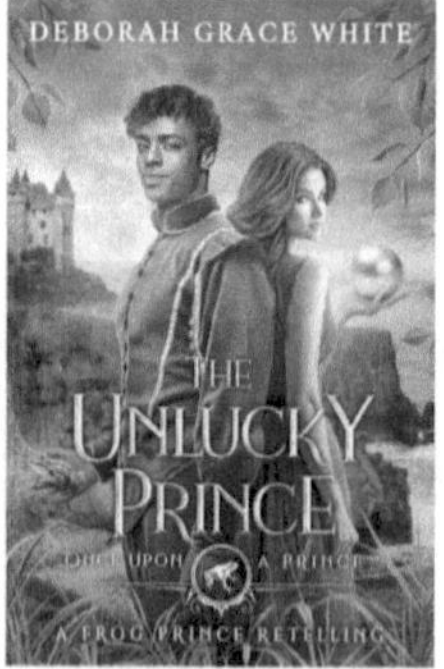

Island of Secrets & Sacrifice: YA Fantasy
(Sacrificed Hearts Multi-Author Series)

ACKNOWLEDGMENTS

Massive thanks to my incredible team—it always feels like such an achievement to reach the end of a series together, and I'm so grateful!

Ray, you're the best husband and supporter ever, and your encouragement and feedback are fantastic. My betas deserve the usual huge thanks: Mel W, Adrian, Tamara, and Dad. Shae's proofread was spot on as always, and of course any remaining errors are my own.

Thanks again to Karri for the cover—I love Jacinta's presence on this one—and to Becca for the gorgeous map that continues to bring Providore to life.

To you, the reader, thank you for giving me the privilege of being an author.

And most importantly, to God, who is the author of second chances and never forgets his promises.

ABOUT THE AUTHOR

I've been a reader since I can remember, growing up on a wide range of books, from classic literature to light-hearted romps. The love of reading has traveled with me unchanged across multiple continents, and carried me from my own childhood all the way to having children of my own.

But if reading is like looking through a window into a magical and beautiful world, beginning to write my own stories was like discovering that I could open that window and climb right out into fantasyland.

I cannot believe how privileged I am to actually be living that childhood dream and publishing my own novels. I do so from my hometown of Adelaide, Australia, where I live with my husband and our little ones.

I've never outgrown my love of young adult stories, so the genre of young adult fantasy was always going to be my niche. Feel free to email me at deborah@deborahgracewhite.com and introduce yourself! Or subscribe to my mailing list at deborah gracewhite.com for free giveaways, sales, and updates.